Praise for THE TROUBLE WITH HATING YOU

"With witty banter and fascinating characters, Sajni Patel takes the classic enemies-to-lovers trope to a deliciously charming level. I loved everything about this book."
—Farrah Rochon, *USA Today* bestselling author

"Liya and Jay are a couple I've been waiting forever to meet in a romance novel. THE TROUBLE WITH HATING YOU has delicious banter, deep wounds, heartwarming friendships, and a path to love that often feels impossibly hard, and the payoff is satisfying enough to give you a book hangover the size of Texas."
—Sonali Dev, *USA Today* bestselling author

"The enemies-to-lovers arc is classic, but the cultural specificity [Sajni] Patel brings makes this rom-com feel fun and fresh."
—*Publishers Weekly*

"Sajni Patel bursts onto the scene with a debut that will make you laugh!"   —Jenny Holiday, *USA Today* bestselling author

"THE TROUBLE WITH HATING YOU was everything I needed—witty banter, explosive chemistry, and a hard won HEA that still has me smiling long after reading the last page. I can't wait for Sajni's next book!"   —A.J. Pine, *USA Today* bestselling author

"An enjoyable debut! The chemistry between Liya and Jay is off the charts. You'll be rooting for these two from their first meeting!"
—Farah Heron, author of *The Chai Factor*

THE TROUBLE WITH HATING YOU

SAJNI PATEL

FOREVER

New York   Boston

Forever
Hachette Book Group
1290 Avenue of the Americas, New York, NY 10104
read-forever.com
twitter.com/readforeverpub

First edition: May 2020

Forever is an imprint of Grand Central Publishing. The Forever name and logo are trademarks of Hachette Book Group, Inc.

The publisher is not responsible for websites (or their content) that are not owned by the publisher.

Library of Congress Control Number: 2019957180

ISBNs: 978-1-5387-3333-2 (trade paperback edition), 978-1-5387-3335-6 (ebook)

Printed in the United States of America

LSC-C

To bae. You know who you are.

Author's Note

Dear Reader,

Thank you! Thank you for being excited about romance, for picking up this book and joining Liya and Jay on their tumultuous, sometimes funny, sometimes embarrassing, always adventurous journey as they navigate falling in love.

Although *The Trouble with Hating You* is a romantic comedy steeped in Southern sass, mouthy banter, hardheadedness, and Indian traditions, the story also deals with (non-graphic) references to sexual assault, death, and trauma.

Some aspects of Liya and her life stem from my personal experience, but Liya is also someone I'd want to be more like. She's opinionated, confident, and resilient. She's also kind and protective, and has a heart as big as Texas that she's ready to share with y'all. And maybe even with Jay if he can keep up.

I sincerely hope you enjoy!

Many thanks and so much love,
Sajni Patel

THE TROUBLE WITH HATING YOU

Chapter One
Liya

My mom absolutely loved the crap out of WhatsApp. She didn't know how to text, but she could do anything on WhatsApp—including sending me a half dozen pictures of the guy she and my dad had chosen for me. And by chosen, I meant the one guy who had even agreed to meet me. Which was a feat in itself, to be honest. He must not have heard about me.

Now my parents were convinced that he was the one, because he'd been the *only* one to not turn and run from the mere whisper of the name Liya Thakkar.

I had absolutely zero interest in allowing my father to arrange my marriage to anyone. While my friends may have ended up in perfectly content matches, I couldn't give in to the archaic practice of this whole arranged marriage business. Or marriage in general. Or commitment, for that matter. No. Freaking. Thank. You.

If I wanted to answer to a man for the rest of my life, I'd just live with my father. Thanks to a culture where our twenties meant draconian aunties swooping in to play matchmaker, I had to battle the nauseating notion of lifelong commitment.

Speaking of the devil from whose loins I came, Dad's name flashed across my cell phone screen for the twentieth time this week, but I muted the ringer. This was likely another demand that I meet this suitor he'd so precisely picked. After all, as one of his multiple voicemails pointed out, finding a qualified man who would even consider me had been a strenuous five-year hunt. Given my reputation and all. We had to act fast to secure this guy before another woman lured him away. I mean, hell, let her drag him away. It would make my life that much easier.

Yet…here I was, at my parents' house because Momma promised this was just an ordinary dinner, just the three of us, and nothing more.

I checked the rearview mirror of my gray Lexus as I drove to their house in the Woodlands on the outskirts of Houston. The car had been a gift to myself, a reminder of how far I'd come and all that I'd accomplished, including my recent promotion. Also, it was physical proof that I didn't need a man to take care of me.

The sun was out, but the towering tree canopy shaded almost every inch of my parents' charming street. When the houses were built years ago, the developer made a point to cut down as few trees as possible, thus pairing fairly contemporary homes with as much untouched nature as possible.

Even though I hadn't always enjoyed spending time with my parents growing up, I loved the neighborhood, and the nostalgia thrust me back to all those mornings running with other kids— the wind in my hair, the faint smell of cedar and cypress trees, and the giggles of girls.

Nostalgia was the past. The present held a different meaning, as was apparent when I parked on the street, providing plenty of room to escape. Why? Because Dad and I had our differences. So I drew a breath, in and out, and reminded myself that Momma was my sole purpose for coming today. She was the calming one, the nurturing one, the only person in my family worth spending time with, and the source of my unconditional love.

The walk up the pebbled concrete driveway was much too short. Leaves crunched beneath my brown Prada riding boots, and the breeze offered a hint of iciness, almost like a foreboding chill telling me to turn around.

I shivered, adjusted the scarf around my neck, and knocked.

Momma swung open the newly polished oak wood door. The woman barely reached my chin, yet she threw her hands around my shoulders and forced me to lean down. My back gladly bent to her command and my senses lit up with pure joy from the smell of her coconut hair oil and rosewater perfume. She smelled like home.

We hugged a few seconds longer. It always hurt to let her go, like maybe she'd wither away. Hugging her was the only way I felt like I could protect her.

She pulled back and swatted the air, her eyes moist. "Why do you always knock? You have a key."

I removed my boots outside the door and followed her inside, the decorated tiles cold beneath my socks. "I know, but it's your house, your privacy."

"We knew you were coming. What were you going to interrupt, huh?" She smiled that genuine, heartfelt smile of hers, the one that made my heart ache because it had become a rare sight over the years.

The spicy aromas of curried vegetables and buttery roti wafted from the kitchen, rolled through the hallway, and greeted me in the foyer. My mouth instantly watered. Who *didn't* melt a little when they smelled their mother's home cooking?

As I made my way down the hall, I saw Dad sitting on the couch in the family room across from the kitchen. His khaki-covered legs were crossed, and a newspaper was in his hand. The gentle swish of turning pages filled the silence as I waited for his acknowledgment, but after a few cold seconds, I said, "Hey, Dad."

"Liya," he stated in that impassive, flat tone of his.

Nice. Not even a smile or eye contact. Something in that shuf-
fling newspaper must've been pretty important.

I walked to the stove and peered into pots and pans, my nostrils greedily inhaling many wonderful scents. Momma pulled
down plates and cups from the cabinets and set the table. We
didn't usually eat at the table, which should've been my first clue.

"You outdid yourself," I said, popping a seasoned slice of radish
into my mouth. A pinch of salt hit my tongue. Curried vegetables
in muted hues of green and orange were piled high in a bowl.
Spicy dhal with a swirl of paprika-induced red glistening on the
surface simmered in a pot next to a platter of saffron-infused yel-
low rice. On the granite countertop, crispy papad with hot spots
of fennel were stacked on a metal dish beside an open container
of creamy raita with bright pieces of mint leaves. My stomach
growled something fierce.

"Just the everyday."

"I can't believe you cook like this twice a day, every day." I
dipped a piece of cucumber into the raita and relished the taste.
There was something calming about the refreshing crunch mixed
with the tangy yogurt.

"You should spend more time in the kitchen with your mother
and learn how to cook," Dad said, his eyes glued to the paper.
"What will you feed your husband and children?"

"Food," I replied as I grabbed a spoon, dipped it into the piping
hot dhal, and took a tentative sip of the tomato-heavy sweet-and-
sour soup.

He scoffed. "Takeout, you mean? A woman should be able to
cook three fresh meals a day. You don't want your husband to
starve."

"I'm sure if it came down to starvation, he could figure things
out," I said, annoyed that his comments took me away from the
beauty of Momma's cuisine.

"He would be too tired after a long day of work. The least you can do is have a hot meal ready when he steps through the door to show your appreciation."

"You do remember that I have an MBA and was recently promoted to lead in my department, don't you? Which means I work long days. Maybe *he* should have dinner ready for *me*."

"Absurd. The plight of a woman is to work in order to make money, but the purpose of a woman is to help her husband by taking care of the home and his needs..." he said in that condescending voice.

I tuned out the rest of his rant about the proper place for women, but unfortunately, my ears wandered back to his babbling when he asked, "Do you even care that people give us such a hard time at mandir about my unmarried daughter residing on her own?"

"I'm not going to argue with you, just like I'm not going to move back into your house. I've been on my own since freshman year in college."

He huffed. "Ha. Ms. Independent." Then he said to Momma, "Make me some cha."

Momma, flustered as she put the finishing touches on an elaborate meal, went to grab yet another saucepan to make cha. I lunged for a ladle to ease down the piping hot dhal before it spilled over and asked, "Can I turn this off?"

She gave a brief nod as she moved gracefully across the kitchen to get milk, sugar, cha, mint, masala, and water, all the fixings for a warm, aromatic drink.

"And hurry," Dad added. "You know I like a cup at this time of day."

So while she sprinted to make a grand meal—and made sure it was just the right temperature by the time he ate—Dad sat there with nothing else to do except read a paper that wasn't going anywhere anytime soon.

I didn't glance at Momma, because she'd give me that curt shake of the head that said let it be.

I tried.

For about two minutes, until Dad said, looking at me, "And get me water."

I held up a hand, embracing my unruly, opinionated self. "You get on me for not knowing how to cook three Indian meals a day, but you can't possibly get off your butt and make your own cha? Or get some water? It's right there. The fridge even dispenses it for you."

Dad glared at me. Boy, if eyes could light things up, I'd be on fire right about now. Momma gently slapped my arm as I brought items to the table.

"Watch your mouth," he growled.

"Don't be so bigoted. Momma, bless her heart, cooks so much because you can't tolerate leftovers. You could help out by making your own cha."

Dad crumpled the paper, his knuckles white. "Liya, you are a girl, perhaps the most rebellious one I've ever known, and you should bridle that tongue of yours. I don't know what I've done in my past lives for the gods to curse me with you."

I raised a sharp brow, my bangled wrist on my hip. "I don't know about your *past* lives, but you've done enough in this lifetime to deserve some affliction."

Momma paled at my side. She turned stiff and stared at her feet while Dad glowered. In his head, he knew damn well what I meant, but somewhere in that black-and-white mentality, he still did not think badly of his actions.

I took in a long breath. There was absolutely no one in the world who made me lose my crap the way Dad did. And I thought for sure that sometimes he did it on purpose. But if he was the rash-inducing irritant that set me off, then Momma was the Tiger

Balm ointment to my wounds. She had a quiet way of calming me, which inspired me to defuse things, if for no one else, then for her.

"I just mean, Dad, would it hurt for you to get your own water once in a while when Momma is running around? You'd never lift a hand in the kitchen, but maybe a little to get a drink?"

Instead of acknowledging my question, he said, "We have company arriving any minute. Go touch up. You look unpresentable."

By "any minute," he meant any second, because the doorbell rang. Since this company was *apparently* anticipated, Dad answered the door himself instead of expecting Momma to.

I unclenched my aching fists and looked to her for an opening to talk about the "forbidden things," but she escaped my gaze and took a pitcher of water to the dining area. The table, now fully adorned with five settings, explained why Momma had made so much food.

She rubbed my arm. "Why must you test him like this?"

"What about what he does to me? Don't you find his attitude demeaning?"

"He does have a point. You must not let your mouth run wild and goad your elders, your parents much less."

My jaw dropped, but I wasn't sure why.

Lots of people said things could always be worse. Sure. He could physically abuse Momma, in which case losing my crap would be an understatement. But it could be a lot better.

Dad's over-friendly voice carried through the hall as it mixed with the upbeat, laughing voices of his company: a man and a woman.

I popped another sliver of radish into my mouth. "I thought it was only us tonight. Who's here, and do I have to eat with them?"

"Jayesh Shah and his mother, and yes, you do have to eat with them."

My eyes widened as I recognized Jayesh's name from Momma's many WhatsApp messages. "Are you kidding me?"

Her expression turned to pleading, a look I couldn't ever seem to deny, but this was far beyond acceptable. "Momma, please," I whispered, "I told you I did not want to meet this guy."

She clutched my arm, and every instinct in my body told me to do whatever it took to make her happy. She needed *someone* in her corner.

"Just meet him, please. You can reject him after dinner. But I don't think you will want to once you meet. Did you see his photos? Isn't he a handsome boy? I thought you would like him."

"You know that's not how things work. There's even more pressure to say yes after agreeing to meet. You can't use passive aggression to force me to marry someone."

I scoffed at the voices mingling in the foyer. I still had time to grab my purse and slip out the back door.

"Please," Momma begged, her voice trembling. "Dad will be so upset if you leave like this."

I clenched my eyes shut, struggling with the prospect of Dad berating Momma because of me.

"He cannot manipulate me every time I come here. I told him no. I'm sorry," I breathed. The words splintered my heart the moment they left my lips.

Before the shadows in the hallway crested into the family room, I fled out the back door. Ignoring my instantly damp socks, I cut through the gate and went around to the front yard. I grabbed my boots on the front porch, slipping one on and hopping haphazardly on one foot before securing the second boot. I hurried to turn the corner of the front porch, around the granite pillar, my attention caught on the stupid pebbles in my right boot instead of looking straight ahead.

My quick, clean getaway hit a wall. A very hard, solid wall of flesh as I bulldozed all six-foot-plus of finely tailored man to the grass. I wish I could've fallen gracefully, or at the least knocked him down and somehow remained on my feet. But no. My body was splayed on top of this stranger, the air knocked from my lungs as I fought to catch my breath. Sugary laddoo and saffron peda rolled across the front yard.

The man beneath me had a hand on my waist and the other above his head holding a red-and-gold box with the lid crushed open. His blue, fitted, button-down shirt scrunched up at the collar.

Momma had been right. He *was* quite handsome, with pitch-black hair, rich light brown skin, dazzling dark brown eyes, and a jawline that could cut glass.

My heart beat against my chest, and not in an insta-crush way. It beat the way it had when I came dangerously close to getting a less-than-perfect grade. It beat as if I were in trouble, as if I had gotten caught doing something bad.

And that feeling did not sit well with me.

"You must be Liya. Would you like a sweet?" he asked in a voice so deep and rumbly, it could've made my legs wobble. If I were still standing.

He brought the nearly crumpled box to my face.

Um…

Well…

All right. This was a definite testament to my stubbornness. Had this been *any other* situation in the entire world, I would've accepted with a laugh. Who didn't love themselves an Indian sweet? But not today. I shook my head.

I wasn't going to avert my gaze first. Keeping my stare locked with his, the mature part of my brain told me to apologize.

I let out a small sigh. Liya Thakkar was a brutally honest person, but she wasn't brutally brutal. My lips parted to apologize, but then two things happened.

One: He spoke again, "A very tempting way to meet, huh?"

What. The. Hell? Tempting how? Like I literally threw myself at him? Did he know? Well, of course he did! Why he wanted to meet me suddenly made sense. Play me to see if the rumors were true? I knew no decent, traditional man would want to marry me, but to use traditions to test those rumors was vicious.

Two: He smiled at me. The audacity! And not a kind, pardon-the-awkwardness-this-wasn't-how-we-intended-to-meet smile. But a flashy, charming, cocky as hell smile. The kind that made women drop their panties in a split second. The kind he probably expected would make me drop my panties. Yep. He'd heard the rumors all right.

As I pushed myself off my *suitor*, the thin scarf around my neck practically choked me and yanked me right back against him. My chin hit his toned chest.

"Do you mind?" I grumbled, verbally smothering his laugh as he moved and lifted the arm that pinned the end of my scarf to the ground.

I snatched it to my chest and rose as Dad opened the front door and shot eye daggers at me. His lips pressed tightly together, and his hands bunched into fists at his side. His words weren't audible, but he was most definitely hissing my name, demanding that I get back into that house while he helped my suitor up.

I did what I had to do. I rolled my eyes at the man flicking grass blades off his dress pants and waved at Dad—an eff-you salute—before hopping into my car. The flare of anger that lit Dad's face was priceless, worth it, but in the back of my mind, I knew that this embarrassment wouldn't go unpunished.

I drove off and eventually parked my car outside my building and rested my head against the steering wheel. More times than not, I was happy to come home to an empty apartment. Peace. Quiet. Freedom. I didn't have to answer to my parents or some man, or hurry to make dinner for anyone. I bought and owned everything to my liking, no compromises.

Ugh. The twenty-minute drive hadn't calmed me as much as I'd have liked. Having someone in my life who reduced me to this emotional mess was not healthy. If not for Momma and my girlfriends, I'd leave Houston forever. That very opportunity had presented itself two weeks ago. A lab position for a giant corporation in Dallas. The offer made my insides tingle. Decent pay, and a reason to leave Houston and all of its hideous memories behind.

I'd mentioned it to my current boss, Sam. He had convinced me to stay because he saw management in my near future. I had taken that chance and it had paid off in big ways at my current company. I was actually putting my MBA to proper use. Perhaps I'd suffer for another year here and land a management role elsewhere once I had this experience under my belt.

I took the elevator to the tenth floor and walked to my loft. I kicked off my boots in the foyer, tossed my dirty socks in the hamper, and quickly dropped onto the couch with a glass of red wine. Time to unwind and prepare for the workweek, but first, I answered a group call from Reema, Preeti, and Sana.

"Hey, Liya! I wanted to see if we could meet the girls at mandir on Saturday?" Reema asked as I put the group on speaker.

The idea of going to the temple sent chills up my spine. It was the place where draconian aunties gathered and vicious gossip made or broke reputations. But for Reema, I'd do anything. "Sure."

"You okay?"

"Yeah. Why?"

"Usually, you have something to say."

I put on a smile, because people often said that they could tell if one smiled over the phone, and explained, "Girl, you would not believe what my parents tried to pull today."

"What?"

"Dish!" Preeti and Sana blurted at the same time.

"You know how I'd told them I wasn't interested in meeting suitors?"

"Yeah..." Reema said.

"They invited this guy and his mother over anyway!"

"No! Stop! That's why they asked you to go over to their house?" Preeti squealed.

"Hey, don't be so quick to snicker, lady. You're next."

"Oh, boy. That time is near," Preeti replied, her enthusiasm suddenly vanishing.

"Is there a guy?" Sana asked, moving the conversation toward Preeti, who, unfortunately, volleyed it right back to me.

"First, let's talk about Liya and her stud! Was it a big Bollywood meet-cute where your dupatta got stuck to his suit and it was googly-eyed love at first sight?"

I could not laugh harder. Anger drained out of me like fat draining out from sizzling bacon in a hot pan. Speaking of bacon, that sounded like the perfect thing to have for dinner. While I relayed the entire stunt to the girls, I pulled out all the fixings to make bacon and jalapeño mac and cheese from scratch because, contrary to popular belief, I *could* cook.

Chapter Two

Jay

I lurched up in bed and hissed from the pain that slashed across my back. Drenched in sweat, I shoved off the covers and grabbed my shoulder as my eyes adjusted to the darkness. My heart beat to an insane rhythm, and my body blazed hot like I was surrounded by fire.

Hold on. *Wait.* I was at home. In bed. Not engulfed in flames.

"Son of a…"

I stomped into the bathroom and splashed cold water onto my face. My eyes were sunken and my lips downturned. The nightmares came and went, fewer and fewer every year, but they were still there. The worst part wasn't the pain or memories, but seeing Dad's face. Smeared with cinder, partially burned and red as he stretched out his hand to push us away. Embers danced around him, grazed his hair, illuminated his eyes. Watery eyes. The kind that spoke immensely about love and life and sacrifice. He made the ultimate sacrifice, and I had not, to this day, forgiven myself for that.

Dad died because of me. Ma kept saying that I deserved a full and rich life, which was why she tried so hard to find a good woman for me. But the truth was that I didn't deserve anything, much less a life. Not when Dad sacrificed his life for mine. But how could I ever tell her that?

I was not really the traditional or religious type. I didn't particularly enjoy going to mandir every week, nor did I entertain the notion of settling down. But I would never be the cause of another stress for Ma after Dad's death. He was the love of her life, a kind and compassionate man. I would never leave her side, but how could I tell her that I didn't deserve the happiness that she wanted for me?

Shaking my head, I twisted and looked at the scars raked down my back. "You're a grown man. Get control of yourself."

Unable to get back to sleep, I pulled out a skillet and made eggs and toast. As I ate, I read over a few legal files for Reinli BioChem, the company I'd recently been assigned to, and sent out email reminders for my first meeting with them for Monday. This was not exactly the type of work I'd envisioned myself doing, but it was what I had in Houston. To do anything else, I had to leave this city, which meant leaving my family, the people who sacrificed everything for me since Dad's death. And that was not about to happen.

I finished up and headed to the mandir to meet the guys for a friendly basketball game. If I had to go to a temple, it might as well be fun.

The makeshift court was small, and the movable hoop was a crying shame, but the room was free, and these boys didn't seem to believe in a gym they had to pay for.

"I can't keep doing this," I said.

"What?" my brother, Jahn, asked.

"This sorry so-called court. We have gym memberships. We need to use the court at the gym."

"What about us?" Samir asked.

"Get a membership!"

"It's not that bad," Jahn said.

"Yes, it is. I can throw the ball across the entire room. We have to dumb down our skills to fit in here. It's hardly exercise."

"Any more complaints?"

"Yes…" I grumbled, agitated in one of those ways where no matter what I did, I couldn't shake it off.

I exhaled and shook my head.

Samir restarted the game, made points, and the ball came back to me. I loved the feel of a rough, rubbery basketball in my hands. I could grip it as tightly as my fingers allowed and pummel it against the floor, aggression flowing from me and through it.

The pounding of the ball echoed against the walls as Rohan tried to block me, but I moved left then right. My back hit his shoulder as I crouched, then shot up to score.

"You mad?" Samir asked.

Clenching my teeth, I only cocked my chin and bent over, my hands on my thighs as I waited for the next chance to get the ball.

"I thought this was a friendly game," Rohan said, bouncing the ball from hand to floor to the other hand.

"Sorry," I muttered and snatched the ball from an unsuspecting Rohan and made another point. His team groaned and threw up their hands.

"Yo, what's going on with you?" Jahn asked.

I shoved a hand through my damp hair. "Sorry. I had a rough night. Not that it's an excuse to demolish you guys. Then again, you're easy to demolish."

And thus, the smack talk began, which siphoned the tension out of the air. The room rumbled with laughter and scuffing sneakers. We didn't keep score, just played. It was enough to ease my thoughts away from the nightmares. Unfortunately, that left just enough room to recall the debacle of meeting Liya Thakkar.

Crap. And just like that, I was irritated.

"Seriously, what's up?" Jahn asked for the third time.

"You know Ma and I met with a woman and her parents. Take a guess."

"Ma hated her? No, she loved her and you hated her? No, wait, she was great, but you couldn't stand her parents? No, I bet—"

"Funny," I said, cutting him off.

"Oh, wait, those have all been done before. Why do you care? You don't want to get married anyway."

Jahn was right. I didn't want to get married, not really. But that was beside the point. I said, "Want to hear something that *hasn't* been done before?"

The guys slowed down to a casual game. Rohan dribbled the ball in place. All eyes were on me.

"As soon as we walked into the living room, she bolted. I had to run back out to grab our gift for her, and she bulldozed me, she was running so fast. Thank god Ma didn't see that."

"Ha! Messed up!" Jahn chortled like it wasn't a big deal. "One look at your ugly face and she ran? That's new."

The guys chuckled.

"It's not funny. Look, I don't care if she thought I was ugly or weird. Whatever. Why agree to meet if you're going to bolt? The worst part was how her parents tried to cover for her. Ma and I felt so bad that we ate with them anyway. She didn't have to run. She could have just said she didn't want to meet me. Ma was so happy about us all having dinner, too. She thought the girl running off was something against *her*. Ma is distraught." My anger surged just remembering Ma's teary eyes and embarrassment, her cheeks pink and burning. With all that she'd been through with Dad dying, I couldn't stand that she'd been brought to tears by some stranger.

"Ma can be sensitive. Maybe the girl will want to meet again when she's gotten her nerves under control. It's kinda sweet." Jahn grabbed the ball.

I glared at him. "Sweet is if she actually ran because of some endearing reason. Selfish is putting us all through that at the very last second. At the very least, she could've just lied and said she wasn't feeling well. But no. She actually snuck out the back door, and I happened to catch her. Literally. She ran into me and knocked me down. And despite that, I tried to be casual and play it off, I tried to make jokes and smile to hopefully put her at ease so it wouldn't be a big deal and we could talk, but she just rolled her eyes and left. Didn't say a word. Didn't apologize or make up an excuse. Just left." Although, admittedly, for a quick minute she did look as if she might rattle off a reason for having to leave. A *very* brief expression of awkward panic crossed her delicate features before she hardened into stone.

"It's for the best anyway. I've heard some things."

"Why? What'd you hear?" I stole the ball from Jahn but lost it to Rohan.

Jahn caught his breath before replying, "Word around the mandir is that she's…well…how to say this nicely. Easy. Gets around."

"What?" I choked. By now the other guys had stopped, curious and nosy.

"You know I don't like to bad-mouth people, especially when I haven't met them. But when *all* the aunties say she's disrespectful, and some of the girls say she gets drunk and sleeps around, then I'm going to be cautious if she's being suggested to my brother as a potential wife."

"What happened to giving the benefit of the doubt, man? Running out on dinner is one thing, but those are serious accusations."

"This is a large community; we can't possibly meet every-one here. But when that many aunties are saying the exact same thing, it makes you think. All we do know is that her parents approached Ma and talked her up. Gave her a picture. The usual. Ma asked if you were interested. You agreed. We should take into account what people who know her have to say. I'm not saying it's all true. I'm just watching out for you."

"Did you tell Ma what you heard?" I ran a hand down my face, half pissed at this woman and her parents and half pissed just to be pissed.

"Not exactly. I can't say something like that to her. She'd ask for proof."

"Ma is smart."

"Be cautious is all I'm saying."

I mulled over his words. Ma was the traditional type, which was fine. She didn't push anything on me. I grew up knowing what had to get done. High GPA. Esteemed college. Prestigious career. Remain Hindu. Marry a Hindu. Raise a couple of Hindu babies to repeat the cycle. I was appeasing my mother by meeting these women, whom I had no interest in actually getting to know, much less marry. I guessed I wasn't any better than Liya.

"Who are you talking about?" Ravi asked.

"Look, I don't want to make a big deal if, by chance, everyone is lying or making crap up, but I'm talking about Liya Thakkar. You guys know anything factual about her?"

Ravi rolled his eyes. "Yeah. Back up. She's a straight-up bit—"

Rohan chucked the ball right into Ravi's stomach. He groaned and bent over. "Not in here," Rohan warned. "Not in a place of worship."

"What's so bad about her?" I asked.

Ravi held up a finger before stating, "She moved out of her par-ents' house after high school."

"To go to college," Rohan intervened. "Not that moving out when you're single is a crime or taboo anymore."

"She never moved back in. She's been living on her own, not even with a roommate, doing whatever she wants."

"Nothing wrong with that," Rohan repeated calmly.

"I went to high school and college with her. Since sophomore year, in *high school*, she was always on some guy. Plus, she hardly talks to her parents, and when she does, she's rude to her father. Ask anyone. Ask her parents, even."

"You actually saw her with all these guys? Or know for a fact that she moved out to spite her parents?" Rohan asked, anger evident in his tone.

"I saw her with plenty of guys. Mostly athletes. At lunch, after school, during class, she got along with the guys real well. I'd overhear them telling each other what she'd done with them. It was like something in her snapped during sophomore year. Same thing in college," Ravi said.

"Maybe she got along with guys better than girls because she didn't have the right girls around her then," Rohan said. "She's got an inner circle of female friends now, but she doesn't mess around with toxic ones. It doesn't prove anything because you don't see her with other women. Even if she was the way you remember her, it doesn't mean she still is. Or that we should judge her. Maybe the reason you don't see her here is because she knows she's being talked about, and no one wants to hang around people who constantly gossip about them."

"You know her that well, huh?" Ravi asked.

"Yeah, actually I do," Rohan spat. "I'm not going to lie and say I know everything about her, but I do know if you're nice to her, she will be a good friend to you. If you're a jerk or start judging her, she'll probably put you in your place. Liya is opinionated and strong and doesn't take crap from anyone. Maybe the

problem here is you and not her. All that judgmental, sexist sham-
ing you're doing isn't reflective of her but defining you." His gaze
wandered to each of the guys, finally landing on me. "If you're
going to label her a bad person, do it on your own experiences
with her, not what anyone else says."

"You feel strongly about her," I commented. Not that a woman
should be labeled as "bad" or "unworthy" because she wasn't
"proper." That double standard always got me. I've had my fair
share of girlfriends, and some of them ended up in my bed, but no
one slapped a label across my face that read *defiled*.

"She's a friend of my fiancée, who is the sweetest," Rohan
continued.

"Definitely. Reema is awesome." I'd been around her at mandir,
and it was easy to see how lovely she was.

"Then you know she wouldn't be best friends with Liya if Liya
was such a horrible person. Now let's play."

While the guys grunted and returned to the game, albeit a little annoyed at being called out, I mulled over Rohan's words. He
was right. I shouldn't judge Liya except on my own experiences
with her. We had one experience. Bailing was something that I
could get over. But being that rude and inconsiderate toward Ma
was an entirely different matter.

We played another thirty minutes, my thoughts alternating
between the game, Dad, and Liya, before a group of women
walked into the room.

A couple of them seemed to recognize some of us guys and
waved. But the last girl, who strolled in with a bright, glossy
smile and the eyes of a Bollywood starlet, ran her gaze over us
and met her friends against the wall.

It was her. Liya Thakkar. There was no denying it, not
with her devastatingly beautiful features and arrogant tilt of
the chin.

After a few minutes, one of the ladies approached us and said, "Are you done yet? We booked this room for five minutes ago."

I was ready to drop the game, seeing that time had gotten away from us, and stepped out, but Ravi said, "Give us ten more."

She shrugged and returned to her friends. After a few moments, Liya approached, hands on her generous hips, one foot tapping, and said in a rigid tone, "Are you done yet?"

"Ah, come on. How many times have we stopped in the middle of a game to let you all take the room?" Ravi asked.

"I wouldn't know. I've never booked this place." She swept a tired glance around the room. "If you're so gentlemanly, then you'll stop now. How many times do we have to ask? You know we've been waiting."

"All right. All right." Ravi and Rohan pulled the basketball hoop stand into the corner while Jahn and others swept the floor, as was the policy after using the room.

"What are you ladies doing?" I asked, digging through my irritation to give her one last chance. Maybe, just maybe, she'd been having an off day and had some hilarious reason to bail on dinner.

"Practicing," she replied, her focus on the area as if mapping out the logistics of the room.

"Practicing what?"

She peered around me without a second glance. Did she not recognize me? "We're going to perform a couple of dances at Rohan and Reema's wedding reception."

"That's pretty cool. Need some guys to help?"

She paused, her sparkly red nail against the corner of her mouth. "No."

"You sure? I can dance pretty well."

"Not interested."

"I'm just saying. Those dances are usually better when you have guys and girls in them."

Every time Ravi walked by, they exchanged surly glances, and her mood was clearly moving toward angry.

"Are you done yet? We don't have a lot of time left, thanks to you guys," she said finally.

Actually, that was Ravi and the guys. I'd immediately stopped and was ready to clean up, but whatever. Instead, I said, "We're putting things away. You don't have to be so irritated."

"Really, when we reserved this room, patiently waited, politely asked, and now I'm being told by some guy that I should be...less irritated?"

"Well, I didn't mean it that way."

"What exactly did you mean? I don't think I'm being unreasonable. Now, are you done?"

"Well, unless you want to play," I said jokingly, to lighten the mood. Maybe if I smiled, if she knew we could be cordial, Liya would relax a little.

"Listen, you are wasting our practice time."

"I was actually kidding. Of course we'll get out of your way." I seriously wondered if this was the woman Ma had actually wanted me to meet, the one whose parents spoke so well of her. Or was I just catching her on a very off week?

"Can you move a little faster? We don't have a lot of time."

"Wow. Liya, right?"

"Yes. Obviously..." she muttered, the only indication she gave that she did indeed recognize me. "I would just like for you and your friends to leave. At this point, you're just being a pretentious ass."

"And you know me so well? I was offering to help you."

"I know guys like you. Good-looking, cocky dudes who strut around thinking girls will give them anything because they wink at them. *Please*. Look at the way you're standing, looking down at me, like you're some god on a pedestal. You don't even know you're doing it. You think you can just smile and expect me to swoon?"

I glanced at our mingling groups, all warmth and conversations, and here we were, bickering. "No. That's not even what I was trying to—Never mind."

"Just say what's on your mind."

"Maybe you just have a stick up your butt. You need help getting that thing out, or do you like it wedged up there?"

She wiggled a little. "Feels good, actually."

"I'm sure it hurts to walk. I'm Jay Shah, by the way. You might know the name? I know you must remember the face."

She opened her mouth to shoot something back, but seemingly stuttered over whatever she was about to say. Maybe she was the tiniest bit embarrassed about what she'd done at her parents' house. Would she apologize? Would she mention an excuse?

Now would've been the perfect time for her to say something.

And she didn't.

Rohan popped up beside us, the court clean behind him as Jahn and the other guys left, and said, "Hey, Liya. What are you ladies doing here?"

As if we were in another realm, her face lit up. Her smile was breathtaking, not that her looks could erase the friction between us.

"Rohan! It's a surprise for your wedding. You have to leave." She beamed at him, her words sweet and almost singsong, the way a girl might speak endearingly to her brother.

Rohan tilted his head and pointed at himself. "I have a really good surprised face that I can use later."

She shook her head, her grin never faltering. "Nope. Sorry. Anyway, how are you? Haven't seen you in a few weeks."

"I'm good. Trying to get into shape before the big day."

"Looking great. Don't get too skinny, though, because we don't have time to order a new sherwani from India." She laughed with him, melodious and perfectly normal, as if we hadn't just been annoying each other.

What the hell? I thought as I watched an interaction too sweet to tolerate.

He laughed and patted his stomach. "I'll take your advice. I'm fiending some Tex-Mex right now." He turned to me. "You in?"

"After we 'worked out'?" I asked with air quotes.

"Please get him out of here," Liya said, although I couldn't tell which one of us she spoke to.

I shrugged, and we followed the other guys out. I elbowed Rohan and asked, "So that's your idea of nice?"

"You must've done something to irritate her."

"She's like a bear? The slightest movement provokes her? I just smiled."

"That did it, then," he joked.

Chapter Three
Liya

A toasted bagel smothered in warm cream cheese hung out of my mouth while I perilously balanced a coffee in one hand and flipped through notes with the other. I wasn't quite sure what had happened since the last lead left, but I might have, for the first time in my life, bitten off more than I could chew. Speaking of, I shoved more bagel into my mouth and felt cream cheese smear across my cheek. Creamy white stuff was the base of all jokes Wendy, my new assistant, made.

She grinned at me from over her purple-rimmed glasses and brushed the corner of her mouth. "You, uh, got something there. Wild morning?"

I tried not to laugh, because, one, encouraging Wendy only added to her power, and two, the last thing I wanted was to spit out my bagel and ruin my four-hundred-dollar Alexander Wang sweater tee.

Covering my mouth, I held up a finger, trying to silence her and quell the impending laugh, but screw Wendy, because she said, "Careful, don't want to choke on all that creamy white stuff."

I absolutely lost it and erupted into very unladylike laughter. At least I didn't choke. Wendy and I had been friends for almost a year now, and I was glad that becoming her boss with this promotion hadn't ruined our relationship.

Tears pooled in my eyes. I fanned my face. "Stop it. Stop, seriously, I don't want to ruin my eye makeup and look like a raccoon for my meeting."

"Oh, honey. You set yourself up."

"I'm so glad that we finally get to work together. You were always the highlight of coming up here to talk to the old boss."

"Yeah. She couldn't handle me the way you can."

"What? She didn't like your dirty jokes?"

"I think she almost fired me at one point!"

I laughed. "Why don't you stop trying to make me choke and help me figure out this abysmal fiscal disaster?"

"Did Lisa leave you that much of a mess?"

"Yes." I sipped coffee and downed the rest of my bagel, and then added, "I'm beginning to think her leaving was not her call. I hope, for the sake of her new job, that she isn't in charge of their budget."

"I'm not a budget genius, but I'll try to help. Give me that one." She flipped through a red folder and nodded her head, then shook it and *tsk*ed.

"You have no idea what you're looking at, do you?"

She dropped the file on my desk. "Nope. That's why you're the boss and I'm your faithful assistant."

"It's okay." I exhaled.

"Just tell the director you don't know."

"That's not an acceptable answer," I replied and paced my office, my nose buried in the red folder. Red meant urgent, right? These atrocious numbers had certainly acquired a rightful status in the red file. A headache thrummed above my nose and behind my eyes.

"I meant more like, you literally just stepped into this position this morning and are looking through files and will have an answer for them as soon as possible."

"Better. I just can't accept that I'm fumbling into my first meeting."

"Not your fault. They won't expect you to have figured this out within the first hour of getting your hands on it."

"Mmm…" I hummed in disagreement. Things changed when an employee leveled up to executive status, and being manager over the entire research division left me only four positions away from CEO. There had to be a better response than "I don't know."

"Have a seat. I'll need you to type some notes while I dictate. Divide and conquer."

Wendy plopped into my cushioned leather chair and swiveled back and forth. "Nice, boss. I'll transcribe for you anytime."

Between the rapping against the keyboard, my Prada heels tapping against the wooden floor planks, and dictating, the nine o'clock hour sped by. This was the distraction that I needed to ignore the pangs in my chest for running out…not on Dad or Jay and his mother, but on Momma. She had messaged and called, but I couldn't quite come to terms with the pain in her blubbering words. I'd selfishly avoided her, but I had to apologize. I had been deceived into that dinner, and perhaps my behavior hadn't been rational, but it was meant for Dad and Jay—who was indeed the cocky type I'd thought he was. I hadn't intended to hurt her. But that was me, always hurting my mom by default.

A subtle alarm went off, and it took a few sentences and three paces before I noticed.

"What is that?" I asked.

"You have ten minutes until your meeting."

"You set an alarm?"

"Yes." Wendy winked. "And ten minutes gives you time to wrap up that last thought, take a quick bathroom or coffee break, and head downstairs to conference room 1-B."

I took the last swig of my now cold coffee. "Thank you."

"I'm not just here to look pretty. I'll finish this document, save it to a shared file, and head back to my desk."

"See you in an hour. Wish me luck."

"You're Liya, who needs no such thing."

"So sweet. You'll make my teeth rot."

Wendy's laugh filled the office behind me as I left. I rushed through a bathroom break and checked my skirt and makeup in one of three large, oval mirrors. The dark circles under my eyes appeared a little more pronounced than usual.

Mental note: try a better concealer.

With an unstressed bladder, poised appearance, and chin up, I stepped out of the floral-scented bathroom. The hallway from my office to the elevator stretched the entire width of the building, and passing through without being stopped seemed impossible. A dozen people congratulated me, stopping to chat. I so valued the welcome, the support and appreciation of a lot of hard work and many long hours. As much as I wanted to stop, I had to thank them on my way to the elevator, checking my watch to realize I was now three minutes late for my meeting. Ugh. Screw me.

The elevator, of course, took forever, but I wasn't about to break an ankle clanking down five flights of metal stairs in these high heels. I impatiently tapped a foot and silenced an annoyed groan when the doors opened to reveal four people and just enough room for me to wiggle in.

And of course people shuffled out at every floor, bumping me along the way, until only one other person remained standing alongside me. The doors slid open, and I hurried out.

To add to the ticking clock, conference room 1-B just had to be the farthest conference room from the elevator. I touched the door handle and took a few seconds to catch my breath. My heart pounded in my chest and my spiked adrenaline decided to stay spiked.

Clearing my throat, I turned the knob and quietly but quickly opened the door, thankful that the hinges didn't squeak. As my gaze flitted across the room, paired with my apologetic whisper, it landed on an empty seat on the far side. I slipped into the chair, straightened my skirt underneath the oak table, and noted every person in the room from my director to the budget committee director.

The man at the head of the room, in front of a board filled with colorful charts, had stopped speaking the second I walked in and now glared at me. Oh, crap on the stick he said was up my butt, it was the guy from mandir, the pompous one who expected me to drop my panties with one smile.

Part of me wanted to just forget this entire mess, walk out, and yell, "Not today!" But there was, unfortunately, nowhere to go. And Liya Thakkar did not run from anyone, much less a man in *her* domain. I'd been here for years. Why was he suddenly here?

Jayesh Shah. He was like a fire ant. A tiny, annoying creature that, if given the chance, only required one minor sting to itch and burn and annoy for days and weeks to come.

He stated, "You're ten minutes late."

"I apologize."

"Liya Thakkar?"

"I am." As if he didn't know.

"Hmm…" he hummed, and leisurely swept his gaze over me.

Oh, hell. I know he did not just pass judgment.

"I know you're new to this upper management schedule, but in the case of meetings, we start on the hour. If you're going to be late, you might as well not come."

My director, Sam, who sat at the head of the table to my immediate left, grumbled beneath his breath and scratched his temple. My skin flared hot.

"If you can't keep up—"

"I can keep up." How about he just finish whatever presentation he had?

He crossed his arms, stretching the fabric of a well-tailored gray pinstripe suit. I couldn't ignore the sharp look of his suit against medium brown skin, the lighter tones in his eyes, and his pitch-black hair. Having been very up close and personal sprawled over him on my parents' lawn, those features could not be easily forgotten.

"Did you even read the emails that were sent out?"

I smiled smugly. "You must've forgotten to include me."

"Apparently, as I see you've come empty-handed. Take a mental note, all of my meetings require a notepad and a report, but seeing that you're sorely lacking in both areas, I assume we won't be getting much information from you."

I tapped a well-manicured ruby-red nail against the table. "Ask anything you'd like."

He smirked, and if I believed in a devil, then I could bet my pretty panties I was staring at him right now. "What is your department deficit?"

I mentally went over the mash-up of numbers I'd read from the red file and replied, "Just under one million."

"We'll need specific numbers from now on. As well as comprehensive lab reports on all MDR products. Maybe you can make that your homework for our next meeting."

"I apologize that I wasn't able to provide an answer that pleases you within my first hour in this position, but I will have the figures for you next week."

He began to roll his eyes but stopped short. He returned to his presentation as if I hadn't responded at all. "Moving along..."

Jay was apparently the corporate lawyer newly assigned to our division, which explained why he took the entire hour to ramble. The basics were this: our company was on the brink of financial ruin, and he had to know how much money we could spare to stay afloat. Plenty of lawsuits were on their way, and he was here to try to curb them, if not stop them, hence needing detailed lab reports. I guess people would not stand for inferior medical diagnostic reagents (MDRs).

I groaned to myself, wondering how I'd ended up with a company that had caused so much suffering to patients.

Others offered a suggestion or two when Jay opened the floor for thoughts. When his gaze fell on me, that incredibly derisive smirk landed on his lips as he said, "Well, I'm sure your hour in your new position wasn't enough time to figure this out."

I could do nothing except stare at him. Was he actually this annoyed with me for not having answers, or was he upset over the whole dinner fiasco? I glared at him, but he didn't seem fazed. He went on, a definite tick in his jaw, but I didn't come this far to get my panties ruffled because of Jayesh Shah.

Everyone gathered their things at the end as Jay concluded, "Thank you all for coming and for your contributions."

"You've got to work on how you handle people," Sam whispered when he leaned toward me.

I released an exasperated breath as Sam filed out of the room behind everyone else. Jay sat down and shuffled his papers together, sticking them inside a black briefcase. We eyed each other as I walked around the table toward the door just to his right. As I did so, he slowly stood up, way up. The man was well over six feet tall. He buttoned his suit jacket with one hand, his chin high, his hooded eyes boring into mine. We both gave each other the slow look-over.

His look lingered on my legs, longer and leaner thanks to the pumps. When his gaze swept back up, he pressed his lips together, and a shallow dimple deepened in his cheek.

"Don't stare too hard, you might be late to your next meeting," I said.

He shook his head and took two strides to reach the exit. Placing his hand on the door above my head and slowly moving it back to open all the way, he shrugged and said, "I'm not frivolous with my time."

He moved past me, bombarding my senses with a mild hint of cologne and a lot of arrogance. I decided not to fume, because why bother? He'd learn not to mess with me soon enough.

I found him facing the elevators and regretted not giving him more of a head start.

"Couldn't stay away from me, could you?" he asked, his focus on the metallic doors as they slid open and we stepped inside.

"Please don't let your inflated head blow up in here. I don't want to die today."

He pressed a button and asked, "Which floor?"

But I'd already leaned past him and pressed the button for the fifth floor. "I don't need you to press my buttons."

"Looks like I already do."

"Are you always this irritating?" I crossed my arms in spite of not wanting to give Jay the satisfaction of knowing how much he got to me.

"Are you always this mouthy?"

"Yes."

"You should put that mouth to better use."

I gawked at him. "Excuse me?"

He shook his head, his features and tone softening when he replied, "I mean by being nice."

"Don't patronize me by telling me to be nicer. I'm kind to likewise people. You don't fall into that category."

"Because I called you out for being late to my meeting?"

"First of all, I apologized for that. Not that you asked, but I was late because everyone kept stopping me in the hall to congratulate me on my promotion. I couldn't just run past them without a word, could I?"

He scoffed, eyeing the floor numbers on the wall. "This coming from Liya Thakkar."

"I neither asked for nor care about your opinion, just like at mandir. You should comport yourself better."

"Yeah," he grunted, "because I was such a tool."

"Your words, not mine."

"Let's not compare your opinion of me at mandir to my view of you walking out on our dinner."

"What?" I asked, tight-lipped.

He chuckled. "Inviting us to your parents' home and then running out without a word. Not even an apology after bulldozing me, much less an apology for leaving everyone, especially my mother and your parents, in a state of shocked embarrassment."

"Let's not assume I invited anyone to anything."

"But you did run out. In fact, you literally ran right into me, and still, you didn't say a word. Why was that?" he asked, his tone inching toward annoyed.

I sucked in a deep breath. I had two options: argue for the sake of arguing, or apologize. But the dinner situation wasn't my fault to apologize for, and I was too tired to argue with some hotshot lawyer who was sure to make my work life a living hell. So I stayed silent.

The elevator slowly came to a stop. I exited without another word, but Jay said, "See you next week, Ms. Thakkar."

"With bells on."

"I'd like to see that..."

I growled beneath my breath. Did he always have to have the last word? Worse than that, I didn't have a snappy comeback.

But I did have an onslaught of messages from Momma, which I carefully perused back at my desk. With my head down and focused on my phone, Wendy didn't ask how the meeting went. Or maybe I actually had fumes coming out of my head.

After closing the door and calming myself, I paced the small office.

And finally called Momma.

My resolve had been to stand my ground, but the moment her shaky voice stammered across the phone, my heart broke.

Apologies came tumbling out. From both sides, surprisingly. Not from Dad, of course. Never from Dad. But I broke down, like a little girl, for my mom. Not because she was disappointed in me, or because I was sorry for walking out, but because Dad had said horrible, abusive things to her. Because of me. Because she couldn't control me.

"Oh, Momma..." I muttered into the phone, my voice shaking with rage and my nails digging into my hand. "I'm so sorry. But...it's not all my fault. Dad took things too far. Have you ever thought of standing up to him?" I asked, knowing full well that leaving him, in our community, was out of the question.

"Don't ever say such a thing," she whispered.

Chapter Four
Jay

Liya was *everywhere*. How could I have gone all this time from never having run into her to having to deal with her at mandir *and* at work? But why did she bother me? Why was I still thinking about that hardheaded woman? I had the right to be upset with her. There was no getting over how she had made Ma feel.

Ma, who still texted me daily to ask if I was okay, and if I'd heard from Liya.

Ma, who still tried to figure out why Liya had left. And ninety percent of Ma's guesses circled back to something against our family.

Ma. Distraught and confused and more stressed than ever.

Liya did that to her.

Nothing mattered more in this world than family. I'd protect them from anything, including a woman who could turn my proud and fierce mother into a quivering mass of doubt.

I grunted and tossed a miniature plush basketball from one hand to the other in my temporary office. It was just two floors above Liya's. I had to work to get this place into shape instead of spending the entire morning simmering over the meeting with her. The rest of the day flew by in a blur. I needed to organize a game plan for these legal woes.

"Hey," my colleague, Nathan, said at the door. "Did you get the files I sent?"

"Yes."

"What's the next step?"

I rubbed the crook of my nose. "I don't know."

"You better know quick. With all the MDR lawsuits being filed, physician and patient complaints, we need every detail of every product under recall. The only way we can even try to save this company is if we have something solid to stand on. Worst-case scenario is fighting and losing, or closed-door settlement, which will look better for you and the law firm. The shareholders knew this when you were brought in."

I almost laughed. Private settlements? That was what they thought of me? The best that I could do? "You keep talking about shareholders like I should be concerned with them. I'm a lawyer, not the board."

"Yes, but they're paying you big bucks to keep this company out of the courts."

"They should've paid attention to other parts of this place."

"True. I could agree with you until the sun comes up, but you should talk to the bio lead about these issues to prevent the press from stampeding over him. Because the press will be after anyone with any sort of position here."

"Her."

"What?"

"The bio lead is a woman."

"She could be a starburst for all the press cares." Nathan huffed out the door, probably in a hurry to get to the next issue.

I slackened my tie a fraction as I took the stairs down to Liya's floor. She'd only recently gotten her position—certainly no one had told her how close the entire place was to shutting down during interviews. Maybe I had even been a little hard on her. It was definitely not her fault that her boss threw her into a sinkhole. She couldn't have all the answers, not yet. And maybe she didn't deserve my anger. At least, not the Liya Thakkar I had to work with. The Liya I saw outside of work, though? Well, there was no way we'd be friends.

According to Wendy, her assistant, Liya liked late afternoon breaks across the street at a café, where I found her at a small corner table sipping from a delicate porcelain cup and nibbling on a scone. Her head was bent over a tablet. Dark hair fell loose from her bun and framed an intent face.

She didn't seem to notice my approach, but glanced up when I asked, "Are you busy?"

Her perfect lips opened in surprise, as if I'd unearthed a secret hiding spot. If she meant to keep this time to herself, then she should mention so to Wendy.

"What are you doing here?" she asked.

Right. I needed a reason to be here. Lawsuits, remember? And apologizing for being a jackass wouldn't hurt. I touched a chair opposite of her. "May I sit?"

"I suppose. Unless you hunted me down to elicit another fight for no reason."

I sighed and sat down. "My job is to keep this company from drowning in lawsuits. You know that I'm only here to help, don't you?"

She nodded, albeit reluctantly, as her focus wandered toward the window to my right. She tucked back some of the more wayward strands of hair behind her ear.

The café wasn't busy, and we were far enough away from others that I was able to explain. "Reinli is on the verge of getting hit pretty hard. The company's diagnostic reagents failed on many accounts, at many levels. The press will likely come after you, after anyone working here, and especially those in management and high up. Be prepared to answer or not answer. Once the company starts to fall apart, your department will be first to shut down."

She stiffened and glared at me.

"Your department is the meat and bones of the company. Once that goes down, the rest follows. Do you see why I'm here now?"

"How do we fix this?"

"Maybe you weren't paying attention during my meeting?"

She scowled. "Listen, jackass, I asked for your opinion, not your sarcasm."

"Placing certain people in charge of various areas. Going over every detail from the lab with a fine-tooth comb to pinpoint errors. I need everything I can get to solidify our defense. Get this place together, correct all the issues that happened over the past few years so there are no cracks in our defense when we hit court. Every employee will have to work very carefully, meticulously, and managers will have to oversee every detail."

She groaned. "Micromanage and be micromanaged?"

"Yes."

She laughed. "Good luck with that."

"That's why we need all managers supporting the strategy. If employees see someone they trust supporting the effort, they'll feel more comfortable working under a microscope. Especially if this department sees you on board and working with them."

"What does *that* mean?"

"You were one of them just last week."

"I'm not going to lie to them."

"No lies. We're about to get hit hard, and everyone needs to do their due diligence even more so than ever. Otherwise, we all lose our jobs."

"Except the lawyers."

I straightened my tie and replied calmly, "It's because of guys like us that you even got this far. This company would've crumbled a year ago."

"And yet it's about to crumble anyway..."

"We have a chance to keep this company afloat, to keep people employed."

"So, you're asking me to keep up morale, rally up the loyalists, work my butt off another two hundred percent, micromanage, dig up research, and do my own work for the *possibility* of keeping my job at the end of the year?"

"Yes."

She pinched her lips. "Don't sound so upset."

"I'm upset, trust me, and stressed beyond what you will ever know. Contrary to your belief, this company going under is more than just a mark on my record."

"I doubt it."

"I could lose my job, too, Liya."

She paused.

"Imagine a young lawyer losing his job. It's a big deal. You'll find work elsewhere, because no one will think you shoved this company into the ground. They'll know it was a long time coming and the timing of your promotion was unfortunate. But me? Not so easy." I slid a folder across the table to her and stood. "Take a serious look."

She tentatively took the folder and flipped through it.

"Congrats on your promotion, by the way. I hear it's well deserved, although the situation it places you in isn't. But if you ever need me, you know where to find me."

She glanced at me disbelievingly. "Tucked away in your little office on the top floor?"

"Yes. You should come see me sometime."

She paused. And there was that annoyance that made Liya Liya.

I smiled. "Two heads are better than one."

"I'll keep that in mind."

I turned away to leave just as a man in slacks and a button-down shirt approached. He grinned at Liya and said, "Am I interrupting anything?"

"No," she replied. "What are you doing here so late in the day?"

"Needed a pick-me-up. One of those days. Glad I ran into you, though. Wanted to see if you changed your mind about getting dinner sometime?" He flashed a smooth, devilish grin, and something inside me flickered. I had no idea why. I didn't even like Liya.

Say no.

She met my gaze, and I realized how tense I'd become. It probably showed on my face because she frowned just a little.

"Probably not, but thanks for the offer," she told him.

"Why do you always decline me?" he asked with a hint of amusement, and I suspected he was flirting.

"I'm not into dating right now, Mike."

Good answer.

He laughed and took a seat across from Liya. "It wouldn't be dating, just a meal."

"You know what I mean," she said with a teasing voice.

The way she wrapped her long, wavy hair around a finger, sat up pencil straight, legs crossed, and looked up at him with batting lashes and a smoldering smile, Liya definitely knew how to bait a man. And it was amazingly difficult not to fall into her tempting web.

I shook my head and silenced a laugh. Why would I ever be interested in a woman like her? Look at her. Flirting with another guy right in front of me. She obviously didn't care about me at all…so then, why was I even the slightest bit jealous?

Whatever he said and whatever she giggled over, I cut right through their sickeningly sweet conversation and said, "Take care of that, Liya. If you need help approaching anyone, let me or your director know. I'd like to take care of this sooner rather than later."

"Right. Thanks," she said, her eyes glued to the guy as he stroked the back of her hand.

I breathed harder. I wanted to knock his hand out of the way, maybe even let him know that Liya was out of his league.

In the end, a trace of rationality seeped into my brain and slapped some sense back into me. Liya was not my type. Liya and I didn't even like each other.

I clenched my jaw, unreasonably pissed, and left. She could date whomever she wanted. She wasn't my girl.

Chapter Five
Liya

Reema yanked open my front door to let Preeti inside, and the hugs commenced. Preeti waltzed in wearing her usual slacks and blouse. She had four gears: sweats, saris, scrubs, and slacks. One of these days, I vowed to get her into a dress or skirt. And high heels. They were the bane of her existence.

I blew her a kiss from across the open space. She shrugged off her jacket, and everyone joined me in the kitchen. We hovered around the granite island where I finished putting the last touches on a giant cheese tray.

"Voilà! Ladies..." I bowed my head to the side and everyone *ooh*ed and *ah*ed over the rectangular plate. I pointed to each group of goodies and explained, "Here we have the cheeses: cheddar, Brie, pecorino, Gouda, Manchego, and a lavender-and-herb goat cheese spread. Honey-glazed pecans, roasted almonds, dried figs, olives, apple and pear slices, grapes, crackers, and a mound of chocolate shavings."

"Looks fancy," Sana commented.

"We have red and white wine, and for the impeccably pure Sana, lemonade. Although I do urge you to allow me to mash up some mint leaves and pretend that you're drinking a mojito."

I pouted, and she waved her hand, caving in. "Oh, fine!"

"Really? After all these years you're finally pretending to drink? I am definitely rubbing off on you."

She carried the platter to the glass coffee table in the living room while I plucked a few mint leaves from my herb garden on the patio, washed, tore, and dumped them into a flute. I added lemonade and handed her the specialty drink.

Nibbling on chocolate, I sat on the couch, tucked my feet beneath me, and toasted, "To my girls. May fate never tear us apart. Thank you for supporting me through life in general."

The ladies raised their glasses, and Reema added, "You know we love you. Thanks for letting us mess up your immaculate place for girls' night."

I went on. "Well, we are celebrating me, so it seems fitting."

"How's the new job?"

"Frustrating. The last person left a mess, and I have the pressure of organizing it. I only have one quarter to show improvements. No one told me this during the interview. Or when they offered the job. Sort of thrown in, sink-or-swim style."

"You're definitely the woman for the job," Sana said before grabbing some almonds.

I blew out a breath and added, "And remember the guy my parents tried to match me up with?"

The girls nodded as Sana mentioned, "The cute one from mandir?"

I shook my head. "Ugh. Sure. He's the lawyer my company hired to stave off some lawsuits, another thing no one bothered to mention during interviews. So I now have to contend with him on a weekly basis as he tries to ride my butt as if any of this corporate mess is my fault."

"And if I'm not mistaken, you have pics of him on your phone?" Preeti teased.

I groaned. *Biodata.*

Both Preeti and Sana made gimme motions with their hands like a pair of toddlers. I pulled up Jay's pictures, even though I hadn't looked at them before. But now, those pictures, both professionally taken ones for work and action shots taken by family or with family, were quite stunning. I handed Preeti the phone, and she and Sana giggled over the pictures as if we were in high school crushing on some hot football player.

"He is so handsome," Sana reiterated.

"Until he opened his arrogant mouth. Within two seconds of meeting him it was clear that he expected me to flounder at his feet just because he smiled at me."

"*I* almost did..." Sana giggled.

"I don't like guys like that. And then he called me out in my first upper management meeting. Should've thrown my phone at him."

"So a guy has actually gotten under your skin?" Reema asked. "Hmm, interesting. Wish I'd been there to see it!"

"Why?"

"Guys don't usually do that to you."

"Well, what can I say? There's just something about his upturned chin and conceited smile that makes me want to punch him."

The girls stared at me. I shrugged and added, "Not that I would. I just...I dunno."

"Rohan mentioned Jay and his brother the other day," Reema said. "Don't worry, I didn't bring up anything regarding the dinner. Rohan said the family was super nice."

I mumbled, "Rohan gets along with everyone."

"He said Jay asked about you..."

My eyes flashed at her. "And?"

"Hmm, methinks you must be somewhat interested in him."

"Why?" I scoffed.

"Just look at how quick you were to ask what Jay asked about you."

Sana and Preeti concurred.

"Do you know him?" I asked Reema, seeing that her fiancé seemed to be friends with Jay.

"I know *of* him," she replied. "I've seen him around mandir and met him a handful of times when Rohan was with him. But I have never hung out with Jay."

"So what did Jay ask about?" I nonchalantly checked my nails as if I didn't care.

"Mainly why'd you run off the way you did."

"I didn't want to meet him. I was manipulated by my dad. So I left."

"You literally ran into him. Knocked him over and just left without apologizing. Did you at least apologize at mandir?"

I grimaced. "Why should I?"

Sana and Preeti stared wide-eyed.

"Come on. I'm not a horrible person."

"Why didn't you just meet him and his mother and say that you had to leave, or apologize that it was a misunderstanding and you weren't ready to meet someone yet?" Sana asked.

"Are you serious? I'm not apologizing to him for anything. *I* was the one who was manipulated."

"Still, there was a better way of handling the situation."

"I suppose, but I did what I did. I think he expected me to apologize at mandir, which I didn't... I'm sure my non-apology is why he embarrassed me at the meeting in front of my coworkers." My face burned from anger.

"Maybe that wasn't why."

"It has to be. Unless he truly is a giant ass."

Reema twisted her lips as she contemplated which was the worst of two evils, but she apparently came up short and shrugged.

"So, that's that. The added drama to my already miserable existence at my new job. But on to happier things. Preeti." I turned to her. "Did you say the other night that your parents wanted you to meet a guy?"

She nodded. "Yes. I'm not sure about him. But he is…you know?"

Her words trailed off, and we all knew what she meant, but I had to hear it. Because I had to correct her. "What?"

She sighed. "The only one who's shown interest in me."

"He's not the only one…" I raised an eyebrow and let the tangy sharpness of my drink slither down my throat.

"*He* doesn't count."

She couldn't even say his name. The once great love of her life. Daniel Thompson.

Preeti rolled a piece of cheese between her fingers as she continued. "Everyone here knows about *that* relationship, but the man my parents want me to meet, Yuvan, seems to be okay with it. He said it was in the past. Part of me wonders how long that might last, seeing that so many people had gossiped about it. How much of that can he take?"

I frowned. "I wish you wouldn't care so much about what others think."

She swirled the remaining red liquid in her glass. "That's easy for you to say. I'm not as strong as you are, Liya. I've always been taught to keep my opinions to myself, obey my elders and parents, and do nothing that could blemish my name or that of my parents. I want to make my parents proud and see them happy. What I did nearly tore my family apart."

"What you did was fall in love. I was raised the same way. I just stopped caring so much about what other people think. All it did was add stress and make me depressed, make me feel that I was never good enough. And it's not that I don't care how my mom feels, especially if someone says something negative about me to her. But that's not how it should be. My mom should be able to put her foot down and stand up for me."

"Is that how you feel? That your mom is ashamed of you and doesn't stand up for you?"

"Of course. So fine, I'm not a virgin, I drink, I date, I flirt, but I'm not just sleeping with everyone. I'm not a horrible person. It's ridiculous and vexing."

"Now you're all riled up."

"I'm being honest and frank, and if that comes across as rude, then that's just another thing wrong with society. For example, you having dated...he who cannot be named in your presence... should never have been a big deal. He's a good guy, educated, loyal, stable, and so into you and liked your family. Your parents respected him until, well, until their daughter fell in love with him. Because what? He's not Indian? Love doesn't see color, just society. And Reema, you aren't going to be a housewife raising three kids and splitting your day between laundry, cleaning, and cooking. Rohan loves to cook. He loves kids, so if anything, he would stay at home."

Reema nodded in agreement.

"But you'd get flak for that. The world is changing, and the older generation needs to keep up or shut up."

"I understand, and no disagreement here," Preeti said. "I just wish I could do it the way you do, with my chin up. I thought love was enough, but the way love broke everything wasn't worth it."

"Love is enough. It's society's views and old-world thinking that broke everything." I bit into a piece of sharp cheese paired with a juicy grape. Oh, if only she knew that there wasn't a concrete barrier between me and the harsh, destructive world. Those same stupid things got to me, too. With Preeti, society wanted to humiliate her because she fell in love with a non-Indian. With me, society wanted to banish me because I wasn't chaste and polite and un-opinionated.

Sana fiddled with the hem of her shirt. "Well, I'm not like any of you. I can't live on my own. I need that safety net of my family and marriage."

"It's fine to want a compliment, but you can't marry a male figure who basically replaces your father." I shuddered at the thought. "Besides, you have a safety net. Us. Always."

"I've decided to accept the offer of engagement," she blurted.

I quirked my brow. "From the guy in India whom you've met once?"

"We talk on the phone every week and email every day."

I sighed, but Reema and Preeti hugged Sana and offered congratulations. I threw my head back.

"I know you don't approve of the traditional ways. We weren't blindly arranged, and I have the option to decline. Arranged does not equate to forced," Sana said.

I softened, the best that I could do. "I know. If you like him, fine. Get to know him more, though. That's all."

She slouched, and Reema shot me a scathing death glare. I bit my tongue. There was a time and a place to get opinionated, but right now with my sensitive and very traditional friend was not one of those times.

"If you're comfortable and really want this, then good. We're happy for you. He just better treat you right."

"Or he'll have to deal with you?" she asked with a light smile.

I grinned. "Don't mess with my sisters."

Preeti added, "But listen, anything can happen to any marriage, no matter how it starts. The person you've dated for ten years before the wedding can be a felon. Who knows? Reema's arrangement worked. So have the matches of plenty of our friends. Be honest, Liya. It's marriage that you abhor."

"It's true." I shrugged. "It's an archaic practice. Who wants to marry someone just because parents and society tells us we need to, or because we're getting too old? Who wants to be tied down to the same man forever? Who wants to have to answer to a man? Who wants to be trapped?" Who wanted to be hurt when they were let down by their man? But there was a critical, heart-breaking question beneath it all: who wanted to marry a broken woman?

I looked to both Preeti and Sana to say, "I do require that you share everything you know about these men, though."

"We have plenty of time for that later. Can we talk about something else?" Sana asked, her face red.

"Same," Preeti said. She seemed happy to have found someone that her parents approved of, but I knew those glistening, sad eyes. She was forcing herself to move forward. Because this was what society told us had to happen? We had to appease family and community, and it was absolute BS.

"How about wedding talk?" Preeti asked.

"Oh, speaking of…" Reema cringed as she finally admitted to Preeti, "He who cannot be named might be at the wedding. Rohan keeps in touch with him, and I wanted to invite Brandy. Would be rude to invite one sibling and not the other."

We all held our collective breath. There was nothing worse than having to see the love of your life and knowing you couldn't be with him.

Preeti gave a gentle nod. "It's fine, guys. I knew Brandy would probably be at the wedding, and of course her brother is still friends with Rohan. Aside from having my ex in attendance, Reema, we have six ladies performing, and they agreed to keep practicing every Saturday at mandir," Preeti said with her usual cheer.

Reema clapped her hands. "Yay!"

"You can't watch, you know," I reminded.

She pouted. "I know, but the dance is going to be amazing at the reception. Rohan said he took a sneak peek."

"What? I told him not to watch!"

Reema laughed. "Just kidding. I wish I could watch and hang out. I got a text from Soniya earlier. They're moving the Sunday program at mandir to Saturday."

"We can do it afterward, I guess," I offered.

"Great! I'll get to see you there, then."

Great. I was bound to run into Dad and a bunch of nosy people who didn't approve of me. Oh, well. It was the same old, same old. What was the worst that could happen?

Chapter Six
Liya

Preeti nudged my shoulder as we slipped off our shoes at the mandir entrance. The large room with idols to the left and the kitchen to the right was filled with noise: laughing, chatting, calling out, and clanking pots and pans. Incense, sweets, and perfumes clashed for attention in my nostrils. I remembered when I'd actually enjoyed coming here. But that was *so* long ago. Another lifetime ago. A time when I was young and innocent and accepted by Indian society. Whatever normalcy and personal peace that I'd obtained over the past few years came from staying away from this place.

The marble floors were ice beneath my bare feet, but at least my wiggling toes shined from a pedicure with a splash of red and silver stripes that made them look like candy canes.

Preeti and I both opted for a comfortable salwaar kameez. She liked them because the long tunic and leggings felt like scrubs, and I liked them because there was no reason to dress garishly for what was ultimately a dance practice.

"Look at you, bindi and bangles and everything," she said, wagging her brows at the length of my sparkly bangle–covered wrists.

"When in Rome," I said. "But I want to see how it feels to dance with all this stuff on or if I should take some of it off."

"I think you'll like how it feels, professional and all. Hey, I know mandir isn't your thing, but thanks for coming to worship with me." She exhaled and slumped as her gaze moved across the crowd.

"Don't worry about them. They can shove their opinions up their...you know? You didn't do anything wrong in your entire life."

"I know, but..."

"Don't let them get into your inner calm, okay? They are no one, not worth an ounce of your worry. You, my darling, are an intellectual queen, and they are but mindless peasants."

"I really wish I could be more like you."

"My outlook took a lot of practice and time, and it's not always easy but definitely worth the effort. Smile if you're happy, keep your chin up, cling to us for support, own this place. This is where you come to worship, not to be judged," I ended with a sneer as soon as Ravi caught my attention. He and his friends turned a little sour at the sight of me.

Although my words were meant to encourage Preeti to the one-hundredth degree, it was easier said than done. As the crowd noticed us in their midst, the two most outcast women in their religious community, it was easy for any newcomer not privy to the latest gossip to see that we were not wholeheartedly welcome here.

Preeti hooked her arm with mine, and we weaved through the masses of sari-clad aunties and kurta pajama-wearing uncles until we spotted Sana and Reema. As protective sisters, we clipped into a circle and maneuvered away from any bickering nosy-bodies.

Our circle grew as Soniya and the rest of the dancers arrived, and we were at a perfect balance in our own world until some auntie pried through our conversation and kindly gave compliments to all of the younger women. Except Preeti.

Her smile instantly turned imitation as she said, "So nice to see you, Preeti."

Preeti nodded.

"I heard an engagement is on the horizon with a nice young man," she said. Rich, coming from her. She did not want her son anywhere near Preeti. Not that Preeti had given any thought to her son, but he had been interested in her at one point. Until his meddlesome, gossip-mongering mother swooped in and convinced him that a good Indian boy would never marry a girl touched by another man. "Such a shame, huh? My boy is your age. You would've made a good match. Too bad that it didn't work out."

Preeti's cheeks turned red, and I almost thumped the auntie on her mouth.

"Well," I said, since my dear friend was lost in a stupor, "Preeti *is* a doctor and your son a what? A business analyst. Oh, no, auntie. That match would be too uneven. A son like yours would probably feel threatened and emasculated to have a wife who makes that much more money than him."

"Oh!"

Preeti opened her mouth, then clamped it shut. She might've tried to smooth over the situation or politely moved on, but I caught her gaze and made googly eyes, and she tried her best not to laugh.

The auntie went around the circle, to Sana, next. "I hear you're thinking about engagement to a nice boy in India?"

Sana grinned and blushed and looked at her feet like a glowing, virginal bride-to-be. "Perhaps, but I haven't made a decision."

The auntie *tsk*ed and pouted. "Mustn't keep a good boy waiting, he won't wait long. What is there to say no to?"

I wanted to gag but straightened my face when her large, brown eyes landed on me. "And Liya! I haven't seen you in mandir in ages. So good to see you. I'm glad that you returned to your senses. I almost didn't recognize that beautiful face of yours."

"You're too kind," I gritted out simply to keep the tension low and away from Preeti, who was in the corner of our group with a downturned face.

"You stress your parents so, living on your own."

And here we went...

"They worry about your safety. My girls didn't move out until they were married. It saved their name. We didn't want rumors to start. And once a girl's reputation is sullied, no good boy will marry her."

"I guess that only matters if I want to get married one day."

"Oh, my! Of course you'll get married one day. You have to. What's the purpose of life without a family, a husband and children?"

"Actually, since you're so inclined to be in our business—"

"It's so good to see you, auntie," Reema intervened. "We should find a place to sit before the program starts."

The auntie was lucky. A sneer rolled off my face just as she nodded and floated away in her green-and-purple sari to meet a group of other older women, more draconian aunties. I caught Dad watching as we sat near the back of the room, passing hundreds of people. Momma waved, and I smiled. I stepped forward to go to her, to hug her, to somehow ease her, but my smile vanished the second she turned away, because Dad shook his head. He silently reprimanded her and me at the same time with the same look.

It never ended. He had his hold, and what could a person do if Momma didn't want to break that crushing grip? I didn't care how it made Dad feel if things were to become public, but I did care how Momma would take it. We, unfortunately, still lived in a society eager to alienate victims instead of protecting them.

So I had to let her be.

Another woman caught my eye. It was Jay's mother, Kokila Shah. I recognized her from the pictures Momma had sent of Jay. She wore a simple sari in white sewn with brown and peach flowers throughout. Her hair was combed back into an elegant bun. She didn't wear any jewelry. Kokila Auntie had a soft, sweet demeanor that made me regret how I'd handled the entire situation by running out on her.

My gut turned heavy and queasy. I let out a breath and marched toward her as she clasped her hands in reverence and greeting to the idols ahead.

"Auntie?" I said.

She startled a bit as she looked me over. Realization must've dawned on her at some point, but there was no single moment in which her pleasant features turned harsh. "Liya?"

"Yes. I just wanted to apologize for what happened at my parents' house."

"Oh?" she said, but the condescending tone I expected never came.

"Sometimes I can be brash and act without thinking it through. I didn't know it was a *meeting* meeting that day at my parents' house. I wasn't prepared for it, and quite frankly, I'm not interested in marriage right now. It had absolutely nothing to do with you or your family. I just didn't want you to be upset or think it was anything against you or that I was some rude girl."

"Do you really care what I think?" she asked softly.

"I don't usually care what anyone thinks of me. I find most people are put off by a woman who speaks her own mind."

She arched a brow, her eyes lit with amusement.

"But I'm not a terrible person who runs around doing rude

things to perfectly fine people. I didn't handle the situation with the maturity and grace that it called for. Actually, if I had stood there in front of everyone and spoke my mind, I'm more than certain that it would've come off just as rude and upsetting."

She paused and regarded me for a moment. Here it came. The annoyance and instant dislike. Oh, well. I was used to those things. But for some reason, I wanted her to like me. She had this way about her; a woman who was strong but genuine. And that was something to be admired.

She beamed and touched my hand. "I'm glad that you told me. I was so worried and fraught over what the problem was."

"The problem was definitely not you or your family."

Prayer chants began, and she glanced at the platform at the front of the room.

"I'll let you get seated. Maybe we can chat later."

"Really?" Hope flushed her eyes.

"Oh! Not about marriage, though," I quickly added.

She smiled, nodded, and walked away.

Amid the throngs of blurred faces and meshed voices, there was always the one who stood out the most. Whatever pride and power I'd built outside this place now withered. Because there he was. A prowling demon in the shadows, something that should've been slain a long time ago. He was among the highest of the respected men in the community, with his devout casing concealing the darkness of his slithering soul. He took care of the temple better than the caretaker. Spent more money and time on it than anyone. He was revered, put on a pedestal for all others to aspire to become. A man who served the poor, took care of the sick, cooked in the kitchens, hung out with the younger men, taught Sunday school, and took the lead in organizing events.

His wife was a saint, that was certain. She didn't have a bad bone in her body, an evil thought in her heart. They had three daughters, all talented and respected, with perfect lives. The two eldest were doctors, one a surgeon, the other a chief of medicine. The youngest had just finished her degree and returned to Houston.

Mukesh. The pious. The unadulterated. The embodiment of a hard-working immigrant who made a rich name in America and remained humble all the way.

Mukesh. The only man I hated more than Dad.

Dad, oh, I could loathe him, argue, slam doors in his face.

Mukesh? I wanted to literally kill him. Because he deserved it.

But without evidence of his sexual assault against me, his word against mine, the saint against the whore, there was no point. He was the reason I was broken. And he was the reason why I wasn't welcomed here, with his malicious fueling of the gossip fire that made me stay away.

Reema bumped into my arm, jerking me back into the moment, and apologized. I waved it off and joined their hushed chatter. Mukesh could creep back into the shadows.

In the back, we whispered, watched others, giggled at the kids, and ignored whatever was being said up front because today's sermon was about the good wife. The diligent, flawless, presentable woman who was educated and obedient, who cooked and cleaned and raised the kids, but also contributed by working. She never spoke out of turn and always agreed with her husband, the head of the house, because any reproach on her was a reproach on her husband, on her family, on her name.

After I rolled my eyes, my gaze dropped on the third to last person I wanted to see.

Jay. Out of the hundreds of people here, why?

Ugh. The thing wrong with going to mandir was these run-ins

with people I did not care to see. I was only here for my girls, to support them. But once Preeti got her confidence back and Reema's wedding was done, there was no reason for me to return here. Ever.

Just like that, my skin puckered into goose bumps and my heart revved up. Why did he irritate me so much?

As he watched me with those golden eyes, I could see why he expected me to flop around like a fish gasping for water around him. Then his lips, full with sharp corners, lifted into a one-sided smirk.

He was doing it again. Smiling. Expecting me to swoon. The only thing that incredibly attractive mouth did for me was annoy.

I pressed my lips together and turned back toward the stage. Not that the sermon was anything better to focus on.

Chapter Seven

Jay

"Is that who I think it is?" Jahn asked, leaning toward me after the program ended and the crowds broke off into smaller groups to socialize.

"What?" I asked.

"That woman next to Reema and Sana. You guys keep looking at each other."

"We do?" I'd only recalled catching her eye once. "That's Liya."

He chuckled. "I knew I should've met her after the basketball game."

"What?"

"I expected you to look at her with some sort of disdain, but you look at her like you want to be friends."

I grumbled, "You're imagining that."

"Nope. I know the difference between a frown and a smile."

"Was I smiling?"

"Yeah. And not just a friendly smile, but a 'hey, *notice* me' type of smile."

"Ah, I don't think so."

"Okay." He grinned, amused.

While I tried to socialize with others, I couldn't keep from searching the room every few minutes for Liya. What the hell was wrong with me?

Ravi popped a sweet into his mouth on his way over and said, "Can you believe she showed up?"

"Who?" I asked, glancing behind him to see what types of food had been offered today.

He cocked his chin in Liya's general direction.

"What's your deal with her?" I found myself asking before I realized it.

"With Liya?"

"Yeah. How do you know she doesn't want to just find her way back into this community? She knows you all, right? Maybe she wants to start over."

He and Samir laughed. Jahn and I were apparently the ones out of the joke.

"Easy girls don't change," Ravi said so matter-of-factly that it made my stomach roll.

My fists tightened at my sides. I growled beneath my breath, steam practically curling out of my nostrils. Why did we waste our time hanging around with this idiot? "Hey, Ravi. Tell me, are you a virgin?"

"Of course, man. I know my culture, my religion."

"Ah. You're a virgin because you're religious, which is fine. But then how can you be so hateful when the same religion tells you to be peaceable and kind to all?"

"I'm not perfect. And I'm speaking the truth."

"That's a tired excuse. She's imperfect, too. We all are. Being imperfect isn't an excuse for you to slander. And she has every right to be here. Sounds like maybe you need to sit in the front row during sermons as much as anyone else."

His face hardened a degree. I could stand here and tell him that I wasn't a virgin and see how he treated me. Based on my experience, he'd be fine with that, since I'm a man. Although I wasn't very traditional, I liked some of our traditions, but the judgment and hate didn't belong. And I could bet that at least half of the people here indulged in premarital sex, just as I knew at least half were likely to enjoy alcohol and meat when our religion forbade all three things.

"Be careful, she's talking to your wife," Ravi warned Jahn, but Jahn casually looked over his shoulder at the unthreatening demeanor in which Liya chatted with Shilpa.

"Right. We'll take care of that right away," I said and elbowed my brother to get the hell away from these morons.

As we moved out of earshot, subtly looking back at them, Jahn said, "I don't think those guys are proper association for you, little one."

I laughed. "Can you believe them? I get that she has a bad rep, but man, come on."

"I wonder if Ravi had tried to date her and she slammed his face into a wall."

I laughed harder.

"What's so amusing?" Shilpa asked, rubbing her swollen belly as she slouched in one of the many plastic chairs lining the room for the elderly . . . or in her case, for the pregnant.

"Just how some guys act," Jahn replied.

She looked at me and pouted. "Was that all? You were laughing pretty hard. I haven't seen something crack you up in a while, Mr. Serious."

I shrugged as Jahn lifted her hand to kiss the back of it. "How are my babies doing?"

Liya, who had been standing at Shilpa's side, arched her brows as if she had never heard anyone speak endearingly to their loved ones.

"So sweet. We're doing just fine," she said. "Have you met Preeti and Liya? This is my husband, Jahnu."

Jahn gave a slight bow of the head. "Everyone calls me Jahn. Nice to meet you, Preeti."

Preeti smiled. "Nice to meet you, too. Nice to see more young faces here."

I said, "Well, youngish. Nice to meet you, Preeti. I've heard a lot about you."

She blushed and swallowed, a wave of discomfort crossing her face. "I hope it's something good," she muttered.

"Just that you're the best medical resident here."

"Oh." She smiled. "Thanks. I'm not usually here often, so I'm just making the rounds with new faces. But I hear you've been here for a while. Guess that shows how spiritual I am."

"Nonsense. You're busy. Education comes first. Besides, this place is huge. If we weren't broken into smaller groups, I don't think I'd actually meet anyone! Just stick to myself in a corner on the edge of the crowd."

At that point, Jahn turned to greet Liya. "Nice to finally meet you, Liya."

"Finally?" she asked him, but threw an inquisitive look my way. She had appeared to be cordial until she looked at me.

"Ah. Rohan speaks so highly of you," Jahn added.

"Oh, yes. I heard someone inquired about me."

I cleared my throat. "Well, you know why I did. Good to see you again, Liya."

"Rein in that enthusiasm; you might burst," she said dryly.

Our little group against the wall stilled, all eyes on me. "You can imagine after being left at a dinner intended to meet a possible marriage match, I might be a little wary of you." I crossed my arms, feeling that irritating tick in my jaw.

"Then you should've asked me if I wanted to meet you." Was she trying to hide a smile? Did she realize, and enjoy, how much she got to me? And so damn easily?

"I didn't even know who you were."

"But by the time we had our first office meeting, you did know. In fact, you knew at the basketball game. And was that why you treated me the way you did?"

I shuffled on my feet. I vaguely recalled where we were, in public, albeit cornered against the side wall between our little group of friends. But damn it, she was so easy to fight with. How the hell could I possibly stop myself?

I lowered my voice. "Excuse me? How exactly did I treat you?"

"You know how," she replied in a calm, undeterred tone.

"Having people popping into *my* meeting late gives me the right to call them out. Those meetings will potentially save your job."

She crossed her arms defiantly and tapped her bare foot against the floor. "You just can't handle someone who actually declined you."

"You think I'm that shallow?"

"It appears that way."

I sucked in a breath and looked skyward to gain my calm. "You love riling people up in a place of worship, don't you?"

"Don't be so easily riled up."

Shilpa giggled, and we glared at her. "Oh, sorry. But you two are just so cute."

Jahn sported a grin, and even Preeti covered a smile. *What* was going on?

"You bicker like an old married couple," Shilpa said. But bless her heart, I could not say a thing against my bhabhi.

So I sorted through all the things that I could throw out there, and instead said to Liya, "See you at work."

Liya shot back, "Bye."

But neither of us moved. "Can I speak to my family?" I asked.

"I'm not stopping you. I'm in the company of friends."

"I doubt my family consider themselves your friends." The words accidentally tumbled out, and I instantly wanted to slap myself.

She paused, and every smile in the group slipped. She swallowed almost imperceptibly. The irritation and anger that usually marred her otherwise pretty features fled. And for a brief second, she was an open book of pain and rejection. I was such a dick.

I went to apologize, but Liya was quick to say, "In case you wondered why I left the dinner, now you know. You're every bit the jackass I pegged you for."

With the best of intentions suddenly shoved aside, my mouth spoke before my brain told it to shut up. "I do know why, and it has nothing to do with me, because you didn't know me. You were more interested in making sure your assumption of me was known instead of excusing yourself properly. Forget if I'm offended. Do you have any idea what that did to my mother? Your parents?"

"Don't pretend to know a single thing about me. I am not going to become some high and mighty traditionalist's submissive and subservient wife. Just because I left before dinner doesn't make me a bad person; or do you just think that because I'm a female, anything I do against expectation is wrong?"

I shook my head; anger sizzled through me. "To think your parents had spoken so highly of you, to have fooled my mother into thinking you were worth marrying." Crap. I did it again. I instantly regretted my words. *Another dick move, man.*

That spark of pain came to life and died just as quickly as she spat, "You clearly want a servant, not a woman, and that is a reflection of you, not me."

I actually gritted my teeth. "Now who's acting like they know something about the other person? You're making an assumption."

"Bailing on you worked out for both of us. People like you are just one of the reasons I loathe coming here."

She turned to Shilpa and Jahn and said in a one-hundred-and-eighty-degree turnaround, pleasant tone, "You are definitely not a reason to hate coming here. It was actually really nice meeting you. It's hard to find people at this supposedly spiritual place who are not here to judge and belittle. So thank you for that. I hear Rohan and Reema invited you to the wedding, so be prepared for an amazing show at the reception."

"We better get ready to practice," Preeti quietly added.

They exchanged kind pleasantries with a baffled Shilpa and strode away to meet a few others. They chatted and laughed, and just like that, Liya's moment of vulnerability disappeared.

Shilpa glared at me.

"What?"

"Was that necessary?" she asked.

"What did I do?"

"I've never seen you behave so rudely with anyone."

I nearly coughed out the words, "Did you hear how she treated me? I only give back what she gives me."

"So, you think Ravi is a jerk because of what he says about her, and yet you act like that?" Jahn asked.

"I don't know where this is coming from. Just last weekend, you told me about the gossip, that it was better the dinner didn't happen. I didn't call her a whore. Ravi is a completely different story."

"No. You just implied that she would never be worthy of our friendship, much less our family," Shilpa spat. "I like her. She's smart and quick and has the funniest sense of humor."

"So you had no issue with how she treated me?"

"Seems like she was doing just fine before you opened your mouth."

Before I could defend myself, Liya's dad approached us. "So wonderful to see you here. Shilpa, you're glowing."

"Thank you, Pranad Uncle," she said as cheerfully as she could manage in all that annoyance toward me.

"Again, I apologize for my daughter's absence," he said to me.

"No worries, please," I said.

"Maybe we can try again at a later time?"

I merely nodded, unable to bring myself to tell him that his daughter was the last woman on earth I'd marry.

"I see that you've spoken with her?" he asked, half worried and half anxious. Poor uncle.

"Yes. We actually meet together from time to time at her company."

"Splendid! Then you know she's a hard worker. Smart girl. Very prestigious role at her company at a young age," he elaborated, as if to clarify her qualifications.

"She is. Definitely a force to be reckoned with." I tried not to look at my brother or the disappointing expression he sported.

Pranad Uncle's hopeful eyes narrowed just a little, and I knew my telltale flickers of unamused honesty peeked through. The same flushed embarrassment from the day he caught Liya running off before dinner washed over him now. My heart truly ached for him. Such an outstanding man with such a difficult daughter.

Chapter Eight
Liya

Dad was, without a doubt, trying to convince the jackass lawyer to give me another chance. But Jayesh Shah had made it perfectly clear that I was not worthy of him or his family. At any minute, he would tell Dad just the same. While I didn't mind someone putting Dad in his place, I *did* mind Jay prying into what I had hoped was a new friendship. Shilpa was a rare rose in a field of thorns. She didn't bat an eyelash when my name, or Preeti's, came up. Even her husband didn't seem to mind.

But, whatever.

Jay glanced at me from across the room, annoyance blatant on his chiseled face. If looks could kill…well, I would've died a hundred times over.

Something in the pit of my belly turned numb, heavy, toxic as it eroded my insides and slowly marched up my throat. I hadn't felt this way since high school, and I was damned if some pretty-boy jerk made me revert to those insecure days.

"Are you okay?" Preeti asked.

"Yeah. Why not?"

"You look a little pale."

"It's just being here. I hate it."

She stole a glance at Dad and Jay. "Does it have anything to do with your dad trying to get Jay back into suitor mode?"

"Let's not even go there. Dad didn't learn his lesson, and I'm assuming Jay is telling him just how much he loathes me."

She frowned, but I waved away her sympathy. "If that doesn't teach him to stop this marriage nonsense, then nothing will. I'll be back in a few minutes. I need fresh air."

"Okay. I'll get the girls together. We'll meet you in the back room?"

I nodded and slipped my shoes on at the door. The air outside was muggy and hot and hit me like a stifling slap. Maybe it was time to just get out of Houston. Maybe that company in Dallas would give me another chance. If Reinli BioChem went down, then there was definitely no reason to stay, aside from my best friends. But Reema and Preeti had their men, their own lives, and Sana would soon get engaged and possibly move back to India. Everyone progressed while I remained stagnant. A new city and a new job were things my life needed.

I checked my phone out of habit. Mike's name popped up on the screen. A text. Asking me out. Yet again. The guy was persistent, but there was definitely something off-putting about getting asked out via text.

The doors behind me swung open, offering a glimpse of Jay, who continued to speak with Dad. The numbing sensation in my gut returned shortly but was outlived by a pang in my chest.

Screw him. Screw all of them.

I texted Mike. I needed a distraction, and Mike was cute and flirty and made me feel tingly in all the good parts. I needed some good-part tingles.

✳

I perused the heavy, embossed paper in my hand, my eyes drifting across appetizers, soups, salads, entrees, desserts, and drinks. None of them were cheap.

"Do you need help understanding anything?" Mike asked from across the round table just big enough for two settings plus a basket of bread in between.

"No, thank you."

"Have you ever had French food?"

"Yes, when I was in France."

My answer seemed to push him back a little, and the slight shake of my head conveyed my disbelief. I placed the menu down and admitted, "Although I'm not fluent in French."

"Neither am I." He laughed just as the waiter approached.

While I ordered the chicken Dijon, Mike ordered the almond roasted duck and a bottle of Burgundy wine.

We nibbled on petite salads and buttery bread before the main course arrived. Mike was a charmer. He constantly made eye contact, smiled, brushed his hand over mine on the table, and sprinkled compliments about my hair and dress. Pair that with an elite taste in restaurants and he quickly fell into favor.

"And those shoes..." He whistled. "So damn sexy."

I gave him a sultry smile and poked my left foot out from underneath the table, displaying my Christian Louboutin pumps with the iconic red sole, a rouge-and-black glittery flower at the ankle, and peekaboo opening to showcase my candy cane toenails. "I know."

He leaned into the table and brushed my crossed legs. His hand trailed my calf to my ankle. Maybe the guy had a foot fetish, or a shoe fetish, because I could see his thoughts materialize on his face. And that's what these expensive-as-hell date shoes did, put a certain image into men's heads.

"I've got some ideas for these shoes and this dress," he muttered.

"Forward, aren't you?"

He shrugged and sat back. "Up front. No games."

"Hmm. Is that what you think? I'm worth an expensive dinner?"

"You are."

I narrowed my eyes just a little. Honesty was a good thing, but it was alarming to realize how easily men objectified women and thought a fancy dinner equated to a night in their bed. Who was I kidding? I was dressed to say the same thing.

As soon as Mike poured the last drops of wine, he called the waiter for another bottle. With one brow arched, he asked me, "If that's okay?"

"Sure. Why not?" I was having a great time. Incredible French cuisine paired with delicious wine and a relaxed atmosphere was just what the doctor ordered after a long week at work.

"Dessert?"

I bit my lower lip. My appetite for sweets revealed itself when my eyes longingly lingered on the desserts page.

"I take that as a yes." Mike laughed. "I'll admit that everything here has been amazing, and I'd love to try the entire dessert menu."

"Oh, you're telling me! I can't decide. I love crème brûlée, but lemon soufflé, raspberry dacquiose…okay." I closed my eyes and touched the menu with a fingertip. Peering through one slit of an eye, I declared, "Strawberry savarin."

"Excellent choice," the waiter commented.

"I've heard incredible things about your tulipes with raspberry sorbet. Let's try that. And a few of the assorted macarons to go," Mike added.

"Excellent choice, as well." The waiter left and returned with my light and fluffy cake with fresh strawberries and cream, and a cookie wafer with a brilliant reddish-purple scoop of raspberry sorbet for Mike. The mint leaf on the side added a nice pop, and I wondered if I could find a blouse in that color.

Mike hadn't offered to let me try his roast duck, nor did he offer a taste of the beautifully arranged dessert. But I shouldn't appear so greedily hungry...even if it was a French dessert that probably tasted as sinful as it looked.

I rolled my eyes. "Do you mind if I taste your dessert? It's so pretty."

He paused in mid-bite, as if my request meant that he might lose his soul if anything went wrong. Well, he paid for dinner, which meant he was entitled to his dessert. But he intended to take me home, so the least he could do was spare a sweet spoonful.

"Sure," he said finally.

I used my spoon and dipped into the raspberry sorbet. Ah, screw it. I ripped almost half of the remaining shell and grinned as I scooped it into my mouth. The shock on his face was unforgettable. If he would only show some type of annoyance, I could walk away and call this a night.

But why was I thinking that? Why walk away? We had a good time. For an hour, he'd kept my mind off all the negative things swirling around in my life. Maybe he wasn't enough. Maybe wine and fabulous French food wasn't enough. Maybe I needed to go to his place more than he needed me to.

Then why was it so hard to turn my brain off? I *wanted* this. *This* made me feel good.

Once we finished, Mike paid and winked at me as he took my hand and pulled me to my feet. In these heels, I was an inch taller than he was, but he didn't seem to mind. He held my hand for only a second before moving to my lower back. He hadn't opened the door for me all night, not when I climbed into his car, not when we arrived, not when we entered the restaurant, and not now when we walked out.

But I didn't believe in that southern gentleman crap. I could open my own doors.

The valet swung around, and we hopped in. The second we started off, Mike's hand was on my thigh, and as he babbled on about doing this again, maybe adding a movie to the mix, his touch gradually moved higher and higher. I leaned my head back and closed my eyes, and his voice silenced.

"Like that, huh?" he asked, his voice husky and heavy with desire.

"Yeah," I whispered, wishing he'd just shut up and let me feel good without interrupting.

He kissed me as soon as he parked the car in the parking garage beneath his apartment building. He didn't waste any time. His hand had moved around to my right thigh, his open mouth kiss a sudden jolt that went straight to my core. And I wanted more. I yearned for more.

I kissed him back harder, feverish, like an addict who couldn't get enough. My fingers roamed through his hair and tugged. He moaned against my lips, muttering profanities of what he wanted to do to me and how hard he was going to do it.

I didn't pay attention. I craved the mind haze this euphoria created, allowing his hands to cup and grope and stroke. I wanted release. I wanted a reason to cry out and scream and, for a minute, have my body turn into mush and my mind explode.

He had my skirt scrunched around my waist, exposing the sexy black lace panties beneath.

"Do you want to go upstairs?" I grunted.

"We can do it right here."

"In a car?" I rasped. "What kind of girl do you think I am?"

"Oh, I know exactly what kind of girl you are," he muttered against my breasts.

"Yeah?"

"Yeah."

"And what kind of girl is that?" I twisted into him.

"The kind who likes to get it whenever and wherever."

The euphoria splintered, but I forced my brain to remain on shutdown and ignored his remarks. "It'll be better upstairs," I promised and bit his earlobe.

He hissed, his grip on my legs tightening. "Nah."

"Nah?" I opened my eyes. "You don't want me in your apartment?"

"Don't take it personally."

I shoved him away. "How should I take it?"

He groaned, exasperated, and a bit miffed, judging by the way his eyes rolled and his lips pressed into a tight line. "I thought you liked quick ones."

"Um, no. And definitely not in a cheap-ass car in a public garage where there's a security camera in the corner."

He flushed. "I didn't notice that there."

"Really?" I crossed my arms. "You live here and you don't know where the security cameras are? Or why you parked in this specific area when there are plenty of spots available? Were you trying to give your security man a show? Or have this on tape?"

He scratched the back of his neck. Caught red-handed, little bastard.

"Ugh. Take me home."

"Ah, come on, don't be like that." He tugged at my arms.

"You don't want me in your apartment so you can set me up to *record* me."

"That's not why. Let it go." He kissed my neck, and I flinched.

"Then why?"

He hit his steering wheel and I jumped. "Girls like you don't get the girlfriend treatment."

"Meaning...?"

"I know your reputation."

"Reputation and fact have nothing to do with one another."

"Fine. Let's go upstairs. If that's what I have to do to get these off you." He slipped his hand underneath my skirt, between my legs. Flashbacks screeched through my head. Harsh hands. Pleading cries. Relentless warnings. And worst of all, no one to believe me.

Well, I wasn't that little girl anymore. I was an adult. A no-fear, badass, will punch a man in his throat adult. I shook, a volatile mixture of anger and fear. A triggered memory. What would my dad say about this? Oh, it was my own fault. Right? Why would I set myself up for this? Maybe I shouldn't have come here, but that did *not* give Mike an excuse.

"Oh, hell no." I pushed his hands away. "Take me home."

"You don't mean that." He kissed my neck again, but this time he stayed there, his hand becoming more aggressive and completely shattering whatever euphoria I'd managed to create.

"Stop, Mike," I growled, shoving his hand and pulling back from his too-eager mouth.

He laughed, as if this were a game, a tease. "I did not just drop two hundred dollars for you not to give it up."

"I'm not a two-hundred-dollar whore. You were not paying for this."

"No, you're worth much more. But you can't just go out with a guy dressed like this knowing what I wanted, and even encouraging it at dinner, to turn me down now."

"You're an asshat. I don't owe you a damn thing. You ruined it by trying to do me here and calling me a whore."

"Don't be ashamed of what you are."

I slapped him. And not a dainty slap, but with the back of my hand so that my rings left red and pink stripes across his face and broke skin. Yes, I was pissed and was only getting angrier, but a bit of my former self trickled to the surface. Anxiety bubbled out. My pulse raged. Sweat formed on my brow. I trembled. Because what if Mike did try something worse? Could I defend myself? Sure, he'd get pretty hurt, but so would I. And emotional wounds were not easily healed. Case in point? Me. Myself. Right here, after all these years.

He grabbed his cheek, now as red as the rest of his face. "You little bitch!"

"Call me a bitch again, and I will cut off that worthless twig you call a penis," I growled.

"Why the hell are you mad that I want to screw you? That's why you came here."

"I wanted a screw, but from a guy who had enough respect for me to take me to his apartment."

He shook his head. "I've heard from plenty of guys how wild you are. Respect is not something I had for you."

"Take me home," I snapped.

"You can walk home."

"Are you serious?" I stared at him. Unbelievable.

"Yep." He turned off the car.

"You don't have the right to be mad, jackass."

"Get the hell out of my car. And don't be mistaken about all the smiling faces around you. We all know what an easy slut you are. Case in point, you almost giving it up to me after one hour. It's the reason I even asked you out."

"You are more worthless than the crap on the bottom of my shoes." I grabbed my bag and crawled out.

"Speaking of, it won't be fun walking home in those screw-me shoes."

I slammed the door. "Asshole." But honestly? I was so glad to get out of that car, unscathed and unbroken.

I stifled a scream. Emerging from the dimly lit parking garage,

I pulled out my cell phone, but the reception was inadequate. With head low, keeping an eye on my surroundings, I walked toward the end of the block just as Mike's car zoomed by.

"Son of a..." I gritted out and walked beneath a tree with a low branch that dropped leaves and little green fuzzy things into my hair.

At least the breeze was nice and refreshing. I was free, not stuck in a car with a creep in the dark.

Swiping my hand through my hair, probably making it worse, I checked my cell.

Screw me harder...

My phone had two bars, just enough to get a call out, but the battery flashed red. I hurried to call Sana. It rang four times. I tapped my foot against the cracked cement. The call went to voicemail.

"Sana! Can you please pick me up?"

I glared at the phone. Dead.

Where was I anyway? No bus stops in sight. No cabs in sight. This night could get worse really fast in this situation.

I stomped a few blocks before a lit diner came into view. Just a few more blocks. Still incredibly pissed, I continued stomping before remembering that my body weight was supported by delicate five-inch heels. But it was too late. My ankle buckled as one foot crashed down into a deep crack in the cement. The heel twisted, and so did my ankle. Pain careened up my leg.

Tumbling forward, I held out my hands to keep my face from scraping the sidewalk. The fall was brief, and the harsh surface scratched my wrists and forearms, as well as my knees. The scream building inside my lungs somehow stayed in check, although my blood boiled hotter than ever.

On my haunches, I tugged off the beautiful pumps and held the broken one up to the streetlamp light. There went fourteen hundred dollars down the drain. The heel was dead, and soon Mike would be, too.

The few taxis that drove by were already occupied. I kept trying to hail them anyway, to no avail.

With every bare step across the rough, disgusting city sidewalk, ripe with nasty germs, possible hookworms, and tetanus, I flinched. My ankle sent a lightning bolt of hot pain racing up my leg. Gritting my teeth, I marched on, and by the time the diner showered the red neon light from its "OPEN" sign over me, my ankle hurt so bad that tears blurred my vision.

Suck it up.

I gathered myself, my precious shoes dangling in one hand, and pushed through the doors. With eyes set firmly on the lady behind the register, I forced a slight smile and asked, "May I use your phone, please?"

She gave me the quick look-over, sympathy bubbling in the creases around her eyes and downturned mouth. "Oh, my. Looks as if you've had a rough night, my dear."

"I have. I'll even purchase something to use your phone."

"No need. Give me one moment to take care of this customer's bill, and I'll walk you behind the counter to use our landline."

"Thank you." Thanks to technology, I didn't have anyone's number memorized, but a taxi would do.

"Here's a glass of water while you wait." She filled one of many glasses behind her, set it on the counter between us, and returned to her customers.

I slumped against a barstool with the weight of many eyes glued to my side.

Chapter Nine
Jay

As I slurped a spoonful of my now tepid soup, a noodle splashed broth against my face, but my focus wasn't on the saltiness dripping down my chin. I, and just about every customer in the place, had paused to notice the gorgeous, dark beauty who had tiptoed in as if she were about to steal a cake right out of the case.

It took a double take to realize who she was. Liya's normally perfect hair was disheveled, frizzy, almost matted in some places. Her usually pressed clothes were smudged and wrinkled.

I leaned over into the aisle, my gaze sliding down her body. She was barefoot. Why was she at a diner this late with her shoes in her hand?

She wasn't any of my concern, though. Her predicament shouldn't bother me.

I wiped my chin and finished the last of my soup and sandwich as Mary, my usual waitress, returned with my card. I signed the receipt and watched as the older waitress met Liya. Together they walked along the counter, where she handed Liya the phone.

Something was most definitely not right, aside from her odd behavior and ruffled look. Why didn't she have a cell phone?

Not my business, remember?

Liya slumped her shoulders while on the phone, then walked back around the corner to sit on a stool. She planted her elbows on the countertop and dropped her face against her hands, heaving out a breath as her body went limp.

I had to walk past her to get to the door, right? And it would kill me if I found out later that she'd been in trouble and something happened because I didn't stop to ask.

Taking my jacket, I approached her continuously narrowing shoulders, as if she were trying to make herself smaller.

"Something got you down?"

"Move along," she grunted without looking up.

"Are you okay, Liya?"

She slowly peered over her hands, her cheeks flushed, her eyes watery and smeared with eyeliner beneath her lashes. I automatically sat down and leaned into her, my heart racing with a hundred possibilities of what had put the all-empowered Liya in such a beaten state. She didn't bother pulling away or telling me to shove off, which worried me even more.

"What happened to you?"

She cleared her throat, sat upright, and looked straight ahead, blinking rapidly a few times. "Nothing. I'm fine."

"You're a bad liar."

She licked her bottom lip in contemplation but didn't have a smart comeback. I leaned an arm on the counter. My knee almost touched her leg. Would she slap me if I brushed some of that unruly hair out of her face? Something told me it was best not to touch her, no matter how much I wanted to.

"Do you need a ride?" I asked gently.

"No."

"How are you getting home?"

Her bitter gaze relaxed. "Don't worry about it."

"What happened to your shoes?"

"I broke them."

"That's too bad. They're pretty."

"And worth fourteen hundred dollars."

What the hell? Were they made of gold and stardust?

"Are you going to hang around here all night?"

"A cab's coming," she said.

"Good. It's late. The diner closes in five minutes."

She groaned.

"The cab is coming before then, right?"

"Why do you care?"

"I'd hate to leave knowing that you had to wait outside, alone in the dark. When's the cab getting here?"

"Fifteen minutes."

"Are you sure that you don't want a ride home?"

"Yep." She kept her focus on the wall ahead, at the stacked glasses and coffee cups.

"Are you hungry?"

"What?" She looked at me, startled.

"Have you eaten? I can buy you dinner."

"I can buy my own dinner."

"Let me guess...you were on a date or something?"

"Leave," she growled, and I had my answer.

"Some idiot left you hanging, huh?"

"I swear to god if you don't leave me alone..."

I tapped the counter. "I'm just trying to help."

"Go help yourself."

"Fine," I snapped and left, casting one last glance over my shoulder at her frigid frame.

I walked out into a gust of wind but waited at the end of the row of windows. I wanted to see if she would change her mind, but Liya didn't strike me as the type of woman who swallowed her pride long enough to seek help.

Through the glass window, I caught her watching me, but she promptly turned back around. Her back stiffened.

What a proud woman.

And what a sap I was, because I waited in my car down the street. Over twenty minutes went by and no cab, no Liya. The last of the diner customers left, and the lights dimmed. A light drizzle sprinkled across the windshield.

Screw this. I didn't know about her, but *I* didn't have all night to wait around.

I marched into the diner. The bell above the door chimed, announcing my entrance, just as the waitress looked at me to say, "Sorry, we're closed."

"I know, Mary. I came for her."

Liya groaned, "Didn't you leave?"

"Where's the cab?"

"They're delayed."

"Okay. Let's go."

"No."

I slipped my jacket around her shoulders.

"What are you doing?" she asked.

"Mary needs to lock up the diner, and I'm not sitting outside any longer."

"No one told you to wait for me!"

"But I'm waiting for you anyway." I stretched my arm toward the door.

Liya hobbled at first, and I caught her when she almost tripped. She cringed every time she stepped on her left foot.

"Did you hurt your ankle?" I asked.

"Yes."

Although she kept my jacket around her, she crossed her arms and stared down the street as if the cab would magically arrive any second. "The cab's coming," she stated.

Mary, after poking her head out to make sure we were good, locked the doors behind us and, inside, turned off the dining area lights. The drizzle turned into a light rain, and Liya shuddered as her hair dampened. Strands and clumps stuck to her forehead and cheeks.

I took her hand and she startled. "What now?"

I shot her my most stoic expression and brought her toward my car. This time, she did not argue. I opened the passenger-side door for her, and she slipped in. Between keeping my jacket on, straightening her skirt, and handling her purse and shoes, she was too occupied to get to the seat belt. So I did it for her, leaned down and across her, our faces so close that our body heat bounced off each other.

"*What now?*" she asked again.

I didn't respond. The answer was obvious. It took everything inside me not to slam the door once I secured her seat belt. She couldn't for a second be grateful, or at least keep quiet if she couldn't say anything nice?

I walked to the other side, slipped into the car, and drove. I kept silent the entire time and didn't ask her directions to her place. She told me. A left here. A right there. Two more lights. The building on the right with the metal balcony railings.

The mood in the car was far different than it had ever been between us. We usually bickered, one insult to meet the last, but this time I kept quiet. Which left her to be quiet. She simmered down and accepted my help.

I opened her door just as the rain increased, and helped Liya out, taking her purse and shoes so she could concentrate on walking on a bad ankle.

"Where?"

"I can walk to my door from here," she insisted.

"*Where?*"

She sighed but replied, "Top floor, first on the right."

I went to slide my arm across her back. Liya nearly jumped out of her skin and shot a death scowl so potent, my bones felt it. I held my hands up and slowly said, "I'm sorry."

She swallowed and scoffed.

"What happened tonight, Liya?"

"None of your business."

I clenched my jaw and slowed my beating heart, my head crammed with all the worst-case scenarios. But maybe she didn't need an angry man making things worse by trying to help.

I took a step back and calmly asked, "May I help you up to your apartment?"

She furrowed her brows, as if she couldn't trust or believe that all I wanted was to get her safely inside. Finally, she nodded and concentrated on the stairs into the lobby as I carefully slipped my arm around her upper waist, her left side against me for support. By the time we reached the elevators, her stamina waned and every step incited a grunt. By the time we walked out onto the top floor, she hobbled miserably and hissed with every movement. She shook under my arm, and when she unlocked her door and flipped on the light inside, the brightness illuminated the scratches on her arms and wrists and a light bruise on her cheek.

A whole new wave of anger overtook me. Not at her, but at whatever had happened, and god help me, if the imbecile who abandoned her on their date hurt her, I might actually punch him.

In the foyer, I closed the door behind us and touched her face. "Did someone hit you? Do you want me to call the police?" I growled.

"No," she replied softly. "I fell."

"Seriously?"

Her attitude returned in the tilt of her head and raised eyebrows as she said, "You think I wouldn't beat someone who hit me?"

"You're right, but it doesn't mean you wouldn't lie about getting hit in the first place."

"I didn't get hit. My heel snagged in a crack on the sidewalk, it broke, and I fell. Hence the broken shoe, scrapes, and twisted ankle."

"Maybe I should've asked before you made it up to the tenth floor, but do you need to go to the ER?"

"No. Preeti is a doctor. She'd tell me to RICE, you know? Rest, ice, compress, elevate."

"If you don't think it's broken." I squatted in front of her, and she stilled as I touched her ankle slowly, looking up to her to make sure she didn't take this the wrong way. She held in a breath but eventually relaxed, her shoulders limp. The ankle was definitely swollen and blotchy. I squeezed gently to gauge the pain. She merely hissed but didn't pull back or kick me. "It's not bruised, doesn't have a bone poking through." I rose. "Hopefully it's not fractured."

"I wouldn't be able to walk on it at all if it was."

"Right." I rolled up my sleeves, took my shoes off, and placed our shoes on the floor and her purse on the kitchen counter.

"What are you doing?"

"What? You allow people to walk into your apartment with shoes on?"

"Well, no, but *why* are you staying?"

I found the glasses in the cupboard and poured water. "Where's your medicine cabinet?"

"In the bathroom. I can do it," she protested, but one step forward and she yelped.

I handed her the water. "Hold this."

"Um. Okay."

"May I?" I asked, now sorely aware that touching her again could trigger whatever the hell had happened tonight.

"Sure…"

Once she took the glass, I scooped her up. She was light in my hold. Her breath escaped her lips in a burst of brief pants as she awkwardly tried to maintain a distance. I readjusted her in my arms, and she finally collapsed against my chest.

There were only two doors past the living room: one cracked open to reveal the corner of a bed, and another revealed a bathroom. I entered the latter.

I settled Liya on the edge of the bathtub and turned on the water.

"Are you going to bathe me?" she asked sarcastically. "Because the medicine is up there."

I roamed through the medicine cabinet until I saw the familiar orange color of a brand-name ibuprofen bottle. "That idea doesn't suck," I muttered.

She took the bottle and popped a few pills while I sat across from her and lathered my hands with her body wash. The scent of Hawaiian flowers filled the room, the smell beneath her perfume.

Lifting her foot, I gently swung it over the lip of the tub. Her cheeks flared red as she shoved her skirt in between her legs, struggled to keep her knees together, and at the same time braced the wall for balance. Anger flashed across her eyes, and I knew she was about to rip me a new one.

I said, "I should've asked. Is this okay?"

She relented, but I knew her well enough to know she had no quarrels in letting me know otherwise.

"Those sidewalks are filthy. You don't want to get all that in between your sheets, do you?"

I gazed up at her as I stroked her feet, hitting the arches and toes. Sparks of pleasure glistened across her face, until I washed her ankle. She bit her lower lip in a whimper, tears flooding her eyes as she blinked them away.

"Do you want me to stop?"

"No…" she replied, her voice soft.

"Does it hurt that badly?"

She nodded. "It'll go away. It's not broken."

"Hmm. You'll have to wear flats for a while at work."

"Ugh."

I chuckled. "There are worse things in life."

I dried off her foot after a good scrub and stood. I grabbed her waist and slid her across the lip of the tub and switched positions. We went through the same routine. Lift foot. Shove skirt between legs. Keep knees ungracefully closed with leg bent sideways. Brace the wall. Lather. Stroke. Pleasure across her face.

After I dried her foot, I handed her a wet washcloth so she could wash her face. Instead of removing all of her makeup with a good scrub, she dabbed beneath her eyes and removed the smudged blackness from her eyeliner.

"The bed or the couch?"

"What?" she asked, her eyes wide in an indignant warning.

"Do you want to RICE in bed or on the couch? I can lock up when I leave, but you need to lie down and put a pillow under your ankle."

"Oh. Um, bed. But I can walk." She stood and buckled, her shoulder slumping against the wall.

I didn't ask if I could touch her again. I let her walk and stood nearby in case she stumbled. We finally made it to her room. Liya crawled into bed after I pulled down the sheets.

She had a canopy bed with lavender and dark gray bedding and gray window drapes. The lavender was unexpected, but somehow the combination put Liya's classy touch on display.

With a pillow propped under her feet, a newly filled glass of water and the bottle of ibuprofen on the bedside table, an ice pack on her ankle, and her phone on the charger within reach, she was set.

She quickly checked her phone as soon as it turned on. I took it before the screen locked.

"What are you doing?" she asked.

"Programming my number." I sent a text to my phone so that I'd have her number, too, and set it down within her reach.

I tucked her in. "Stay off the foot."

Her gaze stuck to the wall in front of her, her lips smashed together. I didn't expect a thank-you or anything, and she wasn't going to give one. But I would go home knowing that she made it safely through the night. And that was enough.

"Well. Good night."

She nodded, and I left.

Chapter Ten
Liya

Jay's footsteps were silent save for the squeak in the foyer when he put his shoes on. The front door opened and closed.

Sitting up in bed, I called out, "Jay?"

Nothing but silence.

"Jay?" I asked louder, only to be met again with the quietness of my apartment.

My head hit the pillow as my thoughts mulled over the events of the night. *Mike.* I was going to beat his ass the next time I saw him. He owed me fourteen hundred dollars for those shoes.

Who was I kidding? Shoes came and went. They were replaceable and dispensable. But for the first time in years, I'd placed myself in a situation that had scared me half to death. Several years ago, fifteen-year-old Liya had been trapped in Mukesh's house, convinced that she had done something wrong to provoke his crude behavior. Worse than that, she'd worried she'd done something wrong by exposing him to her parents. Ever since, I stepped into a position of power with boys, and then men. Things never went further than my realm of control, and most times, they never went far at all. I required full control. At all times. In all things.

I am not a whore, Mike. Not even close.

I was a woman who had physical, *consensual* relationships, and I was not ashamed.

No matter how strong I tried to be, I was not *that* strong. I could hit a man and cause damage, but I wouldn't have been able to fend Mike off if he tried hard enough. My mental state was not barricaded enough to withstand another *situation.*

Stupid tears, hot and messy, cascaded down my face as my vision blurred. Hopefully Jay had really left, because if he knew how I turned over, curled into a ball, and cried into the pillows, I would never be able to save face.

Men should not have control over me.

Men should not have control over me.

Men should not have control over me…

Despite the mantra, my chest heaved as I hyperventilated, and hot tears drenched my face. But the turbulent whorls of weakness and sadness evaporated as I screamed into my pillow. By the time I rolled onto my back, wiped my face dry, and cleared my throat, I had gathered myself. My breathing calmed. My temper, my pulse, and my shaking calmed. I combed my fingers through bedraggled hair.

No man was worth tears. Especially a fading blip like Mike.

As I lay in bed, effortlessly moving between anger and depression, I kept glancing at my phone. I tried to be a strong woman, I swore I did, but being a victim of something did not make me weak. Right?

Asking for help or comfort did not make me weak.

My brain told me to shut up and keep this to myself. But that had to be a residual impact from what happened years ago. Because Dad had said it to me. Girls who get assaulted or harassed usually placed themselves in that situation. Why was I alone with a man?

I punched my pillow in its fluffy gut. "Effing screw you, Dad."
He was wrong.

I snatched up my phone and called Reema.

"Hey, what's wrong?" she asked in a scratchy, sleepy voice.

"Something has to be wrong?" I asked, hating that my voice
wobbled.

"Yes. It's late. Are you drunk? Do you need me to pick
you up?"

I clenched my eyes, and tears streamed down my face. God
bless her sweet heart. She wouldn't ignore my phone call or get
irritated if I had been drunk and needed a ride.

"No. I'm home." The words slipped out with a shudder.

"What happened?" Reema asked, sounding fully alert.

"I had a bad night," I almost sobbed. "I know it's late, but…"

Fabric rustled on her end of the phone, and I knew she'd shot
out of bed. "Preeti is studying in the living room. I'll get Sana.
We'll be right over!"

About half an hour later, she'd texted that she was unlocking
the door, which I was grateful for. I didn't want to descend into a
panic attack, giving Mike power by fearing that he was breaking
into my safe space.

I never felt more overwhelming love for my girls than when we
came through for one another. Reema, Preeti, and Sana crawled
into bed with me with a solemnness in their eyes.

Sana, without a word, popped open a tub of my favorite Blue
Bell ice cream and handed me a spoon first. We quietly gave one
another a half smile as I scooped out some sweetness, letting the
cold melt on my tongue.

Reema turned on the TV and joked, "Netflix and chill?"

✳

The following morning, I dressed to cover any scratches. In the privacy of the bedroom, Preeti examined my ankle and wrapped it. My ankle was bruised and swollen and hurt to walk on, but it didn't look too bad.

For the next week, I would have to say goodbye to skirts and high heels and hello to dress pants, compression wraps, and flats.

It took forever to hobble from my car to the building, cross the hall to the elevator, then down another hall to my office, but I made it to work bright and early Monday morning. Mike worked in the building down the street, and we'd run into each other often during lunch. He wouldn't dare show his face near me again, but if he did, we'd get some crucial things settled. My resolution to face Mike was so vehement within me that I wished Mike *would* cross my path. I banished any lingering fear and anxiety. I was ready.

Since we had our Jay-led corporate meeting today, I went straight to the boardroom, took my time sitting down, and sighed as soon as I displaced the weight from my ankle. It throbbed and thrummed, and I couldn't help but slip off my shoe and gently massage the slightly swollen area. Maybe Wendy could bring ice to my office later.

This moment of peace and tranquility at work was alien. Although nice, it didn't last long. The door opened and Jay walked in, his head down as he read his tablet, a briefcase in the other hand. He wore the hell out of a dark gray suit; tailored lines and expensive fabric that enhanced his physique.

He dropped his briefcase at the end of the table and looked up. He half smiled, but it seemed nothing but sincere.

"You're here early," he commented.

"Took my time. Didn't want to give you a reason to call me out in front of everyone."

"Ah. That first meeting was probably not my best moment."

I arched my brows and poked. "You have best moments?"

He laughed. "Ouch. You seem to be in a better mood. How's the ankle?"

My body warmed, recalling how he'd seen me all frazzled and out of it last night and, to boot, had taken care of me the way he did. "It still hurts, but not as badly."

"Broken?"

"Preeti says it's sprained. Nothing serious."

"Glad to hear it."

Gratitude hung on the tip of my tongue, but Jay nodded and went about setting up. The fabric of his suit stretched across his back as he scribbled a few things on the whiteboard beside the PowerPoint display. He had broad shoulders and a wide back that tapered at his waist. When he reached up to draw a line over the top of his words, his suit jacket arched up and tugged against a very nice backside.

I bit my lower lip and glared at the notes on my tablet. What was I doing?

Within minutes, the awkward silence dismantled as the rest of the attendees filed in. The meeting went on as planned, and Jay revealed the extreme situation we were headed into, but most of us had guessed it was coming. Or in my case, knew because he'd told me.

Lawsuits galore were racing toward us. Payouts and settlements were on the forefront. We would hemorrhage money that was owed to customers and patients, as it was the right thing to do, but where did that leave us? Did this company have enough money to keep going? Did we have enough proof of our formidable, albeit imperfect, practices to evade some liability?

I supposed there was no such thing as a stress-free life, no matter my education, career path, position, or pay. There was always one thing or another, but sometimes it was a wonder that I hadn't given up by now.

Needless to say, my head wasn't into paying attention to the fiscal mess today. There was only so much I could do, but at least Jay was a nice distraction. Easy on the eyes and the ears. Part of me wanted to scold myself for even liking him this way, but the other part kept reminiscing about last night. The way he had taken care of me, asked if it was okay to touch me, made sure I didn't feel threatened or scared or belittled, as if I needed a man to save me.

Because I didn't.

But it was nice to know he was there and willing.

After others bustled out of the conference room, Sam asked, "Are you feeling all right, Liya?"

"Yes, why?"

"You're unusually quiet."

"It's a lot of work on our shoulders. Time to close our mouths, put our heads down, and get to work."

"Spoken like a true leader. I'm proud of you."

"Proud that I can keep my mouth shut?" I smirked, only half joking.

He grinned. "Among other things, but yes. Don't worry too much; we'll work our butts off, and if our best isn't enough to keep this place floating, then I know we will all be fine elsewhere."

I nodded as everyone gathered their things and left. Reassuring words or ominous forewarning? There were three things we could do: quit; work our hardest to keep the company afloat and hope the board appreciated us; or slow down the momentum and do a half-assed job as long as the paychecks rolled in.

Given my work ethic, I did not bow. I rose to the challenge with a game face...unlike how I rose to my feet with little grace and a lot of pain.

"Are you sure you don't want to have that x-rayed?" Jay asked from across the room.

We were alone. Again.

"No. It should be fine," I insisted, and gripped the edge of the table for support as I walked around the corner.

Jay held the door open, and I paused to glare at him. "What?" he asked.

I sighed.

"Get it out. Come on. What do you have to say now?"

I shook my head and glanced away. "I am not a damsel in distress."

"No one ever said you were."

"But you thought it."

"Oh, did I now?" he asked, his right brow arched.

"Yes. You thought it when you saw me at the diner."

He arrogantly laughed. "I would've done the same thing for anyone I knew."

"You would've waited for one of the security guards from downstairs?"

He nodded and replied, "Yes. I would've given them a ride home."

"And you would've helped them to their apartment?"

"Yes."

"And carried them to the bathroom?"

"Well, no. Have you seen those guys? They're like NFL players. I wouldn't have been able to carry them."

I cut down my smile before it had a chance to fully form. "And you would've cleaned their feet?"

"I would've given them a washcloth, water, medicine, and ice. Look. I'm not saying I didn't go the extra mile with you. But what I *am* saying is that no one thinks you're weak or incapable of taking care of yourself. You're human, not a damsel in distress who needs saving. I am not a chauvinistic, egotistical man who thinks you need me. I'm just a nice guy who helped out. That's all. No one's reading anything into this except you."

"That's it?"

"Yes. Trust me, I don't expect a woman to be fragile all the time and unable to figure things out on her own. No one ever doubts that you're an intelligent, capable woman."

"Oh," I breathed. "Good. I wanted to be clear on that."

He tapped the doorknob that was gripped between his fingers. "Now I don't know if I should let you walk ahead of me and risk getting scolded, or walk ahead of you and risk having something thrown at me."

I laughed, which surprised us both. "How about letting the injured go first? That way you can do both—close the door and still pass me in the hall to get to the elevator."

"Sounds appropriate."

I twisted my lips. "Don't sound so sarcastic."

He shrugged. "I can't say 'ladies first' around you. But when that ankle is healed, it's every man for himself."

"Are you saying that I'm a man?" I asked as I hobbled past him.

"You are most definitely not a man, Liya," he muttered.

I'd only made it about three steps before Jay reappeared at my side.

"Do you need a wheelchair?" he asked, amusement lacing his deep voice.

"I don't think that will help. Unless Wendy wants to push me around all day." I shook my head. "No, I'm fine."

We parted ways at the elevator. He was off to his next meeting, and I was heading back to my old lab. Time to micromanage, I supposed.

The lab smelled like chemicals and cleaners, metal and plastic.

The counters were cluttered with pipettes and microscopes, computers and monitors.

I cut through the lobby to get to some of the offices on the other end of the floor, but as soon as I turned the corner, my body flared hot. Why was *Mike* here?

I could go two ways: curl into myself and be scared, awkward, as if last night was all on me. Or I could be pissed, in his face, and remind him not to *ever* screw with me again.

I chose the latter. And while anger wasn't the emotion I wanted to rely on, it sure was a hell of a lot better than feeling like the victim.

What did he think he was doing in *my* building talking to *my* coworkers? Sure, they were friends of his, but if Mike thought he could creep into my space, then he was about to get a serious wake-up call.

Mike chatted with two other guys and boasted about his recent sexual conquest. AKA *me*.

"Was she as hot in bed as she looks?" the one to the right asked.

"So hot," Mike replied, earning pathetic cheers. "That thing she does with her tongue...god *damn*."

I actually felt my blood boil.

"So she's a freak? All nasty in the right ways?" the second guy asked.

"Oh, yeah. And she was begging for it, calling me 'daddy' and telling me to fu—"

"Telling you to *what*?" I growled.

The first guy had the common sense to look away, wipe that lascivious smile off his face, and pretend he hadn't heard anything as he skulked past me. The second was as idiotic as Mike, apparently, since he stayed in the lobby, looking like he wanted to know everything that was about to happen.

Mike shrugged, and for a moment I thought he'd try to play it off. If he had done that, then guy one and guy two might've gotten the hint that Mike might not be telling the truth after all. But Mike, like most lying scum, wanted to save face.

"You knew that I would probably say something to my friends about our amazing night, right?" he said.

"Which part of it? The nice French dinner?" I asked sweetly, and guy two grinned. "Or where you tried to do me in your car for your security buddy to get us on tape?"

Mike took a step toward me, his face still a little too smug.

"Or how about when I bitch-slapped you?"

Guy two's mouth dropped, and *finally* he got the hint. He made his way toward the exit, where I stood, but I put a hand out and said, "Stay. Really. You might want to hear how Mike called me a whore when I did *not* put out."

His face paled, as if this was the last place on earth he wanted to be right now.

"And would you like to hear about how he got aggressive because I didn't open my legs for him? Or how he left me stranded in the middle of nowhere? Speaking of, jackass, I broke my most expensive heels because of you and sprained my ankle."

Then I looked at my coworkers and sternly added, "I'm going to see both of you in one hour in my office. I better not catch you in this type of conversation again or you'll be heading straight to HR. Am I understood?"

They nodded and darted away as I hobbled toward Mike. "You owe me fourteen hundred dollars."

"I don't owe you a damn thing."

"Oh, you think that? I'm going to give you thirty seconds to leave my building."

He clenched his lips and stood over me, as if *that* intimidation worked. There was a certain nauseating feeling that Mike might've done this before. He seemed way too cool and confident, which made me wonder if other women had been too scared to speak out against him.

"What are you going to do, Mike? Hit me?" *Yes, Mike, anger me even more so this nagging sliver of fear slips away.* I could do rage all day. I couldn't do fear. Not again. Never again.

"I have plenty of friends in this building. You can't stop me from talking to them."

"Why are you such a dick?"

"I thought you liked dicks."

I fumed hotter by the second. My knuckles turned ghastly white as I made fists, and if I didn't walk away right now, I would certainly be fired...and then arrested for assault. He wasn't worth the trouble or the jail time.

I sneered. I calmly whipped out my cell phone and took a picture.

"What are you doing?" he demanded.

"Leave now, jackass, or you'll be removed and handed over to the police. Your picture will be with security. Oh, wait. There's security." I flagged down the broad gentleman in uniform.

James, playing his position with authority, looped his thumbs into his belt and marched over. "Hi, Liya. Need something?" he asked in a baritone voice.

"Hello, James. Do you mind showing this man to the exit?"

He eyed Mike when he asked me, "Is there a problem here?"

I glared at a suddenly very restrained Mike. "*Is* there a problem?"

"No." He spoke carefully. "I'm leaving right now."

And although I didn't ask James to walk him out anyway, he followed Mike and glanced back at me. I gave him a reassuring and thankful nod.

As soon as Mike left, I released a shuddering breath. I absolutely hated that he had me shaking, even if it was just one sigh.

Chapter Eleven
Jay

The small and packed restaurant smelled divine—at least according to an empty, rumbling stomach. At this rate I'd eat that unappealing split pea soup on the counter. For a second, I considered taking something up to Liya, something better than green soup, of course, so she wouldn't have to spend half an hour limping back and forth to get lunch, but she had an assistant for that. And why did such a thought even cross my mind?

While stuffing my face with enchiladas and salad, I read over some of my notes at a small table in the corner. The crowd had thickened in the last ten minutes, and so had the lunch hour commotion. I was distracted by a pair of loud guys to my right.

"She was pissed," the first said.

"I thought she was going to fire us," the second added.

I shook my head. Well, if they made a mistake big enough to upset their boss, then maybe they deserved a scare. Also, maybe they needed to quiet the hell down.

"Do you think she slept with him?"

"I have no idea. Mike didn't even look fazed when she caught him talking about her."

Mike? Huh. Couldn't be the same Mike who had asked Liya out. She had turned him down.

"She was probably just pissed because Mike was blabbing about their night."

I clenched my jaw unexpectedly, reeled into their conversation as if it were a blow-by-blow play of the Super Bowl.

"Yeah, for sure. No girl likes that. I don't know, and by how scary she was, I don't even care anymore. Mike can keep his sex scandals to himself."

"She is fine, though."

"Yeah, no doubt."

"There's got to be something with those Indian chicks."

I exhaled. How many Mikes around here recently asked out an Indian woman?

I clenched and unclenched my fists. Had *he* done something to Liya that night she showed up at the diner?

I couldn't finish my lunch. It was about to come up any minute with the disgust and anger raging through me.

The guys went into details of what "Mike the man" had said. The things she did with her mouth, with her tongue, things only pros knew how to do so well.

I slammed down my drink, startling them. Our eyes met, and they clamped their mouths.

"Are you talking about Liya?" I growled.

"Uh, you know her?" the first asked with a snicker.

"Yeah. Are you talking about Liya and Mike?"

The second guy nodded.

I wiped my mouth with a napkin and crumpled it over my plate. "You do realize you can get fired for malicious gossip and defamation of character?"

He raised his hands. "Look, man. We're just talking about something that happened today. We are not interested in them anymore. That's way too much drama."

"I better not hear you talking about Liya or anyone that way."

"Sure…"

I eyed them for another moment, keeping my glare intense. They seemed both awkward and agitated, glancing away but without apology. "Where's Mike?"

"Um…"

"Um, *what*?"

They looked past me at the building across the street. I turned and saw him, the same guy who had been flirting with Liya at the café. He'd emerged from her building with a very stern security officer. Mike spoke to James, but he didn't seem to be in the mood. Not with those crossed arms and stoic features.

I stole a few calming breaths as I marched across the street to a near irrational Mike, who claimed, "Come on, man. I have friends in there. You've seen me all the time. She's just mad at something. Nothing happened. This makes me look bad when I didn't do anything."

But James wasn't having it. He'd been the security officer who cleared me for special access for the next few months while I worked with the company. He was extremely friendly, but also intimidating when the situation called for it.

"Is there an issue?" I asked James and then eyed Mike.

"Just making sure this man found his way out," James replied.

"Mike, right?" I asked.

Mike nodded.

I gave James a thankful glance, and he retreated into the building, behind the glass doors and translucent wall to the lobby. He watched us from behind the security desk.

"You recognize me?" I asked, my voice stony.

Mike squinted in the harsh midday light. "Oh, yeah, I guess I've seen you around."

"I was with Liya at the café when you asked her out. I heard you've been spreading rumors about her."

He straightened up. "You her brother or something?"

"Yeah, because there are only a billion Indians in the world and we're all related."

"You all look the same to me." He sneered.

"And I wonder why in the world Liya ever agreed to go out with you."

"If you heard the rumors, then you know why. She wanted a piece of this and I gave it to her."

I ground out carefully, "Don't lie. I'm not one of your groveling minions you can impress with your BS stories."

"You're some big shot. I get it."

"I want you to straighten out the rumors and then leave Liya alone."

"Rumors are rumors. Sometimes they're true, sometimes they're not. They get passed around and then forgotten about. Who said I started any of them?" he asked defensively.

"Let's not play games. I have meetings to get to and work to do."

"So who's stopping you?"

"Here's what you're going to do, Mike."

He glared at me.

"Before the end of the day, you're going to go up to every person you bragged to and set the story straight. You can start with your two buddies at the restaurant over there who are watching us right now. Then you're going to go across the street, buy the biggest floral arrangement you can find, and march your useless self to Liya's office, security-escorted of course, get on your knees, and grovel for her forgiveness in front of anyone present.

Then, I don't want to ever see you in or near this building, or near Liya, again."

He laughed. "Are you smoking something?"

"Do you know why you're going to do this?" I narrowed my eyes.

"I know why I'm *not* doing that."

"You're going to do this out of the kindness of your heart because you realize what you did was wrong."

He laughed. "Thanks for the joke."

"Legal threats probably don't work for you."

He laughed again. "Get out of my face, man."

"Because Liya has every right to press charges, to get a restraining order against you."

"Don't threaten me."

"It's not a threat. There are cameras everywhere. Whatever you claim you didn't do, just remember there's most likely evidence to the contrary. Our security officer friend on the other side of this wall is probably looking through footage right now. Even if all you did was say something, that's considered harassment. Actions have consequences. You get me, Mike?"

"Yes," he stuttered, his gaze darting between me and the security desk in the lobby.

"Now what are you going to do?" I asked, my voice low.

"Straighten out the rumors, get the flowers, and beg Liya."

"Are we going to have any issues?"

"No." He took a few steps backward, nearly bumping into a passerby.

"Are you sure?"

"Yes. I swear, man, I *swear*."

I watched him until he crossed the street and disappeared into the restaurant where his friends had been watching our interaction.

I walked into the building and toward the security desk. "Thanks for handling that, James."

"It's what I'm here for. Is there anything I should know about that guy?" he asked.

"His name is Mike. There's a tiny chance he might come by later today with flowers asking for Liya. Can you call me immediately if he does?" I asked as I wrote down my cell phone number for James, although he already had my detailed information in his database.

"Sure thing."

Chapter Twelve
Liya

The day could not end fast enough. Between the extra work-load and this killer pain in my inflamed ankle, crumpling into my leather chair with an ice pack hugged against my foot was by far the best thing that happened today.

As I sat in the tranquility of my office, I answered a call from Momma.

"It was good to see you at mandir," she said in her sweet, soft voice.

My heart swelled and broke at the same time. How was that possible, to love someone so much it hurt? "You, too. Is everything...okay?"

"Of course."

"Dad isn't being a giant ass—"

"Liya!" she hissed.

"Is he still upset?"

"A bit. He's trying very hard, you know? To secure a man for you, and you just walk away?"

"I don't want to get married."

"Because of your dad?"

"He's certainly a reason." Although my dad had never been a

leading example of a wonderful Indian husband, I of course saw them around. Rohan would be one. Jahn certainly appeared to be one. There were quite a number who doted on their wives and kids at mandir, those who went all out on romantic nonsense on social media, and those who ran the gossip circuit of having done this simple little gesture or that extraordinary thing.

Momma went on, "He's a good man most of the time. And not all men are like him. Jay is much nicer."

"No, thank you."

"If not now, then when? Men don't want to marry a woman over thirty."

I laughed. "Women these days go to college, sometimes for many, many years. They work and have careers and pursue other interests and *then* get married, well into their thirties. It's fine."

"Well into their thirties? And when are they going to have children?"

How could I explain to my mother that I could not commit to one person to save my life? That I abhorred being tied down by someone? That I loathed the idea of answering to a man? That I...was too broken to be wifey material anyway?

She went on with hope lighting her words, "I saw you speaking with Jay's mom."

"I apologized to her. She needed to know my intention wasn't to embarrass anyone and it wasn't anything against her."

"And you were speaking to Jay?"

"Arguing," I corrected.

"Liya!"

I rolled my eyes but somehow ended up grinning at the same time. "Well...he's easy to argue with."

"You say that about all men."

"Sounds like their problem, not mine. Don't get hung up on this idea of marrying me off to anyone, least of all Jay."

"He's handsome, no?"

"Sure."

"And educated, intelligent."

I checked my nails before adjusting the ice on my ankle. "Mm-hmm."

"What if we revisit the idea next month?"

I groaned. "No. Besides, with a man so…handsome and educated and intelligent, he won't be on the market for long."

"Why are you so stubborn?"

"I'm stubborn? Why don't you leave Dad?"

She gasped at the thought. "Stop that nonsense talk."

"Has he ever hit you? Or does he just verbally assault you?" I gritted, keeping my hands from clenching.

"He has never hit me. We will not talk about your father this way."

"But we can. If you ever need to talk," I replied carefully.

She didn't respond for so long I wondered if the line had been cut.

"I won't say a single word if you want to vent," I added.

There was another long silence between us before she asked, "How is work?"

"Busy."

"Did you work today? You are still working?"

"Of course. I'm at work right now, actually."

"Oh! You should get back."

"It was nice to hear from you."

"You should come by the house again."

I smiled. The irony of that invitation. "Maybe next time you can come by the apartment? You've never seen it."

"You know how your dad disapproves of you living alone like that."

"You can come without Dad, maybe?"

"Silly child of mine. Get back to work."

"You know that I love you, Momma, right?" I finally said. That phrase, that word was not something we expressed. It felt awkward, but it had to be said.

"I know," she replied softly.

We chatted for another few minutes before saying our goodbyes. The day was over. Most headed out, including Wendy, which explained why someone knocked directly on my opened door. A man. I could tell by the slacks and large hands, but not by his face hidden behind a comically large bouquet of roses.

"I think you have the wrong office," I said. "Who's that for? Maybe I can redirect you."

"It's for you," he said, sounding a lot like Mike.

I froze into place, hyperaware of every escape route and every ordinary item that could be turned into a weapon. I hated that his mere presence made me think this way.

He approached my desk and twisted one way and then another before finally placing the basket on one of the chairs.

"Not quite sure where you want this." He looked around, trying to find a spot for the behemoth.

"How did you get in here?" I asked curtly, noting where sharp things were located throughout my office. I could most definitely use a pencil to gouge his eyes out if he got too close. I sort of hoped he would try something. Let's see how he'd like feeling scared and threatened and dehumanized, how he'd like to deal with anxiety attacks and fears whenever he heard a creak in the middle of the night or walked too close to someone else or found himself outside alone in the dark.

"Security gave me ten minutes to bring this gift up."

"They just let you waltz in here? Did your friends vouch for you at security again?" I was going to ream those idiots.

"No. They're gone for the day. Your friend did."

"What friend?"

"The Indian guy. I don't know his name. He's in the hallway."

Jay? His shadow fell across the entrance and I knew he stood right outside the door. I kept my sigh of relief to myself. He wasn't far, then, just in case something happened. "What are you doing here, asshole?"

"Apologizing."

"With flowers? Isn't that cliché?"

He walked around the desk and dropped to his knees, glancing only once at the ice around my ankle but not bothering to ask about it. "Will you forgive me for how I acted last night?"

"No. Are you scared that I might report you? I'd be more terrified of that, Mike. Getting beaten by a woman is bad for the ego, but having a record will follow you wherever you go. To all of your jobs, to all of your relationships. People like to know the truth. And your truth is ugly."

"Please? Don't report me. I got out of hand. Nothing like that has happened before. I just want your forgiveness. I'm on my knees begging you."

"Asking once and saying 'please' once does not constitute begging."

He proceeded to ramble a dozen pleases, one after the other, until I could no longer stand the word or the insincerity. I groaned, trying to ignite anger to disguise the remnants of trepidation he'd left in me.

But then I saw a flicker of something in his eyes. I asked, "Mike...are you afraid of something?"

"No." He scoffed.

I took a pair of scissors from the top drawer. The sound of metal sliding against metal cut through the silence. Mike got to his feet real quick then. Yeah. He was afraid.

"How's it feel to be scared?"

"You're being very cryptic." He gave a hoarse chuckle.

"Cryptic is your last image of me calmly holding these scissors and telling you to forever wonder if I'm coming at you. This isn't over just because you brought flowers and a lame, insincere apology. I may or may not press charges against you. I may or may not have that video from the garage as evidence."

His mouth dropped, and his skin paled. A very *oh shit* look hit him. And it was beyond gratifying.

I went on, "I may or may not punch you in the throat if I see you again. But rest assured, people will find out. If I see you with another woman, she will hear it from me." I limped around the desk toward him as he backed away.

He opened his mouth to spew more nonsense, but thankfully Jay appeared behind him. Jay stood at the door, his arms crossed, his shoulder against the frame. He didn't even have to say anything. His presence was commanding and all-consuming. One knew when Jayesh Shah stepped into a room. There was something about his presence that made the tiny tremors in my body fade away. My grip on the scissors relaxed, something that didn't go unnoticed by him as he glanced at my fists.

Even though he seemed relaxed, the chiseled cut of his jaw was stern. Our eyes locked. He held my gaze with authority and confidence and, strangely enough, it wasn't the least bit domineering. Men like him hardly ever balanced strength without the sort of cockiness that instantly shut me off. Powerful men? Plus. Arrogant men? Minus a million points.

Mike eventually stopped babbling, his words drifting off, and looked over his shoulder.

"Am I interrupting?" Jay asked, his gaze firm on me.

"No. Mike was just leaving," I replied and placed the scissors on the desk behind me.

Jay looked to him pointedly, his tone dropping to something

menacing and terse. "Security is right outside waiting to escort you out. Bye."

Mike muttered something inaudible and skulked away, leaving Jay room to meander toward the floral arrangement. He rubbed a petal between his fingers. "Are you guys dating?"

"No."

"Nice flowers for someone not dating."

"Apology flowers. Did you have anything to do with this?"

"*Me?* I only met Mike the other day when he asked you out at the café."

"Hmm," I grunted suspiciously.

"What was he apologizing for?"

I shrugged. "For being him."

"Does it have anything to do with you showing up at the diner?"

"I don't know you well enough to get into that."

But Jay knew. He had everything to do with Mike's groveling. I couldn't hate Jay for that, because even though Mike apologized for the wrong reason, I was the one who'd scared him. Jay gave me the opportunity to get an upper hand on Mike, handing Mike back some of the fear that he'd burdened me with.

My trembling had fully subsided when I asked, "Do you want to take those home?"

"Why? You don't want them?"

"I love flowers, but coming from Mike, I couldn't be less interested. Besides, there might be a spy camera in there. Please, take them."

"A woman with gift standards?" he teased with a playful smile.

"You don't want to soften your bachelor pad with a giant basket of flowers?"

"Not if they're from Mike."

I laughed, tossed out the ice, and slipped on my shoes. "Too bad Wendy left for the day. Oh, I know the perfect place for these."

"Yeah?"

"The children's center at the hospital."

He watched me as if I'd just spoken alienese. "That's very thoughtful."

I wobbled to the arrangement, trying not to show the pain that worsened with every step, and picked up the basket. The thing was huge. I could barely get my arms around it, much less see around it. I struggled to get it to the door before Jay lifted the flowers from my hands.

"I've got it," I insisted. "I don't need a man to carry my things."

He held it low so he could see over the ferns. "How about me carrying something for an injured person so they don't injure themselves further because they can't see where they're going? Is that acceptable?"

I twisted my lips. "I suppose so."

We walked past the cleaning crew with Jay behind me as I set the pace.

Inside the elevator, he asked, "Did you drive today?"

"No. My friend Sana dropped me off," I said and remembered that I was supposed to call her for a ride home.

"Is she picking you up?"

I groaned. "I forgot to tell her what time. I'll just have to wait a little while for her, I guess."

We stepped out of the elevator as he suggested, "I can give you a ride."

"That's not necessary." I texted while we walked to the lobby.

"How long will she be?"

"With traffic, at least an hour."

"How about I give you a ride to the hospital to drop these off and then to your place? Sana will have less on her plate for tonight."

"I don't think that's a good idea."

"Because I'm a man, and all we want is to try to get into your pants?" he asked from behind the flowers, which made me crack a smile because he looked so ridiculous.

"I'm joking, you know?" he added.

I cleared my throat, mainly because I didn't want to laugh when I responded, "I know."

"Why am I still holding these?" He set the basket down. The tips of the ferns and baby's breath reached his knees. "Why don't you wait here, and I'll bring my car around?"

I nodded. Within a few minutes, the basket was in Jay's back seat, I buckled myself into the front seat, and we headed to the closest hospital, the one where Preeti worked. To elude conversation with Jay, I texted Preeti, and she met us outside of the ER.

"These are gorgeous!" she exclaimed as Jay pulled out the basket. "Wow, you weren't kidding about the size."

"Good thing I warned you, right?" I said.

"Right." She glanced at Jay and then gave me a curious look as he set the basket on a cart, which an orderly pushed through the automatic sliding double glass doors for us. "What are you two up to?"

"Nothing," I said. "Just a quick trip since Sana has my car."

"All right, well, call me later. I want to know all about...where these flowers came from. Nice seeing you again, Jay."

"You, too, Preeti. Have a good one."

She waved as we slipped back into the car and drove off. I hoped he wouldn't start up a conversation, and I even pretended to check my phone for missed messages.

He eventually commented, "Shilpa will be delivering in that hospital."

"That's nice. It's a very good hospital with high-rated staff. Preeti loves working there."

"Preeti is one of the medical residents at Shilpa's doctor's office."

"Are you excited about becoming an uncle?"

"Yeah." He grinned, and his perfectly cut profile shot up three hotness levels.

"Do you, uh, like babies?" I made a face, partly surprised at the fact that he might like kids but also partly disgusted because babies were so…messy.

"You make it sound like they're snakes. I don't mind kids. I'm not especially fond of them, but it's different when they're your niece or nephew."

"Shilpa and Jahn don't know if it's a boy or girl yet?"

"They want it to be a surprise, but they caved and are finding out soon. She's revealing it at their baby shower."

"That's sweet. You must be excited."

"I am. This will be the first grandbaby on both sides. Ma is ecstatic."

"What about your dad?"

He tensed, his voice a little lower when he replied, "He passed away."

"Oh. I'm sorry." I bit my lip, my heart stammering. I hoped that didn't sour his mood. I didn't know the details, although I was curious. All I could do was apologize. I never knew what to say to those who had lost someone. I didn't even know how long ago his father's passing had been to know where to begin.

He didn't say anything after that. Which should've been fine by me, but tension over his dad's death wasn't something that settled without any afterthought. Jay went quiet, his brows knitted and his lips pressed together as if he were in deep thought. I really wanted to ask, but it was absolutely not my business. What happened to him? He must've passed away recently for a grown man to shut down after one mention. Especially when Jay seemed as upset as he was saddened.

We approached my street, and I quietly said, "You can just pull up to the front."

He eased out of the tension and offered, "I'll walk you to your door."

"I'm fine."

"Are you sure?"

"Yes."

He pulled up to the curb, only a few feet from the steps up to the lobby. I opened the door and shifted to the side in order to put all of my weight on my good foot first. Before climbing out, I said, "Thank you."

"No problem. I don't live that far from here, so it's not out of my way."

I slowly added, "I mean, also, for last night. I didn't thank you for that."

The rigidity of his shoulders relaxed. "You don't have to."

"Yes, I do. You helped when I pushed you away. You did a lot for someone you don't even like."

"I don't *not* like you."

I smiled and he grinned. As in a full, all-out grin. The kind that reached his eyes and made little wrinkles at the corners. He had a multitude of faces, from stern and un-yielding to irritating and cocky. But for once, he turned his true face to me, the kind and happy one—the face I'd seen him wear at mandir with his family. I wondered what other faces he had, and if the rest of them were as easy to look at as this one.

"Maybe we can be friends," he suggested.

"Friend*ly*?"

"That works, too."

Once I was inside my apartment, I kicked off my shoes, untucked and unbuttoned my blouse, and slid my pants right off.

A soft tune escaped my lips as I poured a glass of wine in my undergarments and drew a hot bubble bath. I stripped down to nothing, stepped in, sank down, and sighed as the stress and exhaustion of the workday melted away. After today, I didn't mind having nothing else to entertain myself with than a good book.

And an onslaught of text messages.

Preeti: I'm home. Tell me everything! Why were you driving around with Jay? I thought you hated him! Did HE give you those gorgeous flowers?

Sana: How'd you get home? Sorry it would've taken me so long to get you.

Reema: Okay, seriously. Jay. What is up with that? And yes, Preeti and I are tag-teaming you!

Unknown Number: Hi, Liya! I hope this is the right number. And I hope you don't mind that I got it from Jay, but this is Shilpa. I didn't get a chance to give you an invitation to my baby shower. It's on the fifteenth. Hope you can make it. I'm sending it with Jay.

I took my time replying to everyone over the following hour, with Preeti, Reema, and Sana all in group text to save myself. All the details sent them into an emoticon-and-upper-case frenzy. No matter how many times I told them to calm down, that Jay and I were nothing more than slightly friendlier than what they'd seen at mandir, they wouldn't stop.

I then added Shilpa's contact information and replied that I would be happy to attend her shower.

As water drained out of the tub, and I stepped out and dried off, my phone screen lit up with a text message from Jay.

I wrinkled my nose. He did realize we weren't friends, right?

Curiosity got the better of me, and it took a great deal of effort to wait until I had changed into pajamas and started dinner before checking the message.

Jay: I gave Shilpa your number. Hope that's okay. She wanted to invite you to her baby shower.

Me: *Did you have something to do with that?*

Jay: No. It's not MY baby shower. She'd wanted to invite you since she met you.

There was nothing more to say. Still, I was tempted to give his contact info a picture. Apparently, I had plenty to choose from among Momma's many pictures sent via WhatsApp. Although only my friends had rummaged through his excellently selected pictures, I scrolled through them and admired Jay for all his irritating beauty. Finally, I assigned a picture to his name. Not the professional one, no matter how nice his suit. Not the one of him in a sherwani playing garba. But one of him walking down a street in plain jeans and an ordinary shirt. A formfitting shirt. The laid-back style, easygoing smile, and sparkling eyes in that photo were something that would make me pause every time his name popped up on my phone screen.

I sat down to my meal when my phone lit up again.

Jay: Are you going?

Okay, so maybe he was confused as to the difference between "friendly" and "friends."

Jay: You should go.

Me: *Why?*

Jay: Because Shilpa is nice and it would mean a lot to her. You know, if you're not busy that day.

I couldn't help it, and once I recalled his venomous words, a familiar pang in my chest sprouted to life.

Me: *I thought I wasn't good enough to be her friend.*

Calling someone out like that would've made any other guy leave me alone, but in a matter of seconds, he replied.

Jay: I'm sorry I said that.

Me: *Don't be sorry for saying what you mean.*

Jay: We both misjudged each other. Can we leave it at that?

I chewed on the inside of my lip.

Me: *I guess.*

Jay: Is this you admitting that you misjudged me and I'm not so bad after all?

Me: *Um, no. This is me saying I accept you admitting that you misjudged me.*

Jay: Well, maybe one day you'll tell me why you bailed.

Me: *Are we about to get into a texting argument?*

Jay: Only if you're bored and want to spend the evening arguing with me.

Damn it. Why was I smiling?

My fingers twitched over the touch screen.

Well...I *was* kind of bored...and I didn't have anything better to do...and arguing *was* in my nature.

Me: *Let me explain something to you, Jayesh Shah.*

Jay: Hit me with your best excuse, Liya Thakkar.

"Ha!" I said aloud, my laughter filling the quiet.

Me: *I was absolutely ambushed. My father is trying his hardest to marry me off, despite telling him I'm not interested. That dinner was supposed to be just me and my parents. I was vexed when you showed up, all ready to propose.*

Jay: Propose! I hardly knew you. What type of man did you think I was?

Me: *Honestly?*

Jay: Do I expect anything less than honesty from you?

I shook my head and smiled. Or maybe I hadn't stopped grinning this entire time. What was this guy doing to me?

Me: *I thought you were some jackass.*

Jay: Because of traditionally approaching you…or…?

Me: *That and smiling at me.*

Jay: I sort of figured. And noted. Never smile at Liya Thakkar.

I chewed on the inside of my cheek, trying to conjure up some witty remark. But nothing came to me. All I knew was that I never wanted Jay to hide his smile from me.

Chapter Thirteen
Jay

The sound of steel clanking against steel echoed through the weights section of the gym, and drowned out the swish of the cardio equipment on the floor above us. The only thing I concentrated on were the breaths that huffed out of my chest with each thrust of the bar, pushing my limits so I could feel the burn sear through my arms.

Jahn popped up behind me to spot so that the massive amount of weight wouldn't sever my head with an accidental slip. After my set, I sat up, heaved out a breath, and wiped sweat off my face with a towel. We moved on to machine weights.

"Missed you yesterday. I don't know anyone here to ask to spot, so I ended up doing cardio," Jahn commented, our eyes locked on our images on the wall-to-wall, ceiling-to-floor mirrors.

"Liya had me up all night."

His head swerved in my direction and he froze. "Say what?"

"I mean she had me up all night arguing."

He shook his head and did a few reps. "Was it worth it? Missed the gym, probably went to work tired, all stressed out. Why are you even talking to her? Thought you hated her."

"She's not that bad."

"Even if you were arguing all night? And what exactly were you arguing about?"

"Why she ditched the dinner with me."

"Okay." He stopped. "Why? May the mystery of the vanishing arranged could've-been fiancée be solved."

"She doesn't want to get married."

"And that was reason enough to leave?"

"Her side of the story is that she's been arguing with her parents about settling down. She told them she didn't want to meet me, and nothing against me personally, but she went to her parents' house under the impression they just wanted her over for dinner. She didn't realize her parents ambushed her until we walked into the house."

"Still not a good enough reason to bolt the way she did." He shrugged. Jahn wasn't wrong. No argument there.

"My thoughts exactly. At the least excuse yourself or go through the dinner and let me know on the side."

"No. She couldn't have sat through dinner; that would've just led Ma on. But she could've excused herself and saved her parents the embarrassment."

"You see how the argument started." I shook my head, exasperated. Liya and I had two sides to the same story, and we couldn't find a middle ground.

"Yes. But why did it last all night? What else did you guys possibly have to talk about? She doesn't want to get married. She was duped into the meeting. She ran. You didn't agree with how she handled it. That's about two minutes' worth of conversation," he said, and we switched places.

"Then we got into it over her ideas of what she *thinks* Indian men want in a wife, because, as you know, we're all the same."

"That could go on forever, but the question I'm really wondering is *why* did you let it go on all night?"

"It's hard not to argue back with her." I grunted with another push on my machine, working my pecs.

Jahn smirked. "Maybe you like her."

I shook my head before my brother got the wrong idea. "She's tolerable."

"So, then, why are you so agitated?"

"She asked about Dad," I admitted with an annoyed sigh.

"What did you say?"

"Nothing." We switched machines, Jahn on the chest press while I worked on triceps.

"And she probed?" Jahn asked, watching me more intently than I wanted.

"No. She didn't ask anything else. Why would she?"

"So what's the problem?"

"She got me thinking about Dad, more than usual, that is. So now I'm pissed." Not to mention it reminded me that I didn't deserve a happy ending with a wife and kids of my own. Not when I took Dad's happy ending from him.

Jahn sighed in that *brother, we're about to have a talk* sort of way. Resting his hands on his thighs, he bent at the waist. But I kept going, pushed harder, added more weights even when I strained.

"Calm down," he said, "before you hurt yourself. Don't take what happened so hard after all these years."

I slammed the weights down, almost snapping my elbows. "Are you joking? Don't take it so hard? Our dad *died*."

Jahn, always the tempered one between the two of us, replied compassionately, "Yeah, I know, but he died over fifteen years ago. I expect Ma to still mourn, but not so much us anymore."

I scoffed. "Did Dad die because of you?"

"God." Jahn shook his head. "You still blame yourself for what happened?"

I gawked at him. "Are you kidding me? I *am* the reason he

died." I sprang to my feet and returned to the free weights, claiming a bench to use forty-pound dumbbells.

Jahn waited about five minutes before grabbing a free weight for himself, allowing me some time to calm down. "You're not the only one who had to deal with his death."

"How are you even able to look at me and not hate me?"

"You think I blame you? Or hate you?" He eyed me, his features relaxed, kind. We'd had this talk a hundred times. It had been intense at first, mixed with tears and anger and frustration. Over time, Jahn ended up always being the calming one.

As for me? Anger still rose. Rage coated my insides and bubbled through my words. "Of course you do. Maybe you never said it or showed it, but you have to think it."

"You're being an idiot," he said a little harshly to drive the point home.

"So you have no resentment toward me?"

"No. I honestly do not. Never have."

I wiped my brow with my arm but kept pumping. By now, my arms had turned to rubber noodles, but I kept going.

"We were all devastated. We still miss him. Especially Ma. I had to become the man of the house to support us, and still go to college to honor our parents and be able to take care of you and Ma," Jahn said.

"I'm grateful. Believe me. But didn't you wish that you could just enjoy life?"

Jahn replied, "It's my honor. Remember that word? It's what our parents taught us. We don't blame people or hate situations. We deal, accept, move on, and make the best of it. We're fine now. Why? Because we remained strong and kept focused. It was hard, but worth it. I had the honor of taking care of my family and still getting my degree. I married an amazing woman and we're about to have a child. You got through law school. Dad wanted us to live our best lives, be happy. That's how we can honor him. We always had a meal in our bellies, right? A roof over our heads? Love in our home?"

"Yes," I answered. Jahn had a different way of looking at things. Was being happy a way to honor Dad? It felt more like betrayal.

"I hate that he died. I hate how it happened. I hate that you blame yourself and think we blame you, too. What Dad was…he was a hero. If we end up being half the man he was, we'll be lucky. You know what I mean?"

I sighed. "Yeah."

"You just saying that? Or do you believe it?" He grabbed my head and put me in a headlock.

I grappled with him, and he let go real quick. "Yeah. Yeah. I believe you. You wouldn't lie, right? Even to spare my feelings?"

"I'm not lying. You know me too well for that. Are we cool?" Jahn asked with raised brows and a hint of a smile.

I mumbled, "Yeah."

"That doesn't sound convincing. Do I have to put you into another headlock?" he joked.

"And risk getting beat in public? Try it," I jested.

He laughed, and I gently shoved him.

After our gym time, we headed to our cars. I placed a towel on the driver's seat for the drive home.

"So, you're really not interested in Liya?" Jahn asked, still standing next to me.

"I'm not. She's nice enough once you get to know her, but Ma doesn't need her attitude or to deal with the avalanche of rumors surrounding her." I shook my head and jangled the keys in my hand.

"Then you're open to considering a different woman?"

Not really. "Perhaps, eventually, but not right now."

"Why not?"

"Let this mess cool down before I give Ma hope again."

"Is that the only reason?"

I rolled my eyes. "I feel like we're in high school and you're trying to get me a prom date because the girl I want is taken."

"So *Liya* is the woman you want?" He grinned hard.

I punched him in the arm, and he faked a serious injury by grabbing his biceps and cringing.

"I ask because there is a woman who's interested in you. She just finished pharmacy school. Her parents are nice. And she goes to mandir every weekend with her family. We know her parents. You'll be seeing her around a lot now. Her name is Kaajal, Mukesh Uncle's youngest daughter. She'll be at the baby shower, so you can check her out in person."

My face heated, prickled with annoyance. "Did you give her any reason to think I'm at all interested?"

"No. She doesn't know you know about her interest."

"I'll be cordial. That's all I can promise. Rushing into considering someone else doesn't sit right." Not wanting to linger on marriage prospects, I looked down at my sneakers and asked, "Are you sure you're not mad about Dad?"

He gripped my shoulder with one broad hand. He looked me in the eye and said in a stern, authoritative, and promising voice, "I will never lie to you. I have never and will never blame you. What happened was tragic, but it happened because Dad was a hero. *He was a hero.*"

I nodded once. Jahn gently slapped my cheek. "I gotta get home to check on my babies before work. We'll see you at mandir this weekend?"

"Sure."

I drove home and, once inside, peeled off sweaty clothes before reaching the bathroom, tossed them into the hamper, and took a quick shower. As I rushed through the morning routine, my thoughts drifted away from Dad. The assurance that Jahn didn't lie about his feelings toward me, us, everything in regard to Dad, helped. Thoughts of Liya from our time sitting on the edge of her bathtub hit me instead. Was she a bath girl or a shower girl? Was she taking a shower at this very moment? Hopping on one foot and praying she wouldn't slip?

As I rubbed soap down my sore chest, I imagined lather gliding down her body, across her smooth skin, bubbles forming and breaking, teasing glimpses of dewy flesh.

I groaned. What was *wrong* with me?

Shaking my head, I hurried out of the shower, dressed, and picked up breakfast. It wasn't until I took up the entire space of Liya's office doorway that I'd snapped back to reality. How did I get here? With not just my breakfast in hand, but hers as well?

She swiveled in her chair, set her pen down, and stared at me. "Um, do you have something for me?"

What was this strange feeling looming in my gut and swarming around my face? Was it…was it *embarrassment*?

She lowered her gaze to my hands. "Is that breakfast?" Her question was more of a sneer, and while most people's embarrassment level would rise, mine fell flat.

I raised the bag of breakfast sandwiches and the drink carrier with two coffees. "You think I'd bring you breakfast? I just worked out, and I'll need this to keep going in case I don't get lunch, which I sometimes don't."

The briefest splash of red dotted her cheeks, but she rolled her eyes and clamped down what could've easily been a smirk.

"Unless you're hungry. I might be willing to share."

"I'm fine. Why are you here, then?" she asked.

"Checking in on your foot."

"It's okay. Should be back in heels next week." Just as she

finished her last word, her stomach growled like a starving bear. She bit down on her pink-stained lip.

"Are you sure you're not hungry?"

"I can ask Wendy to get me something."

I held the bag up, and she shook her head. Sighing, I sat down on a chair across from her and unloaded the sandwiches on her desk, pushing one wrapped meal and a cup toward her.

She inhaled the steam rising from the coffee without touching it. "I'm very picky about my coffee."

"White chocolate peppermint latte, half skim, half soy, no whip, extra white chocolate sauce on the bottom and a drizzle on top."

Her gaze shot up, watching me over the rim of the cup with a hint of incredulity. "How'd you know?"

I shrugged. "Maybe we like the same drinks." Or maybe Wendy had told me the other day when she balanced three cups of coffee in the elevator.

Liya clamped her mouth shut but covered the warm cup with her petite hands. Her glossy red nails clicked against the sturdy paper cup, drowning out the muted sounds of others in the hallway beyond the open door.

"It's okay," I assured her.

"I don't think you did anything to the coffee."

"I mean it's okay to smile because someone brought you your picky-ass latte."

She took a sip. "We're not friends, you know?"

"No one forgets being told they're not friends," I said teasingly, knowing full well she didn't want to be friends but yet, here we were.

A smile crept across her lips, even though she tried hard to stop it.

Chapter Fourteen
Liya

O f the fifty reports I handed out today, only ten made it back to me. At the end of the day, I sat in my chair and tapped the arms. This wasn't going to make the reports come any faster. I suspected many of my coworkers stayed on board for that lingering paycheck or dwindling hope that the company might survive while they looked for jobs elsewhere. I couldn't blame them. I'd been perusing jobs boards, too. I was even considering a downgrade and taking that position in Dallas. But this type of poor work ethic would unravel the company faster.

I pushed away from my desk and headed to the labs. If they weren't going to do their work, then I'd have to do it.

I donned a lab coat, avoided the janitors as they carefully and meticulously cleaned around me, and worked. I worked like a kid right out of college, desperate to prove myself.

With goggles pressed to my face and my hand cramping from delicately moving and mixing tiny portions of chemicals, a delicious smell floated through the air.

My stomach rumbled, and I groaned, "Dan...how many times do I have to tell you to keep your food away from the labs? That's just disgusting, you know?"

"I think Dan is already gone," a rich voice replied.

I almost dropped the beaker and whipped my head around. Jay stood in the doorway. He held up two white paper bags, and the aroma shocked my senses for a second.

We stared at each other for a moment. He wasn't going to back down, and I didn't know how to respond. We weren't friends. But I was hungry.

Eventually, I caved and removed my goggles and lab coat, and walked to the door to hang them on the hooks. Jay didn't back up, only lowered his hands and looked down at me.

The building was cold with its industrial-strength air conditioner, but the labs were even chillier. Yet, in this particular moment, we might as well have been outside in the muggy, warm night because Jay's body heat invaded me.

I cleared my throat. "What are you doing here?"

"I was going to ask you the same thing," he replied.

"That's not an answer."

"It wasn't meant to be one."

"Okay…Are you stalking me? That's what this feels like."

"No. When I saw that your car was still here, I knew you'd be working late, and I brought dinner on the off chance you'd still be here."

"Wouldn't you have felt silly if I wasn't?"

"Thanks for saving me from an awkward moment with my-self." He grinned.

My stomach groaned painfully.

He chuckled and turned, walking out into the hallway and then into the empty, dimly lit lounge. He pulled out four foil packages, two rectangular in shape, two circular ones, and a bag of chips. I bit my lower lip. Tex-Mex was akin to kryptonite. The air burst with the aromas of seasoned meat, hot tortilla chips, cheese, and grilled peppers. I hardly knew a Texan who wouldn't cave for the rich dishes that were a unique blend of Texan and Mexican tastes. There were just some things most of us were predisposed to like: barbeque, cobbler and pies, iced tea (always sweetened), bluebonnet season, festivals, and Tex-Mex.

He handed me a fork and pushed a soda toward me.

"Are you fattening me up?" I joked as the smell of spicy, cheesy enchiladas wafted up out of the newly opened container. My fork dove into the mass of red sauce, hungrily trying to pick up every element, including sour cream, pico de gallo, and guacamole. So warm and perfect on my tongue.

"Curves aren't a bad thing." He leaned across the table and watched me like I was parading around in see-through lingerie.

"Honey, I got plenty of curves," I retorted and just about snapped my fingers. Then I went after the fried avocado taco smothered in cilantro-lime hot sauce.

"Yeah, I can see that."

Heat washed over my face, but I didn't react, much less look at him. When was the last time a guy made me feel remotely close to flustered?

I only ate a bite of the smoldering black beans in one of the round containers. No need to be bloated and gassy. But the queso blanco in the other container was too delicious to resist. I dipped a crispy, warm tortilla chip into it. Some of the cheese dripped onto my wrist and down my chin. I patted away the warm, gooey trail with a napkin, but honestly, I could've drunk queso straight out of the container.

"Are you not hungry?" he asked, one eyebrow cocked as he dissected a taco with a fork and knife and took a bite.

I gaped at him.

"What?"

"You eat tacos with a fork and knife?"

He shrugged.

"How dare you," I whispered.

He laughed.

"With your hands." I pointedly nodded to the taco.

He sat back and grinned. "You want me to do what with my hands?"

"Eat."

I watched and waited as he lifted the taco to his mouth. On the second bite, the filling spilled out and dripped down his wrists. It was oddly gratifying. I laughed, but he merely shrugged, winked, and licked his fingers. It was just food, right? It wasn't as if Jay licked seductively, or watched me watching him. It wasn't anything remotely sexual. So why in the world was his tongue so mesmerizing?

Clearing my throat, I said, "How did you know I'd like Tex-Mex?"

"It was a guess. There was a pretty good chance that you liked it. Now I know for sure."

"Well, thank you. Although you shouldn't have gone to any trouble. But I'm never going to say no to queso." I dipped another chip into the liquid cheese.

"Noted. And you're welcome. It wasn't any trouble. I was hungry, too. What are you doing working in the labs?"

"The majority of those who stayed on board aren't working as hard. They don't care."

"It's not solely your responsibility to keep bio going."

"Who else will? I'm not going to fail because no one else cares. They might as well leave. Then we'd have a reason to fall short: not enough staff. But with so many still on payroll dropping the ball…If I accepted that, then I might as well not stay, either. It's better to quit."

"Then quit."

"I'm not a quitter. Besides, I still need a paycheck, too." I pushed around the last of the shredded lettuce next to my partially eaten enchilada.

"You're supposed to manage them, file all the details. You can't do this, work around the clock."

I rubbed the soreness out of my shoulder. "I've only been doing it for a few days."

"How long will you keep doing this, though?"

"Why do you care?" I jammed the plastic fork into the remaining bite of food.

He shrugged. "Friend*ly* conversation. Is there anything I can help with?"

"Do you have a bio degree?"

"Nope."

I twisted the straw in my soda, the plastic against plastic screeching in the sudden quiet, and glanced at his nice, cream button-up shirt. He'd left his suit jacket and tie elsewhere. The top buttons were undone, the collar open, offering a glimpse of a white tee underneath.

A wicked curl lifted my lips.

"Uh-oh. What do you want me to do?" he asked suspiciously.

"Oh...I need some stuff cleaned and prepped."

"Grunt work?"

"Yep. Are you still interested?" Of course not. No snooty lawyer in expensive threads was interested in playing lowly lab assistant.

Instead of reminding me of how late it was, that he needed to be up early, or any number of viable excuses, Jay rolled up his sleeves and exposed wide, muscular forearms. His gaze never left mine. There was something extremely sexy about the way he did this.

I shook my head.

He quirked an eyebrow.

I smiled and stood. "That's okay. I'll have the morning crew clean up. It's the least they can do."

"It'll slow them down even more."

"Well, I can't do their job and clean up the mess. That's too much. Again, thanks for dinner." I returned to the lab and slipped a coat back on. I flipped my hair over the collar and jumped when Jay appeared beside me.

His buttons were completely undone. He pulled off his dress shirt before I could protest. I didn't really want him around me all night. He made it hard to think. I wanted alone time, not chat time.

He went to grab a lab coat, but I pointed at the short-sleeved ones at the end, the ones meant for grunt work so the sleeves didn't get in the way. He put one on, buttoned it up, and followed me to the sinks, where I instructed him on how to wash equipment. He finished in no time, and after a quick inspection to make sure he had done it correctly, he moved up to filling bottles and then back down to cleaning when I finished my portion.

The entire time, he kept earbuds in. Once in a while, he hummed or sang, and I was rather impressed. Not just with the voice and rhythm, but his willingness to get dirty and his silent agreement to keep quiet and out of my way.

When Jay finished everything, unable to do one more thing without having lab experience, he pulled up a stool at the end of my table, leaned his elbow on the slab, and rested his chin in his hand. To watch me.

I glared at him through the corner of my eye. "What?"

"Aren't you tired?" he asked, his voice gravelly, fatigued.

"No."

"It's three in the morning."

"Crap. I have to be back in four hours." At a quick glance, it didn't appear that we had done anything all night. The place was clean and organized, but the reports weren't done. I returned to work on the diagnostic reagents.

"You're staying all night, aren't you?" he asked.

"Yep. I want this staff to walk in and realize that I stayed here all night to catch up on their work."

"To make them feel bad?"

I shook my head. Of course not. "To encourage them. A short while ago, I was their coworker and their friend. If they see that I care and will do the work, that I'm not above them, then...maybe they'll step up. But you can go home, get some sleep. You don't need to stay here and torture yourself."

"And leave you here alone at three in the morning?"

"Nothing will happen. We have a security guard."

He ignored me and took out his phone, obviously answering emails or taking notes. But that was okay, because I was back in the zone quickly enough. He faded away, and before we knew it, the doors opened and staff trickled in.

They paused at the door, lab coats and goggles in hand.

"What's going on?" Amar asked.

Jay stood, nodded at me, and excused himself.

"Since we're not reaching our production quota, I've been staying all night to catch up," I replied.

"Oh...are you taking the day off then?" Amar asked.

"Nope." I brushed past him. "I still have my own work to do."

I placed the lab coat on its hook and returned to my office. At lunch, I could run home, take a quick shower, and change clothes. Even if everyone knew that I'd worked twenty-four hours, there was no need to look or smell the part.

✳

A few people upped their game over the next few days, but I kept working extended hours, took naps in the office, and had brief dinners with Jay when he insisted on staying with me during those long evenings. The nights became shorter as more staff worked harder, but getting home before midnight seemed to be a thing of the distant past. Jay didn't talk much, and after the first night, he brought his own things to work on once he finished the underling tasks.

Friday hit hard. We made it to midnight, and I could've passed out. My eyes drooped. Jay's were bloodshot, and I felt a little bad, but not that bad. No one asked him to stay.

He gave me a ride home, which I admittedly took advantage of. I was too tired to drive, and he already knew where I lived.

"See you this afternoon for the baby shower?" he asked, his words almost slurred. Okay. *Now* I felt awful.

"Yeah."

He nodded. We pulled up to the front lobby of my apartment complex, and he leaned over to open my door. His arm brushed against mine. His hair was a black shadow beneath my chin when he froze and slowly backed away.

"All right," he muttered.

"Are you going to make it home safely?" I asked, worried.

"Yes. Don't worry." He struggled to keep his eyes open. I didn't imagine that he had been able to sneak in naps during the day.

I groaned. "Who told you to stay all this time?"

"I dunno. My conscience? I'm fine, unless you're going to offer for me to crash at your place."

My cheeks flared, but he added, "I'll text you later."

"How much sleep have you gotten?"

"A few hours this week."

I rolled my eyes and pointed at the parking lot. "Park."

"Liya, I said I'm fine to drive home," he protested, more alert now.

"Just park the car. I'm not getting out until you do."

"I live less than fifteen minutes away."

I crossed my arms. "This is me being nice. Park the damn car."

He groaned and sloppily parked the car. We walked across the sidewalk and took the elevator up to my apartment.

I tossed the keys on the counter as he locked the front door behind us.

I flipped on the lights and said, "Feel free to sleep as long as you want. Eat or drink whatever. The couch is pretty comfortable."

We slipped off our shoes in the foyer, and I grabbed a prefilled bottle of water from the fridge. Halfway to the bedroom, I untucked my blouse and had it partway unbuttoned before I remembered he was here.

Jay was quiet as he turned away from me. He peeled off his button-down shirt and laid it over the back of the chair. Still in his undershirt, he unbuckled his pants...and I closed my bedroom door.

Chapter Fifteen
Jay

I awoke to the smell of coffee and bacon. I expected to roll onto my side and see my bedroom. Part of my brain wondered who made breakfast before the other part remembered where I was.

Light pushed through the tiny slits between the blinds, and I squinted before fully opening my eyes. I sat up on the plushest couch I'd ever been on. Liya hadn't lied when she said it was comfortable. I stretched my neck one way, then another, and looked around. Liya's door was closed, but a pot of coffee brewed in the kitchen.

Snatching my pants off the chair, I put them on but left them unzipped since I was headed to the bathroom anyway. I'd barely pushed the door open when Liya swung it back and jumped.

"Sorry. Thought you were in your room," I said, my voice miserably hoarse. She wore short pink shorts and a matching tee, her hair pulled back, her face bare. For a passing second, all I wanted to do was back her into the wall and feel her body pressed against mine. I had to stop that thought before it went any further.

"It's fine. All yours." She sidestepped the same way I went, and again the other way.

I finally stepped back and said, "As much as I love bumping into you, we can't keep this up all morning."

She pushed hard against my stomach, and I sucked in a breath. "Don't pee in your pants!" She laughed extra hard and walked away while I made a mad dash for the bathroom.

When I emerged, she was in the kitchen preparing breakfast. I sat on the barstool and stared at her. She was exceptionally beautiful first thing in the morning.

"Yes, this is for you, too." She pushed a cup of coffee and creamer toward me.

"What are you making?" I asked, focusing on pouring creamer and prying my eyes off her.

"My usual Saturday fare: crepes with sweet cream cheese filling and strawberries...and bacon. Because... *bacon*."

I scrunched my nose as she flipped a crepe onto a plate and spooned filling from one bowl onto it, folded it, and added a syrupy glaze from another bowl.

"What? I know you're not lactose intolerant or a vegetarian."

I guess we'd had enough meals together for her to know that. "I'm surprised that you can cook."

"*Because?*"

"Uh. Because you're Liya Thakkar, feminist extraordinaire."

"Don't be an ass."

I smiled. "I thought with all the work and independence, and anti-Indian stuff, that you were also anti-cook."

"You think I have a maid, too? I can cook and clean and do laundry. I can also change my oil and a tire. Just eat."

I grinned and took a huge, sweet bite. Oh, man, I was in heaven. "Did you make this from scratch? It's the best thing I've ever had."

"Yes. And thank you. A borrowed crepe recipe, my own version of sweetened cream cheese, and a strawberry reduction."

"All made this morning?"

"Takes all of fifteen minutes. Bacon?"

I offered my plate, and she dropped four pieces of perfectly cooked bacon onto it. I knew I was about to step into dangerous territory, but I had to ask, "You might throw that pan at me, but there's something I've been meaning to ask."

"What is it?" She poured herself a cup of coffee, a splash of cream, a heaping spoonful of sugar.

"Why are you so against marriage?"

"Seriously? The idea of being tied to one man, for one thing. I don't need anyone telling me what to do, how to do it, or when to do it. I don't need to ask permission for anything."

I laughed. Although a part of me still didn't believe I deserved a happy ending, another part saw imperfections in Liya that matched my own. She was an emotional hot mess and so was I. Maybe...we *would* make a match.

"What's so funny?" She placed a hand on her hip and leaned against the counter as she ate a piece of bacon.

"Marriage doesn't have to be that. Not that it matters now, but I wouldn't want a subservient wife. I want...a queen. Authoritative, independent, decisive, but able to confide in me and consult *with* me, a team player."

She waved off my words. "That's all talk."

"Is it?"

"Guys will say that to get the girl. They'll say anything."

"Except I'm not trying to get you," I lied.

"Whatever idealism you have now doesn't necessarily work out that way post-wedding. I've seen all sorts of marriages start, and they end up with bickering and fighting for control, one dominates the other. There's no way out. There's no room to breathe and think. I love coming home to the quiet. I love not having to jump right on dinner or battle over the remote or argue about which party to go to."

"Maybe one day you'll change your mind and see how good things can be."

"You're one to talk," she said flatly, making me pause. Did she know? Did she know about my past? It wasn't a secret, but my family hadn't discussed it with anyone here. Did she know how it warped my hopes for my own future? She couldn't possibly.

"Explain."

She sighed. "We fight. Even if you do something nice, or I'm feeling relaxed and happy... the calm never stays with us. There's something in me that doesn't want marriage. But there's something in you, too."

Before I could ask what she meant by that, Liya went on, "But anyway, things are good now. Clearly, neither one of us will ever consider the other one for marriage again."

"Clearly..." And yet, here I was kind of wanting to date her. The real her. *This* her. The intelligent, funny, talented, free, laid-back woman who didn't try to put up a hard exterior to keep everyone out.

Liya ate while standing across the counter from me. As the conversation died I noticed she had strawberry cream cheese on the corner of her mouth.

"What?" she asked, catching my stare.

I sighed, leaned across the counter, and gently swiped my thumb across the corner of her lips.

She paused. "You could've just said I had something on my face."

"And miss a chance to touch your lips? Have you lost your mind?"

She laughed my comment off like it was a joke. But it wasn't. With how I was feeling right now, she was lucky I didn't walk around the counter and lick the strawberry right off her. I'd better stop thinking about licking anything anywhere on her.

I glanced around her once immaculate apartment. Shoes piled up by the door. Clothes were strung over chairs. The coffee table vanished beneath several empty glasses. The sink was full. She probably had two hampers of laundry waiting.

The crystal clock on the wall showed it was already ten, and Shilpa's shower started at one. I was supposed to get the sparkling apple cider and sparkling pomegranate juice, the kind in fancy champagne bottles, plus flowers and a fruit tray.

"You don't have to help clean," Liya said when I stood with plate and mug in hand. "It's fine. You have to go home and get ready for the shower, and a few more dishes aren't going to hurt. This place is a mess."

"Are you sure?"

She nodded.

"Thanks for breakfast and letting me crash. Could I offer you a ride to the baby shower?"

"No problem. Actually, I'm going with the girls, and we'll swing by my car on the way. Thanks, though."

I tugged my dress shirt over my wrinkled tee and turned to face a shelf of little multicolored, pointed bottles. "What are these? Miniature stakes?"

"No." She walked around me to get the glasses from the coffee table. "Those are nail polishes."

"Fancy." I eyed the black one with red in the middle and encrusted with crystals all the way up.

"Christian Louboutin."

I put on my shoes. "You mean unnecessarily expensive nail polishes. Those are tiny bottles. They last for what? One, maybe two uses?"

She rolled her eyes. "They also double as eye-gougers. Want to test?"

I laughed and opened the door. "See you in a few hours."

"Yes. Oh, crap. I didn't have time to pick up anything. Quick. Tell me what Shilpa needs."

I raced through mental notes. "I think she has everything."

She groaned and chewed on her bottom lip, her focus on the floor as she considered gift ideas. It was cute that even a baby shower gift to someone she barely knew was a serious affair. It was nice seeing this softer, incredibly thoughtful side to Liya. Even better? The fact that she was letting down some walls and not realizing it. Maybe she was starting to feel comfortable with me. Maybe I was getting comfortable with her, with the idea that having a happy ending was okay. Dad would've liked Liya. I knew that I did.

After picking up my list items, I eased out of my clothes, which still smelled like Liya's apartment, and smiled. By the time I showered, dressed, and arrived, most of the decorations were up. Ribbons, balloons, paper flowers, candies, diapers, and dolls. An aarti tray was set up by the shrine. A long table was covered in confetti and an assortment of food: little square cakes that resembled building blocks spelling out "Welcome Baby Shah," cups with veggie dip and long slivers of vegetables, lettuce wraps, and a watermelon carved into a baby stroller filled with fruit balls.

Alongside that were silver platters of warm vegetable samosas and bowls of a dark green chutney with spicy jalapeño, and sweet date and tangy tamarind chutney. Potato and onion pakora came next, fried golden brown with hints of green herbs and creamy raita.

I knew I had to get some dabeli before those went fast and plucked a small bun of what was essentially a spiced potato burger topped with peanuts and pomegranate seeds.

There was, of course, the traditional assortment of sweets, including peda, reminding me of the fateful day I'd met Liya. I smiled at the once frustrating memory. She'd knocked half the sweets onto the ground, and the others went into the trash the moment I'd gotten home. This woman went from infuriating to picking out a baby gift for my family. How did we get here? How did we get from constant fighting to me wanting to touch her lips?

A smaller table to the right held plates, utensils, napkins, plastic champagne flutes, and five kinds of drinks plus a punch bowl with sherbet melting in the middle like an iceberg. Friends and family had gone all out, but of course Ma had orchestrated it all. She was over the moon and blissfully doting on Shilpa.

Speaking of Ma...I asked her, "Did Bhabhi mention that she'd invited Liya?"

She smiled warmly at the new brood of guests walking in. "Shilpa asked if it was okay."

"Of course, Bhabhi would always ask you first. But are you okay with Liya coming here?"

"Why wouldn't I be? Are you okay?" She arched a sharp brow.

"Um. Yes. We don't hate each other or anything. But I thought, after the dinner gone wrong—"

She waved off my worry. "Liya is a nice girl."

"Liya Thakkar?" I asked, baffled.

"She apologized nearly right away. She explained the misunderstanding and her behavior. I probably would've done the same thing."

"Ah...okay..." How Liya had been so infuriating with me but kind to my family was beyond me. I already knew that I had her all wrong, but leave it to Liya to constantly remind me of just *how* wrong I'd been.

Shilpa made her way inside and hugged me as I took the last

bite of the mini dabeli. Jahn slapped my back and grinned as more guests arrived. The corner table, once empty, was now piled high with gifts. We mingled and chatted. Music played softly in the background. Incense burned. The back doors opened to a wide patio filled with cushioned seats.

The aunties, with Ma and Shilpa's mom, huddled at one end or another unless they were fussing over Shilpa.

"Having you men around will keep them from giving out labor and delivery advice," Shilpa whispered.

"I hope so," I whispered back.

Jahn elbowed me. "What? You don't want to hear about mucus plugs and how to tilt a uterus?"

I cringed as Shilpa added, "It's not even possible to tilt my uterus. I guarantee you, eighty percent of their advice is from old wives' tales."

She laughed as a group of women stole her away. They joined a group of aunties while the guys hung around the food.

"This is good baby shower food," Shilpa's brother said.

"I want some of that barfi Shilpa's mom made."

When I scanned the ever-growing crowd, some of the aunties frowned, their glares glued to the hallway behind us, and I knew Liya had entered. The tension from them immediately thickened. Nonetheless, either immune or not having noticed, Liya cordially greeted Jahn first with Preeti, Sana, and Reema in close tow.

She said, with that starlet smile that started to do some intense things to my gut, "I'm so happy for you guys. And thanks for having me."

He gave her a side hug, welcoming her. She hardly looked at me or my welcoming expression. Instead, she gave me a nod. Which was good, I supposed, seeing that I had the growing need to hug her.

Jahn introduced her to others nearby. Most greeted her like

normal, manner-minding people, but then there were the few who politely nodded and returned to their conversations. Liya didn't seem fazed until her steady, studious glances turned into a glare when she and Mukesh Uncle made eye contact. Something in him shifted as well.

Did he believe all those nasty things about her? Did she abhor his religious sermon every Sunday? What in the world had transpired between them to create this immediate, malicious environment that everyone noticed?

My need to hug Liya intensified. I went to walk toward her, to defuse the tension, but Liya snapped out of the momentary hostile takeover and placed her giant gift bag on the floor next to the table and headed to her mother. There was a fleeting look of annoyance on her father's face, but perhaps he was still upset with how things had gone down with that fateful dinner. Despite my having told him not to worry about it, it wouldn't hurt to remind him that things were fine now, if that meant he would ease off Liya.

Liya ignored him and hugged her mother. I couldn't tell if the awkwardness stemmed from their height difference, as Liya was about a foot taller than her mother, or if it came from the physical contact in public. Still, they embraced for a few seconds and pulled away to chat. Then Ma walked over and joined in, and suddenly the ladies burst into laughter. Ma had that way about her, putting everyone at ease. It was nice to see, and my heart filled. There were lots of aunties here, and many had single daughters, but Ma kept circling back to Liya's mother. Had they become good friends, despite the epic dinner fail? Or were they secretly plotting to try things again?

Either way, it was a warm sight. And for half a minute, my brain foresaw this sort of thing happening a lot in the future. The women in my life having a good time. Moving on, the way

Jahn said Dad would want us to. Finding real happiness in a relationship that was sanctioned by my family. But I dislodged that thought. Getting my hopes up was a dangerous thing.

Then Liya escaped into the backyard.

The air changed the instant she left the room. While we guys seemed unaffected by Liya's presence, the aunties huddled like witches over a cauldron, snapping their tongues about the un-clean girl in their house. I clenched my jaw and took a step forward, but Jahn clamped a hand over my shoulder and subtly shook his head while maintaining his conversation.

At least Preeti, Sana, and Reema had arrived alongside Liya. She wasn't completely alone, although Shilpa wouldn't stand for any negativity at her shower. Shilpa was a lot like Liya in many ways, and she'd put everyone in their place, elder or not.

The backyard crowd filed in when the last of the guests ar-rived. Ma seemed pleasantly surprised when a pretty young woman walked in. She was none other than Kaajal, who walked directly to her parents: Mukesh Uncle and his wife. The way they held themselves, upright and arms in specific positions during conversations; the nice clothes and gold packaged gifts; the clas-sic hairstyles. These people were made of money, or at least acted like they were.

Ma walked the trio toward us as Jahn and I split from the guys to meet them partway. "Kaajal, this is my oldest, Jahnu."

"Nice to meet you. Congratulations," Kaajal said.

"Thank you," Jahn replied.

"And my youngest, Jayesh."

"Nice to finally meet you, too." She smiled invitingly, full lips, great teeth, big, brown eyes lined with makeup. The woman was absolutely stunning.

"Kaajal just finished pharmacy school," Ma added. "She was hired at the drugstore but wants to spend some time relaxing before work begins. I was telling her that maybe she could rent a boat and go to the lake. Maybe you and some of the young ones would like to do that."

Heat prickled up the back of my neck. I tried not to glance at Jahn, who probably grinned like an idiot, or look at Kaajal's parents, who waited for my response.

But Kaajal herself gave plenty of space *and* an out. "I'll have to get your information later and check out my schedule. Let me say hi to Shilpa first, before she gets inundated with gifts and pictures." She held up a gold-wrapped box and meandered toward the girls, while her parents and I were left alone to an inevitable conversation.

It was all grilling from there. Where I went to school, what I did for work, when I planned to make partner. But when they inched into what type of car I drove, I assumed to gather income level without blatantly asking, I clenched my jaw. I thought Mukesh Uncle was supposed to be known for his humility.

"Best car on the lot," I gritted out and smiled at Ma. "Have you eaten?"

She shook her head as Mukesh Uncle opened his mouth to press.

"You should sit, Ma. I'll make you a plate. Excuse us…"

I planted her on the couch, one seat away from Shilpa's "mother-to-be" throne, and took my time piling a plate and pouring a drink before I returned to her.

Shilpa and Jahn stood behind the mystery cake, topped with green and purple, gender-neutral colors. She placed a hand on her belly as Jahn spoke to the crowd. "Thank you, everyone, for coming and celebrating this moment with us. We hope you're enjoying this amazing food, and shout-out to the moms and aunties and sisters who made this party so amazing."

The room applauded.

Shilpa added, "We tried to hold out as long as possible to find out the gender of the baby, but we felt that it would be nice to share with our closest family and friends. I hope we can all be excited together."

"It's a girl, look at how high her belly is," an auntie said confidently.

Preeti rolled her eyes in the corner. Unscientific talk about pregnancy and delivery and anything medical probably sounded like nails raking against a chalkboard to her.

"So, here goes!" Shilpa and Jahn held the knife together and cut a slice, slowly, on the side facing them.

Half the room groaned, "Come on!"

Shilpa giggled as they made the second cut and carefully pulled out the slice. She gasped and Jahn pumped a fist in the air. I knew in that moment that the interior of the cake was blue. A rush filled me. There was going to be another Shah male.

"Yes!" I hollered before the rest of the crowd stood on their toes and nearly toppled over each other to snag a view.

Jahn turned the cake around and everyone cheered when they saw blue. "It's a boy!"

"We're going to have a son!" Shilpa added and wiped tears from her cheeks.

Ma waved her over and embraced her before anyone else had the chance. Once everyone else hugged Shilpa, I wrapped my arms around her last and said with a pounding heart, "Congratulations, Bhabhi, I'm crazy excited for you guys."

She pulled away and patted my arm. "You're going to be the best kaka ever."

"That's right. Kid's going to be a superstar. He won't want for a single thing."

She dabbed her eyes and nodded, her lips quivering as she took to her throne. We gathered around her while she opened gifts.

Some sat on the floor, several had chairs, the rest of us stood off to the side. Liya stood beside the backyard French doors, but straightened up when Shilpa picked up her gift.

Her sister read the card, announcing, "This one is from Liya."

Shilpa gasped and removed the giant basket of soaps, lotions, candles, loofas, and god knew what else. Then she removed a miniature version. "This is one of my favorites! I love the smell of lavender! And I was just getting low on bath bubbles. This silk eye mask is so soft!"

"That has nothing to do with a baby," an auntie beside me muttered.

Liya pushed away from the wall, holding her plastic flute of nonalcoholic drink as if it were a delicate piece of expensive crystal. "It's not the usual baby shower gift, but you'll get so many clothes and toys and books and diaper cakes. But I figured you deserve something to help you relax and unwind. I heard the best things about those foot soak bombs."

"Ooh! I need those!"

"And the mini-basket is for your trip to the hospital. Their soaps suck, right, Preeti?"

Preeti nodded. "Just a generic, tiny bar that lasts a day."

"So you'll have everything you need for an invigorating shower after all that hard work. You won't have to feel like you're in the hospital."

"It's perfect! Thank you, Liya! So thoughtful!" Shilpa chirped, all misty-eyed.

It *was* a thoughtful gift. I wasn't creative enough to conjure up diaper cakes nor would've thought to come up with a relaxation for mommy basket.

The girls clapped and the aunties hushed, but Liya tossed a smug smile their way. One auntie tucked her hair behind her ear, turning her head at the same time to mutter something into another auntie's ear. It sparked a fire in my chest, a need to defend Liya. No wonder she didn't feel comfortable in these crowds. They had a particularly rage-inducing way of alienating Liya.

I had to ignore my gut feeling to speak up, according to Jahn's warning, but when I looked away, I caught Liya's glance at them. Something in her smug features crumbled. But only for a moment. She hardened, sipped her drink, and giggled with the rest of her friends when Shilpa opened a breast pump.

"Try it on!" Jahn teased.

The room erupted with laughter and gasps as everyone threw ribbons and clips at him. He expertly dodged them, and for the love of all this baby stuff, I had to derail my thoughts before I imagined my sister-in-law using a breast pump.

In all the movement, it was easy not to notice Kaajal sneaking up beside me. And even easier not to catch Liya slipping away. But I noticed. And Liya Thakkar wasn't getting away that easily.

Chapter Sixteen
Liya

My heart pounded out a wicked beat. The haunting whispers and gossip of those vicious aunties. If I could slap the snide looks off their faces, the world would be a better place.

Well, I would forget them. This party wasn't for them, but for my new friend. And she was pleased with my gift. How many diaper cakes did one need, anyway? Plus, the aunties were just full of old wives' tales and useless crap.

At least I saw Momma. I loved that Jay's mother seemed to have a radiant effect on her.

I had a good time with Shilpa, touching her belly and giggling over nipple cream. The food was delicious, all sorts of savory and sweet melting on my tongue. Most of the crowd treated me like any other person.

Things were fine. I could deal.

Until one of the girls muttered something about Jay and Kaajal being a good match. Kaajal? Mukesh's daughter?

I glanced up, nonchalantly scanning the room for her. Finding Jay was easy these days. He was tall and commanding, broad with muscles beneath nice clothes. His deep voice carried, and when he smiled that smile, my insides sank like a roller-coaster ride taking its highest drop. The sort of feeling that people loved and desperately craved more of.

The fact that he attracted an equally gorgeous woman was not a head-scratcher. Kaajal was a tall, leggy, delicately curved girl with thick hair, light brown skin, and the features of a goddess.

My stomach turned queasy, and I didn't understand why. I had turned Jay down and hoped he would leave me alone. It was only natural that another woman wanted him, that another auntie tried to hook her daughter onto him. But did he have to seem so comfortable with her? Like a stroll across the park; easy, relaxed.

The way he smiled at her and looked down at his feet every once in a while as he intently listened, pressing his lips so that his dimple showed…

Yeah. I didn't want this. I didn't want to feel like this, attached to someone I didn't want to be with. This feeling was nasty, disgusting, and brought up a vortex of weakness and vulnerability, all the things I refused to harbor.

No matter where I looked, my gaze fell on happy couples and joyous families. Why didn't I have any of this? My relationship with my parents left much to be desired. My relationships with most people were superficial at best. My relationship with a man was nonexistent. I could strive for anything in the world and get it…except this. My baby shower, although I cringed at the thought of having kids, would never be this amazing. Never this sort of turnout and outpouring of love from family and community. Close friends? Yes, of course. Anyone else? Not a chance.

I didn't want this, though…did I? I practically hated many of these people, and yet the way they showed their gratitude toward Shilpa and Jahn peeled away all the layers in my soul and laid open the devastating black hole of emptiness, of wanting, of not belonging.

Ugh. How utterly annoying.

So I said my goodbyes, snuck over to thank Shilpa, and slipped away.

The air outside was humid, but the breeze helped. I slowly walked down the driveway to the street, my hands shaking as I fumbled for my keys and unlocked the car. It beeped twice as the faint sound of running caught my attention.

A hand landed on my car door, and I jumped, swerved around, and readied myself to punch.

"Whoa!" Jay said, craning back to avoid a near swing. He grinned when I blew out a breath.

"What are you doing scaring me like that?" I covered my pounding heart.

"Where are you going?" he asked, seemingly disappointed.

"Home."

"Why?"

"I have a headache." It wasn't a lie. I touched my fingertips to my throbbing temple.

"Are you all right?"

"Yeah. Just a headache. All this work, no sleep, too much coffee."

"No. I mean with them." He cocked his head toward the house, worry cresting over his features.

I crossed my arms and leaned against the car, my shoulder against the cold, metal frame. "You think they faze me?"

"Nothing fazes you. Did you have a good time, otherwise?"

"Yeah. I did."

He leaned into his arm, still across the top of the door, and into me. Our eyes made contact, and we were both too stubborn to break first.

"What?" I asked, tapping my shoe as impatience weaved through me. "Don't you have someone waiting to talk to you in there?"

His beautiful lips curled up. "You sound kind of jealous."

I arched a brow. "I already turned you down, remember?"

"You make me not even want to ask you."

"Ask me what?"

The front door opened, and Kaajal peered her pretty, nosy head out. She looked me up and down, and I expected her to passive-aggressively interrupt us.

"Hey," Jay muttered, drawing me back to his light brown eyes. "What?"

"Can you ignore them?"

"You mean your girlfriend?" I bit my cheek, hating that she even bothered me. At this, I expected Jay to step back, give Kaajal a reassuring word, and return to the party. But he did none of those things.

"I don't have a girlfriend, and I'm not interested in Kaajal."

I casually shrugged, but the words came out bitter when I said, "You don't have to explain anything to me."

"Then why are you suddenly tense?"

"No one is tense."

"This isn't tense?" he asked and took my wrists, gently shaking my fists loose and sending an electrifying jolt up my arms. His touch was warm, all-consuming, and suddenly I hungered for those hands all over me.

I had to gather myself before I could reply, "Are you sure that you want to be seen touching someone so unclean in front of your pious group?"

He moved in, mere inches from me, so close that his body heat and the slight scent of his mind-numbing cologne wrapped around my entire body, making it hard to breathe. But my lungs didn't mind. They didn't need air when he stood so close. Good lord, what was stupid Jay Shah doing to me?

"You look pretty clean to me." He turned me to the side and leaned back to check me out. "Very nice."

I hit his chest. "I bet there are a dozen people watching us through those curtains."

He laughed. "Should we give them something to gossip about?"

Placing a hand against his hard chest, I pushed him. The man barely budged. "Get back to your party before the aunties drag you back inside," I teased.

"Hey," he said, taking my hand before I slipped into the car. "Go out with me."

I scoffed. "Are you sure there wasn't alcohol in those drinks?"

"Seriously, Liya. One date."

"Why?"

"You have time for that answer? Because saying that I like you isn't enough."

Did the humidity spike? Because sweat beaded on the back of my neck. When was the last time a guy had made my stomach tie into knots? My entire body wanted to agree to his terms, but I had to stop myself and remember who we were. We would never work out, so why bother trying when it would lead to failure, to fights and heartbreak?

"No, Jay. I don't want a date with you," I said finally, swallowing the rancid lie down my throat. Glancing at the cross-armed Kaajal now flagrantly waiting on the porch, I replied, "She seems like a nice girl, though."

I slid inside my car and closed the door. Jay didn't move from the spot when I pulled away. Through the rearview mirror, I eyed him as he stuffed his hands into his pockets and watched me leave. Even when Kaajal appeared by his side, he kept his focus on me.

When I reached home, frustrated by the state of my neglected apartment, I took off my shoes and slipped out of my clothes on the way to the bedroom. My usual routine. Before I donned those sexy cleaning gloves to get on my knees and scrub the bathroom, I checked my texts out of habit.

My mouth, subsequently, dropped.

Preeti, Sana, and Reema had group texted me, and scrolling through the messages, a mixture of embarrassment, anger, and flattery pulsated through my veins.

The gist of the twenty-mile-long text chain was this: Jay had asked them to convince me to go out with him! The audacity! Who did he think he was, getting my friends involved? And to make matters worse, of course they were on Team Freaking Jay.

Reema: Do it.

Sana: Go out with him.

Preeti: What've you got to lose?

Sana: He's so into you, we can tell.

Reema: He totally dismissed Kaajal.

All right, the last one made me smile.

Reema: Some auntie tried to grill him on why he was talking to you outside and he shut that down real quick.

I groaned. This was going to become some dramatic, unnecessarily huge ordeal that would add fodder to the gossip.

I tried to convince them to leave me alone, to let this all go, that I was not in the mood to date, much less get married. But they pushed back. For a while, the phone went silent and I scrubbed away, tossed laundry into the dryer, washed dishes, and pulled out the vacuum. Then someone rang the bell.

The girls. All three. Ambushed me.

I placed a hand on my hip, let out an unsteady breath, and opened the door. They barged in, chattering and chirping and clenching my arms, jumping up and down like teenagers. What in the world was going on?

Reema pulled out a bottle of champagne. Sana brought chocolates. Preeti searched for glasses. They hurried me to the couch, settled in around me, popped open the bottle, and poured.

"You better spill *everything*," Reema said.

"There's nothing to tell," I replied.

"Yeah, right, there's nothing to tell. This man came to us asking for support."

"And a fine man at that," Sana added, blushing.

I rolled my eyes. "You're overreacting. He just wants, I don't know, closure or something on why I walked out of meeting him."

"You have to give him something for trying," Sana said.

"I don't owe him anything."

"If you heard how eloquently and matter-of-factly he shut down all those naysayers after you left, you would."

"No one told him to do that."

"But if you'd been there," Reema said, "you'd be all up on him right this second."

They giggled, and Sana's blush deepened. She nodded in agreement.

"Let's be practical for a minute, shall we?" I sat up. "Let's say we went out and it didn't end well. Do you know how much we'd fight? We already bicker all day."

"He's not argumentative," Preeti replied. "He does that because you're so easy to rile up and it's the only way to keep you talking."

"How do you know that?"

"He said so."

I groaned. "You guys are ridiculous. Before you know it, my parents are involved, and other parents want to push their daughters in, and it's a battle to the death, get him before he has a chance to make up his mind, eliminate everyone else at all costs."

The girls were silent for a second before agreeing. Reema said, "Yeah, Gujarati matchmaking is pretty cutthroat. But anyway, that doesn't mean you can't give the guy a fair shot."

I tapped my glass and watched the bubbles race to the surface. "Even worse, what if we like each other? Aunties would be descending upon us like vultures. Having them pry into him and his family…it's a lot. For me, it's just another day. For his family? They'd realize I'm not worth it."

"You're worth everything in the world," Reema said.

My heart swelled, but I had to be honest. "He's not ready to take on that sort of stress. He and his family fit in so well with the community, and I don't. He should consider Kaajal."

"But he doesn't want Kaajal. Trust us, the amount of times he walked away from her was embarrassing."

I choked down a laugh. "He wants to get married. I don't."

"What if he just wants to date?"

"Come on, ladies. Do you really think he's just a 'dating' kind of guy?"

They flicked their chocolate or swirled their glasses, but they all looked away.

My hopes dwindled into nothing as my friends finally realized that I spoke the truth. "Exactly," I said softly.

✳

"Go out with me," a voice called from behind me that following Monday. It was too early in the week for this.

I would recognize that deep, throaty voice anywhere. I smirked and finished sorting through my paperwork before turning to find him at my office door.

Jay sported a deliciously dark gray suit, dapper as always, and his arms were crossed like he was tasked with preventing me from leaving.

"You're embarrassing yourself."

"I think you should go out with me," he refuted.

"Why bother?" I exhaled, placing my blazer on the wall hook beside his head.

He took in every inch of my curve-hugging silk blouse and pencil skirt. "I need to see where things can go."

"What else ya got?"

"I want you to tell me that you're not interested after giving this a serious shot."

I tried to move him aside, tried to squeeze between him and the doorframe, but he gently backed me against the wall, his hand carefully touching my waist, his chest grazing mine.

"Is this okay?" he whispered.

I should've said no instead of nodding, not because his barely there touch wasn't okay, but because I wouldn't be able to deny him a thing if he kept this close to me. Because if he got any closer, we might actually tear off each other's designer clothes and find ourselves in some hot, emotional mess.

He closed the door without giving space between us, his gaze never faltering from mine. And, holy crap, my breath hitched.

"What are you doing?" I asked, out of breath and absolutely hating that he could hear it. I was literally one touch away from wanting him to devour me. He barely touched me, and yet my entire body ached for him.

"Asking you out, again and again," his said, his voice dropping.

My stomach fluttered, and I concentrated on controlling my breathing. "You know that I have work to do."

"There are plenty of people who volunteered to work overtime this week."

"Really?"

He nodded. "There's actually no room for you in the labs. You'd just get in their way."

"I still don't have time for you," I said, my stare stuck to his mouth.

"Are you certain?" He placed a hand against the wall, beside my head, and tilted his face closer to mine.

I didn't understand why my knees practically buckled, or why I wanted to feel the softness of those full lips on mine. Or, more important, why I didn't just take control and kiss him first. But then he'd know that I was attracted to him, and that would encourage him to keep this silly notion rolling.

He ran a featherlight touch down my jaw. Did he expect me to quiver with need? Manipulate me into agreeing to his terms?

Liya Thakkar was *not* that weak.

I pressed against him, our eyes still locked. Gripping his jacket, I raised myself onto my tiptoes and whispered, "If you want to screw me, just say so."

His jaw hardened into a clench so tight, his teeth might've broken. "Why would you say that?"

I had him figured out, and the truth definitely hurt, but what other reason was there? "Because you're a man. Why else would you go through this trouble, knowing the gossip about me? By now, all of it has reached you and your mother, and neither one of you think marrying me is beneficial for your family. Sudden interest after I turned you down *and* explained that I don't want marriage? Why else are you trying to get me? Which rumors got you thinking about how good I am in bed?"

He pulled away from my hands and walked out, all the while his nostrils flaring.

"Didn't think I'd catch on to the truth?" I called after him.

As I stood there, my blood boiling, my lips quivered from the realization that most men saw nothing more in me than a good time. Something cracked in my chest. Maybe...I had hoped Jay would be different.

I startled when he stormed back in. His angry eyes bored into mine, which pissed me off even more.

Through gritted teeth, he said, "If I'd wanted to screw you, I would've said so, Liya. But the fact that you think I'm that kind of guy is insulting."

"Don't be mad at me for calling you out," I spat back.

"I've never met a woman who gets me so worked up in a matter of seconds with that smart-ass mouth."

"I'm sure you've heard of what this mouth is good at, since you're still here."

Smoke nearly vented from his nostrils. "You think others demean you, but you're the worst offender. You're better than that. And I hope by the time the next decent guy comes around, you'll know your self-worth."

"Don't you ever think that you have the right to talk to me that way."

He scoffed. "I hope you grow up."

"You better leave."

He held his hands up and stepped back, but his anger did not dissipate. "I don't know what you see in yourself, Liya, but I see a lot more."

"Don't try to make me feel bad for calling you out, for knowing who you really are. What'd you think? That making up some story of how suddenly my team wants to work overtime and backing me against the wall would make me drop my panties?"

He shoved his hands into his pockets, his chin lifted, and his gaze blazed down at me. "I didn't make up a thing. Your own conduct made your team step up. I sure as hell wasn't trying to get into your panties, either. I don't play games."

"You mean you don't try. Not even flowers."

"Flowers are done. Mike sent you flowers, remember? I did get you something, and it wasn't a cheap bouquet that'll die in three days."

"And where exactly is this gift? At your place, right?"

"At yours, actually."

I opened my mouth to snap at him, but he walked out and said, "You messed this up, Liya. We would've been good together. We could've had something real."

I clenched and unclenched my fists, drowning the need to scream or run after him.

When my rage subsided, I calmly went to the labs, only to find that Jay had spoken the truth.

The labs were filled with team players willing to work overtime to keep the company afloat. And they did so with a smile.

Which also meant that I could go home on time and defuse my anger. Except, when I approached my front door, a box awaited me, the gift from Jay. And when I opened it, my anger erupted all over again.

Chapter Seventeen
Jay

I feel as though we don't see you anymore during the week," Ma said from my dining table.

I hurried through cooking, having forgotten that it was my turn to host our weekday dinner. Weekends were times that our family saw one another at gatherings and mandir, but Ma missed having both of her boys together for weekday dinners. Since I'd been helping Liya, that ungrateful woman, for the past few weeks, I'd skipped out on our meals, which upset Ma.

We'd always been close. Before Dad passed, we ate breakfast and dinner together every day.

After Dad passed, we still tried to be regular in weekly family meals. We kept up the tradition after Jahn married Shilpa, seeing that they lived with Ma and took care of her. It was something I really had to stop neglecting.

I was glad to be back with my family. Family dinners were times of reprieve from daily life, from hectic work, stressful mishaps, and women who drove me insane.

"Let me help," Shilpa insisted, grabbing plates.

"Nope. Bhabhi, you sit, put your feet up," I insisted.

She pouted. "Everyone talks like I'm incapacitated. Sitting

around and eating 'for two' will make me lazy and large. I have to be active so I can push this baby out and recover faster."

"Uh, please don't talk to me about pushing anything out."

She leaned a determined elbow on the counter, like she was about to throw down a daring bet. "You let me help cook or I will stand here and describe in graphic detail the glorious agony of labor."

Jahn laughed. I hoped Ma would argue, seeing that she'd been the most concerned about Shilpa not exerting herself, but she also laughed.

"All right, geez. You play hardball."

She smiled and took over, bumping me out of her way. "Don't mess with a pregnant woman."

"Oh, I won't. Never again."

Since Ma didn't want Shilpa to do too much, she ended up helping, too. Jahn and I set the table, made lemonade and cha, but as we began our meal, someone rang the doorbell.

Before I pushed my chair back, the ring turned into a violent bang against the door.

Ma looked at me with concern, but I held my hand out. "It's fine. I'm sure someone is at the wrong apartment."

My family watched from the table as I checked the peephole. I groaned.

"Who is it?" Jahn asked, ready to jump to his feet.

"Liya."

He grinned. "She sounds pissed."

"You don't know the half of it…"

I swung the door open and stepped out before she could bombard me, and my family, with more wild accusations.

She shoved a package into my arms and staggered away.

"What is this?" I took a few steps after her.

"Your so-called gift. I don't want it," she snapped.

"What am I supposed to do with these?"

She flicked her hand back, as if volleying my words back at me. "Return them."

"Do you know how expensive return shipping is? Just take them. I bought them to replace your broken ones."

Her face turned red. She was on fire.

"Damn, woman. Who the hell reacts like this to a gift?"

She seethed and said pointedly, "You don't do flowers because they're cheap. I guess you figured I was worth a little more. A high-priced lay?"

"You are freaking insane," I gritted out.

"Oh, I was supposed to accept these Louboutin shoes from the kindness of your heart and not think I owe you something in exchange? It's not like you're the one who broke them. What kind of maniac buys a woman he barely knows fourteen-hundred-dollar shoes!"

"You need to keep your voice down, and I'm not a maniac. Unlike you. If you can't accept them, then why didn't you take them to work and drop them off at my office? Instead of raising all hell so my neighbors can hear?"

"And your family . . ." Shilpa said from the opened door, Ma and Jahn behind her.

My neck turned hot and Liya's face looked even hotter. Embarrassment choked out whatever words we had left to throw at each other.

"Oh . . . I didn't know you had family over," Liya muttered.

Shilpa grinned. "Are you seriously mad that he bought you gorgeous shoes? I'd take them if my feet weren't so swollen."

Liya touched a hand to her chest. "I am so sorry for interrupting your dinner."

"They get an apology and I don't?" I asked.

She glared at me. "Shut. Up."

"In front of my mother?" I asked, half offended.

Her face remained bright red as she faced Ma. "I am truly sorry. I'm going to leave." She spun around and headed for the elevator.

"Good," I mumbled and turned to face three angry people. "What?"

"Go get her," Ma ordered.

"But, Ma. She's irrational. Who reacts like that at getting a gift? She broke her favorite shoes, and I thought I'd be nice and replace them."

"There's obviously a misunderstanding, beta."

"Yeah, she thinks she owes you sex?" Jahn asked, and Ma glared at him. "Sorry, Ma. But she did. Maybe some stupid guy did something like this once and he expected her to return the favor." He shrugged. "There's always something more to what women say."

Ma waved me away. "Go. Hurry before she leaves."

I groaned. "Yes, Ma." But I did not hurry.

Jahn took the box, and everyone else, inside.

"And invite her to dinner!" Ma called as I turned the corner.

What? Our family dinners were *not* for anyone else. I clenched my jaw, but there was no point in denying Ma's good heart. I found Liya tapping a foot in front of the elevator and biting her thumbnail.

"That's not going to make the elevator come any quicker," I said, standing beside her.

"Go away," she snapped.

In a more level tone, I replied, "Listen. We were about to eat dinner. Do you want to join us?"

She stared at me, baffled. "Are you joking?"

"No."

"Go away."

The elevator dinged. "Please?"

"So you can parade me in front of your family and rile me up for amusement?"

"Well, you are easy to rile, and that's your problem." The doors opened. "But my family, especially Ma, insists that you come in for dinner."

"Tell them thanks for the invitation." She stepped into the elevator, but I stood in the doorway to prevent it from closing. "You're going to set off the alarm."

"I promise I will not argue. I'm not setting you up. In fact, I don't intend to speak to you outside of work-related matters after tonight."

An uninterested Liya replied, "I have nothing to gain by going in there."

"Shilpa," I reminded.

"I can see her another time."

"She'll be too busy with the baby soon."

Liya took a step toward me, her arms crossed as her discerning eyes met mine. "Are you going to get yelled at if I don't go?"

"How can you sense the truth so easily and still be hardheaded about me truly wanting to date you?"

She narrowed her eyes. "Because good liars can hide well."

"Are you coming inside or not?"

"Nope."

"Fine," I grumbled. I wasn't going to force her.

"Liya?" Shilpa called from behind me.

I stepped back but held my hand out to keep the elevator doors from closing. Liya's defensive demeanor was quickly dismantled. Her arms dropped to her sides, her sour face turned friendly.

"Come on. Dinner's getting cold," Shilpa said.

"Another time. You know? Without him."

Shilpa took Liya's hand and pulled her along anyway. "Don't mind Jay and whatever idiotic thing he did."

Liya quirked her brows at me in passing.

"Why am I the idiot?" I asked as I followed them into the apartment.

"Because you're a guy," they said in unison.

The girls sat with Ma as I pulled up another chair and Jahn grabbed an extra plate.

"What happened?" he asked quietly in the kitchen while I grabbed a cup and utensils for Liya.

"I'm nice to her, right? And I ask her out."

He shook his head. "Rookie mistake."

I ignored him. "And then she flips and accuses me of wanting to screw her. So when she sees the shoes I replaced, she freaks out even more, thinking that I bought those to make her owe me."

"Another rookie mistake."

"You have no idea what you're talking about."

"Why do you bother with her?"

"After tonight, I won't. She's the most maddening woman in the world."

Jahn chuckled.

"And now look, my own mother turned against me. They just assume I'm in the wrong. I should be inconsiderate to women? Is that what they're telling me?"

"There is no way you can win today. Give it up." He slapped my shoulder, and we returned to the table.

I had to follow Jahn's advice, because when it came to women banding together, it was best to leave things alone. Ma sat at the head of the table and Shilpa sat across from Jahn and beside Liya so that Liya was across from me.

Whenever Liya glanced at me, which wasn't often, she had daggers for stares. Her annoyance level was ridiculous. But as soon as Ma engaged her in conversation, she was someone else entirely.

They spoke kindly and fondly, like old friends. Liya, not being at all traditional, displayed genuine respect for her elders with Ma. It wasn't fake or forced, but inherent. They chatted with Shilpa about work and pregnancy and baby stuff. So much baby stuff. Liya laughed and sank her teeth into homemade falafels. Lettuce and red sauce spilled onto her plate, but she casually swiped it up with a finger and a quick lick.

Well, hell. That tongue. It wasn't a lascivious action, or even aimed at me. But there was something mesmerizing about watching a beautiful woman eat, lost in conversation and pointedly oblivious to me.

I'd thought Liya sitting in on our prized family dinner would interrupt our flow, our calm. But once she unwound, it was almost as if she were part of the family. We might not click on every level, but she definitely clicked with my family.

After dinner, while Jahn helped me with the cleanup, Shilpa shrieked when Liya gave her permission to open the shoebox— not that Liya had any claims on it now. She'd been clear that she didn't want the shoes.

"These. Are. Gorgeous! Tell me that you're going to keep them!" Shilpa said as she admired the shoes.

Liya shook her head. "I'll buy my own pair to replace the ones that broke, which I also bought myself."

Shilpa *tsk*ed. Ma didn't seem to understand what the big deal was. They were pretty shoes, and if she'd heard how much I'd spent on them, then she hid it well.

Seeing that we all, with the exception of Ma, had work in the morning, the family called it a night at eight. Plenty of time to drive home safely, shower, and get whatever they needed done for the morning.

"You must come to dinner again," Ma insisted.

"Thank you. This was very nice," Liya responded.

"You probably have family dinners of your own?"

"No. We haven't had a family dinner since high school. Everyone's just so...busy," she replied, and I wondered what "busy" really meant.

Ma smiled and patted Liya on the shoulder on the way out.

Jahn waved goodbye. "Nice seeing you, Liya. You should hang out with us every week." He purposely did not meet my glare.

Shilpa hugged Liya and told her the same thing, but she, on the other hand, gave me a purposeful grin. They all seemed to hurry out before Liya could get her shoes on.

"I'm leaving. I'm leaving," she muttered as she struggled, her hair in her face.

I closed the door. She slowly straightened herself, and held one heel in her hand like a stake. "What are you doing?"

"We need to talk."

"You said you were done bothering with me."

"*After* tonight. Fine print."

She huffed, "Lawyers..."

"I want to know if you really, truly, honestly believe that I'm only after you to get you into bed. That I'm not a nice guy, that I'm using you, that I'm another Mike." I closed the distance between us in a long stride.

"Yes," she replied without a beat.

"Look me in the eye, Liya. Not with all that attitude as a defense. Tell me that I'm another Mike. That all the things I did were selfish. You see how I am with my family, with everyone. Do you seriously think I'm a Mike, or do you just want me to be, so you can keep yourself from taking a chance?

"Because you know what I think? I think, no, I *know* that you realized your ridiculously high walls were shaking, just a little, and maybe even coming down, just a little bit. That you like me, as a person, and instead of believing that I am who I am and that you don't hate my guts, you'd rather believe I'm a Mike, which makes it easier for you to shut me down."

"Are you done psychoanalyzing me?"

"You have yet to look me in the eye and tell me I'm another Mike. I'm waiting…" There could be absolutely no way on this green Earth that she could compare me to that idiot, to someone who hurt her, demeaned her, left her in the middle of the city all alone.

She looked up. "You're…"

"Yes?" I swallowed hard and glanced at her mouth.

"A…" Her gaze dropped to my lips as I licked them. She imperceptibly leaned into me, as if she might actually cave in and kiss me.

"You're not a good liar," I whispered.

She snapped out of our moment and chided, "I don't have to stand here and be coerced into anything. Believe what you want to believe." She stepped to the right, and I matched her move. She went left and I went left. "Are we going to physically fight?"

She pushed me with a cockiness gleaming in her eyes. I stepped backward, taking her with me. As I hit the wall, she hit my chest, our arms flailing as they decided where to land.

I gently took hold of her wrists and slipped my fingers between hers, keeping our hands to our sides. There was an incomprehensible longing when our flesh touched, and even more so when she pressed into my chest, her soft curves melting against me.

"Tell me," I half muttered, half groaned.

She sucked in a breath. "I can't think, Jay."

"Why?" I whispered and tilted into her, my forehead touching hers.

Her breathing turned erratic, hard. Her lips moved and twisted until she bit them, as if words tangled on her tongue and she couldn't bring herself to admit anything to me. "I hate you."

"No, you don't."

"I wish you were a Mike. This would be easier."

"I will *never* be a Mike. And what we have between us isn't going away." I released our interlocked fingers but kept her in place with a hand on her lower back, right where it curved out. With the other hand, I cupped her cheek and turned her head to look at me. Liya wasn't the only one taking a risk. I hadn't accepted that I deserved a happy ending, and going for one felt a little lost on me. But there was something about Liya, a magnetic pull that compelled me to try. "Why won't you give me a chance?"

"I don't want to marry you," she replied.

"No one said anything about marriage." Although I wouldn't mind. Liya would keep me on my toes, and after getting to know some of the real her...it was difficult to imagine any other woman as my wife. Who could possibly stand up against her? Against this feisty, strong, vulnerable, imperfectly perfect woman?

"That's where you want this to head. If I liked you and you liked me and all the stars aligned, yadda, yadda."

"Jumping the gun."

"Meeting to get married isn't jumping the gun?"

"You are way off. If we'd met..." I caressed her jaw with my thumb. "We would've talked. Weeks. Maybe months. Then, if we liked one another, dated. For months, maybe a year. If we still liked each other, hopefully fell in love..." My thumb grazed her bottom lip, and she stilled. "Then we'd get engaged. Then married when you were ready. Does that sound like jumping the gun?"

"I guess not." She knitted her brows together, and some sort of logic wore down her fight. She was almost there.

"Knowing that now, no strings attached, you can walk away whenever you want, or date me for years if you really, really liked me, would you take this chance?"

"Why do you even want to bother with me?" She shook her head as if she really could not understand my wanting this, my wanting *her*.

"Are you serious?"

"Yes." Her eyebrows shot up as if she couldn't believe this conversation was even happening, but her voice was soft and quiet.

I laughed, and she sort of smiled. "You're intriguing, smart, independent, kind, gorgeous, and no other woman has the ability to make my heart beat so hard when she walks into a room. Why wouldn't I want to be with you?"

She took a deep breath. "You're so good at saying the right words. I see why you're a lawyer."

I licked my lips and tilted my head.

"Don't," she protested weakly.

"Don't what?" I asked and leaned toward her. She didn't move away, didn't push me.

I squeezed her waist, and her eyelids fluttered. "So, you don't want to screw me, huh?"

I smiled against her lips. "Who said I even want to kiss you?" I pulled away and went to the kitchen. "Would you like wine? Coffee?"

"Um. No. I should go home," she replied softly, in a daze.

It was beyond me how pursuing Liya Thakkar made me this nervous. This whole concept of personal happiness and moving on with my life and living for myself had me shaking. But I had to take another leap before she slipped away.

Liya opened the door and had stepped halfway out when I said, "Go out with me?"

She gripped the door, her fingers curled over the white painted slab. She didn't lean back to look at me. "Fine," she said with a smile to her voice.

Then she left.

Chapter Eighteen
Liya

When Jay somehow convinced me to go out with him, I anticipated some fancy restaurant where he'd ask me to wear those stupid shoes he bought. Except those stupid shoes were at his apartment. And he advised that I wear *sneakers*.

He took me out on a date, not to a romantic location, but to…laser tag. Glow-in-the-dark laser tag.

I made a face as he fastened the heavy pink-and-white vest around me, playfully jerking me toward him with each snap. Then he laughed as he helped with my helmet, which was much too big for me. It kept drooping over my eyes, he kept readjusting and chuckling, and I managed not to laugh at this entire situation. What were we? Middle school crushes? For the first time in a very long time, I felt like a kid. In a good way. Not weak or vulnerable or the bane of some adult's existence, but carefree.

I watched Jay as he fixed my gear one last time. In this moment, there was absolutely no stress, no wondering what he was really after. If only we could be this way all the time.

He knocked on my helmet. "Are you all right in there?"

"Are you kidding me?"

He flashed that infamously dashing smile. "It'll be fun. Don't get shot."

"Don't get shot," I mouthed when he turned away.

The woman at the front instructed us on how the point system worked, the rules, and other safety information. I followed Jay through double doors, and my eyes adjusted to the dark room, lit with lines and patterns of neon colors.

An alarm sounded after the two teams split and everyone darted away. I stood alone, wondering where to go.

Then my vest buzzed. It lit pink and buzzed again. I searched around and saw a young girl pointing her laser gun at me. Oh! No she wasn't getting any points off this newbie!

"Come on!" Jay said, grabbing my waist and pulling me behind a large box. "The point is *not* to get shot!" He laughed so hard that his arms shook my shoulder.

"I've some business to take care of..." I muttered and went after the girl in pigtails.

"I got you covered," he called after me.

But going after this little girl was literally walking into an ambush. A group of teenagers stole my points in a matter of seconds until Jay and another girl came through and wiped them out. He came out Rambo style, without the yelling, and even took fake laser bullets for me.

We stood back-to-back for a minute, taking all the hits and making just as many. I couldn't help myself now. There was no controlling my laughter.

I hunched over and wheezed, my hand on my chest, his arm around me to protect me from a demolishing spray of laser lights.

"We need to go!" he said, cutting through my giggles.

He took my hand and we zigged and zagged through, over, and around obstacles. He held onto my waist at some points, pulling me back or helping me maneuver around tight corners or climb short ladders. I was nowhere near as fast as he was, but a few more of these games, and I would be.

Jay effortlessly made points, but it didn't take long for my competitive side to roar to life. Our backs hit the plush side of a boxed-in wall.

"Surprise attack on three…" he said with a countdown.

These kids were going down.

Or so I thought. The final takedown was brutal…for us. Our gear lit up in all sorts of colors. When the buzzer went off and the host spoke, I lowered my gun with weak arms. Who knew laser tag was so demanding?

Jay helped me unclip my vest and helmet. He gently rattled the helmet around. "Not bad."

I thought so, too. But according to our scores, I came in second to last.

I frowned. "That sucks."

Jay nudged my arm with his. "It's just a game. It was your first time, anyway."

Two teens from the opposing group walked by, all giggles, and stuck out their tongues. "Oh, I am going to end them. Rematch."

Jay laughed and threw his arm around my shoulder, whisking me away to a gelato stand. "If you want to get really rough, try paintball."

"You're treating me like one of your guy friends." I ordered my favorite flavor, and he ordered the same.

"I don't do pressure dates. Does any of this make you feel obligated to sleep with me?"

"Are we on this again?"

"I don't understand why you think all men are the same, or feel that any nice thing for you is an eternal, damning, binding contract."

"It's the dance of dating. Men buy things hoping women put

out." I took my cup and poked a spoon into the creamy pistachio gelato.

He tapped my nose with the end of his spoon. "You're wrong."

I smeared the light green gelato across the corner of his mouth. "No, you're wrong."

He licked his lips slowly, and a warm tingle filled my insides. He dabbed away the lingering sweetness that touched his cheek and finished his dessert. I wondered if he did that on purpose. Of course he did. Those baiting, sensual gestures.

We leisurely walked down the street side by side. The crowds thinned as we left the busy entertainment center behind. Our swinging hands accidentally brushed, sending a flutter tumbling through my belly. If I didn't feel like a middle school girl crushing on the new boy before, then I sure did now.

I tried not to glance down at our fingers, tried not to indicate what even the slightest touch from him did to me. I blinked a few times just to see if this was real. A man, a hardheaded one at that, made me completely forget where we were.

We stopped at a small hot dog vendor, and Jay bought two hot dogs while kids ran past us. We followed their direction into the spacious park covered in oak and pecan trees.

"This is gross," I mumbled around a bite.

"Yeah…Are you going to swallow before the next bite?"

"Shut up," I joked and butted him away so that I could eat in peace.

He had one hand around his partially eaten hot dog and the other around my waist. I definitely didn't mind the soft touches.

We found a path in the grass to walk along. I inhaled the remnants of my hot dog and wiped my mouth before he saw the mess I had made.

"Missed some." He tossed our trash in a bin, took my hand, and licked mustard off my finger.

Those idiot lightning bolt jitters bombarded my gut. But he would never know that.

I pulled my hand back and wiped it on the side of my shorts. "Is that the best you can do?"

"With my tongue? No."

"I meant with...never mind." But now he had me wondering about all the toe-curling things he could do with that tongue. I could not stop looking at his mouth. Why was it suddenly hot? Was the sun rising instead of setting?

He laughed. "Calm down. Or do you prefer the no-touch rule?"

"Let's do that."

"That's fine."

"What's next?" I asked, looking at my watch but secretly eager to spend more time with him on this gorgeous evening.

He tapped the glass on my watch. "Don't even pretend that you're bored. But that's it. Unless you want to keep walking?"

"That's all? You are so unimpressive right now."

"Fun. Short and sweet. Room to talk if you wanted, no forced one-on-one interaction, giving you the ability to bail."

We paused.

"Do you want to bail?"

Trick question. "Whatever you want. This will probably be your one and only date."

He shook his head and chuckled. "No. That doesn't work."

"Excuse me?"

"You said you'd give this a chance, not enforce a limit because you've already made up your mind."

"Then let's call it a night." *Why* did I say that? I wanted his hand around mine. I wanted to walk into the sunset. I wanted to watch the fireflies and wander around the park until it was too dark to see, too dark for him to notice me shivering every time he touched me.

I didn't want this evening to end. But my big mouth, always out to prove something, had spoken.

He nodded, and we left in our respective cars. Men had taken me to top restaurants and fancy galleries, beaches and resorts. Not a low-key date. But this was by far the best date I'd ever had. It was easy. Casual. No pretenses, no trying too hard. We weren't rigid or trying to put on our best fronts. We were ourselves.

I found myself grinning and delighted all the way home.

And when I slipped into my pajamas, poured a glass of wine, and made popcorn, I subconsciously checked my phone every three minutes. Half a movie later, Jay texted. Simply put, he had a good time.

I didn't realize until the end of the week that Jay and I had actually been on more than just the one date. It had been a build of very cautious, innocent moments. I needed someone to lean on about the situation the company had left me in, and he'd been there. Somehow, those little moments turned into borderline dates and a relationship of some kind. Well, some kind of something that didn't make me want to walk away.

Every morning, he brought a latte with breakfast and we ate in my office before the day started. He pulled me away from a hectic workplace for lunches across the street. When I stayed late, he stayed with me. Sometimes we ate dinners in the lab when my team came up short. Sometimes we ate them on the floor of my office, which sounded disgusting, but was quite comfortable and relaxed when I leaned against the wall and ended the night by resting my feet on his lap. He even gave me foot rubs.

He listened to me talk about my day then talked about his.

When I looked at it that way, we'd actually been on numerous "dates" and had been "dating" for a while now—not that I wanted that information brought to light.

But Jay hadn't mentioned real date plans again, so when Friday ended, I asked him, "What's next?"

"Looking forward to spending more time with me?" he asked, his face lighting up.

"I see you all day, every day."

"Just until either this company goes down or gets rid of its legal issues. Then you'll never see me around here unless we're still seeing each other. And you didn't answer my question."

"Think you're going to last that long, huh?"

"You might be in for a rude awakening if you doubt it. Tomorrow evening. Same time. Same dress code. We're going to the lake."

"Oooh, are we going fishing?" I mocked.

"Yes."

"Ew."

He grinned. When had his smile turned from something I had assumed he flashed at all of the girls to something I knew was sincere and meant only for me?

All those days until our next official date left enough time to fill in Preeti, Sana, and Reema. Those women pried like no one's business.

We met at Reema's apartment for wedding stuff. I was glad to see Momma here, out and about with women, away from Dad. She was a different person. Dad made her insecure, quiet, a shadow. With Reema's and Preeti's moms, she was herself. Free and cheerful and at ease.

The older women sat on the floor and stitched murals of Ganesh for Reema's place, which she would share with Rohan after the wedding. The girls had already stuffed nuts and raisins into gold mesh pouches with gold ties. We were to set one on every seat for the wedding as a snack, seeing how long and tedious a Hindu wedding ceremony could get. Reema placed the last handful of pouches into a box beside the front door.

I sat on the couch behind Momma as she chirped away. I couldn't resist playing with her hair. She always had it in a braid, but it was intensely frizzy. I absolutely had to fix it for her.

Reema's and Preeti's moms were not like the other aunties. They didn't seem to care much about my past or my wayward attitudes about life. It was nice to sit with them and laugh about how hard they tried to get the traditional details down. We seriously needed a how-to book for Indian weddings.

"I heard you had dinner with Jay and his family," Momma said hopefully.

I replied, "Yes. I'm sure you also heard that it went well and I behaved after a big argument with Jay?"

She sighed. "Always arguing."

"He's easy to argue with."

"His mother says you've been spending some time together at work?"

One by one, everyone in the room glanced at me with knowing, arched brows. I groaned. "Yes. He's helpful at work."

"Isn't he a nice boy?"

"Sometimes."

The aunties laughed, but before Momma could delve deeper into the details, which I was sure would be requested via a private phone call tonight, Preeti's mom mentioned how Preeti's intended looked similar to Jay. This I had to see for myself, but something about Preeti's shrugged shoulders and indifferent expression told me that Yuvan didn't make her feel the way Jay made me feel. She was still hung up on her first love and I felt it.

Once the moms left, the girls and I sat around the coffee table and stuffed small gift boxes with assorted gourmet chocolates. These were to be placed at each reception setting.

As much as I actually wanted to discuss Jay, we immediately moved the conversation to Preeti.

"So, what's wrong with him?" Reema asked.

"Yuvan seems like a nice guy," Sana added, always the optimist. She was the most easygoing of us all. I was, by far, the least easygoing. Reema had strong traits, too, that Rohan matched perfectly. And then there was Preeti.

As a doctor, she was intelligent and independent. But she was also tied down to tradition with enough weights to drown her.

She forced a smile and said, "He's fine."

"Fine is not great," I replied. "Something is obviously amiss."

"He's perfect on paper, but we don't have a connection." She slumped a little. "Is that really important?"

"Yes," Reema and I said together, while Sana answered, "No."

We looked to her as she explained, "Connections can be made later. Love can come later. And anyway, both things can fade. His other traits won't fade, or at least not easily or soon."

Logical Sana.

"You're right," Preeti replied. "I put too much emphasis on how I expect to feel that maybe that's why I'm not feeling it. I just thought…that I'd be in love with my fiancé-to-be."

Granted, while many of our friends were either "arranged" or had their spouses approved by their families, most of them were in love when they decided to marry. It wasn't too much to ask for.

Reema and I glanced at one another as Preeti busied herself with boxes. We knew. We knew that once Preeti had fallen in love, she would always try to measure all other guys against the one who got away. I bit my lip because I wanted to ask…

"Just so you remember, Brandy and her brother will be at the wedding," Reema said.

"I know." Preeti smiled big. "I can't wait to see her."

Yet we all tensed at the idea of Preeti seeing he who couldn't be named. She was still in love with her ex. That was the real reason she couldn't scrounge up any feelings for Yuvan. As great as Yuvan probably was, he was *not* Daniel Thompson.

My phone rang. I dug through my purse before it went to voicemail. I hadn't expected to hear from Shilpa.

"How are things with Jay?" she asked over the phone as I finished the last of the chocolate gift boxes with a perfectly tied bow.

"Calm. Why? What did you hear?" I asked.

She giggled. "Wanted to make sure that whatever you guys had been fighting about is okay."

"It's fine. Sometimes we're volatile together. Bad mix."

"I dunno. Jay likes you."

"I'm sure…" I clamped down a giggle.

"He doesn't talk about women. He talks about you."

I perked up. "What does he say?"

"And you're not interested at all, huh?"

"Women always want to know what guys said about them." I waved off the girls as my words caught their attention.

"Let's just say that he's really into you."

"I don't know why." But I was delighted to hear so.

"Don't play that. You know exactly why."

The sun shone high when we met at the lake. Jay rented a nice little boat to take out, and we enjoyed a refreshing breeze, music, and a picnic on board.

"No fishing," he promised.

"Gutting is not romantic," I assured him.

"Who said I was trying to get romantic?"

"What else is a date for?" I asked, trying to control my hair from whipping around my face.

"To get to know someone."

"Oh."

He leaned back on the railing, looking mighty fine on the sun-drenched lake. "Men haven't treated you well before, have they?"

"Don't psychoanalyze."

"All right. I'll just ask questions."

"Boring."

He rubbed his hands together and looked out at the water. "What do you want to do then?"

"Swim."

"Okay." He pulled me up from the bench. Even though he looked absolutely edible in a pair of trunks and a muscle-fitting white tee, he stripped off his shirt and revealed just how much time he spent working out.

Jay was chiseled, from a thick neck to solid biceps and pecs, defined abs, narrow waist, and a faint vein that went down from his abs to beneath his shorts. I mean...damn.

"Did you drop something?" he asked, lifting my chin.

I swatted him away. "I've seen better."

"No, you haven't."

"Ego check."

"And you?" He waved a hand at my shirt.

"Oh, this? I was just joking about swimming. I don't take my clothes off for everyone, you know? But, um, nice effort." I laughed.

"Funny. But remember, this, all this right here." He pointed down his torso. "Will be popping up in your head every time you close your eyes. And that is your fault, not mine."

"Not likely."

He tugged on his shirt, but I held his forearm, as nice and hard as I remembered, and turned him around. "Wait a minute, now. Let's take a look at the back."

"Nope." He pulled away, but I fought with his shirt as he tried to tug it down, and insisted on taking a peek, slipping my hands up his back. Where I expected to feel the dense smoothness of a sculpted back, I felt ridges instead.

"What is that?"

"Nothing." He pulled my hands away.

"Oh. I'm sorry," I said quickly, heat creeping up my face.

He pressed his lips together. "I don't talk about that."

"Didn't you think I'd see if we had gone swimming?"

"Not if I kept my back turned from you. Let it go," he said sternly.

"You said this whole dating thing was to get to know each other."

"So ask a question," he said, struggling to rein his voice back from irritated to normal.

"What happened to your back?"

"Anything except that."

I raised my brows. "Really?"

"Don't get angry. Getting you to open up about yourself is like pulling teeth. You know far more about me than I do about you."

"Fine, *you* ask a question, then," I snapped.

"All right. Why do you get mad so easily?"

"You make me mad all the time. Next question." I crossed my arms and looked away.

"Why are you so defensive?"

"In a world full of people who make assumptions and accusations and judgments? I don't have a choice."

"Am I making any of those?" he asked gently.

"I don't know. Are you?"

"No. So stop being so defensive."

I huffed out a breath. "I don't know why you bother trying with me."

"You ever think that we always fight because there's tension between us?"

"Yes. Annoyance."

"I mean sexual tension between us." He was against me in a heartbeat, one hand on my lower back and the other on my neck. That combination in itself drove me wild, but having his body flush against mine, with nothing but the skimpy material of our clothes preventing full skin-on-skin contact, was infuriatingly intoxicating.

"They say the only way to release sexual tension is to get it over with," I whispered.

"I don't want to have sex with you, not yet," he said gently.

"If you don't want me, then why are your hands all over me?"

"They're barely on you. Trust me, Liya, if I wanted to be all over you, you wouldn't have a coherent thought left in your head."

"Put your lips to better use, Jay, or step back," I teased.

"You want me to want you, don't you?"

"I know you do."

"I *hate* that you think you have nothing to offer me except your body, that it's the only thing I care about," he said softly.

"Isn't it? You're always flirting, always finding a way to touch me."

"I know what you're doing." He raised his brows and gazed right into my eyes, forcing me to look at him.

"Which is what?"

He brushed a knuckle across my chin. "Pushing me away by insisting that I only want you physically, and if I so much as kiss you, you'll convince yourself that you're right and put an end to this dating thing. I'm not falling for that."

He leaned down, his mouth brushing against mine. "Next. Question."

"Are you a virgin?"

He released me. "No. Are you?"

"You know I'm not."

"That's not an answer."

"No. How many girls have you slept with?"

"Two. How many men have *you* slept with?"

"Six."

He didn't seem bothered. "One-night stands or relationships?"

"Both. You?"

"Relationships."

"That your mother and the community know about?"

He shrugged. "I don't blab about it, but I'm sure they know and it doesn't bother me. Ever been pregnant? Get an STD?"

"No and no. You? Got a girl pregnant?"

"No and no. I have one more question, and then you can end this date," he said, pausing to stand in front of me again.

"Gladly."

His next words were spoken carefully. "Why are you so bent on pushing me away?"

I'd been so into this rapid exchange of heated information that I spoke before thinking, "Because nice guys don't come after me."

"What are you talking about?" he asked in what appeared to be sincerity.

I took a deep breath to gather my thoughts. "I know that I have a bad rep, especially at mandir. No respectable guy there takes me seriously."

"So…are you saying that I'm not respectable, or that I don't take you seriously?"

"Why don't you tell me?"

His jaw twitched. "You can't just cram all men into the asshole category, Liya. We're not all the same. I'm not perfect by any means, but I sure as crap am not a walking dick conniving to use you. The fact that you even think I am makes me wonder—"

"Why you're even here?"

He clenched his teeth, working that tick awfully hard now. "Makes me wonder who hurt you so badly."

I froze. Some small part of me knew that telling him would be just fine. That maybe he'd understand or even take my side, but then there were all the hard facts of my life:

Good guys didn't date me.

Bad boys, irresponsible jerks, players, or short-term commitments came around. Those who wanted sex, a good time were constants. Men fell into three categories: ones who wanted me for my body, ones who were intimidated by my personality, or ones who dismissed me because of my reputation.

Those who wanted to take me home to meet their mothers and sisters? Well, that had never happened. The fact that I knew Jay's family was a matter of circumstances. Why was he even here, though? Did he have a point to prove? Did he truly just want sex…and then he'd walk away from us? Because I knew for certain that I was not the type of girl he'd end up taking to dinner with his mom of his own accord.

"Do you think I'd hurt you, Liya?" he asked, cutting through my thoughts.

I scoffed. "Of course you would."

"There you go again, assuming the worst."

"Well, let me ask you this: Would you tell the entire mandir that you want to marry me?"

He let out a long breath. "This isn't about marriage. You don't even want that."

"Marriage is always the end game. Neither you nor your family wants you to be unmarried for the rest of your life. I don't want marriage, so you're wasting your time."

"I'm not wasting anything, because I know once you let down your guard and realize I'm not another Mike, that you might actually want more with me, that marriage can be a good thing."

I took a step back, feeling the hard, cold railing press into my lower spine. "What if I wanted a marriage? Would you, in front of everyone there, in front of the entire community, no matter what they say or think about me, stand proudly with your mom and your brother and say, 'Liya is the right woman for me'?"

"Of course I would," he said without needing a moment to consider his response, his expression full of sympathy and wanting.

"And if they had something profoundly disgusting to say about me, that others agreed with, would you still stand up for me?" I asked bitterly, my hands trembling with both rage and the abysmal fight it took to stave off the pain.

He sighed and rubbed the crook of his nose. "What are you getting at? What would anyone have to say that's so terrible?"

"Something vicious and evil…could be anything. It doesn't matter. But the way they look at me would be the way they look at you. If you stood your ground."

He scoffed. "I don't care what others think."

"And if those insinuating, judgmental eyes were cast over to your brother? Your mother?"

He swallowed but didn't respond. And that's how I knew. Maybe Jayesh Shah was a good guy. Maybe he wasn't another Mike. But he was someone who would protect his mother and his brother, and if that meant keeping me and all those sticky, insidious rumors from touching them…well, Jay had to do what he had to do.

All emotion drained from his face. He parted his lips to speak, but my finger touched them first.

"This date is over," I said softly, as if pardoning him. It wasn't his fault that he cared about his family. In fact, that made him admirable.

And just like that, we drove back to the dock. When he went to return the boat, I disappeared.

Chapter Nineteen
Jay

Kaajal wove in and out of chattering groups of people after the program that Sunday at mandir. She was pleasant, full of cheer, bursting with respect and earning just as much. She was a respectable woman. I saw why some would match us, but she wasn't Liya.

"She's pretty, huh, beta?" Ma asked, standing beside me in a constantly moving crowd.

"She is."

"What do you think of her?"

I shrugged. "She's nice."

Ma gave me a studious glance and pressed her lips together in her usual I-know-what-you're-thinking manner. "But you like Liya," she said point-blank.

I couldn't even manage a stutter. How did Ma know me so well? It wasn't as if I'd been gushing over Liya.

Ma nodded once and left to take prayer. Kaajal caught my eye before moving through crowds to get to me.

"You look lovely today," I told her.

"Thank you. I've had this sari for a while, but I don't usually wear them. Guess I have to get used to it."

"Well, you wear it well."

She blushed.

I cleared my throat. I didn't want her to get the wrong idea, but what else could she think? Her parents wanted us to get together and Ma liked her, and here I was giving her compliments.

We made small talk: work, plans for the year, etc. Conversing with her was as free-flowing as chatting with my brother.

I laughed.

"What?" she asked.

I shook my head. "Uh, getting along with people here is such a relief after the hectic week I dealt with." And the agonizingly few days since Liya bolted.

Her smile dazzled, big and bright, as she suggested, "Maybe we could get coffee sometime?"

Liya's face streaked across my vision. Fiery, distrustful, unwilling to lower her guard.

"Are you there, Jay? I didn't mean to put you on the spot," Kaajal said.

"No. No. Distracted. Sorry. No, I'd like to get coffee."

She beamed. In the distance behind her, her father nodded, and several eyes casually glanced over us as if the entire mandir knew our conversation. Including Liya's friends. They immediately walked over, and suddenly we were thrown into some Indian soap opera.

Reema and Sana squeezed in between us to say hello. Kaajal, undeterred, greeted them and kept the conversation going.

"Have you spoken with Liya lately?" Reema asked, boldly giving Kaajal shade. Kaajal's perfect demeanor cracked with hints of annoyance.

I answered, "Not in a while. I saw her at the office for a second or two. Why?"

"We haven't heard from her, either," Reema replied, her voice laden with worry, a concern that quickly wove through me.

"Have you dropped by her place?"

"Yeah, but..." Reema looked over her shoulder and asked, "Do you mind?"

Kaajal placed a hand on her hip. "I believe that you interrupted us. Do *you* mind?"

"Yes, I do mind."

"Hey, what's going on over here?" Rohan slipped through and landed an arm around Reema's shaking shoulder.

"This is important, so please, give us some space," Reema said to Kaajal.

"Um. Okay," Kaajal mumbled and stepped away as I told her, "I'll talk to you later."

She barely nodded. I felt awful until she daringly looked at me and raised her chin, her voice having lost its quiver, and said, "Call me for that coffee." With a wink at me and a glaring scowl at Reema, she meandered away.

"I'm not quite sure I know what just happened," I muttered.

"Why did you treat Kaajal like that? What did she do?" Rohan asked Reema.

"She's trying to get in between Jay and Liya," Reema responded.

I choked out, "*What?* No, no, no. You have it all wrong. There's nothing between us, with either woman."

"Wait a minute. You asked us to go to bat for you," Reema said.

"And thank you for doing that, but Liya made it perfectly clear that she's not emotionally available for anyone. There's no reason to keep trying, not when she puts up a fight every step of the way."

"Did something happen, then? She stopped talking to us a few days ago," Reema said, worry creasing her brow.

"Our second and last date. She ended it. Good run, though," I added dryly.

"She's gone MIA since," Sana added softly.

I exhaled a rough breath and dragged a hand down my face. "Are you making this sound worse than what it is?"

They shook their heads.

"Liya never shuts down," Rohan confirmed.

I shook my head. "What do you want me to do about it? She doesn't talk to me unless she's spitting fire."

"She still goes to work?" Reema asked.

"That's all she does."

"Okay, then. Hit her where she can't run."

"Why would I want to take part in this? She made it clear she wants nothing to do with me."

"Because you broke her," Sana said.

My heart shattered at the accusation, at just knowing that Liya was in a bad place. "No. I absolutely did nothing to physically or emotionally hurt her. I wouldn't do that."

"But you must've gotten to her. No guy has ever made her close up."

I hated to think that I had had anything to do with harming Liya. How could anything ever get to her, pry through her deftly constructed layers? But if I had something to do with her current state, then how could I leave it alone?

I marched across the fifth floor, earning a few curious looks from passersby and a haggard-looking Wendy. I waved and walked right past her into Liya's office as I tugged on my suit jacket. All I had to do was ask a few direct questions and I'd know for certain if I had hurt her in any way.

That was the plan. In and out. But the moment I registered Liya bent over her desk, I halted dead in my tracks. She leaned over her chair and read files, her blouse sagging in the middle but any cleavage masked by a cascade of black waves. She tugged on her lower lip with her teeth and tapped the desk while humming.

A grin spread across my lips. Look at her, all sexy and hard-working.

I stopped in front of her desk. She stopped humming and peered up at me.

"Hello," I said.

She straightened up. "What are you doing here?"

"Do you know how concerned your friends are about you?" I asked.

She furrowed her brows. "I'm busy. They know that."

"They think you're avoiding them."

She rolled her eyes. "So they sent you? Talk about a fan club, Jay. You've got all the ladies in your court."

"Look, I'm going to be direct, and I'd appreciate some directness in return."

"Sure."

"Did I hurt you?" I asked gently.

She paused. "No."

"Do I have anything to do with your current reclusiveness?"

"You're quite full of yourself." She scoffed. I saw right through her, though. Her walls were coming back up.

"Directness, Liya. Your friends seem to think this is the case."

She looked skyward, her lips puckered—her telltale sign that she was about to give me some serious, undeserved attitude in a circumvented response.

"Don't do that," I stopped her.

"What?" she asked.

"Whatever you're about to say that is not an answer."

She walked around the desk and stood toe-to-toe with me. She smelled of flowers and spice and a certain sweetness that my tongue tingled to taste. Despite how much we fought, my body always responded to her. She woke me up. I came to life. My heart beat as if it had never beat before. My pulse sizzled, my veins throbbed, my gut tightened.

And it was vexing—absolutely, insanely vexing. I hated it.

She said, "I will speak with my friends. You don't have to worry about me, and I'd appreciate it if you didn't come here outside of work-related issues."

"Don't worry. With lawsuits in full force, you won't have to see me much longer. But I came because I was concerned."

"You're like a puppy."

I scoffed and looked at my watch. "This puppy has a date in twenty minutes."

"Sure you do."

"Across the street at the café with Kaajal."

Her jaw clenched.

"If you feel the need to see proof, drop by," I said and left.

Liya didn't snoop around, and that disappointed me. Despite the accomplished and well-respected Kaajal in front of me, who didn't hide herself and offered her entire background story, I found myself scouring the café for Liya.

The coffee date came and went, as boring and disenchanting as I'd presumed it would be.

Every day afterward, I fought the overpowering desire to go to Liya's office with breakfast, to stay late with her. When we had to take up space in the same room during the weekly meeting, she was more distant than ever.

Every time she walked by, she did so with her head held high and her gaze always ahead. We never made eye contact, but her flowery perfume lingered long after she'd walked past. The scent took me back to all those non-dates, all those moments where we'd been around each other and where she had lowered her guard even the slightest.

And that made me miss her even more. I found myself glancing at her in passing or at meetings, willing her to smile or laugh, to see that shimmer in her eyes, to hear her voice again. I even found myself wanting to argue with her. *Anything*.

I left my tie and jacket in the car and headed up to her tenth-floor apartment. She didn't answer after several knocks, or even after a few texts. But her gray Lexus was in the parking lot and light glowed through her closed curtains.

I paced the hallway. Was this stalking? Was I going too far? Would she think I was off my hinges?

I sighed. Well, the truth was... I needed to tell her the truth.

The front door finally opened, very quietly, as Liya ducked out of her place in a short, tight, cherry-red dress with shoes and lips to match.

Those lips. Good lord.

She jumped when she saw me, her hand clutching her purse like she was about to take a swing.

"What—what are you doing here?" she asked, closing her door but not yet locking it.

"I've been texting you, waiting out here like a—"

"Desperate weirdo?" she asked, her words toughening up her appearance.

"I can't get you off my mind."

"Says the guy who walked away and—"

"You wanted me to! You're still making all kinds of excuses. Hypotheticals in worse-case scenarios. Tell me what that's about."

"No."

I arched my head back and took in a deep breath.

"Am I taxing you? I have to go, I have a date."

I slowly returned to her. "With whom?"

"None of your business."

The thought made my stomach turn inside out and leak acid all over my guts. Some other guy was going to have her attention? Be on the receiving end of her smile? Touch her? Kiss her?

"Yes," she stated.

"What?"

"That look on your face? You're wondering if we're going to have sex, and yes, we will."

I mentally shoved down a lump of anger and jealousy. "So you really don't want us to be together?"

"There is no 'us,'" she declared.

"Why don't you just tell me to my face that you don't like me."

Her glare turned hot, her cheeks flushed, her lips pressed, holding back a heap of icy words.

"I know that you assume the worst about me, Liya. That I— if I have my facts straight—am just after you for sex, I wouldn't support you no matter what shady history came out, that aforementioned shadiness would make my poor, weak mother distraught—"

"Now wait a minute—"

I took a step toward her and interrupted her just as quickly as she'd interrupted me. "Because obviously my mother has to be weak if a few rumors can dismantle her. Which means I'm just as weak. I'm so consumed with what others think that the mere thought of displeasing strangers makes my balls shrink? I guess? I'm not man enough to stand up for you? Or would I be so thoroughly disgusted with your history that I wouldn't be able to stand the sight of you?"

She tapped a foot and glared at her watch. "You're making me late. Any more patronizing analysis that you want to throw at me?"

I released a harsh breath. "Your friends are convinced that you're depressed, that I had something to do with it. And I am so sorry if I did."

"Don't give yourself that much credit."

"Is this what you do? Have sex with whomever to make yourself feel better?"

She opened her mouth to bite into me, but her words deteriorated into nothing.

"No matter how much I like you, and Liya, I *really* like you, I have no right to tell you not to sleep with another guy. But don't. Please."

"Because it's harmful behavior?" she gritted out. "You don't get to tell me what's right and wrong. My sex life is none of your business. We are not dating. We are not friends."

In an instant, I had her soft body crushed against mine, one hand around her waist and the other on her jaw. Her breath hitched, and all the fight left her.

I tilted my head, my mouth close to hers, and said, "If you want therapeutic intimacy, then you can get it from me, not some random idiot who probably doesn't want anything more or who doesn't see anything more."

"You think you see more?" she sneered.

"I see so deep into you, Liya, that you can't hide yourself from me. Even things you don't want me to see. I love every piece of beauty, every imperfection, and I can't get enough."

My lips crashed down over hers. I meant to be sensual and slow, but she was hungry and so was I. Our kiss was deep and passionate, my tongue sliding over her bottom lip and tangling with hers. A delicate moan escaped her and a deep one rumbled through my chest. Liya tasted every bit as sweet as I had expected.

Her fingers fisted in my hair as she pulled me into her, desperate and dominating. Searching through the dizziness and battling for control over myself, I managed to pull away and slow the kiss. Sensual. Sweet. Caring.

I nipped her bottom lip and sucked, her gasps slowing as she caught herself.

"What are we doing?" she whispered.

"I don't know anymore."

"Why are you here?"

"You're not this quiet, lost person. Where did you go?" I cupped her cheek and searched her eyes for the vibrant, full-of-life fighter that was somewhere in there.

"Most people like me to shut up," she said quietly.

I grunted, "Not me. Where's the snarky, smart-mouthed, opinionated woman?"

"She's still here."

"I miss her," I confessed.

She craned her head back. "You miss that woman?"

"The world feels incomplete without her."

She momentarily glanced away, her lips quivering as if she were trying not to smile. "You talk like a man who has it bad."

I caressed her cheek as I let go. "I am a man who has it bad."

Chapter Twenty
Liya

I'd like to believe that the half-empty bottle of wine on the coffee table was to blame for my light-headedness. But I'd be lying.

I'd never been kissed like that before, with urgency and passion, and something that stirred my entire being right down to the bones. Other guys had given me the roller-coaster feeling, the need to hurry up and release as soon as possible. But with Jay? I wanted this phenomenon to slow down and last for eternity. It was as if my entire life had been broken into obscure pieces and his touch brought everything together, clarified the whole, and made me stronger.

He watched me from the other end of the couch, patiently waiting for me to speak. When I couldn't, he lifted my feet onto his lap and rubbed the soles. The massage on the arches was delightful and erotic, and I just about lost my mind.

I wanted him to go higher and send those wondrous fingers and lips to scour every last inch of my body. My chest ached. He made it hard to breathe, to concentrate.

"How's your ankle?" he asked.

I gave him a sheepish smile. "Is that why you're rubbing my feet? Concerned?"

"Why else?" he asked, his eyes never leaving mine as his hands slid up my calves, massaging as they went. So much of me wanted him to keep going, all the way up, unraveling me bit by maddening bit. Instead, he promptly returned to the arches and the once-injured ankle.

My skin burned. "Didn't you say that if I wanted to get intimate with someone, it would be with you?"

"Intimacy doesn't have to be physical."

I almost face-palmed. How did he just say that to me? "Do you not see what I'm wearing?" I arched my back, displaying a tight, deep neckline, and crossed my legs over his lap so that the already short hem rode even farther up my thighs.

He closed his eyes and bit his lip, but then raised his hands. "Intimacy with me is not quick, meaningless sex."

"But what if that's what I want?"

His gaze fell upon me with penetrating eyes that pierced straight to my soul. "Is that all you really want from me?"

"It's a start," I teased.

He laughed. "I'm never quick. And meaningless? That doesn't work for me."

"Ah…so you tricked me?"

"Are you going to kick me out?"

I smiled, feeling those hardened layers around my emotions soften just the tiniest bit. All right. *Fine*. It wasn't all that bad to have a decent man around, to know he wasn't going to be another one-night stand. Not that it meant I was ready to admit such a thing out loud. "How would Kaajal feel about you being here?"

"She probably wouldn't care. She was annoyed that I didn't pay any attention to her during our coffee date," he replied.

"Oh?"

"I was distracted."

"By what?"

"By you. Waiting for you to walk in, wondering where you were, what was wrong."

I sipped my glass of wine.

"I really missed you," he confessed. Yeah, I had missed him, too.

Dragging my finger over the back of the couch in patterns, I admitted something to both myself and to Jay, not really knowing why I wanted to share. "I missed you, too. But you *need* to understand why this won't work." No more secrets. He had to know about Mukesh, about how awful things could get for his family if he chose me over Kaajal.

Jay caressed my leg. "I don't care what others think. If it hurts you, I'll talk to them, but only because I don't want you to hurt."

"So calm, aren't you?"

"Well, I almost punched someone for saying something."

"That is the problem, isn't it? It bothers you. You shouldn't have to defend me all the time. And what about your mom? I don't want to be the cause of any pain if she heard how vicious some people can be toward me."

"Ma is strong. She doesn't take any crap."

"Jay. There are some terrible things in my past. Things that almost destroyed me, things that destroyed my relationship with my parents. And they will come out."

"So tell me first."

I swallowed. Hard. How did someone go from never trusting a man to telling one about being assaulted? By the most respected man in the community? What if Jay didn't believe me? I blinked back a tear, suddenly realizing how fast my breathing had become.

"It's okay," he said softly and took my free hand, the one that I'd clenched into a fist. "I'm not going to judge you or blame you."

"Will you believe me, though?" I asked.

"Of course."

"You say that now—"

He sighed. "Stop. We're past this. Stop assuming how I'll react."

"Okay. How about I tell you in the morning? When I'm refreshed and less tired and mentally prepared?" Because even though I couldn't quite bring myself to say everything aloud, I really wanted to tell Jay the truth that very few people knew.

"Deal. *If…*"

I groaned. There was always an "if."

"If you answer this question: Are you sleeping with anyone now?" he asked, both gently and sternly.

"No."

"Do you want to be?"

"Are you asking me to?" I bit my lower lip, which didn't go unnoticed by Jay. Lord help me, it would be impossible to deny him if he even hinted with the slightest nod. How incredible would he feel? Even if he walked away the day after, or a few weeks later, or months down the line, having gotten all the physical goods before getting bored, this entire thing might still be worth it.

He explained, "I want to know if other men are coming around."

"No," I admitted. I was not even remotely interested in other men.

"Not even this guy you had a date with tonight?"

I swirled the wine in my glass and arched a brow.

"There was no guy, was there?"

"Can't a girl treat herself?"

He leaned his head back and laughed, then said, "I want all of you. The bad liar, too."

I pushed my foot against his chest, and his hand accidentally fell to my thigh, grazing my skin on the way to the cushion. He shifted across the couch so that I was snug against his chest.

Okay. This was unexpected. Him kissing my neck? Yes. But him holding me and caressing my arm? Totally new.

I rested my cheek against his shoulder and closed my eyes, trapping the tears. I was never meant to have someone this good, this decent. It would eventually end, and that would end me.

Jay brushed a thumb across the dampness of my cheek, and I startled.

"Are you crying?" he asked quietly, pulling away to look at me.

"Too much eye makeup and sleepiness makes my eyes water. I should wash my face."

He kissed my cheek, his lips gentle against the wet trail. "Do you want me to leave?"

"No. Why don't you find a movie and I'll change?"

"All right."

I washed off all the makeup and stared at my teary-eyed reflection in the mirror. Jay was genuine, and he really liked me for me? He still wanted me, still chose me over another woman as the one to bring home to his perfect family?

I managed to control my emotions and slipped into pajamas. Not the everyday ones: a pair of dark green bottoms and a matching three-quarter-sleeved top. Not the intimate ones: an assortment of revealing, lacy lingerie. But the nice ones. The kind I wore to sleepovers with the girls or when I wanted to feel nice all on my own: gray, white, and pink pinstriped short cotton shorts and a pink tank top.

Jay sucked in a breath when I returned. He pulled down the throw from the side of the couch and covered me.

"Okay…What's wrong now?" I asked.

"Nothing."

I threw off the sweltering blanket, letting it lie in my lap as the movie began. Jay glanced at me through the corner of his eye, biting his nail, and keeping to himself.

"Spill it," I demanded.

"Liya, you're making it very difficult for me not to take you into your room."

My gut clenched. "I thought you didn't want to have sex with me."

"I wouldn't have sex with you," he said so matter-of-factly that a hefty dose of pain shot through me. "We'd make love. We'd turn down that bed. I'd have you making all kinds of noises and calling out my name like you'd lost your mind."

"You sure are full of yourself."

"And you'd be full of me."

I swallowed. "Why are you holding back, then?"

He grinned. "I've got other parts of you to unlock first. Doesn't mean I'm not turned on by you."

I grinned and slid the blanket off my shorts. "Does this bother you?"

"Testing me, woman."

I laughed, and although he kept his hands to himself, after a while, I bundled up as the night chilled. Only then did Jay wrap his arm around my shoulder and hug me, tender and protective, and all the things that made me warm inside. All the things men had never offered.

I awoke in bed, beneath the covers. Not remembering Jay leaving, or even which movie we tried to watch, I yawned, stretched, and crept out of the bedroom. I stilled at the sight of Jay tugging on his pants, his wretched back turned to me. Scars and welts seared his flesh. My heart ached at the sight. He had a painful past, too.

Mesmerized, I tiptoed toward him, carefully, quietly, the sound of his zipper a booming rumble in the silence.

Jay's back was tall and broad, the color of dark caramel, rich and creamy, with swirls of mismatched hues on marred, rough, rigid skin.

My hand reached out and my fingertips touched the creases. Jay spun around and grabbed his shirt. His eyes blazed.

"What happened to your back?" I asked softly and watched as his hands expertly buttoned his shirt.

"Nothing."

"Jay…"

He paused, as if he were conjuring all the words to explain his scars, but not a single word made it past his lips. There was a surge of miserable anguish that crested his features and, in that moment, the hellish black clouds lingering over our heads became one. There was a whorl of misery that our pasts had created, that followed us around, but seeing Jay's in the flesh somehow created a protective cocoon meant for just the two of us.

"I…"

He watched me carefully. "Liya?"

A harsh breath shuddered through my chest. Here. Went. Everything. "I really like you, Jay."

His expression softened, but he didn't attempt to speak.

"I think this, whatever we have and could have, will dissolve because I'm wild and untamed and you'll get tired of either my ways or the rumors. And I know you believe you'll never let that happen, but wait until it's constant and external. You'll decide we're not worth it after all."

"Do you want this to be worth it, or are you just using this excuse to spare yourself the pain?"

"Both."

"Who hurt you so badly that you think like that?" he asked.

"The question is: who hasn't?"

He ran his hand down my cheek, his touch warm with the right amount of roughness. "Tell me all the bad things that have happened to you, that make you doubt any man would or could make a life with you."

I pulled away and went into the kitchen. "I told you last night that I would tell you the truth, and I keep my word. I can't watch you watching me while I tell you something that I don't usually share, though."

"Okay," he said softly.

I busied my hands with coffee, lots of coffee, and toast while he made scrambled eggs.

"This doesn't leave us," I said.

"Agreed."

"I started having sex when I was fifteen."

"Okay. Why?" he asked like any other casual conversation. No judgment. No assumption. No accusation. No negative anything.

Two mugs clanked in my hands and the calming aroma of coffee filled the air. "Because I wanted control over something, and when I realized how much a girl could control boys with sex, it became natural," I replied, waiting for the undiluted disgust that never came.

"Just did it one day and liked it?"

"No. I hated it. I hated being touched, being used. I hated the man who first touched me, who made me feel like a cheap, defenseless child. Sex was the only way to validate myself, take power back, be the dominant one in a world where I had no authority."

I saw the lines of his face harden from the corner of my eye. "Were you assaulted?"

"Yep. I was at his house because his family was friends with mine, and his wife had me over after school until my parents came. She, um, left the apartment to do laundry and he came home." My chest burned as I relived that warm afternoon. Mukesh didn't have a lot of time to do as much as he could've, but he did enough damage. "And you know society. It was, of course, my fault. Certain people were quick to villainize the victim."

"Liya, I—"

I quickly looked to him, meaning to give a confident face that showed how much it didn't bother me, but it came out weak and shaky instead. "It doesn't define me. I made sure that I worked hard in school and made a career and found independence so I never have to rely on a man."

He took a step toward me and touched my hand over the coffee mug. "What happened to this asshole?"

"Oh, he's still there, running the show with no one to drag him down."

"Did you report him?"

"I told my parents. My mom was scared, but my dad said it was my fault."

"What the hell?" he growled.

"He said I must've done something to lead that guy on. And then he..." I looked down at our comforting hold. "Instead of protecting me, he profusely apologized to him. My dad was the first to label me a whore. He blamed me, then he blamed my mom. Ever since I finished college, he's been pushing someone on me to marry because, according to him, girls who get assaulted are broken and useless, and finding a man to even consider me was an exhaustive ordeal."

"Oh, my god, Liya." Jay wrapped his arms around me and held me tight. In his embrace, the truth didn't hurt so much. What my dad had done disintegrated. I'd only ever known men to hurt me, but for the first time, this man was gluing me back together. "And you think this secret would come out and make us run from you?"

"It's not that simple."

"I am so sorry you went through all of this," he added, kissing

my head. "You are amazing and strong, and I'm incredibly hon-
ored that you shared with me."

"Don't get all emotional," I joked, my voice cracking in the
process. "And you're burning the eggs."

"Crap!" He jumped aside and grabbed the handle of the pan
with a towel, moving it off the heat while gingerly trying to
scrape the eggs into a plate. "I'll make you better ones."

"It's fine. I like burnt eggs."

He went to work cracking more eggs. "All these idiots in your
past distorted what a real man is and how a healthy relationship
works."

"Well, hell. Don't hold back now."

He paused. "What happened to my back is the past, but you
still want to know. Whether you like it or not, the past still
affects us."

I swallowed. A numbing sensation crept over my chest and
burrowed into my skin, and spread like thick tar.

Jay deftly made a new batch of scrambled eggs and plated them
while I brought the coffee to the counter. "I'm glad you told me. I
know it's not easy."

He leaned over and tenderly kissed my forehead before taking
a seat beside me.

I took a bite of eggs and made a face.

"Don't tell me my eggs are gross. I perfected scrambled eggs."

I laughed. "This needs salsa. How do you live with yourself?"
I hopped off the barstool and rummaged through the fridge,
grabbing a half-empty bottle of homemade, oven-roasted salsa. I
shook it in my hand like a martini. "Extra spicy."

He grinned. "Keeping the moment light?"

I handed him a spoon to dip into the jar. "The heavy stuff has
passed. Unless you want to share something?"

"Come here," he said, pulling me onto his lap.

He wrapped an arm around me while I took a bite of spicy eggs. He cleared his throat and explained, "When I was a kid, I got caught in a fire. Actually, I started the fire. By accident. Our apartment went up in flames. Hence the scars on my back."

"Oh. Wow. I'm sorry. That must've been traumatic. But you're okay, you survived."

"Yeah…" he replied softly, and I knew that someone else hadn't. As much as I hated talking about my past, I couldn't hold him to telling me more, not when I hadn't told him my entire story.

"Do the scars hurt?"

"Sometimes they're sensitive, phantom pain, but otherwise, no."

"Can I see them?" I asked.

"Why do you want to look at my ugly side?"

"Jay, you don't have an ugly side."

He watched me thoughtfully for a moment before shifting me off his lap. He kept an intense gaze locked on mine as he unbuttoned his shirt and peeled it off.

He turned away as I carefully ran my fingertips over the ridges, studying and memorizing them, feeling his pain and terror. To have been a small child, consumed by flames, melting, screaming in agony, certain of death? Tears welled in my eyes as I could, unfortunately, relate. To that night when a grown man slid a hand over me, explained to me the things good girls do for him.

I swallowed hard, my throat dry and aching, and blinked back hot, stinging tears.

I didn't know what possessed me, but I spread my fingers over his back in a gentle caress and kissed one of the scars. My lips moved up to his shoulders, his neck, near his ear, where I whispered, "Everything about you is gorgeous."

Jay swiveled back to me and pulled me between his legs. He took hold of my mouth with his, his hands alternating featherlight touches and gripping commands on my waist.

I'd wanted men before, simply for their bodies, for wild flings and mind-numbing sex, but I found myself wanting Jay on a different level, a new plane. All of him. Physically, emotionally, eternally.

I pulled back after he landed a final soft kiss to my lips. We stared at each other longingly.

We still had boundaries: His not to cross anything beyond kisses. Mine not to venture anywhere near love.

An impasse. A resolve that was quickly falling apart.

Chapter Twenty-One
Jay

Things returned to normal after spending the night with Liya, but normality now included sharing all meals—including my family weekday dinners. Liya added a lot of laughter. And we now had actual dates where heels were sanctioned. Those freaking expensive high heels, to be exact. At nearly five inches taller, she didn't have to look so far up to reach my eyes. But she was still shorter, and I liked that. We were a perfect fit.

Those shoes made Liya's already long legs leaner, and the short red dress she wore made them stretch for days. The dress hugged every flawless curve.

No matter what she wore, the woman was drop-dead gorgeous. It was a no-brainer to see why she made heads turn wherever she went, why men drooled over her. Case in point, she waited by the bar while the staff cleared a table for us. After I washed my hands, the hostess informed me that our table was ready. I returned to Liya to bring her over, when another man leaned against the counter and tried to buy her a drink.

I stopped just behind Liya to blend into the line of people waiting beside the bar, the guy totally focused on her. She giggled, and my heart constricted.

"A pretty thing like you shouldn't have to buy her own drinks," he said with a wink.

Some deep, dark, dank part of me worried how she'd react to other men hitting on her, or if I'd end up an emotional, jealous, constantly worried man-child.

Liya tucked hair behind her right ear. "I can buy my own drinks. And I'm not a thing."

The man's grin wavered. "Oh, I didn't mean it like that—"

"And I'm here with someone."

"I don't see him."

"You don't have to…" she replied curtly and swerved away from him, startling when she nearly walked nose-first into my chest. "Oh! You scared me."

"Sorry. Our table's ready. Are you all right?" I asked her before glancing at the stranger over her shoulder. I placed a hand on her lower back, rubbing my thumb across her spine.

"Yeah, just telling this guy that I have a man," she replied loudly enough for him to hear.

I chuckled, immediately at ease, as we weaved through tables to get to our seats near the window. Leave it to Liya to make sure she was heard. Definitely no blushing and playing it off or apologizing for things that weren't her fault.

I never thought I'd be the type of guy who wanted a woman who commanded so much attention, like, man, I'd have to deal with this *all* the time? How far would another guy go to get her? But I was working on not worrying. I was appreciative of everything about her. And yeah, feeling a little cocky that she was with me. I definitely felt like I'd won at life being with Liya, and somewhere in the recesses of my mind, my brain started to pick that up.

As I pulled out her chair, she backed into me. The curve of her backside so perfectly aligned with my body, the slight scent of her flowery, and no doubt expensive, perfume, and tickle of her hair against my throat made me shudder. I gently pushed her chair in as she sat down and crossed her legs.

Clearing my throat, I took my seat across from her, but not without noticing all the looks.

"Is this what it's like taking you out?"

"What do you mean?" she asked with a frown.

"All the looks?"

"What looks?"

"Come on, you don't notice all these guys gawking at you?"

"All these women undressing you with their eyes, you mean?" she teased with a smile, and presented a side I'd thought I'd never see. So far removed from her tough-girl, in-your-face image that one wouldn't believe such an easy side of her existed.

From that point on, it was just the two of us as everyone else ebbed away into a sea of colors and faint sounds. We ate lightly and shared a bottle of wine and a dessert. Time flew by. Had it been an hour already? Two?

Maybe she read my thoughts and didn't want the evening to end just yet, because she stood and gave me her hand. "Dance?"

I stood, my eyes never leaving hers, took her hand, and walked her out to the dance floor. A slow song played, and several couples swayed to the music as we found ourselves in the middle. At first, she maintained distance, that awkward/respectful few inches, but I pulled her in close. I never wanted her too far from me.

She gasped as her chest hit mine and my hand slid down her back, but she didn't fight it. Gradually, her arms wrapped around my neck, her cheek against my shoulder as I leaned down. She shivered as my lips landed on her neck, her arms tightened, her breathing a little heavier.

Why hadn't every man in the world fallen in love with Liya Thakkar by now?

We danced for three songs straight, the music effortlessly melting together, before we parted. I pulled her back into me and asked in her ear, "Do we have to call it a night?"

"What do you have in mind?" she muttered.

"Come on." I took her hand, small but powerful, in mine.

The valet pulled my car around, and I opened her door before he could. Once inside, I reached over the console and took her hand in mine, threading my fingers through hers. She studied our hands, thoughtful. What went through her head?

"Where are we?" she asked when I pulled into a parking lot.

"The park."

"Isn't it dangerous at night?"

"Not here. Come on." I pulled her out of her seat and grabbed a blanket from the trunk before trekking through the soft grass.

"You always keep a blanket in your car?"

"Yeah, for emergencies. Never know when you might need it. Food, water, first-aid kit, too."

"Oh!" she grunted and caught my arm as one of her heels pierced the soft dirt and sank.

"You should take those off."

"And walk around barefoot? Hello? Ever heard of hookworms and tetanus?"

"Ever heard of snapping your ankles as you fall flat on your face in the dark?" I asked as I squatted in front of her and slipped her foot out of the high heels.

"What are you doing?" she gasped, tumbling forward and grabbing onto my shoulders for support.

"Removing your obstacles."

She landed a bare foot on the grass as I undid the other shoe. "So now I get tetanus?"

I looked up at her, my hands lightly stroking her ankles up to her calves. "You worry too much."

"It's a real risk. Ask Preeti."

I stood slowly, moving up her body, and hovered above her.

"How...how far are we walking?" she asked.

"To the river."

"In the dark?"

I nodded and handed her the shoes.

"Took these off and you won't even carry them?"

"I'll carry them," I replied, swooped down, and threw her over the blanket on my shoulder.

Liya yelped. "Put me down!"

"So you can get tetanus?" I asked and walked toward the river.

She laughed. "I hate you!"

"You love it."

She slapped my butt and then poked her pointy elbows into my shoulder as she arched her back. "Enjoying the view of my backside from over there?"

I slid my hand up the back of her thighs and tugged her dress down to keep her covered.

"This isn't so bad," she said.

"Oh, yeah?"

"Yeah." She slapped my butt again. "Giddyap!"

"All right. You asked for it."

Her next words were swallowed up in a scream as I took off at a full sprint.

She gripped my shirt, clutching for my waist, as the breeze broke around us. I ran the short distance to the riverside in no time, slowing only when the moonlit gleam on the water's surface appeared.

I placed Liya on the grass, but she swayed away. I grabbed her by the waist to steady her and chuckled. "Are you okay?"

"You try doing that upside down."

After laying out the blanket, we sat arm to arm and watched

the ripples on the water. Sitting soon turned into lying down. My head rested on my hand while Liya constantly shifted to get comfortable on the ground.

"Never been camping, have you?"

"Camping's disgusting," she retorted.

"Here." I slid my arm beneath her waist and hoisted her against me so that she was on her side, her cheek against my chest. "How's that?"

"Better," she muttered.

After a minute, her rigidity faded, and her hand snaked over my stomach to find a comfortable resting position.

The stars twinkled around sparse, slow-moving clouds. The full moon shone bright. Crickets chirped in soothing harmony, a ballad of nature in the middle of a sleeping city.

"I had a good time tonight," I admitted.

"Me, too."

"Are we doing this again?"

"I hope so," she said.

"Do you want to come to mandir tomorrow?"

"And worship with you? Be still my heart." She laughed.

"That would be nice."

"I'm never going to be a religious girl. Does that bother you?" she asked.

"Honestly, I'm not that into it, either. I go for Ma, and it's family time."

"That's sweet. But I still don't want to go."

"I actually meant in the afternoon. We have a basketball tournament."

"Oh. Maybe. Do you want me there?"

"Of course I do."

"Okay."

✳

My competitive side roared to life during the three-game tournament. Sure, we were just a bunch of men from temple competing for a non-trophy, non-glory spot, but it didn't mean that we didn't go for it. But, since the game was held at mandir, we left the trash talk at home.

On the benches, the other teams watched along with friends and family. In the throngs of colorful clothes and sweaty jerseys sat Liya. She watched me with her head turned toward Reema, whispering and giggling. I knew she was throwing her don't-care wall back up in this place. But that didn't stop her from cheering when we made points or getting into the game.

In the end, we won, but it didn't matter. Not because this was a friendly tournament, but because all of my focus was on the woman who rose in the parting crowds.

Kaajal appeared in my peripheral vision, but I made a beeline up the benches to Liya. She crossed her arms and hinted at a smile. "Congratulations."

"Oh, that? That was nothing. I'm just a beast." I grinned.

"A beast against non-athletes. I could've won. In my heels."

"Ah, you think that's funny?" I teased and swiped a sweaty forearm against her dry, smooth arm.

"Ew!" She jokingly gagged and wiped the sweat on my shirt, which just made her sweatier.

I laughed.

"Disgusting."

She sucked in a breath when I made the last step and stood in front of her, heat exploding around us, my blood raging, my adrenaline still pumping on high. "What did you say?"

"You heard me."

I cocked an eyebrow, parting my lips to say something smart-mouthed, when Mukesh Uncle cleared his throat at the bottom of the near empty bleachers.

"Your admiring groupie," Liya muttered. "Listen, I need to practice dance with the girls for Reema and Rohan's reception. I'll talk to you later." She trotted down the bleachers without another word, throwing serious evil eye at Uncle, who responded in kind. The hostility between the two was so thick, I could've choked.

I met the elder at the bottom, snatching my towel and water bottle. As I guzzled, he said, "Nice game."

"Thank you, uncle."

"Since we're practically alone, I wanted to inquire on your thoughts about any interest in Kaajal."

I sputtered. Well, that was certainly direct. "I never thought about it."

"Really? When we met at Shilpa's baby shower, I thought you were aware of our intentions. Your mother said you were available and that she'd discuss it with you."

Every time I saw Ma, she either chatted with Liya during our family meals or earnestly prayed at mandir, and everything in between *except* bringing up Kaajal. We hadn't discussed Liya, but Ma must've known with the regularity of having her at weekly dinners that something was happening between us.

I dragged the towel down my face and neck. "I appreciate the consideration, but I'm not interested."

"Oh? Why not?"

I shrugged. "Your daughter's lovely, respected, accomplished, and any man will be lucky to marry her, but at this point, I'm not drawn to her."

Something changed in his appearance: a narrowing of the eyes, a flare of the nostrils, a clench of the jaw? Something that skewed his polite features. "I understand that at one time, Pranad Thakkar presented Liya."

I nodded, not particularly happy about his venturing into my personal life.

"You speak to her often?" he inquired.

"Yes."

He sighed and rubbed the bridge of his nose as if speaking to a child in need of much discipline. "You should be aware—"

"I'm aware," I interrupted.

"That she has quite the negative reputation? And you continue to talk to her? If you know, then did she refute or acknowledge her behavior?"

"She told me what I needed to know."

"You must be careful not to fall into her *traps*."

"What *traps*?" I snapped.

"If you know her reputation, then you know what I mean. It would be unfortunate to be sullied by her."

"While I appreciate your concern, I think you should focus more on bringing people to God rather than gossip."

That was the end of that…for about ten minutes.

When I caught Mukesh Uncle talking to Ma, inciting varying levels of alarm and embarrassment in her, I stormed toward them.

"If you can just speak to Jay, help him see reason," he said.

"Speak to me about what?" I asked, trying to remain calm.

He spun around, his face a combination of dark brown and bright red. "I was suggesting that your mother speak to you about reconsidering Kaajal."

"Didn't we just have this conversation?"

"You're a young man, brash and not seeing the future, someone who benefits from the mature advice from his trusted mother. She has one son taken care of. Only one left."

"Don't harass my mother," I said, irritated.

"Beta," Ma warned.

He backed away. "I only meant for you to consider Kaajal."

"Seeing that you and I already discussed this, we have nothing else to say."

He shook his head and glanced at Ma with a look that said, *What sort of rude son did you raise?*

I stepped in between them, and stared at him until he turned from us.

Before facing Ma, I released a breath and then apologized for whatever he said that made her upset.

"What did he say?" I asked calmly.

Ma replied, "He wants me to encourage you to marry Kaajal."

"What else?"

She looked at my feet.

I lifted her chin with my finger and leaned down. "You can tell me anything," I said gently.

"He warned me about Liya."

"What exactly did he say?"

"That she's a rude, hardheaded girl who does nothing but argue. She's not marriage material, or good daughter-in-law material. She's...very American," she whispered.

I didn't need any further explanation to know what "American" meant. It meant Liya wore revealing clothes, partied, drank, had sex, cursed, everything anti-traditional. I kept my fists from clenching, kept my body from tensing. Was Ma traditional? Yes. But not close-minded, not judgmental, not persuaded by gossip.

Unfortunately, Liya's words echoed through my thoughts. Of course I'd support Liya and stand up for her no matter what. I'd like to believe that Ma would, too. But Liya worried that such a sweet woman like Ma would get the short end of the stick and have to deal with all of this. Was she right? Or would Ma back Liya up?

I knew Ma better than anyone. "I'm sorry if that upsets you. Are you okay?"

She nodded and touched my arm. "Beta, I'd already heard this about her."

"You have?"

"Mukesh had mentioned this to me months ago when I told him about meeting Liya and her parents. He advised against it."

"I'm confused. If you heard so much negativity about Liya, then why did we go to her house to meet with her and her parents?"

"Because you never judge someone based on rumors. This girl hadn't hurt us. I haven't seen her doing any of the things he claimed."

I released a pent-up, anxious breath. God, I loved Ma. Now if only everyone else around here would have her logical point of view. "What do you think of her now?"

"After the debacle of our dinner, of course I felt humiliated. And what sort of girl would do such a thing to her parents? But she apologized as soon as she saw me at mandir. Her behavior at the dinner was brash, but her way of apologizing was mature. She's been a very sweet girl, although honest and forthright, but since when is honesty a bad thing? I've seen her angry, that time you fought outside your apartment during dinner. She's not perfect, but she's human, and a good person. She's full of life. Otherwise I would not have her at our dinners and I would've told you to leave her alone."

"Does it bother you that our community thinks the worst of her?"

She took my hands in hers. "I trust my son. You've always made good decisions, made me proud. So if you see enough good in her to be with her, then who cares what others say? You're with her, not with all these fickle, judgmental people," she said matter-of-factly.

"So you don't care?"

She waved in Mukesh Uncle's general direction. "What I don't care for is some man talking to *me* like that, telling me what to do with *my* sons."

I chuckled. I loved that Ma didn't take any crap. Oftentimes, I was so occupied with protecting Ma that I forgot just how strong a woman she was.

Chapter Twenty-Two
Liya

"Are you and Jay still talking?" Reema asked as she stuffed noodles into her mouth with chopsticks. She sat on the floor across from me, eating her dinner on the coffee table in my living room.

"Yes," I replied, and she stared at me.

"Uh, okay, well, do tell. God, it's like prying teeth with you. You've never closed up about a guy before. You're usually very... graphic..."

I laughed, and Reema added, "Are you two dating? Friends? Thinking about something serious? What? Have you had sex?"

"No," I admitted, feeling heat prickle my neck.

"Because...?"

"He's different."

"He seems more traditional. As in serious. He doesn't seem like the fling type. I'm guessing if he had sex with you, things would have to be very serious, like impending engagement and wedding serious, and holy crap, he's madly in love with you serious."

"You're right, which is why we're never doing it. I'm still waiting for him to change his mind about me."

"Why do you say that? You're a true catch, Liya. Brains,

beauty, independence, street smarts, you can take care of your-self. Are you worried about him finding out about all the guys you've been with?"

"He knows. Not as if six partners is a lot these days."

"It is if you're traditional. I'm not that traditional, and I've only ever been with Rohan, but god forbid if our parents found out."

"Jay definitely isn't a virgin or a hypocrite. He's worried about my view of healthy relationships. Look, I'm straightforward. I told him a little bit about the assault, how things could get messy for him and his family. It didn't deter him. I honestly think he'll wake up one day and think I'm not worth the trouble."

"Wow. I've never heard you doubt yourself. You must really like him to have told him about the assault. And he handled it well. He's a keeper."

I shrugged. "He's looking for seriousness, long-term, marriage material. I'm not that girl. But I was honest and upfront with him, and he's fun and sweet and I like having him around, so I'll keep it going until he walks away."

"And if he doesn't?"

"I'm sure he will. He'll eventually want a wife, and I'm not a wife."

Reema leaned forward. "Not that being a wife is the ultimate goal in life, but being a wife for someone like Jay means you two love one another and want no one else. You know you'll work through your problems. It's not always perfect, but you're com-mitted and comfortable. You might even have kids. You become one. There's no force on the planet that can pry you apart. That's what I think, anyway, when it comes to marriage. In which case, you are definitely wifey material. And for the record, you are absolutely worth whatever trouble you think you're giving him."

I smiled, my chest warming up and tears prickling my eyes. "Shut up," I managed to joke.

"No. We, your friends, all see it because we all see the real you. And he sees the same thing."

I rolled my eyes, pretending that my friend's view of me wasn't heartwarming or tear-jerking.

"Want some advice?" she asked.

"Unsolicited advice is the best!" I said sarcastically with a toothy grin.

She flicked a piece of shredded lettuce at me, and I dug it out of my hair.

"Let yourself go and just see where this takes you. Fall in love," she said.

"Are you out of your mind? Love will lead to heartbreak."

"It doesn't have to. Is Jay worth it, Liya?"

I shrugged, but I wanted to yell, "Yes! Oh, god, yes! He is worth everything to me right now!" And that freaked the crap out of me.

"So let's assume that's Liya talk for 'yes, he is.' I've never known you to not go after what you want. Where's the determination?"

I shrugged.

"Or are you scared?"

"Me? Scared? Ha!"

"Oooh…Liya's afraid of some good loving!" She giggled and lightened the mood.

"Shut up!" I laughed and tossed a pillow at her.

"If Jay likes standoffish you, imagine how hard he'd fall for you if there are no bars holding you back. I want to see that: all fire and passion and heart."

My face flared up, and I couldn't understand why. "How about we discuss what's going down this weekend for your bachelorette party?"

"No. Let's talk more about Jay!"

"Hey! Did I tell you that we're going to a strip club?"

"No! Liya, no, you promised."

I grinned. Oh, how easy it was to derail her with the right topic. "Then let's talk about this party, shall we?"

"Ugh, fine, but afterward, back to Jay. What are we doing?"

"Swanky club, may or may not have strippers."

"Rohan is going to kill me." She slouched and pushed around her food, but then she giggled.

"What happens at the club stays at the club. Listen, the bridal shower begins at six with all the aunties and moms and whatever. Gujarati finger foods, pretty cake, nonalcoholic bubbly drinks, presents, you know, classy. That should end at nine. Kick those old biddies out, slip out of our nice saris and bangles and put on some short dresses and high heels, and hit the club at ten."

"I don't know if I can keep up."

"It's okay. I got a private booth, so you can sit and sip all night, we can keep up the energy or slow down. Everything is on your schedule. But if a stripper comes over, well…"

"Liya!" she rasped.

We burst into laughter. To see some fine, ripped guy grinding on poor Reema as she freaked out would be something hysterical to witness, but I would never do such a thing to her. She was not a woman who enjoyed being touched by any man except her own.

"Are there seriously going to be strippers?" Reema demanded as she wiped away tears with both hands.

"We'll see, sweetie…"

I had to sit against my desk for support. Shocked, my lips parted but I lacked the words to express the mess tumbling through my head. "Can you… can you please say that again?"

Sam cleared his throat and averted his gaze, as excited to tell me the news as I was to hear it. "Despite some of the lawsuits against the MDR products being closed with quiet settlements, most have us reeling. No surprise, but we're closing."

"But all the people who stayed on board, who worked their butts off?" I croaked, my eyes misting as I thought of every single face who believed in me and believed enough in this place to keep going. "All that time wasted?"

"Not wasted. Enough to break even, to close without being as deep in the hole as we could've been."

"That doesn't mean *anything* to me and everyone else who continued to work here when we should've been looking for a new job."

"We understand that." He held his hand out to what? *Calm* me? I glared at his gesture, and he retracted his arm. "Everyone will get a nice severance pay."

I scoffed. "What? A month or two? That's not enough to make up for the fact that it can take far longer to find a new job. When are you going to announce this?"

"Next week."

"Why not now? They deserve to know *now* so they can get their finances and résumés in order."

"I'm fighting to send out the announcement now, trust me. I can only do so much."

"Then why'd you tell me?"

"Because we put you in a bad position."

"Yeah? No crap. And you expect me to keep my mouth shut for a week?"

"I also wanted to tell you that we recommended you to manage another company, higher pay, better benefits. In Dallas. The one that offered you a job before."

I paused. "Well, thank you for your consideration, but I'm still pissed. There are dozens of people below me who won't get that treatment."

"We've written outstanding recommendations for all of them, which is why we're taking a week to announce. They can have their recommendations with the announcement."

"It's still BS."

"Yes. I agree, but I'm also not the person who handled things this way. Believe me when I say that you're one of the first people I looked out for, especially when I knew that you took this job over the one in Dallas. Their CEO would personally like to interview you via a video call, and then fly you up to Dallas for an in-person interview to show you around. It would be a fresh start. You always said Houston was a sweltering hellhole filled with idiots."

I sure did. Mainly Dad and the gossipers. But I had my girls here. I had Jay, sort of, didn't I?

"I would take the offer if it comes through," Sam added.

I checked my nails. "I'm not keeping my mouth shut this week."

"You're legally required to."

"What are you going to do? Fire me?" I snapped, pushed past Sam, and stormed out of my office. I wanted to scream. What was this company thinking? I wanted to tell everyone everything, warn them, tell them to get on their way, but I knew that I could do no such thing. I had to get out of here. I could not, for my sanity, look anyone in the eye right now and not feel the soul-crushing need to hug them and tell them the truth.

I walked right into Jay as he rushed out of the elevator. He had his cell phone stuck to his ear, his eyes darting across the office spaces.

"Yeah. Okay. Are you sure? I'm on my way, but there's traffic," he spoke into the phone.

He grabbed my wrist and took me with him into the elevator

as he continued in short bursts. "Stay calm. I know, I'm sorry. I'll try to find him. Right! Coming over first! Ma will take care of you, don't worry."

He hung up the phone and blew out a hot breath.

"What's wrong?" I asked.

"I came by to see you before heading home when Shilpa called."

"Is she okay?"

"She's in labor." He hurried out of the elevator on the ground floor, and I jogged after him to his car in a nearby parking space. He opened the door for me, and I slid in without question. All the work drama rushed out the window.

He white-knuckled it all the way to Shilpa's house, muttering, "She can't find Jahn. I called his phone, his office, he's not there."

"Maybe he's stuck in traffic and can't hear the phone ring, or at the market, or something."

"That guy. I told him to take paternity leave when Shilpa started her maternity leave to be there for this moment."

"He could've gone out for milk and this exact same thing could have happened. It'll be fine. Did she call an ambulance?"

"No. We have instructions from Preeti for when Shilpa should call the hospital and have us drive her. It's not an emergency, considering it's Shilpa's first baby, water hasn't broken yet, contractions still ten minutes apart…"

"You know a lot."

"She just spilled it to me over the phone. I take her word that she knows what's best."

I fished through my purse for my phone.

"Who are you calling?" he asked.

"Preeti. Isn't she Shilpa's resident doctor? She has to be there for the delivery. And I can ask her if Shilpa should call an ambulance instead of waiting, what, an hour to get there and get her to the hospital?"

"At least."

I caught Preeti between patients and gave her a rundown on the situation. She agreed that Shilpa not call an ambulance but remain calm, take a shower, eat something light, and pack her things. She'd meet her at the hospital.

Jay eased his white knuckles, but he drove like a maniac, as if this were his wife about to have his baby.

I touched his lap. "Is your mom worried?"

"No. Just Shilpa, but mainly because she can't find Jahn." He blew out a breath, anxious and annoyed.

"Where's your phone?"

"In my front pants pocket."

"Who puts a phone into their front pocket?"

"Someone who was going to put it into the console and forgot. What are you doing?"

I slipped my hand into his pants pocket. He practically jumped out of his seat.

"Whoa!"

"Sorry!" I couldn't help but giggle. "Trying to get the phone in case Jahn or Shilpa calls."

"The phone is the flat, hard thing."

"Not the other hard thing?"

"Liya…" He half grinned.

"Sorry, not the time, but your face is so cute. Okay. Got it." I sat back and checked his screen for messages and calls, noticing Kaajal had texted. From the locked screen, the text notice cut off partway, but said, "I missed talking to you after the tournament. You did a great…"

I almost asked Jay if they still communicated, but that would come across as jealous and bitter. If he trusted me not to flirt with other guys, then I had to trust him, too, right? So then why did her text drive me freaking crazy? That woman needed to back off.

"Anything?" he asked.

"Not yet. Shilpa must be calm enough. Just concentrate on driving safely."

"If these idiots would get out of the way..." he muttered, agitated but absolutely adorable about getting to his bhabhi.

I took the liberty of texting Shilpa from my phone about Preeti's directions and to update her about our whereabouts. She was ready to go, anxious, scared, nervous, all the things a new mother could be.

"Stay here," Jay ordered as he shot out of his car in Shilpa's driveway. Five minutes later, Jay's mother emerged, helping a waddling Shilpa to the car as I crawled out, offering her the front seat. She waved me away and slipped into the back seat.

Jay sprinted to the car just as I closed the door on his mom's side. He tossed two black duffel bags into the trunk, and we took off.

I twisted in my seat and waited for the pain to subside from Shilpa's clenched face before asking, "Are you doing okay back there? Need water?"

"No. Just want this baby out," Shilpa said in between panting.

"Did you remember my gift?"

"First thing I packed." She winked.

"I called Preeti. She'll be waiting for you at the emergency room entrance. She'll get you to a room and we'll park the car."

"Thank you, Liya."

"Any word from Jahn?"

"Yes," Jay's mother responded, a pink phone in her hand as she answered and told him where to meet us. She flinched as Jahn yelled into the phone, enthusiastic and completely freaking out. I'd never heard a man so excited to become a father.

I laughed and turned around in my seat, catching Jay's eye. He chuckled and landed a hand on mine over my thigh. I froze.

We weren't alone. His mother was in the back seat and could see our hand placement if she leaned to the left. Shilpa could see us if she wasn't in a pain-induced haze.

He licked his lips and gave me a slight nod, as if to reassure me, to tell me this was all right. Were we serious? Was I ready for this?

What *did* his family think? Was I good enough? Did they disapprove? Why did I care so much?

I was tense the entire way, even when Jay squeezed my hand. He didn't release it until we pulled into the emergency entrance. He hopped out, opened the car door for Shilpa as Preeti walked out of the sliding glass doors with a wheelchair. Once Shilpa was on her way, with Jay's mother right behind them, we parked and weaved through the endless halls to the labor and delivery unit.

"You go first," Jay said outside of Shilpa's room.

I touched his stomach. "It's fine. She's not stripped down naked and pushing a giant baby out of her vagina just yet."

He cringed. "God, why, Liya, why?"

"Because it's cute to see how anxious you are." I kissed his cheek and knocked on the door before entering.

Jay's mother called for us to come in, but he needed some convincing, as in me taking his hand and pulling him through the door, past the curtain, and to the bench seat across from his mother, who sat in a chair at Shilpa's bedside.

Shilpa was already in a gown, under the sheets, as a nurse hooked her up to machines and took her information. Preeti pulled up a rolling stool. Shilpa threw us a smile and grinned even bigger seeing Jay tensely bent over, his arms on his thighs.

Even though this wasn't my family, I was ridiculously excited.

Preeti glanced at the monitors, the one that recorded contraction intensity and fetal heart rate. "Are you okay with everyone here while we get the belts on?"

"Yeah," Shilpa replied anxiously.

Preeti pulled the sheet down to Shilpa's waist and lifted her gown to expose a giant belly. Jay silently groaned, his hands fists in front of his face, as he turned into me and pressed his head against my shoulder. I touched his head and whispered, "It's okay. You won't feel a thing."

He chuckled against me. "I'm going to be sick."

"The fun stuff hasn't even begun."

In another minute, we heard the baby's heartbeat like sonar pulsating through the room. Preeti pulled out gloves and a little packet of lube. Snapping on the gloves, she beamed at Jay and said, "Guess what's next?"

Jay shot to his feet. "My cue to leave. I'll be right outside if you need me."

"I'm in good hands," Shilpa said.

Preeti winked at us as I followed him out. We paced for a few minutes before an anxious Jahn ran down the hall, stopping in front of us to wheeze.

"Is she?" he gasped.

"She's still pregnant," I assured him.

"Should I go in there?" He looked at the door quizzically.

"You did this to her, I'm sure she wants you in there."

"Can you check?"

"Unlike me, you've already seen her lady parts. Just knock and go in. The curtain is closed in case she yells at you to leave."

"Okay."

"You got this." I slapped his shoulder as he walked inside. "You guys are both hilarious. Why are you so worried?"

"She's had some difficulties," Jay explained.

I frowned. "Oh. I'm sure she'll be fine. She's made it this far. Just a little further to go. Preeti will make sure she's taken care of."

"Right. I know."

I rubbed his arm. "You're going to be okay, too, kaka."

He scratched the back of his head. "I better get used to being called that."

"I'm excited." I grinned so hard that my face actually hurt.

"Me, too. Do you think about having kids?"

Way to knock my smile off... "And put myself through that? No, thank you."

"Eventually your ovaries will be exploding every time you see me." He wagged his brows and then winked at me.

I laughed so hard that I had to cover my mouth. It was funny until someone down the hall screamed bloody murder. "Oh, no. I can't give birth. I don't know how anyone does this."

Preeti slipped out a few minutes later. "You guys can go in."

"Is she okay? Is she close?" Jay asked.

"She's fine, baby is great. And she's only dilated to four. She was two in the office yesterday. Her contractions are closer, and her membrane is thinning."

"Ugh, please, Preeti..." Jay groaned.

"This means she's in labor and progressing. We're going to keep her and see if she keeps progressing or if her water breaks."

"She might get sent home?" he asked.

"It's a possibility."

"She's going to be miserable if she has to go home pregnant."

"Don't worry. We'll do our best to help her as much as possible. You're welcome to stay as long she wants visitors, but I recommend letting her get some sleep tonight. I don't foresee her delivering today," Preeti said.

"Thanks." He walked past her but looked back at me. "You coming?"

"Yeah, in a minute," I replied.

When he disappeared into the room, Preeti grabbed my arms

and muffled a squeal. "Tell me! What is this? You guys are freaking adorable!"

"*Adorable?*" I'd been called many things, but adorable was not one of them.

She batted her eyelashes and grinned so hard, her face might actually have gotten stuck that way. She nudged my arm with hers. "Look at you right now."

"What? Something gross?" I went to touch my cheeks, my nose.

"You're glowing," she whispered, "like you're in love."

And that's when a sudden truth hit me. Adrenaline pounded through me, both terrifying and exhilarating. Oh, lord. Was this real? Was this fantasy that only happened in other people's lives happening to me?

"Oh, my god. You are..." Preeti cut off her squeal by clamping her lips together.

And just like that. Just like biting into a tiny, unexpected green chili in the middle of a bowl of sweet lilo chevdo snack and bam! Life, much like those unsuspecting taste buds, got a hell of a wake-up call.

Chapter Twenty-Three
Jay

I was incomprehensibly glad for this moment. My nephew was due to arrive soon. A baby in the family, a new life, joy with endless potential, and I had the privilege of being a part of this day.

This was a family moment, but only one person was missing. He would've loved this. He would've been smiling and laughing and telling old-school dad jokes that he, no doubt, would've continued to tell his grandson for years to come. He would've had boxes and boxes of sweets to give away to every family member, uncle and auntie, and showered the nurses and doctors and staff with cookies. A dozen bouquets for Shilpa and Ma. The best chocolates from Europe flown in for Jahn. He would've placed a big hand around Jahn's shoulders and walked him down the hall to get coffee and tell stories of when Jahn was born.

Dad should've been here for this.

My chest squeezed, and for a moment, I couldn't breathe. My head buzzed, and I dragged my fingers through my hair. My hands shook.

This child was going to be born and it would be one of the happiest days of my life. But it also foreshadowed the anniversary of Dad's death. Looking around the room at my family, I didn't know how they did this. How they could be so happy but not torn the way my heart was? They saw the best, and I kept reliving the worst.

I concentrated on my breathing, on the goodness of what was happening all around this room. Ma was safe and happy. Shilpa was calm and healthy. Jahn was a frazzled mess but excited. Their baby was doing fine and prepared to meet us. Liya was a refreshing sight in a chaotic storm.

My nerves settled around eleven, only when I had dozed off for a few minutes. Shilpa hadn't delivered, but she dilated to five, which meant they'd probably keep her and hopefully she would deliver tomorrow.

I needed sleep. I didn't have the excuse that Jahn had to miss work. Liya was slumped against me on the bench seat, her bare feet tucked beneath her, my jacket over her as she slept off and on. I nudged her cheek with my lips and bit her earlobe, rousing her from sleep.

"I'm taking you home."

She nodded and blinked away drowsiness.

"Want me to take Ma home so you can stay here?" I asked Jahn.

He shook his head. "I'll take her. I have to shower and get some clothes and food anyway. Shilpa will be fine for a few hours. She needs sleep. Preeti said they'll call me if anything happens."

"You're leaving her alone all night?"

"No, no. Of course not. Shower, eat, grab stuff, come back. Let Ma sleep in her bed and I'll sleep on this bench."

"Are you sure?" I asked.

"Yeah." Jahn stretched.

"Shilpa's okay with you leaving?"

"She insisted. She's passed out. Who knew this labor stuff required so much energy?" he joked.

"You're wrong for saying that, and I hope she bites you during labor."

He chuckled. "Here's hoping for tomorrow."

I slapped his chest with the back of my hand. "Soon-to-be father. God. Can you believe it? A baby. A life that's totally dependent on you."

"Yeah, I know. Wish Dad could be here."

I swallowed, my throat raw and aching. In that moment, I relived the stories Dad used to tell us about when we were born. Men didn't usually stay in the room when their wives gave birth back then, but he helped Ma just the way Jahn helped Shilpa, always making sure that she was as comfortable as possible. All the pillows, all the blankets, water, and cold washcloths she wanted. "Me, too."

He gently slapped my cheek and kept his hand there. "But this is a happy time. So be happy with us."

I nodded, but it was a hard request to fulfill. Dad should've been here giving Jahn advice, keeping him collected, laughing at him for being anxious, and able to hold his first grandchild.

"I mean it," he said. "Take your woman home."

I smirked. Jahn always knew what to say to lighten the mood.

Liya curled up beneath my jacket in the front seat as I drove her home. "Do you want to grab something to eat?"

"No," she groaned. "I'm dead tired."

"Okay. Do you still have my phone?"

"Oh, yeah." She plucked it out of her purse and handed it to me when I pulled up to her place. We glanced at the lit screen at the same time. Kaajal had sent me three text messages.

She released the phone into my hand and commented, "I forgot to mention that she'd texted earlier when I was looking for texts from Shilpa and Jahn."

"It's nothing. I don't text her or call. I don't know how she got my number, but I programmed her in so that I know when it's her."

"It's fine. You don't have to explain. It's not as if we're exclusive or anything."

I took her wrist and gently pulled her back inside the car. "What you do mean we're not exclusive? Are you seeing other men?"

"No," she replied, her voice calm, sleepy. "I meant that if you change your mind about us, I understand."

I cupped her cheek and kissed her, deep, passionate. Fire sparked around us, and she woke up instantly. Pulling away, I said, "Don't think for a second that there's even a chance of me walking away from this. You understand me?"

She nodded, her eyes dazed, her lips swollen.

"Should I walk you upstairs? You look as if you're about to pass out."

"No," she breathed. "Unless you want to come inside."

"And sleep?" My gut clenched.

"Yeah…"

"On the couch?" I swallowed. No. I wanted to sleep in her bed, with my arms around her, some sort of comfort and peace before my emotions blew up. The time around the anniversary of Dad's death was the hardest out of the year. Jahn had dealt with it. Ma had dealt with it. But I couldn't let it go.

Every year, I immersed myself in something—school, work, exercise—but tonight I had nothing except a bottle of one-hundred-and-forty proof to drown myself in.

"Jay?" she asked.

Having someone see the wretchedness of my weakness was not something that I could share yet, even with a woman whom I tried to get to open up to me. Hypocritical? Yeah.

I replied, "I need to get some rest and be on my game tomorrow.

I just found out that Reinli BioChem is closing for certain. I don't know if they told you. They were supposed to talk to management today. Don't worry. I'm confident you'll be able to find better work."

"Yeah, they told me. I don't want to think about it right now." She covered her yawn.

"My firm couldn't save the company."

She kissed me. "Not your fault."

"Sure feels like it. I have a lot of paperwork to handle tomorrow. I should get home and prepare."

"Understandable. I'll see you tomorrow. Good night." She smiled and crawled out. She texted me when she locked her front door, then I left.

Silence. Even though we hadn't spoken most of the ride back, Liya offered a distraction, a tranquility. Without her, that serenity rippled and disbanded. The car provided sound; the engine, the radio, and other cars on the dark roads. At home? Memories pried through.

Terrifying flames rose around me, high, bright, scorching. There wasn't an escape route for two scrawny boys. But there was Dad. There had always been Dad. He was a superhero, swooping in at the last minute to save us; courageous, confident, selfless. He picked us up, one boy in each arm, and rushed this way and that. He stumbled, falling debris almost hit us, but he was able to get us out.

Dad's leg fell through a floorboard, and he lunged forward, throwing us out. "Go!" he ordered.

I'd whimpered and pleaded, but he growled, "Jahn! Get your brother out!"

Jahn tugged on me, scratching my arm to get me to run. But I didn't. I lurched back toward Dad. He couldn't pull his leg out and shove me away at the same time. With one final push against me—the stubborn, stupid son who distracted him—we stumbled backward while he tumbled in.

What if I'd just run like he told us to? He would've been able to concentrate on getting his leg free, crawl out with two arms instead of using his hands to shove me away.

What if I'd not been playing with the stove trying to make dinner? None of what happened afterward would've mattered, none of the what-ifs, because there wouldn't have been a fire to begin with.

Jahn ended up with scratches and bruises and a few burn marks on his hands.

I ended up with a marred back and a lifetime of guilt.

Dad ended up dead.

Ma ended up a widow left raising two kids.

I ruined my family.

But things turned out okay, Jahn always said.

I glared at the bottle of bourbon in the cabinet. Grabbing it, I ran my hand down the glass. Straight out of the bottle, right?

My phone pinged.

Jahn: Get some sleep. Don't do anything stupid. I need my child to have a levelheaded kaka tomorrow.
Liya: Thanks for tonight. Let me know if you go to the hospital tomorrow and maybe I can come? GN

Then Jahn sent me a baby and heart emoji, and Liya sent a kiss emoji.

Damn emojis.

I slammed the bottle down and went to the bathroom. I rinsed my face with ice-cold water and downed a couple of nighttime ibuprofen. I'd rather struggle with getting up after six hours of medicine-induced sleep than struggle with a self-loathing hangover.

After stripping off my suit and hanging it over a chair, I crawled beneath the covers in my boxers, set my alarm, and played a soothing R&B playlist that always took me back to happier places.

Because I had picked up Liya from her office yesterday and took her straight home, her car was still at work. I offered to give her a ride the following morning, and the instant I saw her, I definitely woke up. She jogged down the steps in high heels; how anyone could do that and not fall flat on their face was beyond me. She deserved a medal for that talent.

The morning light shone on her sleek, black hair, always a different mixture of curls and waves when she wore it natural.

Her white blouse glowed in the light, making her skin radiant, a goddess descending the stairs. A dark gray skirt wrapped around her thighs and ended in a dark purple hem, matching her shoes. A giant white purse bounced against her side as she expertly checked her phone while walking.

She hopped into the car, fully rested and alert, her energy a viable entity that breathed life into me. Her rosy perfume hit my senses, and in the span of half a minute, the entire world changed. For the better.

Liya grinned, her plump lips painted pinkish purple. She'd probably get upset if I kissed her and messed up her perfectly placed makeup.

I shrugged. Riling her up was the fun part. I weaved my hand through her hair, and she almost batted me away, complaining, "You're going to mess up my hair!"

I planted a soft kiss on her lips and she quieted. I smacked my lips. "I always wondered how pink lipstick would look on me. What do you think?"

I puckered my lips, and she laughed, swiping a finger across my lips to take off the color.

"You look more like a burgundy man," she teased.

I chuckled and we headed on our way. "Not upset about the company closing?"

She shrugged. "Like you said, I'll have something lined up. Worrying doesn't do anything. Besides, I have something more important to focus on right now. Shilpa asked me to be her delivery photographer."

"Really?" I asked, surprised.

"Yeah. I didn't think we were that close yet. I'm going to go right after work, unless she delivers earlier. Apparently Jahn bought this fancy new camera and she's not sure that he knows how to use it."

I laughed. "Sounds like him. Good. No one will ask me to take any pictures. I don't plan on being in the room when she delivers."

Liya cringed. "Oh, right. I'd have to be there for that part. Wonder if she thought of that."

"I'm sure that's what she meant."

"Never seen a delivery."

"Me, either."

"It's kind of gross and horrifying, I hear."

"Better you having to watch than me!"

"But that means I'll get to see your nephew before you do!" she teased and stuck out her tongue.

We pulled up to the front lobby. "I hope you have a good day, Liya."

She frowned. "We sound like a couple."

"We sort of are a couple."

She nodded in agreement with a genuine smile. "Thanks for the ride. Meet you at the hospital?"

"Yep."

The first half of the day slogged on in a groggy daze full of paperwork over final lawsuit and closure details. I had to concentrate on meetings and getting myself together. Part of me, thanks to the medicine, was numb. Part of me fought against the myriad of sorrows from the approaching anniversary of Dad's death. Part of me remembered that my brother was about to have a freaking baby. Once that joyous realization took center stage in my thoughts, I was antsy to get the day over with.

Jahn texted once in a while with updates. Shilpa was doing very well. Ma was impressed, and Shilpa wasn't screaming her head off...yet. Baby looked good on the monitors.

As soon as work ended, I went straight to the hospital, anxious to meet my nephew.

I walked through the labor and delivery hallway, busier than it had been last night. It was filled with doctors in white coats, handfuls of nurses in matching blue scrubs, and occasional family members.

I walked into Shilpa's room. "Hi, I brought pizza!"

"Oh, no, you did not..." Liya chided and jumped up from the bench, ushering me back out.

"What did I do?" I asked.

"You and Jahn and your mom can eat that in the waiting area. Don't bring food into Shilpa's room! She can't eat! Do you know how miserable that'll make her? Smelling this delicious food while you chow down in front of her?"

"Oh, crap. I didn't think about that."

"Mm-hmm..." She looked me over like I'd lost my mind, went into the room, and out came Jahn and Ma.

We ate quickly in the lobby and returned to the room, but only when Liya ascertained that we didn't smell like mouthwatering food.

"How are you?" I asked Shilpa.

She gave a weak smile as she lay in bed. "Tired."

"Did you get any sleep?"

"Some last night, but all day someone's checking me, or the contractions get worse. I'm exhausted."

"Can the nurse give you anything to sleep?"

"Not at this point. I'm so close. I'm fully dilated, and the baby just came down all of a sudden."

"In a few hours, then?"

"Hopefully not that long! If I'm this tired now, I don't know if I'll be able to push!"

"You can do it. You're strong," Jahn encouraged as he replaced the cold, damp washcloth on her forehead. I walked toward Liya as Jahn cooed over Shilpa.

"What are you doing?" I asked Liya.

She turned from the room, her back to me, and fidgeted with the camera. "Why is this thing so complicated?"

I chuckled. "You don't know how to use it, either?"

"I'm not a photographer. I use my phone camera. Why does a camera need so many pieces? And why are there so many buttons?"

"Let me help you," I offered.

"Like you know?"

"I messed around with Rohan's camera; it's not as complicated as this one, but it's close, same brand, older model."

I wrapped my arms around her, and she stilled as I worked with the camera in her small hands. Her hair, thick and tickling my throat, smelled like shampoo from her morning shower. Her blouse was untucked but unruffled, and she wore the same high heels from work so her head landed closer to my shoulder than my chest.

"Your mom's here," she muttered.

"I'm aware."

"She isn't going to snatch you by the hair and ask what you're doing?"

I chuckled against her. "No. And I thought you didn't care what other people think."

"I don't, but I'm not heartless. I don't want to look like we're rubbing something lewd in her face."

I kissed her head. "There."

"What there?"

"Zoom in and out, capture, focus, video."

I released Liya, and we sat down.

"So...do you want raw footage or adorable moments?" Liya asked.

"Both," Shilpa replied.

"Uncensored stuff or social-media-ready material?"

"Both. I want to see the baby come out. But no video."

We both cringed, and I patted Liya on the back. "She's your girl."

She shot me a dry look but asked Shilpa, "Are you sure you want me to see all your business?"

"At this point, I don't care if my lady parts are televised, but I do want to see him come out. I can always delete the pictures later," Shilpa replied.

"You don't want Jahn or his mom to do it?" Liya verified.

"I need Jahn to hold one of my legs and my hand. Ma doesn't want to look, but she can help support my neck during pushing."

"Isn't your family coming?"

Shilpa readjusted herself a bit in bed. "They have tickets to fly in this weekend. The baby is a few days early. Are you okay doing this for me?"

Liya nodded. "Yes, whatever you need me to do."

"Great," Shilpa hissed as she curled forward and clamped her teeth around a silent scream. "Because I think it's time."

Chapter Twenty-Four
Liya

Having a baby was no less disgusting than I'd imagined. But Shilpa didn't scream until Preeti said, "This is called the Ring of Fire. It's going to feel like your vagina is on fire, but it's the baby's head. He's past the pelvis, so it won't be much longer."

During the next contraction, Shilpa pushed three times, each a count of ten seconds. Her lady parts widened and stayed that way as a head rocked back and forth with each heartbeat. It was the weirdest thing I'd ever seen. Preeti massaged the baby's head. I stood corrected. *That* was the weirdest thing I'd ever seen.

"He has so much hair!" I said.

Jahn, half excited and half about to pass out, grinned proudly.

In the next contraction, the head came all the way out and Jahn choked out a laugh as his son slid out in a mess of fluids. Preeti placed the baby on a blanket on top of Shilpa's stomach as the nurse vigorously dried him and suctioned the gunk out of his nose and mouth.

Shilpa cried. Jahn cried. Jahn's mom cried. The baby cried. I freaking cried.

Preeti clamped the cord and handed Jahn scissors. I caught every moment. And when the nurse took the baby to the warmer,

I photographed the measurements, weight, and Jahn timidly giving his son his first bath and fumbling with the tiny diaper and onesie.

They wrapped the baby up and handed him to Shilpa, who fed him after Preeti repaired her destroyed lady parts. The baby smacked his adorable little mouth, looking for a boob.

After the nurse and tech cleaned the birthing mess, quicker than a few blinks, and Shilpa had nursed and bonded, she let Jahn hold the baby for a minute, then his mom, before Shilpa asked me, "Do you want to hold him?"

She held up the bundle like an offering. I shook my head, blinking back tears. "Not before Jay."

"Okay, did anyone tell him?"

"I texted. He's coming," Jahn responded as Jay hurried in, a giant, cheesy grin on his face.

"Where's my nephew?" Jay beamed.

Shilpa proudly handed the baby to him. Jay immediately melted. This child had everyone wrapped around his fingers. Jay swayed side to side and cooed to the baby. There was something very, very sexy about this six-foot-four man in his dress clothes, button-down shirt with a few top buttons undone, sleeves rolled to his forearms, biceps bulging against the tightened fabric, holding this tiny, helpless baby.

And damn everything if my ovaries weren't actually rumbling. Although not quite exploding yet.

I captured him on film, as I had with everyone else, but now that he'd returned, I felt that I should've left the family to enjoy themselves.

I placed the camera down and reached for my purse as Jay walked over and asked, "Did you hold him yet?"

"No. I would never do that before you had your chance."

"Give him to her," Shilpa encouraged as she devoured her dinner.

"Oh, no, I don't…" I stuttered over my words.

Jay's warmth crowded me, and his arm pressed against mine as he slipped the bundle into my arms. "Sit down," he whispered.

We sat together, and my eyes watered at the sight of this tiny, perfect boy. "You guys made a nice-looking kid," I said.

They grinned.

I sat against the bench. Jay stretched his arm over the top of the back and rubbed my opposite arm. Was this what it would feel like to hold our baby together? And was I actually thinking of having babies?

"What's his name?" Jay asked, stroking the baby's cheek with his free hand.

"In the tradition of the Shah men, his name is Joshil," Jahn said.

"Josh…" Jay hummed. "Perfect."

When he glanced at me, his eyes twinkled. Of course they did. He was an uncle. I didn't notice Jahn taking pictures of us until I rose to hand the baby to Jay's mom. She gratefully took him as I congratulated all of them.

"Is there anything anyone needs?" I asked.

They shook their heads as Shilpa and Jahn profusely thanked me.

"It was my pleasure. Thank you so much for allowing me to be here. I'll let you guys bond and gush, and I'll see you soon?"

"You better see us soon," Shilpa said as I slinked away.

I hurried once I left the room, hoping to avoid Jay. But the man was fast and agile and was at my side before I hit the lobby.

"Running off so fast?" he asked.

"This is your family time."

"You're family."

I swallowed, a little dizzy from that simple yet profoundly overwhelming statement. I still had to deal with employees, and the interview for the job of my dreams. I wanted to tell Jay about

Dallas, I really did, but how could I tell him now? How could I tell him that I had spent this entire morning updating my résumé and filling out a lengthy application? "I have a lot of work, early morning. Who knew closing down would be so busy?"

"Yeah. My firm will send me elsewhere, but what about you? Have you looked for work yet?"

"Yes. Sam is actually trying to help me out in that area with tips and recommendations. I'll be fine. But you should definitely stay a while longer."

"I will. Thanks for helping." He kissed my cheek. "See you at work tomorrow. I'll be wrapping up my last few days with Reinli BioChem. Oh, and this weekend? Still on for family dinner?"

Did I want to see him so soon? His family had integrated me into their fold with open arms. My ovaries actually tingled, *tingled*, at the sight of Jay holding a baby. What the crap? I needed to take a step back, clear my head, make sure that I wasn't losing myself in whatever this was.

Was I softer? Emotionally dependent on a man? Or was this how things were supposed to be? Loving, caring? Would that turn into marriage? Worshipping? Having to answer to someone?

"No. The bridal shower for Reema is this weekend. Lots of preparation."

"Ah, that's right. Rohan is having his bachelor party," he said.

"What are you guys doing?"

"Strip club, naturally," he responded with a serious face that broke my heart. He was going to let some woman grind on him? He'd let someone else rub their boobs in his face? The thought of him touching someone else, of someone else having the privilege of getting that close to him—that was not going to happen.

I opened my mouth, fully prepared to snap back with an, "Oh, hell no."

But he chuckled. "Kidding. Can you imagine poor Rohan in a strip club? He'd freeze up in a corner."

My lips lifted in a shaky smile. How was I supposed to handle this? I'd never cared about a man like this.

"All right. Have a good night. I'll text you later?" he said.

"Sure. Have fun with your brand-new nephew. Josh is the perfect addition to your family."

It was Friday and there were still another few days left until the big announcement, making every minute at work keeping the secret to myself agonizing.

And then there was…the job. Not just any job, but THE JOB FOR ME. The dream company that I had applied to months ago was now considering me for a management position instead of the lab position that they'd originally offered.

The phone and video interviews had gone so well on Wednesday that they'd brought me out to the site in Dallas for the final interview yesterday. It went *extremely* well. Which meant they might offer, and I'd have to leave behind my friends. It was hard to make real friends, and I wasn't ready to say goodbye.

But this job also meant leaving behind Jay. I was not about to turn down a job that I desperately wanted for a man. Even a man like Jay…a man whom I might be falling for…a man who scared me with all the possibilities of normalcy that came with a healthy relationship.

For all the blunt attributes I'd developed over the years, they sure knew how to fail me now.

Wendy swung through the door, her hair flowing and her makeup on point.

"Where are you going all pretty?" I asked.

"*We're* going to a bar."

"Um. Sure?"

She frowned and peered over her shoulder. "Look, I know what's going down."

I jumped to my feet and pulled her into my office, checking behind her to make sure no one overheard. "How did you find out?"

"Well, I'd caught a few comments here and there through the door."

"Eavesdropping?"

"Coming to give you coffee or messages or the files you'd asked for. Not intentionally. And I had my suspicions with the way you've been acting, especially every time Sam came around. I wasn't sure until now, to be honest."

"Oh…confirmed it myself. Rookie mistake," I groaned.

She took my hand and squeezed before letting go. "I'm about to be out of a job. Unemployed. Miserable. Scrambling to pay rent. I need an evening of getting hammered."

"Uh, you know? Bars are expensive. Maybe we should hit up a liquor store? My treat." I offered a probably not very convincing smile, hoping she'd take the bait. The idea of going to a bar unhinged me. Having guys hit on me would be an annoying flashback to the old me that I didn't want to get near again.

"Please? It won't cost us anything…I mean…with you as my wing girl?"

"You're using me?" I smirked, amused.

"You get so many free drinks. Teach me your ways."

I laughed. "I'm sorry, Wendy. I have so much to deal with right now…and bars aren't my scene anymore."

"What about the super nice ones at the fancy hotels?"

"I don't know."

"Please? Please? Please? I don't feel like going out alone or getting slammed at home and doing something stupid like email-ing an all-caps letter encompassing pure rage to Sam and all the higher-ups."

I rubbed my forehead but couldn't find any valid excuse to deny Wendy. She, like so many others come Monday, would be in a world of financial hurt. Besides, it wasn't as if I would accept any drinks from men. I mean…how full of myself was I to think anyone would offer me anything?

"Okay. But I'm not drinking…" I warned.

"There's no fun in that!"

Yet, after work, we grabbed our jackets and purses and drove downtown to one of my old favorite hot spots. The ambiance was chill and laid back, and patrons dressed in business attire drank off the day in the glimmering bar.

Wendy had changed out of work clothes and into a cute little green dress and heels before we burst through the gold-rimmed double doors.

We sat at the counter and perused a menu of items that we had no intention of paying for.

"No matter what's going on in your head, if you pretend to be confident and act like the only woman in the room, then you've done the job," I said calmly.

"I can pretend."

"Now arch that back and look like you're living your best life. The guys will come around. They almost always go for the classy, got-your-crap-together-and-don't-need-them vibe."

"So much to learn. So little time. Uh, one of these drinks is half of my weekly lunch budget," Wendy muttered.

"It won't take long." I tapped my fingernail against my cheek and smiled at the two men down the bar who watched us. With that single look, the game began.

This started out as Wendy's thing, but showing her my techniques, as basic as they were, lured me back to a place where I didn't want to be. But it was also a comfort zone.

"I miss this, being out with you," Wendy said smugly as she nudged arms with a handsome man in a suit.

"Me, too," I lied.

"Want to go upstairs?" a man asked me, one of several.

I clenched my jaw every time. "No. I'm neither available nor interested."

"But I just bought—"

I held a finger to his lips. "Shh. There's no sign on the door that says you can buy sex with a few drinks."

He scoffed. "That's usually how this works."

"Well, next time ask before you buy the drinks."

He shook his head and muttered some obscenities.

Hours passed, cocktails and drinks were downed, appetizers were eaten. The food tasted more like acid than high-quality dining. The drinks turned bitter and foul in my stomach.

But I kept on. I wasn't sure why. Maybe because I didn't want to make a scene or leave Wendy alone. Maybe I had to stand by to make sure she'd be okay. I didn't miss this at all, and I abhorred the touching. I was one minute away from retracting all the drinks and footing the several-hundred-dollar tab on my own when I realized the reason behind my sudden shift in this old lifestyle.

It was the past. I wasn't interested anymore. It wasn't therapeutic or fun or unwinding.

"Are you there?" Wendy asked me, her speech slurred. "What are you thinking about?"

I gave her a soft smile. Jay. I was thinking that I'd rather be snuggled on the couch with Jay debating TV shows.

Easing off the high barstool, I said, "I'm thinking we should call it a night."

Chapter Twenty-Five
Jay

It was Saturday night, and Rohan's bachelor party meant being treated to luxurious shaves and treatments.

We had dinner at an upscale restaurant, made toasts, and relaxed. Rohan was a happy, happy man with a lovely bride, and he couldn't stop smiling. His joy was most definitely contagious and took my mind off Dad's death for those couple of hours.

"Whoa!" Rohan sat back and read a text. "Reema just messaged."

"That's against the rules of the bachelor party," I said and snatched his phone.

"The girls ended up at this swanky club, like reservations are booked for a year out. They have a huge, private booth and want us to join them."

"That's the opposite of a bachelor party, man!"

"Yeah, but our night's winding down. We've had some drinks here, and it's been fun, but they're at the ritziest club in town! I just want to see what it looks like!"

The others agreed, so we headed out.

Liya came down and grabbed us from the lobby, throwing out a group hello and hooking arms with Rohan to lead him first as we followed. We didn't hug or kiss. We were...still a little awkward around each other in front of our friends.

Liya was as stunning as ever in a snug gold dress with red heels. Her waves flowed down her back and her cheeks flushed the moment she saw me. She gave a shy smile and focused on Rohan. I grinned to myself, somewhat satisfied knowing that she didn't look at any other man the way she looked at me. I stuffed my hands into my pockets and followed the guys.

The club was nice, and we immediately took in the grandeur of shimmering gold and crystal chandeliers. Women walked around with trays of complimentary champagne with gold flakes. Everyone was dressed to the nines, bling twinkled on every wrist and neck. Even the servers looked like their cars cost more than mine.

The music was loud, and dozens of clustered booths created a circle around a dance floor of writhing bodies. We walked up a grand staircase, following the banister that overlooked the crowd below, and headed into a private booth. The kind with curtains, a huge table, and curved bench seating that could hold ten people.

It was a little quieter up here, and Reema squealed as soon as she saw Rohan. She threw her hands around his neck and kissed him.

I cleared my throat, not that they could hear the subtlety. Inside the booth, tiered plates with meticulously created finger foods filled the table, along with cocktails and bottles of champagne. We ate and drank and admired the spacious area before everyone went out to the dance floor, leaving Liya and me alone.

She kept her hands in her lap and bit her ruby-red lips. The things that simple little act did to me. Electricity practically ignited the air between us.

"We don't know how to act in front of our friends, do we?" she asked.

I laughed and slid closer to her on the semicircular bench, my arm on the back behind her shoulders. She smelled amazing, hints of flower and vanilla and spice.

"Guess they don't all know, huh?" I touched her hair, and she melted into me.

"Jay?" she asked and turned in to me.

"Hmm?" I leaned down to kiss her. I couldn't help it.

I pulled her closer as our kiss deepened. My hand dropped to her bare knee and skated up an inch. Maybe two. Her fingers pressed into my shoulder.

"Were you going to say something?" I muttered against her mouth.

"I love—" She froze, her eyes wide as she caught herself.

I chuckled, but my heart wasn't as calm as my voice. "Yes? You love what?"

"Your family."

"Is that all?"

She relaxed a bit and added, "And I love being with you."

"I love being with you, too."

"My closest friends know that we've been dating, but I'm not ready to be public beyond them and your family. It's so much pressure. You know my parents will jump straight to wedding talk, and I can't handle that."

"I absolutely understand. I just need to make sure that I'm hearing you correctly. Is there an *us*?"

Liya replied without needing a moment to consider the implications of her answer, "Yes. There is definitely an *us*."

I brushed featherlight kisses across her jaw. Maybe it was the few drinks I'd had earlier. Or the many drinks I'd had since arriving at this club. Or maybe it was simply the intoxicating allure of Liya. But her words made my heart beat like never before. They made my skin tingle. They made my gentle kisses turn passionate and consuming.

She gasped as she gripped my shoulder. "You should stop," she said and pulled away.

"Why?" I moaned.

"Because anyone can open the curtains and walk in. All the food and drinks are here. Someone will be coming back any second."

"Right…"

She took a long drink of champagne, shimmied out of the booth, and looked down at me, offering a hand. "Come on. Dance with me? Maybe I'll let you take me home tonight."

As fast as she moved through these drinks, I had every intention of making sure she got home safely.

What I hadn't planned on? Sleeping over.

Chapter Twenty-Six
Liya

I woke up to one of the worst headaches in history, the kind that had me seeing double. Even the slightest chirping outside transformed the room into the inside of a war drum. Nausea rolled around in my gut, and everything hurt.

Oh, no, how much did I drink during the club phase of Reema's bachelorette party?

The clock glinted eleven in the morning. The sunlight tried to pry through the closed blinds. Rolling over, I found a glass of chilled water. Beads of moisture skittered down the sides, and a puddle edged toward a bottle of ibuprofen. Strange. I gulped three pills with water and threw the covers off, suddenly cold from lack of clothing.

Sluggishly tumbling out of bed, my hair all over the place, my joints aching, my face sticky, I wandered around my dresser and pulled on cotton shorts and a tank top. Glancing at the mirror, I smoothed down a wild nest of stiff waves and wiped raccoon eyes. I needed a shower.

As soon as I swung back the bedroom door, a whiff of ginger cha and bataka pooha hit my senses. For a second, I thought I was still in high school, at my parents' house, and Momma had made breakfast. I didn't see a lean woman scrubbing away in the kitchen, but the broad shoulders of a man working over a wok.

"What are you doing here?" I flinched and touched my forehead. Ugh. Why was my voice so loud?

"Morning," he said, his voice hoarse.

"How did you get in here?"

Jay turned to me and dished up spicy potatoes and flattened rice and then sprinkled chopped cilantro and a squeeze of lime on top. "Don't you remember last night?"

I looked over my shoulder at my bedroom. He must've left the water and pills on my bedside table. "Did we...?"

"No."

Slowly, pieces of last night floated together. My annoyance levels had reached an all-time high with the aunties last night, and I compensated by having too many drinks at the club. Jay must've brought me home. I licked dry lips. I made a sharp turn toward the bathroom. I had to pee and wash my face and brush my teeth and pull back this mess of hair before I could talk to him.

I re-emerged and asked, "We didn't do anything last night?"

He pushed out a bowl of bataka pooha with a dollop of mango chutney and a cup of cha. "I brought you home and you passed out. Hope it's okay that I slept on the couch."

"Oh. Yes, of course. Thank you." I pulled out a barstool across the kitchen counter from him, sorely embarrassed for what drunk me might've done last night. I spooned a flavorful bite into my mouth.

He furrowed his brows and glared at his plate.

"Jay. What's going on with you?" I touched his hand.

Sweat gleamed at the edges of his brow. His nostrils flared, and his chest expanded with every deep, uneven breath.

"Jay?" I asked, my shoulders trembling.

"I'm going through a lot right now."

"Me, too." Like losing my job and probably landing a new one many, many miles away. Which I still had to tell him about.

"There's another reason why I crashed here last night. It's the anniversary of my dad's death. I couldn't be alone."

"Oh, Jay…You don't have to deal with anything by yourself. You can talk to me. You can lean on us."

He walked around the counter to stand in front of my chair. "You have no idea what that means to me."

I wished that I could've enjoyed his tender kiss instead of closing my eyes from this headache careening out of control. I rested my head against his chest. His heart pounded. He held me firmly. His muscles tensed. His breath escaped fast and hard against my skin, into my hair.

He released me and stretched his neck as I watched him from the barstool. He was a behemoth of a man. I touched his cheek, and he stilled, the pain gruesome and evident in his furrowed brow and distant stare.

"Will you come to mandir tonight?" he asked.

"That place?"

"Please? There's a program tonight, and it's Josh's first outing. Shilpa was asking for you. And being at mandir helps me deal with Dad's death."

"Of course, Jay." I fell back into him.

He wrapped his arms around me. For the longest time, he held me. We didn't speak, but his heart pounded faster than ever.

Dad always said patience was a virtue I'd never had. Well, look at me now: patient as hell.

Jay ran his hand down my back and finally said, "I know you don't like that place, and I appreciate your willingness."

"Oh, it's not the place itself. Just the idiots there." I laughed but flinched.

"Do I need to carry you back to bed to sleep this off?" he asked.

"No. I should shower. I'm a gross mess."

"Do I need to carry you to the shower?"

"Don't be starting stuff now."

His chest rumbled against me with laughter.

"You don't have to leave, you know?" I said, and held him a little tighter.

"Oh, yeah?" he replied.

"Who's going to make lunch and rub my head?"

"I'd love to, but I've got some things to take care of. See you tonight?"

After Jay left with a very knee-wobbling, wanna-break-the-bed kiss, I locked the door and leaned against it. Why couldn't I tell him about Dallas? *C'mon.* Where were those big girl panties?

I screamed into my hand and pushed off the door. I showered and did my hair and makeup and got dressed in my best interview clothes to put myself into the right mind-set. Sunday seemed like an odd day to have a video interview, but with the Dallas company wanting to expedite the process and our hectic schedules, it ended up being the only day that worked out.

Then I sat down and waited for the call, tapping my fingernails on the counter. There was still time to text Jay or any of my friends and tell them.

Or...hear me out, brain...I could wait until an official offer came through. Why worry everyone or have to confront Jay about the mere possibility of moving?

Then the phone rang. A Dallas number lit up the screen. On the second ring, I exhaled. And answered.

✳

By the time six rolled around and I'd pulled into the mandir parking lot, I felt halfway decent. My head hurt less, and a newfound hope bubbled through me.

Most people had filed into the grand room, and the parking lot was nearly full. I parked a bit farther away and walked across the newly paved areas, my heels clacking along the way, and reached out for the glass double doors.

Not too far from the entrance, in clear view, stood Kaajal and Jay. He had his arms crossed, standoffish, and that had me snickering. But then she not only touched his arm, but *caressed* it.

She had better get off him.

All I had to do was walk in there, stand beside Jay, and say hello. Facial expression, body language, and tone did the rest.

A hand slammed the door closed.

"What the—?" I jumped.

"Hello," Mukesh said, having formed from the primordial darkness like the nasty little shadow he was.

"What?" I snapped.

"Why are you here?"

"Not here for you, so move away," I said dryly.

"Don't sully the temple," he said, his words cutting through the air like sharpened knives.

"Excuse me?"

"Do you know how many hours I spend wiping everything down after you've been here? Afraid that your touch leaves a residual uncleanness that the gods detest, that others may touch what you've desecrated and have their prayers and worship denied. Many may be too nice to say anything to you, to tell you to leave before you bring ruin to this holy place, to turn you away before your disgrace burns everything."

I replied sardonically, "Nice job at being a pious man. It's no wonder why I hate religion. That's something you'll have to answer to God for."

"Make no mistake, God is forgiving, especially for someone who tries to protect His place. However, you should be aware that there are some things that even God cannot forgive."

"Then that explains why you try so hard to seek His forgiveness, because if God can't forgive me, then He's already sentenced you to burn for what you've done," I hissed.

Mukesh's smile singed into a condemning frown. "Leave this place."

"Or what?"

"Or you and your parents will regret the moment you defied me by walking inside. Do not come between Kaajal and Jay. Do not defile him, a good boy who deserves a good girl."

From behind the glass doors, Kaajal caught my eye through the emptiness between us that was both a small distance and a gaping one. One corner of her mouth lifted in a determined, satisfied way, as if she'd won something.

"Does he know?" Mukesh asked.

"Who doesn't know?" I growled.

"Does he know the slander?"

"The truth, you mean?" My voice rose. "Of what you did to me?"

"Slander. If you walk through these doors again, I will make sure everyone knows of your little treacherous, lying tongue," he said calmly, implying that he would finally tell people what had happened between us…his story, anyway. A story of a little "slutty" girl who came on to him. A story of a "pious" man who rejected the advances and kept it secret to protect my parents.

"They'll hear the truth." The truth that Mukesh had sexually harassed and assaulted me as child. The truth that he hid, in partnership with my father, to make the few who knew about the assault believe that I had done something to provoke him.

He barked, "What is the truth? Will they accept the dirty words from a foul girl or the story from their most respected elder? The girl who hardly attends worship and is known for her perverse lifestyle, or the man who is here every day, working, praying, associating, building?"

I gripped the door handle when he let go.

He dared me. "Go ahead. Go to him. And watch his face as he realizes the horrors and reproach that you bring when I tell him your accusations against me. Or do you think that he cares so much for you that he'll believe you instead?"

"You know nothing." Because I knew Jay would believe me, that he would side with me.

"Then if you believe he'll take your side, stand up to me in front of his mother and family, and stand beside the known whore...by all means, Liya. Go to him. Interrupt my daughter. Become the center of a spectacle. Throw your parents, your poor mother, into another scandal. But what happens if he doesn't take your side? Will you crumple and die from heartache? Will your mother die from heartache? Hmm. Perhaps it is better if you go to him. I'd love to see how fast you shrivel."

I tugged on the door, breathing fast, hot air. My jaw clenched, and he was lucky I didn't punch him in the throat for bringing my mother into this.

Until he added, "You wouldn't be the only one to shrivel. Your mother...women like her tend to unfold quickly."

"What do you mean *like her*?" I snarled.

"Quiet, shy, submissive, concerned with what others think. Would be a shame if she couldn't come here again, lose all of her friends. I let it pass before, when you accused me of trying to defile you. Your parents and I kept your lies between us. But now you're disrupting my family..." He *tsk*ed.

"Threaten my mother again, jackass."

"You can take my words because you don't care about anything, but stop and think what it will do to her. That is, if you even care for her."

I blinked. I could take the humiliation, the turmoil, the attention if Mukesh told everyone that I came on to him. I might've been able to handle Jay publicly siding against me, not that he would believe Mukesh. But my mother?

My hand fell from the door handle.

"That's a good girl. Run along."

"This isn't the end," I promised through tight teeth.

"It is tonight."

I straightened my back. "One day...I'm going to ruin you, and I'll enjoy watching everyone realize the truth of what a disgusting, pitiful, lying blob of walking crap you are."

"Watch your words at mandir."

"Watch out for your soul at mandir." I stormed away but added over my shoulder, "Oh, and since you dragged my mother into this, I'm going to have a fun time dragging your daughter through this."

He seethed, and I tossed him a promising smile with a hint of malice. He threatened my mother? I was going to rip through his family and leave nothing untouched by these *sullied* hands. Jackass thought he could manipulate me? Mandir was off limits?

I'd have to text Jay and have him meet me outside. I wanted to be there for him while he grieved, but I couldn't risk the chance of Mukesh trying to publicly humiliate my mother. I muttered all the way to my car, yanked the door open, slipped inside, and slammed the door.

"Whoa!" a voice yelled.

I wasn't in the mood to talk to anyone. Someone knocked on the window. I intended to ignore him, until he leaned down and revealed his face. Instantly, every drop of anger leaked away.

Rolling down the window, I said, "Sorry!"

"Where are you going?" Jay asked.

"I'm sorry. I have to leave. Come with me. Please tell Shilpa I suck because I couldn't go inside."

He opened the door and crouched. "I saw you talking to Mukesh Uncle. Did he say something that upset you?"

"When does he ever not upset me?"

He growled, "What is his deal?"

"Isn't it obvious? He thinks I'm a dirty whore and that you should marry Kaajal."

He gripped the door. "Are you kidding me? He said that? I'm going to talk to him *again*. This is harassment, and I'm not having it."

I grabbed his arm as he straightened. "Don't bother."

"He said something to Ma that upset her over this, and now to you?"

"He talked to your mother?" Horror engulfed me, but she already knew the worst about me, didn't she? She must've heard the gossip.

"She dismissed him," he added. "She takes you for how you treat us, not for what others say. And then I put him in his place, but apparently that didn't get through to him. I'm sorry, babe."

"Did you just call me 'babe'?" I twisted my mouth.

"Yeah."

"Oh. Okay." I smiled.

"Guess who's watching?" He pulled me out of the car and hugged me in full view of Mukesh and Kaajal.

I laughed, taking in his scent and feeling the strength of his body.

"Do you have any last gestures for them?"

"Am I allowed to? In such a holy place?" I teased, watching them scowl and mutter.

"It's just a parking lot."

I kissed his neck and tossed Mukesh the middle finger as Jay swung me around and settled me back inside the car. "Let's get out of here."

"What about being at mandir to help you cope with your grieving?" I asked.

"No chance that's happening right now. Besides, my family isn't even here. Shilpa was too tired to leave the house, so the whole family stayed home to help her and the baby."

"Where do you want to go?"

"Your place?"

"Sounds perfect."

He closed my door and gave a wave to Mukesh and Kaajal as he jogged to his car and followed me home. That was *almost* as satisfying as an orgasm.

Chapter Twenty-Seven
Jay

Giving Mukesh Uncle a clear message was a lot of fun, but the solemn ride to Liya's wasn't. My heart sagged with all the emotions that gathered and overflowed at this time of year. Mandir helped to lift some of the burden. I wasn't religious, but it made me feel closer to Dad on the anniversary of his death.

Jahn and Ma had Shilpa and Josh to ease any suffering. I had them, too, but my pain couldn't level out around them right now. All I thought of was how Dad would've loved seeing his first grandchild, holding him, spoiling him from day one, and showing him off to everyone he saw. He should've been here to complete the picture.

I undid the top button of my shirt in Liya's parking lot and tried to calm my ragged breathing. A happy family didn't draw me out of this depression. A bottle of bourbon wasn't going to help. I was in dire need of something bigger, better, all-consuming.

Liya waited for me at the top floor of her complex, looking beautiful in her brightly colored outfit. Her hair was back in a loose bun and chandelier earrings twinkled against her neck.

"So?" She tossed her keys from one hand to the other in front of her door. "Seems like we end up at my place a lot these days."

She lowered her hands; the smile faded from her lips as I came into clear view beneath the glow of the overhead lights. Perhaps I looked as wrecked as I felt. Could she see the bags under my eyes? The paleness of my skin?

"Jay?" Panic crossed her features as I clenched my jaw.

"Can I stay the night?" The question came out haggard, lifeless.

She touched my cheek, dragged her hand over my shoulder and down my arm before grasping my hand and leading me inside. She locked the door behind us as we took off our shoes. On her tiptoes, she weaved her fingers through the hair at the nape of my neck and kissed me.

A soft kiss, yet completely devouring. Everything else slipped away. Liya was intoxicating, addictive, and she drank away my sorrows in the sweetest ways. My hands wrapped around her waist and pulled her into me. Who cared if she misunderstood my request? Maybe we were ready for this.

I lifted her onto my hips, wrapping her legs around me, and pushed her against the wall. A delicate moan left her. I kissed her neck, nipped and licked as she rolled into me.

"How do you take these things off?" I asked, biting the collar of her salwar kameez.

She pulled back and asked softly, "Jay? Do you need to talk?"

My breath crashed past my lips, close to heaving. "Why not ask instead if we can take this to your bed?"

"As much as I would love to have you all over me, something is bothering you. Is this about your dad? Or is it Mukesh?"

"Don't mention his name," I groaned and lowered her.

She took my hand and led me to the couch. Pulling down the throw blanket and covering us, she snuggled against my side, and I held her in silence for a long time.

My chest constricted every time she tapped a finger against

mine in a random pattern, back and forth. Sweat tickled on my brow, but I didn't budge to wipe it away. It skittered down my cheek. I twitched.

I tried my best not to clench my fists or tense or scream or just lose my crap. So I closed my eyes and tilted my head back and let the silence linger.

"I'll wait as long you need me to," she whispered and kissed the back of my hand.

Looking down at her dark, soft waves, consumed by her flowery scent and vibrant fight-for-life attitude, things had never been clearer. She was the one. And she would be the first woman I ever told my story to.

"Twenty years ago today, my dad died."

She peered up at me. "I'm sorry, Jay. Were you very close to him?"

"Yes."

"Do you want to talk about what happened?"

I told her the story of how my childish decisions had led to the fire and added bitterly, "God. Why did I try to cook that day? We weren't supposed to use the stove without someone there. And then instead of listening to him and running out, I ran back to him like some stupid little kid. And that's what ended him. He was too busy trying to make me run that he couldn't pull himself out."

Liya hugged me and quietly said, "Jay, you were being brave trying to help him."

"But I didn't help him," I snarled. "I distracted him. If I'd ran like he ordered us to, then he would have had enough focus to pull himself out and get away."

She pulled back to look at me. "You can't blame yourself."

"I caused the fire. I was the reason Dad ran into a burning building. I was the reason why he got caught inside and couldn't focus long enough to get out. You can't say that it wasn't my fault."

She blinked, and her eyes glistened with tears. "You were a child," she said in a soft voice. "You can't keep blaming yourself. Does your family hate you, knowing the truth?"

"No."

"Then don't hate yourself."

"Easy to say, isn't it? Hating myself feels right. Believing that I don't deserve a happy ending when Dad didn't even get the rest of his life feels right."

She sat up.

"I'm sorry."

Liya rubbed my shoulder. "It's okay. You can vent with me. Whatever you need, I can give it to you."

I released a long, rough sigh. "Thank you."

"This is a heavy burden to carry around for so many years. Do you talk to Jahn about it?"

"I try to. He tells me to let it go. I'm convinced he hates me for it, even though he says otherwise."

"I don't think Jahn or your mother hate you. They love you very much."

"I usually just down a bottle of something strong this time of year. I'm fighting it." I twiddled my thumbs. "I think about Dad all the time. He should've been there to see us graduate, to see Jahn get married, to see Josh. I made a widow out of my mother, fatherless boys out of us, a grandfatherless child out of Josh and all of his siblings and cousins to come. I can't even look at myself in the mirror, much less at the scars on my back."

She ran a hand up my back, and I jumped at the odd feel of someone else's touch over the ridges. "You have to let it go before it completely consumes you."

"How do I do that?"

"Approach and embrace the bitterness. Look it in the eye and give it all you have, your tears, your fears, your anger. Then release it like a breath you've held for too long. Remember the good things about your father."

"You're not going to think I'm some emotional man-child if I cry?" I smirked.

She smiled. "We'll cry together."

And that's just what we did. We ordered pizza and drank soda instead of alcohol. And Liya listened to every detail I wanted to tell her. She was right. Tears and fears and everything came out. I couldn't believe how much I'd held in, how immense a burden, and how light I felt when she took it from me.

Liya rubbed my shoulders as I yelled at myself. She didn't interrupt to tell me I was wrong or that things were okay. It was a powerful thing, having someone simply listen and not worry about how I looked: weak, depressed, clinging to the past…

After what seemed like an hour later, when all the rage had subsided, I said quietly, "You would've liked him."

"Yeah?"

"He always told jokes that weren't funny until he added, 'It's an old Indian trick.'" I chuckled. "Every day, he always had hard caramel candy for us. He could cook, too. Ma would always shoo him out of the kitchen, but on weekends he'd wake up early and make breakfast. She'd scold him and then hug him, and we'd all eat in the living room. He taught us how to cook. We'd decimate the kitchen." I laughed. "I'd just wanted to surprise him that day, show him what we'd learned."

She patted my leg and rested her head on my shoulder again. I pulled the blanket across our laps.

Liya helped me to give in to my bitterness, and somehow it didn't scare her away. She cried into my side when my tears slipped and held me tight. She laughed at the fun memories. She unlocked a chest of aggression and repressed emotions as we floated and crashed through all the hard-hitting truths.

One night didn't free me from the guilt, but one night with Liya at my side as we navigated through the grief unleashed more than the last nineteen anniversaries combined.

It was midnight before she changed into shorts and a tank top. I stripped down to my boxers and we went to bed. Together. She pressed her cheek against my chest, her body soft against mine. I held her in my arms and played with her hair as she ran her nails gently over the scars.

"We're finally going to sleep together?" she asked and yawned.

"Looks like it."

"Best night of my life." She kissed my chin.

I didn't think that I could sleep, but Liya's warmth lured me into dreams, not good, not bad, but the kind one doesn't remember in the morning. For the first time in twenty anniversaries, nightmares didn't plague me. When I woke up a few hours later, somewhat rested, relaxed, I knew that I could never let this woman go. She had become my remedy, my everything.

"Liya?" I muttered in her ear, then bit her earlobe when she didn't stir. The woman could sleep.

"What?" she groaned.

"You hit your alarm three times."

She stretched against me. "You know, there are better ways of waking me up if you're going to be sleeping in my bed."

"Next time, I promise, but don't you have to get up for work?"

"Don't *you* have to leave to get ready for work?" she muttered, and just like that, all the sarcasm returned.

I grazed her side, and she yelped. "Oh, are you ticklish?" I asked innocently.

She held my hands in place at her waist with a death grip. "Do. Not. Tickle. Me."

"Then get up for work," I teased.

"I'm not going to work," she groaned.

"Are you going to call in?"

"Are you?"

"I only have some paperwork left that I can do from home." I let out a rough sigh. I couldn't believe I couldn't help save this company. Granted, it wasn't all my fault. Or even majority my fault. But it didn't look good for me to have this loss following my career. And now Liya, among hundreds of others, would be out of a job.

"Oh. Screw work." She closed her eyes and loosened her grip.

"That doesn't sound like you."

"The company's closing. I'm supposed to be there when all those people get laid off, and they'll know that I knew. I don't want to. I don't have to. I'm not going to be upper management's little monkey who does the dirty work and gets the brunt of crap flung at me. And there will be a lot of crap flying. Let them deal with the mess they made."

"Have you had any luck with finding another job?"

"I might have something lined up."

"Well, that's amazing and fast. Where?"

She rolled onto her back. "You're awfully chatty at six in the morning."

"Sorry, princess."

"No one's ever called me a princess. Does that make you a prince?"

"Only if you're marrying me."

She pried open one eye, and I expected her to crawl off the bed and take my joke the wrong way. Instead, she cracked a smile and stuck out her tongue.

"Don't tease me, woman."

"You always say that." She winked.

"This time I'm half naked in your bed." I pulled the covers down to reveal the tank top that had scrunched up over her stomach during all that tossing and turning, revealing the toned flesh of her abs and the hem of her shorts. "Nice."

"Now who's a tease?"

I pulled the covers back up and said, "Thank you for last night, for listening and helping me through everything."

She gazed up at me, now fully awake. "Did it help any?"

"You lifted the weight. Not all of my guilt is gone, but my shoulders aren't about to break from the burden."

"It was my honor. Seriously. I'm glad that you could share it with me, that I helped. I'm not usually good in that department, sad things and kind encouragement and the sort."

"You did really well."

She smiled and slid a hand across my cheek just as I pulled back to lie down. Her hand accidentally trailed down my chest and stomach. I sucked in a breath and tightened my muscles beneath her palm. I froze. She froze.

Liya bit her lower lip and dragged her eyes down the length of my body.

Swallowing, she sat up and swung her legs over the side of the bed. "I'm going to make coffee if we're going to keep this talking at six in the morning thing going."

She piled her hair high on her head and stretched on her way across the room. Her shirt rode up and revealed a sliver of skin, and her shorts dropped an inch to reveal the curve of her narrow waist where it tapered out to generous hips, nice thighs, and a mighty fine butt.

Emotionally drained, I lay back, the silence interrupted by faint noises in the living room. Closing doors, running water, and the smell of coffee that accompanied Liya when she walked back in with two mugs. She placed them on the bedside table.

"You gonna get back into bed with me?" I asked, reaching for her hand.

She placed one knee on the mattress and watched me. "Are we going to be lazy bums?"

"Yes."

"I don't know." She tapped her jaw. "I don't like lying around with a handsome man all day when I could be dealing with all the pissed-off people at my company."

"Comparable, huh?" I grabbed her thigh and hoisted her onto me.

Liya yelped and laughed, falling on top of me, her body landing with a soft crash. "You're going to pay for that!"

"Yeah? What are you going to do, *princess*?"

"Don't call me that!" She giggled as she delicately punched my shoulder.

"It's not nice to hit." I tickled her sides, and she thrashed violently over me. "Damn, woman. Calm down."

"Don't tickle then," she screamed around her laughter.

I flipped her over and landed on top of her, calming her outburst as she heaved beneath me.

"Don't," she pleaded.

"Don't give mercy?"

"Don't, Jay, please. I hate being tickled."

"Like this? But you're laughing. Laughing indicates enjoyment." My fingers danced up her sides, beneath her shirt.

She bucked against me. "I'm going to end you!"

"I think you're just going to laugh. Not very threatening."

She scratched down my shoulders, and I hissed, grabbing her hands and trapping them above her head. I cocked an eyebrow.

"Don't you have somewhere to go? Or a nephew to visit. Oh! Let's go see Josh," she suggested.

"You want to see him?"

"Of course I do. I miss him. He looks a little like you, you know?"

"Oh, yeah?"

"His eyes. And that little roll in his chin."

I chuckled. "This chin?" I nudged her neck with the stubble on my jaw, the frisson sending her into another bout of giggles.

Somewhere between torturous tickling and desperate wriggling, her scent invaded my head, reminding me of where we were. Half naked. Wrestling in her bed. Her soft curves writhing beneath me, bucking against me when I tickled her.

Her laughter filled the air. Her loosening hair glided over my arm.

My chin lowered to her collarbone for a final brush, giving my lips access to her neck. Once my mouth touched her flesh, she sucked in a breath.

And stilled.

Chapter Twenty-Eight
Liya

My lungs burned from gulping in air between giggles. My head throbbed from laughing too hard. I hated being tickled, but I didn't mind the heaviness of Jay's body pushing me into the mattress. His hand let up on my wrists and slid down my arm, leaving a white-hot trail of goose bumps. The tickling friction of his chin scratching my skin turned into soft kisses.

How did we get here?

I never fathomed feeling so good. I floated on a high, a slow-building euphoria that I hoped would never end. Everywhere Jay touched awoke my senses as if they'd been asleep my entire life.

I breathed against his hair, my arms falling around his broad shoulders as he kissed lower and lower. My fingers delighted in the play of his muscles and wandered to the fringes of his scars. He paused.

"I'm sorry," I whispered. "Does that hurt?"

He shook his head.

"Do you hate that I touch them?"

"I could never hate you touching me."

I swallowed. "Should I keep touching you?"

He craned back and looked down at me through heavy lids

before sitting back and pulling me up onto his lap. His hands supported my butt as he rolled my hips against him. "What do you think?"

I gasped at the feel of his excitement. The next roll incited a deep rumble in his chest as he kissed my cheek, my jaw, my lips—first gently, then passionately as his tongue danced with mine.

We pulled away to gulp air, our foreheads against each other, his gaze full of desire.

"You're going to get into trouble if you keep this up," I muttered as his hands moved up my back, sliding my shirt up...and off. I gasped at the cold air hitting my bare skin and shivered against Jay, needing to feel his skin against mine now more than ever.

"There's no one else I'd rather get into trouble with." His mouth crashed over mine in devouring kisses, accepting me mind, body, soul, everything. All of me. Imperfections, faults, insecurities, confidences, all mashed together and laid open and bare for him to cover with affection and adoration.

This wasn't a lustful moment where we eagerly consumed each other in order to reach the end. There was something else here, something that bubbled out of me, filled me to the brim with longing and...love? The way he cared for me and my needs, ran featherlight kisses on the back of my hand and up my arms, how he took his time, asked, held my gaze...

For the first time in my life, I *felt* loved.

This was love.

"Congratulations, Ms. Thakkar. We thoroughly enjoyed your interviews last week, and the review committee has reached a decision. There's no doubt that we want you working for us. Please give us a call back to discuss the terms of an offer, which include a company-paid, fully furnished apartment for the first three months available as early as next Monday. We're delighted to have you join our team."

I hung up the phone and stared at the voicemail screen. I could delete it and ignore them. Getting a job was imperative, and landing one so far away from the mess here, including Dad and Mukesh, was something that I'd dreamed of for years.

That was before Jay.

I'd already group texted the girls about how hard I was falling for Jay, which ended up in a squealing marathon. I'd even told Momma that I'd give him a try because she was right. Jay was amazing. She was ecstatic.

I bit my lip. Maybe Jay would be happy about Dallas. He should be happy for me, for finding work, for bouncing back from this company, for hitting a higher pay scale, a higher level. What would that mean for us? I'd finally found someone, but I knew deep down that he wasn't going to leave his family, his baby nephew.

I dropped my head. I wanted to celebrate, call Momma and my friends and even Jay. But at the same time, I was not ready to leave any of them.

Wendy walked into my office, cradling a box of her things.

I smiled weakly. "Didn't think you'd stay the rest of the week."

"Hell, no. I love you, and hate to leave you, but screw this place."

"I feel you. I'm just here to help anyone I can."

"That's sweet of you. Ugh. Can't believe they screwed us all over like this. It's not your job to take care of everyone else. You need to look for a new job, you know? What we should've been doing for months instead of saving this crap place from completely drowning. I knew a few days earlier than most, but not enough time to find work."

I spun my cell phone on my desk. "I have something lined up. Not that I knew this place was going to use me. It fell into my lap."

"That's great news!"

I nodded.

Wendy frowned. "But what? Don't tell me you're sad about getting a new job when I'm floundering for one."

"Aside from feeling awful for everyone who's getting laid off, the job's in Dallas."

"Wow. That's a nice change!"

"It would be."

"You've always talked about getting away from this muggy, smoggy hellhole."

"Yeah."

She twisted her mouth. "Is it a guy? That fine-as-wine lawyer who keeps coming around?"

I couldn't keep my lips from twitching into a smile.

"Look at you. The glow, the glazed eyes, you're in love." She dropped her box on a chair and rushed over to hug me.

"Oh, my god. It's not that big of a deal," I said unconvincingly even as heat prickled my cheeks.

"Yes, it is. You've been like this unobtainable chick for years, all the guys coming after you, and finally one landed you and you didn't automatically kick him to the curb? I'm happy for you, but do not let a man step in between you and your goals. Not to be a negative Nelly, but what if things don't work out with him? Or if you can't find a job here? You can only put your life on hold for so long. He has to meet you halfway."

"Ever thought about a career in counseling?" I eyed her.

"You're a train, not to be stopped, not meant to slow down."

"An eventual train wreck?"

She laughed. "Okay. Don't turn down this job yet."

"I just got the call."

She waved her hand. "You'll make the right decision, but don't give in just because friends and family and a man want you to stay. You have to do what's best for you."

Wendy was right. I had to take everything into consideration. I didn't want to leave Momma, but it would be best to leave Dad behind. My friends would understand. Dallas wasn't that far. And Jay should understand. A man shouldn't hold me back.

Even if that man was quite possibly the love of my life?

As in all things that required advice, I invited the girls over after work.

"It's been a while since we had a wine and cheese party," Reema lamented as she gobbled up a glass of Merlot.

"Slow down there," I warned. "You don't want to get sick the week of your wedding."

"I'm so nervous."

"Why?" Preeti asked. "You've been ready for this since you guys started dating, and lo and behold, it's been sanctioned by all the parents since before you two met."

"It's a big step, and there are so many people who are going to be there, and any number of things can go wrong," Reema admitted.

"Like what?"

"For starters, are you aware that weddings for one's child require that the parents invite everyone they've ever met? One of my invitees to ten of theirs. I won't know most of the people at my own wedding! It's going to be huge. And the caterer can mess up, the cake can fall on the floor, the flowers could dry up before the ceremony, what if my choli is too tight, I could trip in my heels, Rohan could get cold feet—"

"Let me stop your neuroticism right there," I interjected. "Things will go smoothly, and so what if they don't? The important thing is sitting through the ceremony and getting the legal papers signed. Anything else will be laughable. Rohan will not get cold feet. You will not trip. But if you do trip, Rohan will catch you and it'll be romantic. So there."

She nodded briskly and carefully smothered a baguette slice with goat cheese. "What's new with you? How are things with Jay?"

"Jay," Preeti and Sana sang.

I wanted to roll my eyes and brush it off, but, just like with Wendy, my lips twitched and my smile couldn't be contained. They leaned in to hear every juicy word.

"We're good," I managed to get out.

"Just good?" Sana asked.

"Or hot as Hades?" Reema winked.

"That second one," I muttered, my face heating.

"You guys did it?" Preeti stated more than questioned.

I nodded in silent, gleeful confirmation, biting down on my lip to keep from grinning like a fool. The girls squealed and practically flung themselves back into their seats like a bunch of teenagers.

I expected them to ask for details, but Preeti added, "It was inevitable."

"What is that supposed to mean?"

"C'mon, Liya. We could all see it. He's insanely into you, and you are head over heels for him."

"Sort of."

Sana nudged my shoulder. "Admit it. You like a man. *Like* like."

"Yes. I admit it. We are very into each other, we're actually in a committed relationship. I was such a prick to him, but he fought for me."

"Like I said, Jay is a good man. If he can fight you and win, then he can and will fight anyone and anything to keep you. I love

it! What a romance!" Sana swooned. "Have you told your parents?
They must be elated."

"My mom knows. Although we're not thinking about marriage."

"Isn't that where this goes, though?"

"Traditionally, but we all know I'm not traditional, and Jay is
fine with that." I laughed. "*That* would be the best conversation
with my dad. Yeah, that suitor you tried to force me to meet,
remember, the one I ran out on and mortified you over, well,
turns out we ended up together anyway. *However*, don't expect an
engagement, much less a wedding, anytime in the next decade.
We're just going to date, get it on, maybe move in together."

Sana turned bright red, her chestnut eyes wide and gleaming.
"That's horrible. Your poor parents will be crushed."

"You can't always live for someone else. Live for yourself. I'm
with the man they wanted for me. That's all they can ask for, and
that's all they're going to get for right now. I admit…Jay makes
the idea of marriage attractive. But let's not start planning a wedding anytime soon."

"I'm very happy and excited for you, Liya. You deserve a good,
strong man who loves you," Sana said.

All right. Time to get down to business. After a long swig of
wine, I confessed, "So, my company is closing."

"No!" Reema said. "What happened?"

"They screwed us over. Got me to cheer on a bunch of
coworkers who trusted me, to rally them and keep them working despite all the lawsuits that had been coming at us, only to
dump us all."

"I'm so sorry. Are you freaking out?" Reema asked.

"No. I have cushy savings."

"Are you sure?" She looked around, her scrutinizing gaze
sweeping over my expensive style and landing pointedly on my
Christian Louboutin collection.

"Yes, I'm certain. I live within my means. I pay bills, live debt-free, buy luxuries, and save money. I'm not completely irresponsible."

Reema shook her head. "Sucks they didn't tell you months ago. You would've had a new job by now."

I drew in a breath. If I couldn't count on my friends, then what good was our friendship? "They actually recommended me to another company, higher position, better pay. It's a company I've had my eye on for years. I applied to them before, but they wanted me for a lab position instead of management."

"That's wonderful! I was about to worry. Where is it? Downtown?" Reema's face lit up.

I played with the fringes of the throw blanket. "It's in Dallas. They made an offer today."

"*What?*"

The ladies gawked, panic quickly spreading through each of them like wildfire. I swallowed down my trepidation and went on, "I've never been this nervous to say something. I don't want to leave you guys, but let's face it, Houston has ruined me. I can't stand being near…*certain* people. It's exhausting. And I want to be with you forever, but you're all moving on. We're growing up."

"Forget them!" Sana exclaimed.

"It's understandable," Reema interjected. "I'm proud of you for making it this long. We'll miss you, but it would be nice to have a place to stay in Dallas. It's far enough for you, but not too far from us. We will be there every month."

I grinned, anxiety easing out of me until Preeti asked, "What about Jay?"

"I haven't mentioned it to him. How do I? I don't want to feel bad for leaving, but I can't stay here for him."

She sighed. "Well, sounds like you have something great, either way, and a serious discussion to be had. I'd suggest talking to Jay about it as soon as possible. He's understanding and seems supportive. I don't think he will try to make you stay. When would you start?"

"Um. They have a furnished apartment for me for the first three months and they want me to start right away. The place will be ready...on Monday." I grimaced, expecting their worst reactions to such a big change happening this fast.

Reema almost choked on her drink. "What! Like *this Monday*, Monday? The day after my wedding, Monday?"

"I wouldn't start that early. I don't have to move up right away, either. I haven't decided anything yet."

"I'm going to miss you. This is so soon, so sudden," Preeti said, her shoulders slumped.

I took her hand and gave it a squeeze. "I may not be as loud, but you'll still hear me all the way from Dallas."

She laughed and wiped away a tear. "I believe it! Maybe you and Jay can check out the apartment together?"

That was certainly one way of breaking the news to him. As if Jay's ear tingled from being talked about, my phone buzzed with a text message from him. I opened the picture and my heart melted.

Jay: Jahn took this picture when we weren't looking.

I caressed the screen. What a perfect moment captured of us sitting on the bench seat in Shilpa's delivery room. I held Josh in my arms and smiled down at him. Jay had one arm behind me, on the bench, his hand on my shoulder, his body against my side, his other hand on Josh's head, a proud smile on his face.

Reema snatched the phone. "Is it a sexy picture from your heartthrob?"

"Oooh! I want to see!" Preeti landed on the couch beside her.

I didn't fight them or the onslaught of *aws* that echoed around the room.

"This is so sweet!" Preeti crooned.

"Imagine if you two had a baby. This would be you!" Sana cried.

I sucked in a breath. My cheeks warmed. The ladies gawked at me. And here it came...

"Liya Thakkar did not immediately balk at the idea of having a child," Reema said.

"I don't want a baby," I promised.

"But..."

I grinned and replied sheepishly, "But yeah, my ovaries kind of exploded at that moment."

We flailed with hysterical laughter, holding our stomachs and wiping tears.

I hadn't ugly laughed like this in a long time.

Chapter Twenty-Nine
Jay

"D id she like the picture?" Jahn asked.

"Yeah," I replied and helped Ma cook in the kitchen at Jahn's place.

"Is she coming over for dinner?" Ma asked.

"She said she would."

"So, what's going on?" Jahn asked.

"Nothing much."

"I mean with Liya. You guys look pretty couple-ish there."

"Yeah, with your baby."

He grinned. Ma grinned. Even Shilpa grinned as she walked around burping Josh.

"Tell us, beta, do you think I can rest now?" Ma asked. "Not having to look for a girl to marry you. I'm getting tired of fighting off all these women asking about you for their daughters."

"I think we're good. Maybe not engagement anytime soon, but—"

"That's enough for me." She touched my arm. "Do you understand what a headache it is to find the right girl for you? Too short, too quiet, too far, too traditional, too much trouble..." She sighed. "I hope this works out and that you keep her happy."

"You like her?"

"Of course I like her! Do you think I would've kept my mouth closed if I didn't? Or that I would allow her to sit in our family dinners? Or that I wouldn't have shoved her out of Shilpa's delivery room?"

Shilpa cackled from across the room. "Ma would've kicked her out!"

Ma added, "Her parents asked for another dinner, you know, to sit down as a family and discuss if you two are interested in moving ahead with dating. She must not have said anything to them."

"We haven't discussed where we're going. We're just going. We'll see when we get there."

"That sounds very romantic," Shilpa said and opened the door when the bell rang.

Liya's energetic voice carried through the hallway. Ma hurried around the counter to greet her and hug her. Jahn and I watched, sort of dumbfounded. He grinned and pushed me toward her.

"Oh, hi," Liya said when I was suddenly forced in front of her.

"Glad you could make it," I said, moving my hands behind me because suddenly I didn't know how to greet her in front of my family.

"I wouldn't miss it for the world."

"Really?" I asked, smiling.

"Yes. I must see this handsome little man named Josh. Gimme, gimme." She went straight for the baby, and my family laughed at my expense.

Liya held him with natural affection, at ease, and smothered him in kisses, alternately saying, "So cute!" over and over. And then she broke down into baby talk, and Ma looked at me with arched brows and cocked her head, like, go get her pregnant right now!

Jahn cracked up and whispered, "Marry her first."

Liya held Josh for most of the evening, even while eating. How could she not read the looks my family gave her?

"You're attached to him, aren't you?" I asked, sitting beside Liya at the table.

She ate while Josh slept peacefully in the crook of her arm. "Aren't you? He's freaking adorable."

"My family is looking at us like we should go back to my place and do something about this baby business," I muttered in her ear.

She paused, her cheeks pink. "Oh, no."

"Oh, yes."

"Not every woman wants to be a mother," she said even as her skin flushed.

Shilpa took Josh to feed him when he squirmed and cried. Jahn helped Ma clear the table. I placed an arm on the back of Liya's chair and whispered, "You look good with a baby."

"You better shut up with that baby talk," she warned, her mouth stern but her eyes playful.

I stroked her thigh under the table. "I mean if you want, I could take you home and put a baby in you."

She laughed. "Hell, no."

"You don't want my baby?" I teased.

"You want me to have your baby?"

"Yeah." I licked my lips and her gaze dropped to my mouth.

"How did we go from monogamous dating to baby-making?" she asked, tilting her head in amusement.

"You didn't answer my question. You don't want my baby?"

"You must have me confused with someone else."

"That's not a yes or a no," I teased.

"I…"

I touched her cheek.

"Your mom is watching."

"She'd love another grandchild."

"Maybe. One day. Not this year. We've only…once…" she whispered.

"Then let's practice." I grinned.

"You are so much trouble. I'm telling your mom."

"Telling me what?" Ma asked, and we both shut up quickly.

I moved away from Liya and cleared my throat.

Ma smiled and sat down in front of us. "I'd like to speak with you two."

Liya sighed. "I know what this is about."

"Do you?" Ma asked.

"About how much time Jay and I spend together. I knew that you'd eventually hear the gossip and step in."

She waved off Liya's remark. "I don't care about what others say. All I need to know is that you're dedicated to Jay as much as he is dedicated to you and that you won't hurt him. It's obvious to all of us that you're good for him and that he's crazy about you."

She blushed. "Thank you. Aren't you in the least objecting to us?"

"No. Believe it or not, you remind me of myself when I was much younger."

"Really?" we both asked in unison.

"Yes. I had such a smart mouth on me. My parents practically died every time I opened it. Sarcastic and witty. Oh, no one messed with me, and it took a brave man to marry me. He never expected me to change, saw me for every good deed and every blemish, but loved me like in the movies. You better believe how mean people were to me. In India, at that time, pushing myself to become educated and independent, society did not like that. I enjoyed a party or two, I tried a drink. Jay's father and I snuck out a time or three before the wedding."

"Oh, lord," I muttered, not wanting to know this side of my mother.

"We were full of passion and fire, and yes, we argued sometimes, but we never stopped loving one another."

"Ma..." I mumbled.

"Oh, hush. You're an adult now. You know what we did to make you."

"Lord," I muttered under my breath and offered Liya an apologetic glance.

She laughed. "I love your mother."

Ma went on. "You can be different, free, opinionated, be all those things but be a good person."

"Were you a feminist?" Liya asked.

"Still am."

"But this whole finding a wife for your sons?"

"It's a parent's duty, isn't it? To make sure their children are loved, fed, taken care of. That they get through college, build a career, and marry the right person to spend their lives with, someone who will make them happy. I've always kept an eye out for special women for my sons, but it's always up to them. I don't force them. I wouldn't force my daughter to marry a certain man, either.

"Notice that Shilpa is not a quiet girl. Oh, no. She will stand up for anything she believes in. She's a hard worker, an equal partner in her marriage. She respects me, I respect her. She doesn't expect me to tell her what to do, and I wouldn't expect her to obey me if I did. She's independent and, thankfully, out of the goodness of her heart and the fact that we get along so well, she's more than happy having me live with her and help with the baby.

"And don't you think I know how hardheaded, competitive, and assertive Jay can be? He wouldn't want a quiet girl, either, but a special woman who can put up with him, put him in his place if need be, but more than ever, build one another up."

"I'm sure by now you've heard all the rumors, in detail, about my wild ways. Aren't you concerned?" Liya bit her lip and glanced at the table between us and Ma.

"No. Some of us have had our wild times. Yours is in the past and Jay is your present. Love is love. If you're committed to my son, and only my son, I'm happy. What else is there? You're everything to him. On top of that, you come from a good family, have a career, good friends, are a hard worker. It's not as if you're having relations with other men at the same time, or are you?"

Liya shook her head vigorously. "Oh, lord, no."

"Good. I approve, in case either of you were concerned."

"That means so much to me," Liya replied, her eyes glistening.

I took her hand beneath the table and squeezed.

"I enjoyed dinner. I'll leave you two," Ma said and went upstairs.

"I didn't mean for us to get ambushed like that," I said after Ma left.

Liya shrugged. "That's not an ambush."

"Look, I know where you stand on marriage and kids and all that, and you know where I stand and what I'm willing to compromise on. There's no pressure here."

"There was no pressure from her, either."

"Good. As long as we're honest with one another, we'll be good."

She squeezed my hand a little more. "Speaking of, you know how I said I might have a new job lined up?"

"Yeah."

"My boss actually recommended me for a job," she said, albeit a little nervously.

"That's great! Is it nearby, or do you have to drive through this nasty traffic?"

She rubbed her hands against her lap. "The job is in Dallas, and they just made an offer."

"What?" My heart sank at her words.

"I've been debating another city for a long time, particularly this company in Dallas."

I swallowed. "What's there to debate about?"

"I hate living here. You know that. Been trying to get away for a long time, and this company has been on my radar since graduation."

"You're trying to run?" I clenched my jaw.

"Not from you." She touched my cheek. "I promise I'm not. But there are tumultuous things here, corrosive people. I also have my friends here."

"And *me*," I reminded.

"And you," she said gently.

"But the fact that you're aiming for Dallas says a lot about what you think of us."

She swallowed. "I have always wanted to get away from Houston. I didn't think you'd be the type of guy who would hold me back from this kind of opportunity."

"Hold you back? You mean get upset because you're considering leaving me?"

"I'm not leaving you." She shook her head as if this conversation was exasperating her.

"How long do you expect a long-distance relationship to work?" I asked, trying to keep my anger, my panic, down.

"We'll try. Maybe you can get a job there."

I scoffed and pulled away. "And leave my family? I get that you hate yours, but I love mine. I can't leave Ma, I won't leave Josh. I thought you were starting to love them, too."

She sat back, her face rigid. "Are you telling me not to accept the job?"

"There has to be a company here."

"That I want to be with? In a management position? With better pay? No. There isn't."

"You're running away from me again."

"Jay. You're not hearing me. I am not running away. This is the type of job I've worked very hard for over several years, at a company that I've tried to get into before, a company that I really want to work at and a position I believe I'll thrive in."

"In Dallas!"

"What should I do, then?" she growled. "Stay here, work at a place that I hate *if* I can even get a job here? Play housewife and go to mandir and deal with those idiots who I hate?"

I rubbed my eyes. "Are we fighting again?"

"Sounds like it." She pushed away from the table and stood. "Now you're pissed at me. It's not the situation I want, either."

I shot to my feet and went out the door, Liya right on my heels. "Tell me when you got things figured out."

"I already do. I'm taking the job, Jay."

She reached for my hand when I pulled out my car keys. "This is not the end of us," she said softly.

"I can't leave my family. You won't stay here. That sounds like the end of us."

"Jay—"

But I wasn't hearing it. I got into my car and left.

Chapter Thirty
Liya

An Indian wedding was a larger-than-life ordeal. Comprised of several ceremonies and parties, mendhi to get done, pictures to take, and in every aspect, I had to put on my best, happiest face. I *was* happy for Reema and Rohan, but I had to deal with Jay later. He was upset. I got it. But he didn't fully understand why I could never stay here.

I had to tell him. I had to tell another soul, after all these years, the name of the man who assaulted me. I knew Jay would believe me, side with me, but there was a vicious niggling that he wouldn't believe such a pious man could have done such a thing. After all, my own father hadn't believed me.

But after the wedding. After all of my exuberant duties and dance numbers.

Stepping back into the mandir after Mukesh's very real warning haunted my thoughts. He had me nervous, but my best friend's wedding was enough to shove thoughts of Mukesh to the side and show up proud and jubilant. Not even that lying maniac could keep me away.

Reema had transformed into Houston's most elegant bride in a flowing crimson-and-gold lengha. Intricate maroon mendhi designs trailed up her hands and forearms and on her feet. Chiming anklets with teardrop bells wrapped around her ankles. A dozen sparkling glass bangles lined her wrists to match her outfit. A giant diamond engagement ring weighed down one hand. Her ears drooped with heavy gold chandelier earrings to match a thick necklace. Her eyelids glimmered with glitter, her eyes were lined with kohl. Her lips were ruby red.

"I'm not going to cry," I promised, my voice cracking.

"Don't cry! If you cry, then I'll cry," she said.

The swarm of women around us warned against my making Reema cry, but their eyes misted first, and then it was a downhill battle from there.

"Don't ruin your makeup!" I chided. "We still have a million pictures to take."

Preeti fanned her while the majority of the women walked out of the back room where we waited for the big cue. Reema's doting mom lovingly pulled Reema's dupatta over her face. The doors opened, and we paired up with the groomsmen and walked down the aisle. Mukesh caught my eye as I smiled big. He would not take this from me.

We stood poised and watched the double doors open. Reema walked down the aisle with her two uncles, holding her bouquet, her smile shaking as she tried not to cry on her way to the intricately carved altar, its golden poles wrapped in red-and-gold silk. Marigold and rose garlands hung from the top in a curtain of aromatic flowers.

Once Reema took her seat across from Rohan, I glared at Mukesh on the way to my chair.

To the right, Dad silently shunned me. It wouldn't be a surprise if Mukesh had given them an earful. And here we found ourselves again, the same place we were years ago and kept returning to. When someone tried to ruin me, where were the parents who would stand up for me? To deny those claims? To fight for me?

To the left, Jay wore a splendid green sherwani with gold beading along the hem. His lips lifted in an imploring half smile, and I smiled back. I'd missed him so much the past few days. I wanted to hug him, to kiss him, and never let go. On my way past, I touched his shoulder.

I sat near the back with Preeti. We deserved a front row seat, but she, much like myself, needed the exit in sight. This place and its judgmental, hypocritical people were stifling. And with her ex present, Preeti was definitely a flight risk.

She held my hand, and I leaned my head against her. Jay turned back and glanced at me with that heartwarming smile that said everything without saying anything.

I nodded, knowing we'd have to sit down and talk later, and glanced away, only to find Mukesh watching us from his seat near Dad. *Focus, Liya, just look at Reema.*

I wiped a tear, and Preeti squeezed my hand. "Don't make me cry. Do you know how many attempts it took to get my makeup right?"

"Okay." I giggled, hoping to ease her and convince my heart that it shouldn't be so heavy.

The ceremony went on without a hitch, but partway through the modernized, fast, one-hour version, Jay stood and walked past me.

He crouched behind me, his mouth at my ear. "You look beautiful," he said simply.

My heart skipped several beats.

My hands shook as he stood and walked away to stretch beyond the double doors. I went to him.

I breathed. In and out. Slow, methodical, cleansing.

"You don't look half bad yourself," I said when I found him alone down the hall.

"Look, I—" we both started at the same time and then chuckled. Were we two awkward teens here?

People filed in and out of the hallways, breaking my concentration. "I need to talk to you, Jay."

"Yeah."

"After the reception. I have several more bridesmaids' duties to get through. I have to get back."

He kissed my temple. I breathed in his scent, felt his warmth wash over me. I would've kissed him, except we were in the middle of my best friend's wedding at mandir.

After the wedding and ceremonious traditions, we cleared the hall. Dozens of people rushed through to transform the area into reception mode while the couple took care of even more traditions. Then we all changed into elegant party gear. Reema and Rohan sat on red velvet thrones on a dais beside the wedding cake and catering table.

Reema grinned at us. I smiled back and waved. What a perfect day for her.

Between walking past Jay and getting to the dance floor, Mukesh managed to creep by and mutter, "I warned you what would happen if you returned here, if you kept Jay away from Kajaal."

My breath stalled, and I blinked away the shock of terror as he walked toward the back, toward Jay and his family. I squeezed my eyes tight as we took our places barefoot on the wooden makeshift dance floor. Now was not the time to curse him out. It was not the time to run off with Jay.

Hold it together. Just dance. Concentrate on Reema and Rohan. My palms turned clammy and perspiration crawled down my neck. My head spun, and all the staring, watching faces blurred as the music revved up.

My nerves were wrought and coiled tight as we stepped into

formation and the Bollywood beat came on, pounding through our ears, vibrating the walls, and earning cheers.

We did our thing, danced, spun, tapped, clapped, swayed our bodies and hips, and flicked our wrists in all of the cinematic Bollywood glory that the song demanded.

At the end, applause erupted all around, and we caught our breath, sweat dripping down our temples. Afterward, Reema and Rohan would enjoy their first dance, cut the cake, and feed each other, and then the dance floor would open to everyone. The caterers would unveil silver pots of food. The cool air would fill with spicy aromas and pounding music, laughter, and conversation.

I made a beeline toward Jay, my heart pounding and my limbs heavy.

My parents stood off to one side, waiting to approach me, without a doubt. Dad called me toward him with a crook of his finger, as if I were a child caught eating cookies before dinner. Mukesh was at their side. Jahn approached him, worry creasing his face, and said a few words. His mother was summoned, and they walked into a smaller, private room.

Oh, hell no. Anger rippled through me. Mukesh was *not* about to pull Jay's family into this. I gathered my heavily beaded chaniya into my hands and marched into the room after them, throwing open the door as Mukesh pleaded with Jay's family.

"What are you doing?" I growled.

"Wait outside. Adults are talking," he rebuked.

"Listen here, old man—"

"I warned you, didn't I?"

I looked to Jahn and his mother. "I'm so sorry."

"You weren't sorry while you stole Jay away from my daughter? Seducing him? Defiling him?" Mukesh barked.

"I meant that I'm sorry this senile bigot dragged you into the fictional drama in his head. Look, whatever you're trying to tell them, they've heard it all. Don't embarrass yourself any further."

Jay's mother spoke to him. "Mukesh Bhai, we've heard the gossip, and you've already spoken to us. I don't care what you have to say. Liya is a good girl, and we're pleased that she and Jay have chosen each other."

Momma breathed a sigh of relief, but Mukesh's following words cut through her happiness like a blistering knife. "This is something that we've kept private, secret."

My heart spasmed. "Don't do this."

"Do what?" Jay asked. He looked at Mukesh with a restrained ferocity, and then at his brother and mother with concern. Finally, he glanced at me, his concern ever deeper.

Mukesh said solemnly, "As much as this hurts me to say."

"Then don't," I responded, my expression stoic, a plea, a warning. This was not for *him* to tell, to distort and lie about. This was *my* truth for me to tell my side when I was ready, not in a back room in the middle of my best friend's reception.

"I don't care what you have to say. I thought we made this clear weeks ago," Jay said, his voice rough but calm.

"It's time to reveal this disturbing truth because you're making a huge mistake with Liya," Mukesh warned.

"That's none of your business," Jay growled.

"Your manners!" Mukesh said, appalled, and gave Jay's mother a pitiful look.

"Don't look at her," Jay retorted, standing between Mukesh and his mother.

"You should hear this..." Dad interjected.

"*What?*" I balked. My mouth gaped, my chest splayed open by the ever-deeper betrayal. He had never backed me in these heartrending claims, but to give Mukesh the room, to silence everyone, to be his pillar while removing mine? How could Dad do this to me? *He* wanted to push me onto Jay. He wanted this alliance. I was his flesh and blood, but he took the side of the viper. Instead of shielding me, he held the venom to my veins and allowed the serpent to sink its fangs into my flesh.

Tears filled my eyes. My body turned to lead. I hadn't felt this abandoned since childhood, since Mukesh started this atrocity.

I trembled at the thought of telling this room my story, of being forced to relive that day and the years that followed when those who were supposed to protect me broke me.

Jay cast a worried glance my way, but I turned from him and walked past Mukesh. The least I could do was leave, to let this play out without the added mortification of being present. But someone grabbed my arm with a tight grip and pulled me back. I assumed it was Mukesh, and I was so ready to hit him.

Dad's aging hand gripped my forearm. He yanked me back into the room with another tug. Having caught me off guard, I stumbled backward and glared at him.

"Who do you think you are, handling her like that?" Jay snapped and gently touched my back. "Are you all right, Liya?"

Too many tears flooded my eyes, too many to see through. Once I blinked, they slithered down my cheeks. I could hate Dad all I wanted, but the debilitating pain from his betrayals never lessened. After all these years, he still wielded the power to reduce me to a whimpering child.

"I meant to tell you right after the reception," I muttered, my chest heaving, my stomach trying its hardest not to puke.

"Tell me what?" Jay whispered, his body turned into my side.

I closed my eyes for a second. "Mukesh—" I began to tell Jay. If I couldn't tell the room, I could at least tell Jay while he blocked my view of everyone else.

"You all know what sort of man I am," Mukesh interrupted.

My hands fisted at my sides. "Shady," I offered.

"Insistent in overstepping boundaries?" Jay added.

"Well, I am a pious man, a religious sort, a man of God," Mukesh said.

I scoffed.

"Liya," Dad snapped.

Mukesh went on, "I'm at mandir every day, devout in my worship. I help with all functions, meals, I even clean and cook in the kitchens. Ask any patron, ask my family, your friends, my coworkers, the friends and teachers of my children. And true, I'm a bit forward with this situation, but only because you can't make this mistake, Jay. Even if you don't want to marry Kaajal, it's in your best interest to walk away from Liya. You don't know her."

"I know her better than you," Jay said as he took my hand. His face turned rigid, hard, scary when he glared at Mukesh, but it softened to something so fiercely protective when he returned his gaze to me.

My breathing turned ragged and raspy. "The man who sexually assaulted me, molested me when I was a kid," I said calmly, quietly, void of all the anger I'd held for the past ten years.

"*You're* the one?" Jay snarled, whipping toward Mukesh. His fists turned white as he took a step, but Dad stopped him with a hand near his chest.

"That is the lie she tells herself," Mukesh replied. "This is why we kept this between us. I'm an elder in this mandir. I'm here to help those who stray, but Liya is a special case that has worsened over the years."

"You're the liar," I said as ire whirled through me, awakening me, pushing me toward the breaking point.

"We all tried to help. Do you dare call your parents liars?"

Dad was a liar, and I'd called him out on it. Momma was... scared. Even now her lips trembled. But then she did something that I didn't expect. She narrowed her teary eyes. Her terrified expression turned angry, protective. She took a step forward and opened her mouth, but Dad reeled her back, and they fought.

She finally stood up for me? She finally stood up to Dad?

I let out a shuddering breath.

Mukesh had never stopped talking. "This is the truth, Jay. This is for us only, but you're hearing it because she has seduced you to the point that you cannot see the dangerous, disturbing truth. Your mother and elder brother are here as witnesses, to help protect you against her if you don't believe the truth. At only *fifteen*, she managed to get me alone at our home and seduce me."

"You manipulating, lying piece of crap," I snapped.

"See! She gets out of control like this all the time. Do you really want to be with a woman as volatile as her? And I'm certain that if you've spent more than five minutes with Liya, you've seen this side of her."

From the corner of an eye, Jay studied us, but I couldn't look at him, couldn't watch as realization unfurled across his features. Maybe he wouldn't forsake me, but if there was the slightest chance that he would, I couldn't bear to see that truth.

"How could I lie in this place of worship? After she tried to seduce me, and I kindly rebuked her, she told her parents that *I* made advances on her." He solemnly shook his head as Dad agreed.

My heart skipped two beats and slammed against my ribs with the third beat.

Dad's white-knuckle hold bore into Momma's arm, silencing her. My hands trembled to touch her, to hold her, to apologize that these jackasses existed.

"See the shame? Her seduction didn't stop there. She tried hard to convince her parents about her lie, and then turned hostile toward me for not giving in to her. Since then, she's turned her wiles on all sorts of boys. Her lifestyle didn't change. It worsened. Drinking, partying, cursing. She became a whore. She still is one."

There was a scuffle behind me, Jay no doubt, but I couldn't look.

"Women are like dishes, no? Once broken, of what use are they? Some pieces may be glued back together, but she will never be whole. In Liya's case, there are too many tiny pieces, some that left her long ago, stuck to someone's bed. Go ahead, ask her father if this is true or not."

"This is the truth," Dad pushed out, making direct eye contact with me. How much could a father hate his own child?

He went on as I watched him through teary, blurred eyes, "I'd hoped that she could find a husband, and that was my fault. To believe that a man would marry her, want her after being so used. But to slander a good man's name... We're indebted to Mukesh Bhai for keeping this between us. I would've been indebted to you, Jay, for marrying her, but that would be unfair to you."

"I hate you," I growled. "How could you believe him over me? All these years you stick to his side and disown your daughter? I was just a child!"

"You were a whore even then!"

"I *wasn't*. You're my father! Where the hell was your parental protection?"

His slap was swift and hard and echoed against the walls, reverberating to shake my very core. My hand lifted to the hot, stinging sensation across my cheek and lip. My tongue tasted a metallic drop of blood. A disconcerting calm fell over me, cleared my thoughts, dried my tears, pacified my words.

"Pranad!" Momma wailed and pushed Dad away.

"I'm so sorry," she wept as she touched my cheek, tears sliding down her face.

Behind me, Jahn was holding Jay back, but the horrid disdain on their faces was enough to finish whatever we could've had. Even if they believed me, they would never want a lifetime tied to this drama. Not their close-knit, perfect family. This would not be the family Jay's mother would approve of. She knew I had a past, but nothing like this, nothing that would disrupt her worship and her way of life here, something that could chisel her right out of the community.

"Liya, are you all right?" Jay asked, pulling away from his family's grip as they pulled him back. They pulled him back...I'd lost them, which meant Jay would either decide not to be with me, or choose me over them and eventually hate me for it.

I wiped my face, lifted my chin, and said, my voice aquiver, "That is enough. I have no father."

I shoved Dad aside and prowled past Mukesh without giving in to the need to punch his snide face, for that would only add fodder for his claims.

As I slammed the door behind me, the rumblings and shouting escalated. Maybe Jay yelled my name? Did I imagine that? But he didn't run out after me. And that was enough of an answer.

The upbeat mix of Bollywood music and club songs drowned them out. It was an entirely different world out here. Dancing, lights, laughter, cheer.

Reema and Rohan cut across the room full of joy, meeting and chatting, dancing and eating. I tried my hardest to grin at them and gave a carefree wave. But I had to get out of here.

Preeti popped up beside me when I pushed through the front doors. A light chill hit us as she asked, "Can I join you? I can't be near my ex for this long. Where are you going?"

"Anywhere."

"What happened? Are you okay? Have you been crying?"

I nodded, intending to put on my don't-give-a-damn attitude, but I completely broke down.

"Oh, my god!" She put an arm around my shoulder and helped me to her car.

"Can we leave?" I hiccupped in the passenger seat. I was completely drained.

"Anywhere. Call it."

"Your place?"

She nodded. "Of course. What about Reema? She'll wonder where we went. Where you are."

I bit my lip. "I don't want to ruin her perfect day. She can't know any of this. Not yet. Can you have Sana cover?"

"Of course." She texted Sana and crawled into the car.

"First I need to go home to get something."

"Anything," she said and we took off.

We had driven to the reception together, after having prepared at the apartment she shared with Reema. Preeti drove me home first to get my car. There, I hurried up to my apartment and quickly shoved as much as I could into a suitcase with any and everything I thought I'd need. Preeti quietly, worriedly watched. I was ready to go to my new place. I did not want to stay a minute longer in case anyone showed up to wag their judgmental finger in my face.

Then I drove my car and followed her to her apartment.

When we crashed on her couch, our chaniyas fluttered around us in sparkling waves. "Wine? Coffee? Tea? Cha?" she suggested with a warm smile.

I shook my head as Preeti took my hand in hers. "What happened?" she asked.

Biting my lip, I pondered what to say. "I'm leaving tonight," I blurted. "My new apartment is ready. The job is ready. I'm not coming back."

"No. Don't say that." She hugged me tight, and neither of us let go.

But I had to. I had to let go of all of this. "We'll keep in touch, promise. And you'll come visit and we'll do girl trips as usual. Let's change. I have to get out of this heavy outfit before we stain it with ice cream and tears."

"Agreed. I actually think I have bruises from mine."

We changed and pulled out a pint of Blue Bell Rocky Road and a half gallon of Bride's Cake ice cream.

Preeti sat on the couch and I sat on the floor as I devoured the cold amaretto sweetness like there was no tomorrow.

After we suffered a few ice cream headaches, I relayed the entire story, half pissed, half mortified.

Her face was red and her fists clenched. Preeti was actually shaking with rage. "He's one of those men who supports shunning women who don't do traditional things. He definitely had something to say about me for dating a black man. He stopped talking to my dad after everything that happened. I *hate* him. What a moronic, piece of scum, dirtbag. I can't believe he did this to you! That you suffered so much! Ugh! I want to punch him in the throat!" she screamed.

I coughed out a weak chuckle. "With some scalpels between your knuckles to really damage him?"

"Yes. Son of a bitch," she growled.

"Hey. Calm down," I muttered. Unlike me, Preeti did not have a mouth on her. I'd never seen her so angry, and it was a bit alarming.

"No. I will not calm down. He ruined your name, your life. And your dad? This is so wrong. I won't stand for this. Mukesh has to be punished. People have to know."

"No. Stop. Please. I can't deal with more of this."

"It's not right, Liya. He will go on with his perfect life, walking around the place with his pretentious head held high and have everyone's respect. He doesn't deserve that. Why are you the only one who suffers?"

"Because it's society. Girls get the short end of the stick. It happened so long ago, people won't take it seriously now. Especially coming from me."

"He needs to get taken down. He has no place being a high authority figure in a religious organization, leading a community. Men can't keep doing these things and getting away with it, and on top of that, ostracizing the victim!"

"I'm so tired of it, Preeti. I've fought my entire life. I can't fight anymore."

"Okay. Okay... What did Jay do?" she asked.

"Nothing," I cried, the pain in my chest unbearable. "He didn't even come after me when I left."

"Shhh," she cooed and caressed my hair when I laid my forehead on her knees and wept. "He was probably stunned."

"That's never stopped him before. Let's face it. It's over. Mukesh won. Even if Jay didn't believe him, he wouldn't want this drama."

"Has he called?"

"I don't know. I haven't looked at my phone."

"Check it."

"Why bother?" I sniffled.

"Because he could be looking for you. You have to go to him."

"When he didn't come to me in the moment I needed him?"

"What are we going to do, then?"

"Eat more ice cream?"

Preeti continued to caress my hair as I sobbed on her lap, hiccupping and wheezing. A void clawed itself open in my soul, and I shoved tear after tear into it. It wasn't enough. Nothing would ever be enough to fill that gruesome hole.

I'd never cried so much, so hard, not since Mukesh distorted the truth all those years ago. I was empty, hollowed out, by midnight.

Liya Thakkar might've lost this one, but she would not stay down. No matter how much this hurt, no matter how long this would hurt, even if I had to stumble and crawl, I would rebuild my life. Elsewhere.

Chapter Thirty-One
Jay

Didn't Liya hear me call after her? She'd run out so fast that I couldn't catch her because I saw red. Bloodthirsty rage. Reason and logic weren't even in my vocabulary right now. The most aggressive level of indignation seized control of me, to the point that Jahn used his entire strength to hold me back from beating Mukesh's ass (he did not deserve the respect of being called Uncle anymore). Even Ma's touch couldn't soothe me, help me see reason. I grappled out of Jahn's grip and went after Liya when she stormed out, but her father and Mukesh stood in my way. Her father had even snatched his wife's arm when she tried to go after their daughter.

"You better move," I warned.

"Let her go," her father said.

"How could you let this happen?" I yelled.

"I'm sorry. It's not something a parent tells a prospective suitor from the beginning. What would you have done?"

I clenched my jaw. "I would've believed my daughter."

"She's a known liar," Mukesh insisted. "You understand this was hard to do, to tell another soul after we decided to put it behind us so long ago."

"You worthless asshole. And *you*." I glared at Liya's father. "The worst thing you can do is not believe your child about being molested. And siding with her accuser? Why? So you can save yourself from having him turn the community against you? Pathetic."

"You don't know what kind of child she was, what sort of woman she turned into."

"The problem is that *you* have no idea. You missed out on an amazing person. She already told me she was molested, why she turned to sleeping with guys, how many she'd been with. It still didn't matter. You both should feel lucky you weren't dealing with me. I'd have kicked your ass long ago, old man, and thrown you in jail. And I would've disowned you as a father."

I went for the door when Mukesh touched my shoulder. I had my fists around his collar and his back against the wall before anyone could stop me. "Touch me, or her, or anyone else, and I will dismember you," I growled, baring my teeth. "Don't even look at or think of her, or get near her or my family, or I will open an investigation and find every dirty detail from the day you were born. I will have you behind bars so fast, you'll be a sniveling old man in the blink of an eye. Even if she doesn't let me unleash the justice system on you, because your fate is in her hands, then just know that whatever fear you put Liya through, I will make you drown in it *every* day. Do you understand me?"

He gulped and nodded, his hands up in defense. "You're making a mistake, son."

"No, *you* made a mistake when you did this to Liya. You messed with the wrong woman and crossed the wrong lawyer, because guess what? There is no statute of limitations in Texas, and I will personally open up that case and have you in jail. And by next week, everyone at mandir will know what you did to a *child*. You will lose every privilege and respect that you have here. You are not a role model and don't deserve to be looked upon as one."

"You're going to destroy this community," he barked.

"Make no mistake, *you* did this to our community. *You* are responsible for what happens now. *You* are the *only* person to blame. I am going to shred you apart."

Jahn pulled me away, but Liya's father didn't bother making a move.

I ushered Ma out first, then Jahn. I approached Liya's mother and pressed my palms together in a sign of reverence. "I apologize for all the things you've gone through. This is not a reflection of you, and if you need anything, my mom and I are here. And I promise you that Liya will be in good hands with me, and if we ever have children, they will be an extension of you, not your husband, and we will never let anyone touch them and get away with it."

"Thank you," she wept.

I wished she could've left with us, or had followed Liya out, but I knew she would do neither. I knew it was beyond my reach to take her. But before I turned away, Ma's arm brushed past me. She took a hold of Liya's mother's hands and said, "Chalo. Let's go."

Of course, Liya's dad tried to stop his wife from leaving, but we were here and she wanted to leave.

Then it clicked. Liya's mom was deathly afraid of her husband. It was in her eyes, in her trembling lips, in her submissive body language. Ma would never have let Dad dismiss us if we claimed something so terrible. Even if she disagreed with him, she would've backed us up with the ferocity that only mothers had to protect their children. Unless that fierceness was severed by a domineering husband...

"It's okay. Let's just go for a walk," Ma said gently, glaring at both men.

Liya's mom brushed at her tears and gave her husband the coldest expression ever. Dynamics were shifting. The women walked out ahead of me.

I paused beside Liya's father and said, "If I even think that you've hurt her, I will come for you."

"She is not my daughter anymore," he said, convinced in his beliefs.

"I mean your wife."

He startled.

Then I left, having forgotten that we were in the middle of a wedding reception. The music was loud, the movement roaring, but nowhere did I see Liya. I searched everywhere, but the crowds were so big and the temple grounds vast. Would she have left her best friend's reception? After all that? Dumb question.

I found Jahn at the edge of the dance floor. "Have you seen her?"

"No. We're looking, but she probably left," Jahn replied.

I groaned and ran out the doors. I didn't see Liya's Lexus.

All of my calls went straight to voicemail and my texts went unanswered. I found Sana to inquire of Liya's whereabouts as dread crept through me, but she hadn't seen her since the chore-ographed dance. Preeti was nowhere to be found. Shilpa hadn't seen her, either.

"All Preeti said was that Liya checked in with her and was fine, but didn't want to talk to anyone and turned her phone off for a while," Shilpa replied.

"Preeti asked me to cover for them so Reema didn't find out," Sana added.

"Does Preeti know where Liya is?" I pressed.

"Preeti won't say anything else."

"Do you think Liya is with Preeti?"

"I hope so, but Liya tends to fly solo when she's upset," Sana quietly admitted.

I panicked and drove my hand through my hair. Where did she go?

"Beta," Ma said with a gentle hand on my arm. "You must find her. What happened... it was not good. Don't let her slip away. She did nothing wrong. She has to know that. We'll look for her, too. Keep making calls, Shilpa. Make sure she's okay, beta?"

"I will."

I went to Liya's apartment first, but she wasn't there. I drove around all night, searching in every park, bar, restaurant, and club that she liked. If Liya flew solo when upset, then where else could she be?

I returned to her apartment at the end of the night into early morning. She wasn't home. Her lights were off. So I waited.

I jolted awake. The sun was out and bright, and the car was already sweltering hot. I checked my phone. Liya had not responded, but others had. Jahn and Shilpa checked on me to make sure that I was all right, wondering if I'd found her.

Then another text.

Preeti: Was sworn to girl oath. Liya's devastated and humiliated and left for Dallas. She's not coming back.

"Damn it!" I snarled and threw the phone against the dashboard, cracking the screen protector.

"You gotta be kidding me!" I yelled.

Why would she leave like this? She couldn't have possibly thought that I believed them over her. She couldn't have believed that this was something that we wouldn't come back from, that I wouldn't care for her and love her.

I shouldn't have gotten so angry with her for wanting to move to Dallas. I should've told her I had accepted it and would support her, anything for her to be happy. But hadn't she seen my texts or listened to my voicemails? Of course not. She was mad that I was mad, busy with the wedding on top of that. And yet I didn't take the opportunity at the wedding to tell her.

Liya hadn't left just because her dad and Mukesh pulled that stunt. Liya left because of me.

My heart split—into two, then four, splintering and sending shrapnel through my veins. I breathed heavily for a long time, in and out, until my chest burned. I hadn't felt this vulnerable, this guilty, this erratic and helpless since Dad died. I thought I was over this when Liya guided me through the anniversary of his death. But I never thought I'd feel this way over someone else leaving. Not like this.

My tires screeched as I backed out of the parking lot and called Shilpa, demanding Preeti's address. She reluctantly gave it to me, adding, "Don't do anything rash. Preeti is just the messenger…"

"I know that," I snapped. "But she's the only person who knows where Liya is. How else would I find her in Dallas? I just walked out on her when she told me about getting a new job there. I can't believe I did that, left before she ever had the chance to tell me where she would end up."

"Be calm."

"Would you be calm? If some manipulating jackasses did that to Jahn and forced him to leave forever?"

"Be calm…but go get her."

"Damn right I'm going to get her."

I parked the car and took the steps two at a time to get to Preeti's apartment. She didn't open after a few knocks, so I pounded harder and texted.

"Come on, Preeti. I know you're in there."

After another minute, she quietly opened the door. Her eyes were red and puffy and her skin a little pale. My heart broke. How much worse did Liya look right now? Had Liya been crying when I wasn't there for her?

"Jay. What are you doing here?" she asked, her voice hoarse.

"Is Liya seriously gone or is she hiding in your apartment?"

"She's gone."

I exhaled. "Then I need her address."

"No can do. Breach of girl oath. She entrusted me, and only me, with that information. I'm not going to completely lose her. Give her some space, some time."

"How long?"

"A few weeks, months."

"That's too long to go without her, without Liya knowing that what happened doesn't change a thing for us, for her to have to go through any of this alone."

"Trust me, I tried to reason with her. She's so shaken and...Jay, I've never seen her as anything but resilient. But she's broken. She cried for hours."

I clenched my eyes shut and pushed back the all-too-familiar sting of tears. Why hadn't I just taken her hand, pushed through the doors, and taken her home before anyone said a word? I was supposed to protect her, shield her when the accusations came. But no. I was too stunned at first, then too enraged to think straight.

"I'm not going to lose her, Preeti. That intelligent, *fierce*, beautiful woman is the love of my life."

She smiled. "I know."

"Then give me her address."

She frowned. "Girl oath. I honestly think we'll all lose her forever if this chain of trust breaks. She scared me when she said so."

"Okay. What about the name of her new company? That's not breaking your word."

"Are you going to stalk her?"

"Whatever it takes. I need the name and I need to leave for Dallas right now."

She chewed on her lip. What was there to deliberate about?

"I'd never hurt her, Preeti. We can't lose her. We won't."

She blinked away tears as I held my breath for her next words. "Fine. I'll tell you her new workplace. I want you guys to work out because you're good for her and she's happier for it. She's meeting with HR today at one. Which means she should be walking out of that office by two."

I dropped my head back. I could've kissed her. "Thank you, Preeti. I owe you an eternity for this."

It was seven in the morning right now. Which meant I had time to call my law firm on my way home to grab a carry-on size roller suitcase. I didn't know what I needed, so I literally just threw stuff in there for a few days' stay. I had ample time to weave out of Houston traffic before it clogged up and make the three-hour drive to Dallas.

My dad. I lived my life trying to make up for his loss, by sticking to my mom and brother, by making him proud. If he were here, he'd want me to go after Liya. He'd go after Ma without a second thought. It was time. It was time to leave Ma in the care of Jahn and make my dad proud in a different way. Ma would understand. She'd want this for me, too.

I yanked open the front door to head out, the handle of the roller carry-on in my hand, just as Jahn had his fist raised to knock. Ma stood behind him.

"Where are you going?" he asked.

"He found Liya," Ma said with an approving and proud nod.

"Yeah. She moved to Dallas for a job offer," I stated.

"You're driving there right now?" Jahn asked.

"Yes."

He stepped aside, "Well, hell. Go get her."

"Thanks!"

Ma took hold of my elbow, and I paused to face to her. She touched my cheek and said, "You fight for her and never let go."

"Of course. After all this—"

"After all this," she said with determination, "is why I'm reaching out to Liya's mother and not letting her go. After all this is why I'm taking these matters to others in mandir. Mukesh is madness that will infect the community. We won't stand for this."

"No. Don't. It's too much stress for you. I'll take care of it."

"I'll help," Jahn added. "Shilpa and I will both help. We already discussed this. In fact, there wasn't anything to discuss."

"Good," Ma said. "But I will still help as well. We need more voices. And if Liya was my daughter, granddaughter, niece, sister, cousin, mother, friend, stranger...I would still raise my voice. This is corruption, and I will not stand quietly by. We have to protect other girls and support girls like Liya. Do you understand me?"

Jahn and I nodded and glanced at each other. How could we expect anything less from Ma? She loved our culture and religion and tradition, but she was the strongest woman I'd ever known. No wonder she loved Liya, too.

"Now go!" She shooed me down the hall. "And Jayesh!"

"Yeah, Ma?" I called back.

"If this means you must move to Dallas, then you must move to Dallas."

"What?"

"You've lived your life for me, for us, but at some point, you have to live life for yourself. Besides, you don't let a girl like Liya Thakkar get away."

Chapter Thirty-Two
Liya

Dallas was a large city, but calmer than Houston. I vowed to be a different person here, no longer running from problems and dealing with the past by being wild.

I'd just finished my preliminary HR round and headed to my new place, a short drive away. While parked in the parking garage beneath brightly lit ceilings, I went through my phone. Finally.

I sniffled. I missed Jay. *So* much. I knew I'd miss my girls, but I never imagined ever missing someone as much as I missed Jay. His relentless banter and willingness to volley with my arguments, his consideration, his smell, his touch. The way his lips made me feel at peace, and the way they made me unravel and shatter in bed. I could cry forever without him.

I'd finally found the courage to read Jay's texts. He'd sided with me, believed me. I was too horrified and ashamed to respond to him. Wasn't that ironic? I hadn't done anything wrong, and yet I felt shame. I wanted to crawl into a dark corner and die. I didn't want to see anyone, even if they sided with me.

His texts were to be savored like the last slice of bacon in the world. I could never face him again after that humiliation. And so what if his texts said that he didn't believe Mukesh? Or that he loved me unconditionally? Why hadn't he come after me when I walked out? What kept him in that room for so long? Why didn't he say anything to stop them from talking?

I wiped my tears and called Momma to tell her I was in Dallas.

"Good," she said, a smile in her tone.

"Are you okay with me living in Dallas?"

"I want you to be happy. You need this and you worked for this."

"I worry about you, still. With Dad. Now things are out in the open."

"Things are rough."

I let out a ragged breath. I never intended to hurt her.

"But things are changing," she added. "And Jay's mom is a *very* strong woman. She is just like you, and she's stuck to my side. She is helping me to learn how to stand up for myself."

I wiped my tears and caught my breath before I could reply, "I'm eternally grateful for her."

"Things will change slowly."

"Is Dad enraged with you?"

"He hasn't said a word to me, and I don't care."

"Just remember that you always have a home with me, Momma."

"I know. I'm sorry for all of this. For not standing up for you. What kind of mother am I?" she asked, her voice cracking.

I did a poor job keeping in my sobs when I replied, "A good mother. You were scared, just like me."

"Did you speak with Jay?" she asked with a shuddering breath. "Did he find you?"

"What?"

She told me what had happened after I left. She told me how

Jay stood up for me, how he acted against Mukesh and Dad, how he and his mother protected her.

After we hung up, I leaned my head back against the seat and dried my face. I needed to call Jay. How could I ever have doubted him or felt too embarrassed to face him? We had to meet and speak in person. Maybe I could drive down so he wouldn't have to come all the way up. Maybe he could get off work early and we could have the rest of the day to chat.

I drew in a very long, deep breath and called Jay.

He picked up the phone on the second ring. "Hey," he said, his voice throaty but calm.

"Hi."

"I'm sorry—" we both started at the same time and then chuckled at ourselves.

I climbed out of the car, my heart racing and aching. What I wouldn't give to be in his arms right now.

"How are you?" he asked.

"I don't know. My head is clearer."

"In Dallas?"

I locked my door and began walking when someone three spots away got out of their vehicle. I kept an eye on him, his back turned to me as he closed the door. That car had come in shortly after I had, but the person sat there this entire time? The man was tall and broad with a tight white shirt and blue jeans. He reminded me of Jay. Hearing his voice on the phone made me light-headed, thinking every man could be him.

"Yes," I replied. "We need to talk. I can...I can drive down."

"There's no need."

My gut clenched. Why not?

The guy ahead locked his car. He had a phone to his ear. The sound of his car alarm echoed off the phone. Then he slipped his phone into his pocket and turned toward me.

I buckled. My hands lurched out to grab onto something. They reached for him, for *Jay*. He was faster than possible and caught me. My thoughts reeled.

I was in his arms. He leaned down and asked, "Liya?"

That voice. That deep, throaty, sexy voice.

I closed my eyes, my lashes wet with tears. As I caught my breath, he helped me upright but didn't let go, and I hoped he never did. I swallowed hard and admitted, "I um, maybe shouldn't have left like that."

Before I could formulate another sentence, Jay pulled me into him. He kissed me.

Passionately.

Fervently.

Desperately.

Longingly.

My mouth had missed his. It knew the taste of his tongue, the play of his lips. My body surrendered to the very familiar, very real feel of his wide hands on the small of my back, gripping my body.

He pulled away as we panted and caught our breath.

"Don't apologize for a thing," he said.

"What are you doing here?"

He licked his swollen lower lip. "I came for you."

"How did you find me? Preeti?"

"She only promised not to tell anyone your address. She told me your new workplace, and I might've been stalking you for the past couple of hours."

"You're a weasel." I laughed.

"Lawyer." He pointed at himself, proud and amused. "I came because you're the one," he rasped. "You're mine. I'm yours. We don't belong with anyone else. I don't stand in front of you, or run after you. I walk alongside you. I will be damned if anything breaks us. Do you understand me?"

He gently took my jaw in his hand. "Do. You. Understand. Me?"

I bit my lip and nodded. "What about your family? Are they still okay with us?"

"They love you, and you know that."

"What about how embarrassing my drama is? That I'm too much of a mess after all? That your family is appalled by the drama, how vile my dad is, the fight ahead bringing to light what Mukesh did?"

"None of that is true. I should've stopped them from talking, should've taken you out of the room, but I was in shock. And then I just wanted to bash Mukesh's face in. I didn't think. I was always going to come after you, no matter how fast or far you ran, but they weren't going to get out of that room without knowing where we stood, where *they* stood. I am *so* sorry if you felt alone or abandoned or humiliated."

"I was afraid that you might believe them."

"Never, ever think that I wouldn't believe you."

I swallowed and blinked away tears.

"Your dad won't bother your mom that way again. Mukesh *will* be removed from his responsibilities and his position at mandir. He will go to jail if you want to press charges. I will take care of it. I will be by your side. You will never stand alone ever again."

I nodded, relieved beyond reason to finally hear those words. I gulped in several deep breaths to keep myself from getting emotional. "Do you understand why I hate Houston now?"

He cupped my face and wiped my tears with his thumbs. "I do. Baby, I'm so sorry that you endured all that pain alone for so long, that you hurt so badly last night and I wasn't there to hold you."

I hiccupped. "You're making me cry."

He pressed my forehead against his chest. "Then I'll just hold you while you cry."

His shirt soaked up all of these stupid, dreadful tears, but his arms around me made everything one hundred percent better.

When I managed to control my crying and pull away, he kissed my nose and softly asked, "Can I see your new place?"

I squeaked out a laugh, took his hand in mine, and went upstairs. We took off our shoes and snuggled on the couch as he looked around. "Not bad. Kind of big for one person. Maybe you need a roommate?"

"Are you...offering to move here?" I squeaked. My heart fluttered with anticipation, that we would move ahead and get our happy ending.

He sucked in a breath. "Liya, you're wild as hell, a whole lot of trouble cushioned by a whole lot of amazing. I can't sleep when you're not next to me. I can't keep my focus not knowing if we'll be together. You challenge me. You keep pace. Hell, sometimes you even leave me in the dust. I love that. I adore you. You're the madness I need, the passion I breathe, the spark that brings me to life. I will go wherever you are."

I swallowed hard, afraid to ask, "Won't you hate me for making you leave your family?"

"I talked to them. Before I even opened my mouth to *tell* them, they told me to go. With happiness. With blessing. With support. I wasn't going to ask them for their permission or advice. I already knew, the moment you walked out of that room, I knew that you had to get out of Houston and that I would go wherever you needed to be."

"But your job."

He laughed. "I wasn't anywhere near making partner with my law firm after the debacle with your company. I can start over. I have connections here. Things will work out. I've been eyeing Dallas and some other cities. Honestly, I was afraid to leave Ma after my dad died, but my dad would've wanted me to live my life, to be with you. My dad would've loved you as much as the rest of us do. Besides, Houston isn't that far. It's a long weekend at worst."

"Do you mean to say that you're really going to move in with me?"

He kissed me with absolute need. The answer was in his eyes, swirling with resolution, determination. "Do you think you can escape me so easily? What? Just drive off to Dallas and think I won't find you?"

"I tried." I half smiled, and he grinned.

"I'll follow you to the ends of the earth because you are most definitely worth it." He traced my temple down to my jaw. "Do you have those shoes that I bought you?"

"Yes."

"Put them on," he said.

"Now?"

"Yep. Are they in that suitcase by the bedroom?"

"Um. Yes."

Jay returned and lowered himself to his knees in front of me. He caressed the side of my calves and looked up at me with irrefutable longing.

"I should get dressed first," I said.

"Actually, I want you *undressed*, but just wearing these heels."

I bit my lip at the implication of his words, of the images that swept through me.

"There's something you should know first," he said.

"What?"

"There's something wrong with these heels."

"If they're fake, I didn't even notice." I laughed.

But then Jay handed me a shoe upside down, the sole facing the ceiling. I blinked twice to make sure I wasn't seeing things.

Around the tall, spiked heel rested a white gold ring.

My breath shook. What was happening?

I looked to Jay for an explanation, but he shrugged, and we both returned to looking at the ring: not a diamond ring, but a sapphire one, one that sparkled with every deftly cut facet more brilliant and colorful than any diamond.

"What—what is this?"

Jay took the delicate ring from me and slid it on my *right* hand.

"I know you're not into marriage and arranged engagements and such, but here's a ring. A symbol of my devotion, whether it's officially on paper or just officially in our hearts. Liya Thakkar?"

"Yes?" I whispered.

"Will you be mine? Forever and always?"

I couldn't speak. I could barely nod my answer.

"I am *so* in love with you, you may never know the full extent of my devotion, but I promise to show it every day. In how I treat you, not like a *princess*, but a queen. Not as my submissive other half, but as my equal. I know you can take care of yourself, but should someone try to hurt you, they'll still have me to deal with. Not one day will go by without you feeling my love, in action, words…or when we turn down that bed every night."

My breath hitched.

He trailed his fingers down my calf and slipped on the shoes, his eyes never leaving mine. "I've been in love with you since the day you walked into that diner, when I took you home and decided to buy these damn shoes."

"You're going to have your hands full."

"As long as they're full of you. What do you say?"

"I say…that I love you *so* much, Jay. I never thought that anyone would love me, or that I'd fall in love." The words flowed out of me, more natural than anything else in the world. "I thought it was always just me, and always would be just me, walking alone, fighting this world alone, defending myself alone."

"You will never be alone. This is our world, and we're about to own it. Together."

He pulled me down onto his lap and kissed me. The sort of kiss that was meant to last lifetimes, the kind that shouldn't end, the sort that would never be forgotten. Everything turned upside down, blurred together, and pulled apart, then realigned into crystalline clarity.

Everything finally fit. And it fit perfectly.

Acknowledgments

It takes a village to publish a book, and my journey to publication, at times, has felt endless and daunting. Things really took a drastic, positive turn when I signed with my agent, Katelyn Detweiler. Katelyn brings a massive amount of continued support that makes whatever happens easy to deal with, the highs and lows. She truly is the best advocate that I could've asked for. It took a while to find her, but the wait was worth it. Thank you, Katelyn, for everything that you've done. Your support, dedication, hard work, expertise, skill, communication, advice, editorial visions, and jokes (so many jokes) are invaluable. Thank you to the entire team at Jill Grinberg Literary Management for providing answers to endless questions and guiding me, and for working so hard on my behalf.

I'd like to thank the entire team at Forever for loving my book as much I do, for seeing its value, for supporting the characters and their stories and underlying themes, for never once saying a strong, opinionated female main character is unlikable but instead rallying her on, for not thinking that one Indian romance author on the list is enough or that stories about South Asians are niche. I'll never forget that whirlwind Friday before Thanksgiving when everything happened so quickly and changed my career. I want to thank everyone for your overwhelming support and dedication, but especially my editors,

Lexi, Amy, Leah, and Madeleine. I have been blown away by the welcome.

A lot of my creative aspirations wouldn't be possible without a strong network of family, friends, and the writing community. I'm blessed by the bountiful love from my parents. Thank you to the hubs for being there for me, Parth, Rohan, Meet, and the "London Girls," and for not dismissing this path as something silly and fleeting, but encouraging it, getting excited over it. I don't come from a creativity-supporting community, but I am grateful for having family show their pride and excitement for my stories and never saying (and I'm pretty sure not thinking) that the creative path is a lesser path or time wasted. AKA: Why aren't you a doctor?!?

A big shout-out to my bae, Lizet, and special thanks to Jocie. A gigantic appreciation for Christina, for reminding me that I'm "a motha-freaking unicorn," ha! Thank you for many years of writing dates, listening ears, advice, consoling moments, and open hearts to Anna Banks, Marissa Meyer, Rori Shay, and Lish McBride.

Many endless thanks to all of the readers out there. You make the world spin with your insatiable love for stories. I sincerely hope that you enjoy this adventure with Liya and Jay and will join me for more wild rides in the years to come.

Eager for more romance by Sajni Patel? Don't miss Preeti's story, coming in Summer 2021!

About the Author

Sajni Patel was born in vibrant India and raised in the heart of Texas, surrounded by a lot of delicious food and plenty of diversity. She draws on her personal experiences, cultural expectations, and Southern flair to create worlds that center on strong Indian women. Once an MMA fighter, she's now all about puppies and rainbows and tortured-love stories. She currently lives in Austin, where she not-so-secretly watches Matthew McConaughey from afar during UT football games. Queso is her weakness, and thanks to her family's cooking, Indian/Tex-Mex cuisine is a real thing. She's a die-hard Marvel Comics fan, a lover of chocolates from around the world, and is always wrapped up in a story.